The Best AMERICAN ESSAYS 2021

GUEST EDITORS OF
THE BEST AMERICAN ESSAYS

1986 ELIZABETH HARDWICK
1987 GAY TALESE
1988 ANNIE DILLARD
1989 GEOFFREY WOLFF
1990 JUSTIN KAPLAN
1991 JOYCE CAROL OATES
1992 SUSAN SONTAG
1993 JOSEPH EPSTEIN
1994 TRACY KIDDER
1995 JAMAICA KINCAID
1996 GEOFFREY C. WARD
1997 IAN FRAZIER
1998 CYNTHIA OZICK
1999 EDWARD HOAGLAND
2000 ALAN LIGHTMAN
2001 KATHLEEN NORRIS
2002 STEPHEN JAY GOULD
2003 ANNE FADIMAN
2004 LOUIS MENAND
2005 SUSAN ORLEAN
2006 LAUREN SLATER
2007 DAVID FOSTER WALLACE
2008 ADAM GOPNIK
2009 MARY OLIVER
2010 CHRISTOPHER HITCHENS
2011 EDWIDGE DANTICAT
2012 DAVID BROOKS
2013 CHERYL STRAYED
2014 JOHN JEREMIAH SULLIVAN
2015 ARIEL LEVY
2016 JONATHAN FRANZEN
2017 LESLIE JAMISON
2018 HILTON ALS
2019 REBECCA SOLNIT
2020 ANDRÉ ACIMAN
2021 KATHRYN SCHULZ

The Best AMERICAN ESSAYS® 2021

Edited and with an Introduction
by KATHRYN SCHULZ

Robert Atwan, Series Editor

MARINER BOOKS
An Imprint of HarperCollins*Publishers*
Boston New York

marinerbooks.com

ISSN 0888-3742 (print) ISSN 2573-3885 (e-book)
ISBN 978-0-358-38175-4 (print) ISBN 978-0-358-38122-8 (e-book)

Printed in the United States of America
1 2021
4500835412

"Clarity" by Ruchir Joshi. First published in *Granta,* #151, 2020. Copyright © 2020 by Ruchir Joshi. Reprinted by permission of *Granta.*

"Oh Latitudo" by Amy Leach. First published in *Granta,* #153, 2020. Copyright © 2020 by Amy Leach. Reprinted by permission of The Wylie Agency, LLC.

"Insane After Coronavirus?" by Patricia Lockwood. First published in *London Review of Books,* July 2020. Copyright © 2020 by Patricia Lockwood. Reprinted by permission of Patricia Lockwood.

"Love in a Time of Terror" by Barry Lopez. Published in *Literary Hub,* August 7, 2020. Copyright © 2020 by Barry Holstun Lopez. Reprinted by permission of Sterling Lord Literistic, Inc. This essay originally appeared as the foreword to an anthology, *Earthly Love: Stories of Intimacy and Devotion from Orion Magazine,* published by *Orion* in 2020.

"What I Learned When My Husband Got Sick with Coronavirus" by Jessica Lustig. First published in *The New York Times Magazine,* March 24, 2020. Copyright © 2020 The New York Times Company. All rights reserved. Used under license.

"What Money Can't Buy" by Dawn Lundy Martin. First published in *Ploughshares,* 46/1, 2020. Copyright © 2020 by Dawn Lundy Martin. Reprinted by permission of Dawn Lundy Martin.

"Two Women" by Claire Messud, first published in *A Public Space,* #29, 2020, and later included in *Kant's Little Prussian Head and Other Reasons Why I Write* published October 13, 2020, by W. W. Norton. Copyright © 2020 by Claire Messud. Reprinted by permission of The Wylie Agency, LLC.

"My Mustache" by Wesley Morris. First published in *The New York Times Magazine,* October 18, 2020. Copyright © 2020 The New York Times Company. All rights reserved. Used under license.

"Apparent" by Beth Nguyen. First published in *The Paris Review,* Spring 2020. Copyright © 2020 by Beth Nguyen. Reprinted by Beth Nguyen.

"The Designated Mourner" by Fintan O'Toole. First published in *The New York Review of Books,* January 16, 2020. Copyright © 2020 by Fintan O'Toole. Reprinted by permission of Fintan O'Toole.

"Going Postal" by Max Read. First published in *Bookforum,* Sept/Oct/Nov 2020. Copyright © 2020 by Max Read. Reprinted by permission of Max Read.

"In Orbit" by Dariel Suarez. First published in *The Threepenny Review,* Winter 2020. Copyright © 2020 by Dariel Suarez. Reprinted by permission of Dariel Suarez.

"Witness and Respair" by Jesmyn Ward. First published in *Vanity Fair,* September 2020. Copyright © 2020 by Jesmyn Ward. Reprinted by permission of Jesmyn Ward.

Contents

Foreword ix

Introduction xxi

ELIZABETH ALEXANDER *The Trayvon Generation* 1
FROM *The New Yorker*

HILTON ALS *Homecoming* 9
FROM *The New Yorker*

MOLLY McCULLY BROWN *The Broken Country* 22
FROM *Virginia Quarterly Review*

AGNES CALLARD *Acceptance Parenting* 30
FROM *The Point*

GABRIELLE HAMILTON *The Kitchen Is Closed* 37
FROM *The New York Times Magazine*

TONY HOAGLAND *Bent Arrows: On Anticipation of My Approaching Disappearance* 52
FROM *Ploughshares*

GREG JACKSON *Vicious Cycles* 55
FROM *Harper's Magazine*

RUCHIR JOSHI *Clarity* 73
FROM *Granta*

AMY LEACH *Oh Latitudo* 80
FROM *Granta*

PATRICIA LOCKWOOD *Insane After Coronavirus?* 84
FROM *London Review of Books*

BARRY LOPEZ *Love in a Time of Terror* 92
FROM *Literary Hub*

JESSICA LUSTIG *What I Learned When My Husband Got Sick with Coronavirus* 101
FROM *The New York Times Magazine*

DAWN LUNDY MARTIN *What Money Can't Buy* 109
FROM *Ploughshares*

CLAIRE MESSUD *Two Women* 121
FROM *A Public Space*

WESLEY MORRIS *My Mustache* 136
FROM *The New York Times Magazine*

BETH NGUYEN *Apparent* 150
FROM *The Paris Review*

FINTAN O'TOOLE *The Designated Mourner* 164
FROM *The New York Review of Books*

MAX READ *Going Postal* 175
FROM *Bookforum*

DARIEL SUAREZ *In Orbit* 182
FROM *The Threepenny Review*

JESMYN WARD *Witness and Respair* 192
FROM *Vanity Fair*

Contributors' Notes 201

Notable Essays and Literary Nonfiction of 2020 206

Notable Special Issues of 2020 220

Foreword

DEVOTED READERS OF this series will have noticed how often Montaigne and Emerson have appeared in these annual forewords. As they represent two of world literature's finest essayists, the literary reasons for their persistent presence should be clear. But less obvious may be my personal reasons for always circling back to them. So for this year's foreword I will indulge in a bit of intellectual autobiography.

For those of us who encounter the world with a defective intellect, life can be an exasperating struggle. Whether the result of brain circuitry, formative early experiences, or an evolved sensibility, a chronic skepticism can amount to a troublesome affliction. One of my first intellectual heroes, Bertrand Russell, put it well: "people hate sceptics far more than they hate the passionate advocates of opinions hostile to their own." Skepticism can lead to indifference, indecision, apathy, disengagement—all attitudes despised by those passionate in their beliefs and opinions. It can also lead to a contrarianism that delights in taking a vacation from prevailing orthodoxies. In a fine 1997 essay, the writer and free speech advocate Wendy Kaminer—a former president of the National Coalition against Censorship—called this tendency "A Civic Duty to Annoy."

My parents—both high school dropouts—apparently didn't realize that my skeptical temperament would not suit the urban parochial schools they sent me to from first to twelfth grade. I doubt I would have fared better in our public schools, but I very early on grew skeptical of what I learned in religious instruction.

This caused constant friction with the priests and nuns, or—as we called them—the fathers and sisters. Yes, in those days they really did rap your knuckles with a yardstick, and it stung. I respected religion—I even served as an altar boy—but the beliefs just led to too many questions, and I wasn't often satisfied by the answers supplied in our *Baltimore Catechism*. Much of the time I learned to simply keep my mouth shut, keep my doubts to myself, and do my work.

My first scientific experiment involved miracles. We heard a great deal about miracles in our school and church, and to a child's mind the difference between a miracle and any surprise event or sheer coincidence is hardly clear. I was in third grade when I conducted the experiment. Two years earlier, a week or so before I would start first grade, I'd been out playing with other kids in the parking lots of the old Riverside Terrace apartments, where my grandparents lived with my Ayatollah-bearded, unconverted Muslim great-grandfather, near McLean Boulevard in Paterson, New Jersey. Maybe we were playing tag or just running around or possibly I was pushed—but however it happened, I fell flat on my face. As I got up, I noticed a large piece of jagged blue glass sticking out of my bleeding left hand. In the emergency room, a doctor (I assume) cleaned the wound and applied stitches. I don't recall feeling much pain, but a few days later, I noticed I couldn't bend my left ring finger. Nor could I over the next few years.

The grade school I attended was attached to a Roman Catholic church, Our Lady of Lourdes. (I was not a Roman Catholic, however; like many Lebanese and Syrian Christians, I had been baptized into the Eastern Maronite Church. But that's another story.) Now, as every student at Our Lady of Lourdes knew from countless reminders, the small French village of Lourdes became a famous holy site after the Virgin Mary miraculously appeared to a fourteen-year-old peasant girl, Bernadette, in 1858. On one of her eighteen apparitions over a period of a few months, the Virgin told Bernadette to dig a small hole, and when she did, it released a gushing spring that would soon become a holy destination for millions of pilgrims from around the globe, many hoping to drink or bathe in the holy spring water that could produce miraculous cures.

Someone, either clergy or a parishioner, visited Lourdes while I was in the third grade and returned with a generous amount of the miraculous water. Some of it was poured into the holy-water fonts scattered about the church so people could bless themselves with it. But I wanted more. Somehow I figured out a way to sneak a small bottle of the water home, where I set up in my bedroom a little table with a statue of the Virgin, added some flowers I had picked—most likely backyard dandelions—and placed the holy water in a small container. Then for several days—when I would find myself alone—I knelt by my tiny shrine, placed my paralyzed finger in the water, and prayed. I don't recall how long it took, but I eventually realized the ritual was pointless. The finger would never bend again. The Lourdes water could not work miracles. I had proved that to my own satisfaction.

A few years later, when I told the story to a classmate who had spent some time at a seminary studying for the priesthood, he said my experiment had proved nothing at all. It showed only that I lacked the unwavering faith such miracles require. The Virgin Mary knew I'd been skeptical of the cure, and my doubting attitude stood in the way. Had I not designed a test and stolen the water, but simply immersed my finger in the church's holy-water font and uttered a sincere "Hail Mary," I might now have a functioning finger. I wasn't sure about this argument—and how could anyone realistically suspend their skepticism?—but still, I saw what he meant: I didn't begin with the absolute belief that the water would cure the finger but rather wanted to see if it would. For me at that moment, it was more a matter of hope than faith. I thought how disappointing it must be for those who made a long and costly pilgrimage to Lourdes, fully hoping that the water would cure their blindness, cancer, or paralysis, only to discover that after bathing they retained the infirmities they had started out with. My disappointment came with an odd satisfaction: it confirmed my innate skepticism.

This mental defect grew only more troublesome in high school, where I often suffered the consequences of asking the wrong questions. I had never learned early on that questioning counted as a form of implicit criticism, a sure sign of what Stalinists condemned as "insufficient zeal," a crime I confess I'm often guilty of, in both thought and action. One particular question that I asked in my senior year landed me in the principal's office, where Sister Grace Alma informed me that because I'd posed such an outrageous question, I would receive no college recommendations from the school. Luckily, some admissions officer at the only college I applied to approved of my SAT scores and overlooked my lack of references.

In high school I had two loves: chemistry and Dostoyevsky. I didn't realize they would soon be at odds. Dostoyevsky's novels were forbidden at our school, so I read them in secret, a situation I found comical since so many Cold War jokes often centered on silly-sounding kinds of censorship in the Soviet Union. And here I was, cloaking my paperback of *The Brothers Karamazov* with the cover of my Roman Catholic missal. My love of chemistry brought me to an engineering college, where I excelled in that one course but remained indifferent to all the other requirements, so that I barely managed to pass. I was a C– student in everything but chemistry. Then, one icy cold March morning, an Air Force ROTC officer discovered me, in full uniform and stiff overcoat, huddled in the back seat of a friend's car, deep into *Crime and Punishment.* My crime: skipping drill; my punishment: long hours cleaning the supply room. I realized by the end of my first year that, except for chemistry, my college experience had been an enormous disappointment.

I dropped out for a year to work in a chemistry lab. It was a life experiment: if I liked it, I'd apply somewhere to study just chemistry. I enjoyed the job so much, I almost didn't want to leave, but in the end the choice remained: Would it be chemistry or Dostoyevsky? Science or literature? Literature won (barely), and I transferred as a full-time student to the small inner-city college where I'd been attending night school. At this small Catholic commuter college—a branch of Seton Hall University—students had to take a series of courses in philosophy. That seemed initially inviting, but the catch was that course after course—logic, metaphysics, epistemology (my favorite), cosmology, and so on—all followed a rigid Scholastic dogmatism, or, more specifically, the philosophy of Saint Thomas Aquinas. Doubt and skepticism did not play much of a role; Faith always triumphed over Reason.

In one of our textbooks by a prominent Thomist whose name escapes me, I read (I paraphrase here) that any number of reasons could explain why there would be a Descartes, but there could be no reason for anyone to be a Cartesian. So Descartes too seemed forbidden. This of course instantly drew me to his *Discourse on Method.* I still have the Penguin Classic edition, which cost ninety-five cents and is dated "5/8/62." The edition also contains *The Meditations,* the opening sentence of which I had neatly underlined:

> Many years have passed since I first noticed how many false opinions I had accepted as true from my earliest years, and how flimsy a structure I had erected on this treacherous ground; and so I felt that I must one day rid myself of all the opinions I had hitherto adopted, and start the whole work of construction again from the very foundation, if I aspired to make some solid and lasting contribution to knowledge.

I found this enterprise thrilling. I began to meditate on how few things I knew for certain and began to draw up lists. But I soon discovered I was no Descartes.

I was learning, however, that there are degrees of skepticism, that only the most extreme skeptics doubted the mind's ability to know anything for certain. Didn't Descartes's quest for certainty demonstrate his openness to the possibility it could be achieved? I was learning too that skepticism was not just a philosophical problem but something that pervaded all areas of life and thought: To what extent do we believe in authority, data, experts? Does scientific consensus end debate? When do we consider the evidence sufficient for establishing a true belief? Perhaps I didn't immerse my finger in Lourdes water long enough? How reliable is information, even when it comes from trusted sources? Did I really know for sure that the water came from the miraculous fountain at Lourdes? Perhaps it was from the sacristy faucet. Most of our information is mainly based, as the journalist Walter Lippmann once said, on something we heard from someone who heard it from someone else, who in turn heard it from someone else.

Although by my senior year in college I'd read a smattering of Montaigne and Emerson, I was more influenced at that time by the philosophical and scientific essays of William James and Bertrand Russell. Eventually, within a few years, all four would come to shape my thinking, and they would be joined by John Stuart Mill. The five, I realized years later, comprise a fairly tight circle: the great skeptic Montaigne represented one of Emerson's intellectual heroes; Emerson would famously "bless" the infant William James; William James dedicated his book *Pragmatism* to the "memory of John Stuart Mill"; and Mill lived just long enough to serve as Russell's godfather.

This intellectual circle would influence my general approach to literature. I developed a wariness of certainty and a fondness for an open-minded skepticism. I began to prefer writers who either avoided or resisted aligning themselves with a dominant theory, school, or system— whether social, cultural, or political—avoiding those who, as D. H. Lawrence put it, wrote with their "thumb on the scale." I enjoyed the quirky, the deviant, the outsider. I liked to recite in my head memorized passages of Allen Ginsberg's "Howl," "America," "Sunflower Sutra," or "A Supermarket in California." Like essays, Ginsberg's poetry always seems to be in conversation with someone: "What thoughts I have of you tonight, Walt Whitman . . ." As did the poetry of someone who might appear Ginsberg's complete opposite, Robert Frost, another whose memorized lines could, even when unsummoned, entertain me at any moment during the day. I relished too the skepticism of Frost, a student of William James and a poet with an Emersonian consciousness. I read many poets as though they were essayists. I could admire their poetic genius and still be impressed by the dynamics of their thought.

The critic Irving Howe apparently took a similar delight in Frost. In a 1963 essay, he observed that "Frost's best lyrics aim at the kind of wisdom that is struck aslant and not to be settled into the comforts of an intellectual system." Howe goes on to describe this "wisdom":

> It is the wisdom of a mind confessing its nakedness, caught in its aloneness. Frost writes as a modern poet who shares in the loss of firm assumptions and seeks, through a disciplined observation of the natural world and a related sequel of reflection, to provide some tentative basis for existence, some "momentary stay," as he once remarked, "against confusion."

We can learn a good deal about what makes essays come alive by paying close attention to the underlying thought processes of Frost's poetry as they oscillate between the invitations of an easy conversational style and a skepticism that doubts whether effortless communication can ever be achieved.

The disquiets of doubt struck me as more alluring than the satisfactions of certainty. And, of course, given such affinities—though I never lost my love of poetry—I grew especially attached to the genre of the literary essay, where doubt, skepticism, uncertainty, and the aesthetic enjoyment of "not knowing" often reigned. (I found it perfectly appropriate that the inaugural volume of this series in 1986 contained Donald Barthelme's wonderful essay "Not-Knowing.") For centuries the essay—first shaped by Montaigne's guiding principle, "What do I know?"—had been the primary genre for the skeptical imagination, always welcoming what John Stuart Mill called "the liberty of thought and discussion." Mill's robust defense of free expression in *On Liberty* would serve as a model for one of Bertrand Russell's finest books, the 1928 collection *Sceptical Essays.** In his introduction to the 2004 Routledge Classics edition, the philosopher John Gray calls Russell's collection "some of the most beautifully written and engaging essays in the English language." A lifelong skeptic, but not of the cynical or pessimistic school, Russell wholeheartedly believed in the power of reason and the possibilities of human progress. According to Gray, his purpose in these essays is "to show that sceptical doubt can change the world." Or as Russell himself said of his book: "These propositions may seem mild, yet, if accepted, they would absolutely revolutionise human life."

Like Mill, who had been arrested in 1823 at the age of seventeen for distributing pamphlets promoting contraception, Russell practiced a skepticism that didn't stand in the way of his activism. Nor did it result in a foolish consistency: a pacifist during World War I, Russell gradually came to support the Allied Forces during World War II, considering Nazism a greater threat to civilization than warfare. After the war he became internationally known for his tireless protests against nuclear weapons; he famously served jail time at the age of eighty-nine for his participation in antinuclear demonstrations. I recall at the time seeing news clips of his arrest on television.

Sceptical Essays is largely a book about politics, the way political parties betray the public they have promised to assist, and the need for the public to cultivate the habit of "political scepticism." One point Russell insists on throughout the collection: political parties function by instilling hatred. To succeed, a political party requires an enemy. "No political party," he writes, "can acquire any driving force except through hatred; it must hold up someone to

---

* For an engaging, brief, and well-balanced view of Mill, I recommend Richard Reeves's "John Stuart Mill," *Salmagundi*, Winter/Spring 2007.

obloquy." Such hatred is in turn abetted by the press and its techniques of propaganda. He thought one of the goals of education should be to teach students the art of reading a newspaper so that they would eventually come to discover that "everything in newspapers is more or less untrue." By learning to weigh the biases of different news sources, "a practiced reader could infer what really happened."

Much of what Montaigne, James, Emerson, Mill, and Russell stood for may seem antiquated by today's standards. One sees very little skepticism in a media that apparently thrives on belligerent and simplistic assertions of certainty that would surely frighten our five philosophical essayists. The past few years have also seen increasing challenges to the traditional liberal ideals of free speech and open inquiry. A 2015 Pew Research Center Poll found that millennials were less likely than older generations to give "offensive" speech First Amendment protection. Some offensive speech doesn't have much protection anyway, but as more and more opinion begins to fall under various categories of "offensive," the limits of free speech may indeed be narrowing. To many, this isn't a serious issue but a necessary containment of harmful expression, which may have been long overdue. Many journalists approve of censoring "misinformation" and support a greater degree of "content moderation" in publications and social media.

Although some of this censorship might be justified on the grounds of public safety, the issue becomes complicated when "misinformation" or "disinformation" becomes equated with doubt itself. If, to express doubt about something one feels is dubious, unlikely, or perhaps just ongoing and not fully investigated constitutes an "information disorder," then a habitual skepticism, as I suggested earlier and that Bertrand Russell believed was essential to a healthy democracy, will be regarded as a psychological defect in need of correction. A challenge for skeptical individuals as we move into a new decade will be in figuring out the line between "acceptable" and "unacceptable" skepticism. Perhaps the time has come for a new cabinet position, a Secretary of Truth.

It could be that a pandemic-spooked public has grown more comfortable with authoritarian regulations, less tolerant of disagreeable speech, and more prone to issue taboos on what can't be said. During the worst stretches of the pandemic, I was very careful not to express in public even the slightest skepticism about Dr. Anthony Fauci or the Centers for Disease Control, for fear of being reviled, even arrested, or perhaps just having my knuckles thrashed again with a yardstick. It was like being back in parochial school: I kept my mouth shut, I put on my mask, I put on two masks—hell, once I even added a third mask, and then I absolutely couldn't utter anything objectionable. I completely muted my "civic duty to annoy." Sister Grace Alma would have been proud.

I'll conclude with remarks not from Montaigne, Emerson, Mill, or James—each of whom I've cited often in these forewords—but from Bertrand Russell. In 1959, just before his eighty-seventh birthday, Russell gave several television interviews that are now available on YouTube. In one he was asked that if that interview could one day resurface, as did the Dead Sea Scrolls, to be seen by future generations (as it now can be), what wisdom would he like to impart? He replied that he had two things to say—one intellectual, the other moral. Here is my transcription from the video:

> *The intellectual:* When you are studying any matter or considering any philosophy, ask yourself only what are the facts and what is the truth that the facts bear out. Never let yourself be diverted either by what you wish to believe or by what you think would have beneficent social effects if it were believed, but look only and surely at what are the facts.
>
> *The moral:* Love is wise; hatred is foolish. In this world, which is getting more and more interconnected, we have to learn to tolerate each other, we have to learn how to put up with the fact that some people say things we don't like. We can only live together in that way, and if we are to live together and not die together, we must learn the kind of charity and the kind of tolerance which is absolutely vital to the continuation of human life on this planet.

Two appeals to the future: respect facts and practice tolerance. But issued, of course, with some skepticism as to whether they could ever be achieved. Or, some sixty years later, even be appreciated.

The Best American Essays features a selection of the year's outstanding essays, essays of literary achievement that show an awareness of craft and force of thought. Hundreds of essays are gathered annually from a wide assortment of national and regional publications. These essays are then screened, and approximately one hundred are turned over to a distinguished guest editor, who may add a few personal discoveries and who makes the final selections. The list of notable essays appearing in the back of the book is drawn from a final comprehensive list that includes not only all of the essays submitted to the guest editor but also many that were not submitted.

To qualify for the volume, the essay must be a work of respectable literary quality, intended as a fully developed, independent essay (not an excerpt) on a subject of general interest (not specialized scholarship), originally written in English (or translated by the author) for publication in an American periodical (or an English-language periodical with a strong US presence) during the calendar year. Note that abridgments and excerpts taken from longer works and published in magazines do not qualify for the series, but if considered significant, they will appear in the list of notable essays. Today's essay is a highly flexible and shifting form, however, so these criteria are not carved in stone.

Writers and editors are welcome to submit published essays from any eligible periodical for consideration; unpublished work does not qualify for the series and cannot be reviewed or evaluated. Also ineligible are essays that have been published in book form—such as a contribution to a collection—but have never appeared in a periodical. All submissions from print magazines must come directly from the publication and not in manuscript or printout format. Editors of magazines that do not identify their selections by genre should make sure all essay and nonfiction submissions are clearly marked. Editors of online magazines and literary bloggers should not assume that appropriate work will be seen; they are invited to submit clear printed copies of the essays after consulting the website for the most up-to-date mailing address.

The deadline for all submissions is February 1 of the year following the year of publication: thus all submissions of essays published in 2021 must be received by February 1, 2022. Writers should keep in mind that—as is the case for many literary awards—the essays are selected from a large pool of nominations. For this award, unlike many, writers are invited to nominate their own work. Also, though many prominent literary journals regularly submit issues to the series, others do not. We continually reach out with invitations to submit and reminders of deadlines, but not all periodicals respond. Writers should check to see whether their editors routinely submit to the series.

For more detailed information and updates on the submission guidelines and current submission mailing address, please consult MarinerBooks.com/BestAmerican.

Please note the following recent changes to guidelines for the essay series:

- Editors of print journals and periodicals that include the series on their subscription lists need do nothing further in the way of submissions. I will review all appropriate material and consider the essays and literary nonfiction in each issue as nominations. If editors prefer to highlight or nominate certain essays for special attention, they are welcome to do so. If their periodicals also publish original essays in a separate online outlet, they are invited to select and submit no more than seven candidates in hard copy.
- Because of the overwhelming number of submissions from online-only sources, the series will now limit submissions to a total of seven from each periodical. These must be submitted in hard copy. They can be submitted either all at once or over the course of the year.
- Individuals who submit to the series will now be limited to no more than seven selections. They are welcome to submit these candidates all at once or over the course of the year.

A further note: It is surprising how many submissions omit the name of the publication or its date—and sometimes I can't even find the name of the author! Separate submissions from print or online sources that do not include a full citation (name of publication, exact date, issue number, and author contact information) will not be considered. When submitting multiple essays, please remember that cover letters can sometimes get separated from selections, so please clearly indicate the full citation on each essay nominated.

For this edition of *The Best American Essays*—the thirty-sixth in the series—I'd like to thank Kathleen Lee and Debra Gwartney for providing the contributor notes for their respective spouses, Tony Hoagland and Barry Lopez, who both passed away recently, the distinguished poet Hoagland in October 2019 and Lopez (an outstanding essayist featured often in this series) in December 2020. I'd like to also thank John Freeman for calling my attention to Barry's essay, so sadly his last.

I didn't expect the work on this edition to be more difficult than last year's book, which coincided with the outbreak of the pandemic, but the 2020 collection had been pretty much assembled by the time offices shut down and everyone began working remotely. So I'm enormously grateful again to my editor, Nicole Angeloro, for all her efforts in overseeing and coordinating the remote environments we are all still enduring. A special thanks to others on the Houghton Mifflin Harcourt staff who helped make this year's book possible: Mary Dalton-Hoffman, Jenny Freilach, Susanna Brougham, and Megan Wilson. I also thank my London-based son, Gregory Atwan, for his expansive knowledge and support throughout every edition. Again, the work during this long pestilence was lightened by the loving support of my wonderful daughter Emily, who thoughtfully made sure her "high risk" dad had company, groceries, and bourbon through months of relative isolation.

It was a special treat to work with one of my favorite writers, Kathryn Schulz, on the 2021 book. As she notes in her introduction, 2020 felt like two years, and it seems odd to consider this edition as a 2021 publication. I know what she means. But thanks to FedEx, email, the internet, and instantly exchanged PDFs, twenty fine essays from a tumultuous year came together in an exceptional volume that will long depict what that year was like for many who lived through it. As I mentioned to Kathryn, I hope young readers who come across this collection in 2031 will find much of it surprising and respond, "Oh, so that's what it was like!" and not "Oh, so that's how it all started!" But in the meantime, readers in 2021 will find plenty here to reminisce about, cry about, think about, and occasionally laugh about.

R.A.

Introduction

I AGREED TO edit *The Best American Essays 2021* in August 2019. The title is, as always, somewhat misleading: it refers to the year of publication of the book, not of the essays. Thus my task, when I accepted it that summer, was to choose the best essays published in 2020.

Little did I know; little did any of us know. Back then, I assumed that in making the selections for this book and writing its introduction, I would be grappling, like my predecessors, with the questions implicit in the project. What do we mean by "best," that convenient but exasperating critical summation? What do we mean by "American": written by American authors, appearing in American publications, in some way expressive of the status or essence of our nation? And what do we mean by "essays"—a word that is a kind of philosophical opposite of "American," in that it resists the very notion of definite borders? In the end, though, all of these considerations, while never far from my mind, felt much less pressing than one that didn't even occur to me back in 2019. By rights this volume should be called *The Best American Essays 2020,* and it was a strange and challenging honor to edit it at a time when the most salient part of that standard formulation turned out to be the year.

To be clear, it is not that the preceding era had been conspicuously calm. No year in this country's history, or for that matter in history more generally, has ever has been free of tumult and trauma; the illusion that there was a time when our nation as a whole enjoyed tranquility and prosperity is the fantasy of MAGA Americans. But even by the standards of a difficult age, last year was notable. Mostly, it was notably bad. At first, that badness seemed consistent with the immediate past—as when, on January 16, an impeachment trial commenced without the benefit of crucial witnesses and relevant documents, after the Republican-controlled Senate voted not to admit them. But its specific character began to reveal itself five days later, when the Centers for Disease Control confirmed that a novel coronavirus, which had emerged the previous month in Wuhan, China, had been detected in the United States. On February 1, a man who had recently disembarked from a cruise ship fell sick with the disease caused by that coronavirus, SARS-COVID-19. By February 20, the ship, by then under quarantine off the coast of Japan, had more than half the world's known COVID cases outside China, and the rest of us had an alarming analogy for how we would feel in the coming months: captive, adrift, simultaneously too close to yet too separated from our fellow humans. Three days later, in another early indicator of the nature of the year, an unarmed twenty-five-year-old Black man named Ahmaud Arbery went out for a jog and was pursued and murdered by three white residents of Glynn County, Georgia. Five days after that, on February 29, the CDC announced the first confirmed COVID death in the United States.

Then came March, a month that soon began to resemble its grimmest noun form: a slow, forced slog to nowhere, or nowhere any of us wanted to be. One week into it, thirty states had confirmed the presence of the coronavirus within their borders and seventeen Americans were known to have died of the disease. On March 13, plainclothes police officers in Kentucky entered an apartment after midnight on a no-knock warrant and shot and killed a twenty-six-year-old Black woman named Breonna Taylor, an emergency room technician and former EMT for the city of Louisville. Four days later, the CDC announced that COVID was present in all fifty states. By that time, in a development that was unthinkable one month earlier and unprecedented in American history, virtually every elementary and secondary school across the country had closed, sending some fifty million children home to caregivers suddenly scrambling to figure out how to keep them attended, educated, and safe. By March 21, 3.3 million Americans had filed for unemployment, a thirteenfold increase over the previous week. A week later, that number had doubled, and 75 percent of Americans were living under lockdown orders.

And so it went. March felt eternal and April felt like March and May felt like March, except that all the terrible things kept getting worse. The mad president, who had already demonstrated a striking lack of interest in governing, now proved himself unable or unwilling to rise to one of the most critical moments in our nation's history. Privately aware of the dangers of COVID, he publicly downplayed it, refusing to wear a mask and ridiculing those who did, defying the medical establishment by promoting the use of a drug that proved ineffectual at best and dangerous at worst, suggesting that people could ward off the disease by injecting disinfectant directly into their veins, and memorably declaring that one day, like a miracle, the pandemic would simply disappear.

It did not. By the end of April, nearly seventy thousand Americans had died of COVID. By the first week of May, almost 15 percent of the country was out of work. On May 24, four Minneapolis police officers murdered George Floyd, in broad daylight and with appalling casualness, while bystanders tried helplessly to stop them. Floyd, as it turned out, had COVID; the disease wasn't what killed him, but by the end of the month, an additional forty thousand people were dead of it, bringing the total to 108,000 Americans—more than died in the Korean and Vietnam Wars combined, although with an analogously disparate toll on people of color. By the end of June, Black Lives Matter activists, galvanized by Floyd's murder, had organized more than forty-five hundred protests around the country, the mad president had once again made plain that his loyalties lay with white supremacists, five thousand National Guard troops had been deployed to fifteen states, and the death toll from COVID had risen by another 20 percent.

All of this, and we were only halfway through the *annus horribilis*—thinking, like the ancient Egyptians, that the final disaster was upon us when more and more plagues were preparing to descend. In August, a derecho tore across the Midwest, leveling swaths of Iowa and Illinois, leaving some areas in a weeks-long blackout, and causing $11 billion in damage. Farther west, heat, drought, and lightning conspired to cause the worst wildfire season in American history: at a time when much of the country was obligated or inclined to stay home, more than one-tenth of the population of Oregon was ordered to evacuate, and people all across the region repurposed their coronavirus masks to protect their lungs from a different threat as ten million acres of land went up in smoke.

Meanwhile, the nation seemed to be figuratively on fire as well. On September 18, Justice Ruth Bader Ginsburg died, creating an opening on the US Supreme Court six weeks before the presidential election. The Senate majority leader, Mitch McConnell, who had famously refused to consider any nominees after the death of Justice Antonin Scalia in February of 2016, on the constitutionally dubious grounds that President Obama had less than a year left in office and therefore should not be permitted to fill the vacancy, immediately pledged to move forward with a confirmation hearing. Eight days later, the mad president announced his nominee for the position, Amy Coney Barrett, in a ceremony at the White House Rose Garden, followed by an indoor reception. Six days after that, in a development that was no less shocking for being entirely predictable, the president was hospitalized with COVID and the White House ceremony began to reveal itself for what it was: a superspreader event known to have infected at least forty-five people. A week later, the FBI announced that it had foiled a plot by a right-wing militia to kidnap Gretchen Whitmer, the governor of Michigan, in retaliation for measures she had implemented to stem the spread of the pandemic. On October 30, three days before the election, a caravan of Trump supporters tried to run a Joe Biden campaign bus off the road. On November 7, when it was clear that the mad president would be president no longer, his attorney Rudy Giuliani, tasked with announcing plans for the GOP's desperate and disingenuous effort to impugn the election results, held a press conference in the parking lot of Four Seasons Total Landscaping, a previously unexceptional business venture sharing a desolate city block with a sex shop and a crematorium, in a last-gasp event that summed up better than any parody ever could the ethos of an ersatz, vulgar, and utterly ruinous administration. All that remained was for the president to rant and lie his way to the end of his only term, by which time, under his watch, more than 400,000 Americans had died of COVID.

This compression—a whole year in six paragraphs—does no justice whatsoever to the experience of living through 2020, one defining feature of which was its notable *lack* of compression. Time grew palpably strange last year, as insistent yet also as attenuated as the Doppler wail of an ambulance siren. The endlessly long days combined oddly with that famous fierce urgency of now; the fierce urgency of now combined, also oddly, with an acute awareness that we were living through history. Everyday items (toilet paper, thermometers) became difficult to obtain, while previously ancillary items (antiseptic wipes, face masks) became everyday. Unusual words and phrases entered our vocabulary: "R-naught," "essential workers," "HEPA filters," "flatten the curve," "Zoom" as noun, "Zoom" as adjective, "Zoom" as verb. Meanwhile, all of us, whether total strangers or dear friends or close family members, became, unto each other, a potential mortal threat. The number of COVID deaths rose constantly—in the worst weeks, by as much as four thousand a day—alongside another toll, that of grief, which still remains far beyond our reckoning. Grown children said goodbye to their dying parents through an iPad held up by a stranger at a hospital; grandparents said hello to their infant grandchildren through the closed windows of a nursing home. Even those who lost no one to COVID lost something to the pandemic: a job, a wedding they had spent the previous year planning, enough money to put food on the table, a much-anticipated first year of college, mental and physical abilities that had succumbed to the mysterious aftereffects of the disease, simple human contact, time with family, time alone. For all but the luckiest, and sometimes even for the luckiest, the daily texture of the era was simultaneously fraught, gripping, tragic, and boring. A friend from Alabama wrote to say that life in 2020 reminded him of being in high school: the gas was cheap, but there was nowhere to go.

In a peculiar search for silver linings, or perhaps in a grand act of public shaming, a great many pundits have pointed out, over the past year, that certain magnificent works of art were produced during earlier plagues: Boccaccio's *Decameron,* Tony Kushner's *Angels in America,* Shakespeare's *King Lear.* Perhaps in the coming years, we will learn that some genius of our own time absorbed its particular ambience—its fear, its grief, its absurdities, its few but stirring triumphs, chief among them the ousting of a mad president and the forging of what by many estimates is the largest civil rights movement in this nation's history—and found in them the makings of something bracing and beautiful. Be that as it may, it is clear that in the meantime, this era provided uncommonly rich fodder for essays. Only the most restrained of writers has ever commented on the form without pointing out that the word for it comes from the French verb *essayer,* "to try." Well: these have surely been trying times, and so many essayists felt called to grapple with them that it would have been easy to compile an anthology of the best coronavirus essays or the best essays on the Black Lives Matter movement.

But that was not my mandate, and anyway, W. H. Auden and the Old Masters were right about suffering—about how, inevitably, it takes place while the rest of the world is simply carrying on with its usual business. That is why, to name just a few examples, Jessica Lustig's "What I Learned When My Husband Got Sick with Coronavirus"—the first-person recollection that educated and terrified so many of us back in the earliest days of the pandemic—shares space in this anthology with Dariel Suarez's "In Orbit," an account of the ties between family members and nations and what it was like to grow up admiring astronauts in the small, hot island nation of Cuba under the comically distant cultural influence of the Soviet space program. It is why "Love in a Time of Terror," the last published work by the nature writer Barry Lopez, shares space with an essay that could almost share its title as well: Jesmyn Ward's "Witness and Respair," about the sudden death from acute respiratory distress of her beloved partner, a few months before coronavirus and "I can't breathe" weighted that diagnosis with the burden of an entire nation's rage and grief. More generally, it is why there are essays here not just about the most virulent sicknesses that plagued our nation this past year, but also about social media, regular media, parenting, suicide, desire, mustache politics, politics-politics, small businesses, family dynamics, the age of human beings relative to petunias and platypuses and the planet, and life and death as they look from the up-close perspective of a man in hospice care.

I have always taken Auden's poem about suffering—the lovely "Musée des Beaux Arts"—to be an indictment of our indifference to even the most proximate pain, so long as it isn't our own. But reading through this year's essays, I was reminded that it is possible to think quite differently about the chronic coexistence of suffering and well-being, grief and joy, extremis and everyday life. Ignoring suffering is the alpha and omega of iniquity, but ignoring everything else is the road to depression and despair—the high road, perhaps, but one that nonetheless leads to an emotional and ethical dead end. The world is abundant even in bad times; it is lush with interestingness, and always, somewhere, offering up consolation or beauty or humor or happiness, or at least the hope of future happiness. And so I tried to choose essays for this volume that reflect both the specific calamities that so unmistakably dominated 2020 and all those aspects of life that were touched by them only lightly, if at all: the vast rich realms of thought and experience both within and mercifully beyond the anguish of this past year.

KATHRYN SCHULZ

The Best
AMERICAN ESSAYS 2021

ELIZABETH ALEXANDER

The Trayvon Generation

FROM *The New Yorker*

THIS ONE WAS shot in his grandmother's yard. This one was carrying a bag of Skittles. This one was playing with a toy gun in front of a gazebo. Black girl in bright bikini. Black boy holding cell phone. This one danced like a marionette as he was shot down in a Chicago intersection. The words, the names: Trayvon, Laquan, bikini, gazebo, loosies, Skittles, two seconds, I can't breathe, traffic stop, dashboard cam, sixteen times. His dead body lay in the street in the August heat for four hours.

He was jogging, was hunted down, cornered by a pickup truck, and shot three times. One of the men who murdered him leaned over his dead body and was heard to say, "Fucking nigger."

I can't breathe, again. Eight minutes and forty-six seconds of a knee and full weight on his neck. "I can't breathe" and, then, "Mama!" George Floyd cried. George Floyd cried, "Mama . . . I'm through!"

His mother had been dead for two years when George Floyd called out for her as he was being lynched. Lynching is defined as a killing committed by a mob. I call the four police officers who arrested him a mob.

The kids got shot and the grown-ups got shot. Which is to say, the kids watched their peers shot down and their parents' generation get gunned down and beat down and terrorized as well. The agglomerating spectacle continues. Here are a few we know less well: Danny Ray Thomas. Johnnie Jermaine Rush. Nania Cain. Dejuan Hall. Atatiana Jefferson. Demetrius Bryan Hollins. Jacqueline Craig and her children. And then the iconic: Alton Sterling.

Eric Garner. Sandra Bland. Walter Scott. Breonna Taylor. Philando Castile.

Sandra Bland filmed the prelude to her death. The policeman thrust a stun gun in her face and said, "I will light you *up*."

I call the young people who grew up in the past twenty-five years the Trayvon Generation. They always knew these stories. These stories formed their worldview. These stories helped instruct young African Americans about their embodiment and their vulnerability. The stories were primers in fear and futility. The stories were the ground soil of their rage. These stories instructed them that anti-Black hatred and violence were never far.

They watched these violations up close and on their cell phones, so many times over. They watched them in near-real time. They watched them crisscrossed and concentrated. They watched them on the school bus. They watched them under the covers at night. They watched them often outside of the presence of adults who loved them and were charged with keeping them safe in body and soul.

This is the generation of my sons, now twenty-two and twenty years old, and their friends who are also children to me, and the university students I have taught and mentored and loved. And this is also the generation of Darnella Frazier, the seventeen-year-old Minneapolis girl who came upon George Floyd's murder in progress while on an everyday run to the corner store on May 25, filmed it on her phone, and posted it to her Facebook page at 1:46 a.m., with the caption "They killed him right in front of cup foods over south on 38th and Chicago!! No type of sympathy </3 </3 #POLICEBRUTALITY." When insideMPD.com (in an article that is no longer up) wrote, "Man Dies After Medical Incident During Police Interaction," Frazier posted at 3:10 a.m., "Medical incident??? Watch outtt they killed him and the proof is clearlyyyy there!!"

Darnella Frazier, seventeen years old, witnessing a murder in close proximity, making a record that would have worldwide impact, returned the following day to the scene of the crime. She possessed the language to say, precisely, through tears, "It's so traumatizing."

In Toni Morrison's *Sula*, which is set across the bleak Black stretch of Ohio after the First World War, the character Hannah plaintively asks her mother, Eva Peace, "Mamma, did you ever love us?" To paraphrase Eva Peace's reply: *Love you? Love you? I kept you alive.*

I believed I could keep my sons alive by loving them, believed in the magical powers of complete adoration and a love ethic that would permeate their lives. My love was armor when they were small. My love was armor when their father died of a heart attack when they were twelve and thirteen. "They think Black men only die when they get shot," my older son said in the aftermath. My love was armor when that same year our community's block watch sent emails warning residents about "two Black kids on bikes" and praising neighbors who had called the police on them. My love for my children said, *Move.* My love said, *Follow your sons,* when they ran into the dark streets of New York to join protesters after Eric Garner's killer was acquitted. When my sons were in high school and pictures of Philando Castile were on the front page of the *Times,* I wanted to burn all the newspapers so they would not see the gun coming in the window, the blood on Castile's T-shirt, the terror in his partner's face, and the eyes of his witnessing baby girl. But I was too late, too late generationally, because they were not looking at the newspaper; they were looking at their phones, where the image was a house of mirrors straight to hell.

My love was both rational and fantastical. Can I protect my sons from being demonized? Can I keep them from moving free? But they must be able to move as free as wind! If I listen to their fears, will I comfort them? If I share my fears, will I frighten them? Will racism and fear disable them? If we ignore it all, will it go away? Will dealing with race fill their minds like stones and block them from thinking of a million other things? Let's be clear about what motherhood is. A being comes onto this earth and you are charged with keeping it alive. It dies if you do not tend it. It is as simple as that. No matter how intellectual and multicolored motherhood becomes as children grow older, the part that says *My purpose on earth is to keep you alive* has never totally dissipated. Magical thinking on all sides.

I want my children—all of them—to thrive, to be fully alive. How do we measure what that means? What does it mean for our young people to be "black alive and looking back at you," as June Jordan puts it in her poem "Who Look at Me"? How to access the sources of strength that transcend this American nightmare of racism and racist violence? What does it mean to be a lucky mother, when so many of my sisters have had their children taken from them by this hatred? The painter Titus Kaphar's recent *Time* magazine cover portrays a Black mother cradling what should be her child across the middle of her body, but the child is literally cut out of the canvas and cut out of the mother, leaving a gaping wound for an unending grief that has made a sisterhood of countless Black women for generations.

My sons were both a little shy outside of our home when they were growing up. They were quiet and observant, like their father, who had come to this country as a refugee from Eritrea: African observant, immigrant observant, missing nothing. I've watched them over the years with their friends, doing dances now outmoded with names I persist in loving—Nae Nae, Hit Dem Folks—and talking about things I didn't teach them and reading books I haven't read and taking positions I don't necessarily hold, and I marvel. They are grown young men. With their friends, they talk about the pressure to succeed, to have a strong public face, to excel. They talk their big talk, they talk their hilarity, and they talk their fear. When I am with them, I truly believe the kids are all right and will save us.

But I worry about this generation of young Black people and depression. I have a keen eye—what Gwendolyn Brooks called "gobbling mother-eye"—for these young people, sons and friends and students whom I love and encourage and welcome into my home, keep in touch with and check in on. How are you, how are you, how are you. How are you, baby, how are you. I am interested in the vision of television shows like *Atlanta* and *Insecure,* about which I have been asking every young person who will listen, "Don't you think they're about low-grade, undiagnosed depression and not Black hipster ennui?" Why, in fact, did Earn drop out of Princeton? Why does Van get high before a drug test? Why does Issa keep blowing up her life? This season, *Insecure* deals directly with the question of young Black people and mental-health issues: Molly is in and out of therapy, and we learn that Nathan, aka Lyft-Bae, who was ghosting Issa, has been dealing with bipolar disorder. The work of the creative icon of their generation often brings me to the question: Why is Kendrick so sad? He has been frank about his depression and suicidal thoughts. It isn't just the specter of race-based violence and death that hangs over these young people.

It's that compounded with the constant display of inequity that has most recently been laid bare in the COVID-19 pandemic, with racial health disparities that are shocking even to those of us inured to our disproportionate suffering.

Black creativity emerges from long lines of innovative responses to the death and violence that plague our communities. "Not a house in the country ain't packed to its rafters with some dead Negro's grief," Toni Morrison wrote in *Beloved,* and I am interested in creative emergences from that ineluctable fact.

There are so many visual artists responding to this changing same: Henry Taylor, Michael Rakowitz, Ja'Tovia Gary, Carrie Mae Weems, lauren woods, Alexandra Bell, Black Women Artists for Black Lives Matter, Steffani Jemison, Kerry James Marshall, Titus Kaphar. To pause at one work: Dread Scott's *A Man Was Lynched by Police Yesterday,* which he made in the wake of the police shooting of Walter Scott, in 2015, echoes the flag reading A MAN WAS LYNCHED YESTERDAY that the NAACP flew outside its New York headquarters between 1920 and 1938 to mark the lynchings of Black people in the United States.

I want to turn to three short films that address the Trayvon Generation with particular power: Flying Lotus's "Until the Quiet Comes" (2012); his "Never Catch Me," with Kendrick Lamar (2014); and Lamar's "Alright" (2015).

In "Until the Quiet Comes," the director, Kahlil Joseph, moves us through Black Los Angeles—Watts, to be specific. In the fiction of the video, a boy stands in an empty swimming pool, pointing his finger as a gun and shooting. The bullet ricochets off the wall of the pool and he drops as it appears to hit him. The boy lies in a wide-arced swath of his blood, a portrait in the empty pool. He is another Black boy down, another body of the traumatized community.

In an eerie twilight, we move into the densely populated Nickerson Gardens, where a young man, played by the dancer Storyboard P, lies dead. Then he rises, and begins a startling dance of resurrection, perhaps coming back to life. The community seems numb, oblivious of his rebirth. That rebirth is brief; he gets into a low-rider car, that LA icon. The car drives off after his final death dance, taking him from this life to the other side. His death is consecrated by his performance, a ritual that the sudden dead are not afforded. The car becomes a hearse, a space of ritual transport into the next life. But the young man is still gone.

What does it mean to be able to bring together the naturalistic and the visionary, to imagine community as capable of reanimating even its most hopeless and anesthetized members?

What does it mean for a presumably murdered Black body to come to life in his community in a dance idiom that is uniquely part of Black culture and youth culture, all of that power channeled into a lifting?

A sibling to Joseph's work is Hiro Murai's video for Flying Lotus's "Never Catch Me." It opens at a funeral for two children, a Black boy and girl, who lie heartbreak-beautiful in their open caskets. Their community grieves inconsolably in the church. The scene is one of profound mourning.

And then the children open their eyes and climb out of their caskets. They dance explosively in front of the pulpit before running down the aisle and out of the church. The mourners cannot see this resurrection, for it is a fantasia. The kids dance another dance of Black LA, the force of Black bodily creativity, that expressive life source born of violence and violation that have upturned the world for generations. The resurrected babies dance with a pumping force. But the community's grief is unmitigated, because, once again, this is a dreamscape. The children spring out into the light and climb into a car—no, it is a hearse—and, smiling with the joy of mischievous escapees, drive away. Kids are not allowed to drive; kids are not allowed to die.

What does it mean for a Black boy to fly, to dream of flying and transcending? To imagine his vincible body all-powerful, a body that in this society is so often consumed as a moneymaker and an object of perverse desire, perceived to have superhuman and thus threatening powers? In the video for Kendrick Lamar's "Alright," directed by Colin Tilley, Lamar flies through the California city streets, above sidewalks and empty lots, alongside wire fences.

"Alright" has been the anthem of many protests against racism and police violence and unjust treatment. Lamar embodies the energy and the message of the resonant phrase "Black Lives Matter," which Patrice Cullors, Alicia Garza, and Opal Tometi catapulted into circulation when, in 2013, they founded the movement. The phrase was apt then and now. Its coinage feels both ancestral in its knowledge and prophetic in its ongoing necessity. I know now with certainty that there will never be a moment when we will not need to say it, not in my lifetime, and not in the lifetime of the Trayvon Generation.

The young Black man flying in Lamar's video is joyful and defiant, rising above the streets that might claim him, his body liberated and autonomous. At the end of the video, a police officer raises a finger to the young man in the sky and mimes pulling the trigger. The wounded young man falls, slowly—another brother down—and lands. The gun was a finger; the flying young man appears safe. He does not get up. But in the final image of this dream he opens his eyes and smiles. For a moment, he has not been killed.

Black celebration is a village practice that has brought us together in protest and ecstasy around the globe and across time. Community is a mighty life force for self-care and survival. But it does not protect against murder. Dance itself will not free us. We continue to struggle against hatred and violence. I believe that this generation is more vulnerable, and more traumatized, than the last. I think of Frederick Douglass's words upon hearing slaves singing their sorrow songs in the fields. He laid waste to the nascent myth of the happy darky: "Slaves sing most when they are most unhappy." Our dancing is our pleasure but perhaps it is also our sorrow song.

My sons love to dance. I have raised them to young adulthood. They are beautiful. They are funny. They are strong. They are fascinating. They are kind. They are joyful in friendship and community. They are righteous and smart in their politics. They are learning. They are loving. They are mighty and alive.

I recall many sweaty summer parties with family friends where the grown-ups regularly acted up on the dance floor and the kids d.j.'d to see how quickly they could make their old-school parents and play-uncles and aunties holler "Aaaaayyyy! That's my jam!" They watched us with deep amusement. But they would dance too. One of the aunties glimpsed my sons around the corner in the next room and said, "Oh, my God, they can dance! They've been holding out on us, acting all shy!"

When I told a sister-friend that my older son, during his freshman year in college, was often the one controlling the aux cord, dancing and dancing and dancing, she said, "Remember, people dance when they are joyful."

Yes, I am saying I measure my success as a mother of Black boys in part by the fact that I have sons who love to dance, who dance in community, who dance till their powerful bodies sweat, who dance and laugh, who dance and shout. Who are able—in the midst of their studying and organizing, their fear, their rage, their protesting, their vulnerability, their missteps and triumphs, their knowledge that they must fight the hydra-headed monster of racism and racial violence that we were not able to cauterize—to find the joy and the power of communal self-expression.

This essay is not a celebration, nor is it an elegy.

We are no longer enslaved. Langston Hughes wrote that we must stand atop the racial mountain, "free within ourselves," and I pray that those words have meaning for our young people. But our freedom must be seized and reasserted every day.

People dance to say, *I am alive and in my body.*

I am Black alive and looking back at you.

HILTON ALS

Homecoming

FROM *The New Yorker*

BY THE LATE summer of 1967, when I turned seven, we'd been living in the house for six years. By "we," I mean my mother, two of my four older sisters, and my little brother. And although we shared the place with a rotating cast of other relatives, including my mother's mother and an aunt and her two children, I always considered it my mother's home. The house was in the Brownsville section of Brooklyn. Like all the moves my mother engineered or helped to engineer for our family, this one was aspirational. Despite the fact that Brownsville had begun its slow decline into drugs, poverty, and ghettoization years before, my mother's house —the only one in her life that, after years of work and planning, she would even partly own—symbolized a break with everything we had known before, including an apartment in Crown Heights, with a shared bathroom near the stairwell, where, on Sunday nights, my mother would line her daughters up with freshly laundered towels so that they could take their weekly bath.

Privacy was something my sisters had to get used to. Our new house had doors and a proper sitting room, which sometimes served as a makeshift bedroom for visiting Bajan relatives. (My mother's family was from Barbados.) The sister I was closest to, a poetry-writing star who wore pencil skirts to play handball with the guys, composed her verse amid drifts and piles of clothes and kept her door closed. My brother and I shared a smaller room and a bed. My mother had her own room, where the door was always ajar; she didn't so much sleep there as rest between walks up and down the hall to watch and listen for the safety of her children.

The Brownsville summer of 1967 was like every other Brooklyn summer I'd experienced: stultifying. Relief was sought at the nearby Betsy Head Pool, and at the fire hydrants that reckless boys opened with giant wrenches. The cold water made the black asphalt blacker in the black nights. Gossip floated down the street from our neighbors' small front porches and from stoops flanked by big concrete planters full of dusty plastic flowers. Nursing a beer or a Pepsi, the grown-ups discussed far-off places like Vietnam. So-and-So's son had come back from there all messed up, and now he was on the methadone. Then the conversation would shift to the kids. Every kid in our neighborhood was everyone else's kid. Prying, caring eyes were everywhere. Sometimes the conversation stopped—just for a moment—as girls in summer dresses passed. Men and women alike looked longingly at those girls, for different reasons, as they ambled down the street, pretending to pay no mind to the fine-built boys who called to them from a distance.

In short, what one saw in that place on those nights was what my mother had been searching for: community. She was a proud member of Mary McLeod Bethune's National Council of Negro Women, and had attended Martin Luther King Jr.'s 1963 March on Washington. When she reminisced about that march, it was with a vividness that made her children feel shy: sometime in the long ago, Ma had been part of history. Nonviolent organization, picket lines, and marches: all these strengthened our mother's conviction that inclusion worked, that civil rights worked, that the Black family could work, especially if welfare officers and other professionally concerned people—journalists and sociologists, say—paid attention to what a Black mother built, rather than to how she failed. ("I don't think a female running a house is a problem, a broken family," Toni Morrison said in a 1989 interview. "It's perceived as one because of the notion that a head is a man . . . You need a whole community—everybody—to raise a child.")

If Ma failed, then we failed, and she never wanted us to feel that. Something else Ma wanted: for Black people in Brooklyn, in America, not to forever be effectively refugees—stateless, homeless, without rights, confined by borders that they did not create and by a penal system that killed them before they died, all while trying to rear children who went to schools that taught them not about themselves but about what they didn't have.

And yet there was no way to save Ma's idea of community and hope when, in September 1967, our neighborhood changed forever. Someone, or a bunch of someones, heard that a young boy, a fourteen-year-old Black kid, Richard Ross, had been killed by a cop—a detective named John Rattley—in Brownsville. Apparently, Rattley believed that Ross had mugged or was mugging an old Jewish man; as Ross tried to get away, Rattley shot him in the back of the head. In those years, Black boys were locked up or killed all the time; you didn't think about it much, because to think about it was to remember what a killing field New York was, and how easily you too could become a body in that field. The detail we hung on to in the flurry of hearsay and speculation was that Rattley was Black. The activist Sonny Carson was big then; it was said that he was leading a demonstration, and it was coming our way.

Marches, protests, and the like were, we knew, a prelude to the racially motivated violence that had already cropped up in nearby Newark and other places, such as Detroit. For sure, Brownsville would get more messed up if the cops were involved; that was how demonstrations became riots. I remember that night—or was it late afternoon?—our mother walking us swiftly into the house and shutting all the doors and windows. Inside, it was lights-out. The air was close. We could hear our hearts beating. Peeking from behind one of the living-room curtains, I watched as the protesters started flinging bottles and stones at the cops, and our real world turned into a movie, a horror film in which everything we'd built together—home, hope, the illusion of citizenship—was torn to the ground. Black people, mostly men, were roaming the streets, periodically smashing car windows or overturning ashcans and torching rubbish. They were claiming what they felt to be a kind of freedom. As refugees, we knew that none of it belonged to us—not that shop, not that newly built pigeon coop—even as we knew that it did belong to us, emotionally speaking: it was all part of our community. Still, why not trash a universe that has trashed you?

Standing by my mother's living-room window, I tried, tentatively, to ask her why our world was burning, burning. She gave me a forbidding look: *Boy, be quiet so you can survive,* her eyes seemed to say. Did I want to be another Richard Ross, one of the hundred or thousand Richard Rosses out there? So many questions I could not ask—among them, had our desire for community also been reduced to rubble and ash? The chaos that night—it would last for two days before life went back to "normal"—was more vivid to my burgeoning writer's mind than what I could not see: our mother's vivid memories of King's promise of a promised land. Where was that? And was it different from—or superior to—the world my poetry-writing sister was gradually entering, through her admiration for a number of the musicians and poets associated with the Black Arts Movement? A world that promised a cataclysmic end to whiteness, if only we could carry arms and follow the teachings of early Malcolm X? Was my mother a "better" forecaster of what was to come than my sister? Martin and Malcolm, like protest marches and riots, belonged to different generations. Because I loved my sister and wanted to think as she did, I was, presumably, part of the "riot generation"; I knew about violence from the teasing, taunting Black boys in my neighborhood, and Sly and the Family Stone's dark and furious live album *There's a Riot Goin' On,* released four years after the Brownsville uprising, stayed in my bones more than those of any weepy folksinger. But what about Ma and her dreams? I belonged to and was part of them as well.

Who would I be when the revolution finally came? A soldier for peace, or a man who might appear in "The True Import of Present Dialogue: Black vs. Negro," a poem by the activist and writer Nikki Giovanni that opens: "Nigger / Can you kill"? But my brother and I weren't niggers. And if called upon we wouldn't have been able to protect our mother and our sisters. Whom could we rely on to protect them, let alone us? Would the young Black men with bats and other weapons who were flitting down our street—they seemed to leap as they walked—come for us? Would they save us? Or destroy us too? No door or lock could keep them out.

Ma had her girls first. I wonder what it was like for her to try to understand boys—to rear boys who were not a threat to women, who would grow up to support women's dreams and protect them. In her world, men came and went and were Something Else. My brother and I were different, and, although we were our mother's familiars, I wonder if she eyed our difference unbelievingly at times, even as she nurtured it.

When we finally left our house in Brownsville, we walked out into a changed world. Apparently, while we were inside, Lloyd Sealy, who was then the commander of Brooklyn's North Borough, had ramped up the police presence in the area. One way to control unruly, ungovernable refugees, of course, is to remind them that they are guests of a mighty police state. Every billy club that cracks open a Black skull anywhere is proof of that. Once we learned that Sealy was Black too, we bent low in sorrow, or rose with arms high in grief and anger. What had civil rights wrought? Were powerful Black men mere functionaries for a white administration? Did Black lives not matter to them, then or ever?

Brownsville was not their home. Was it even ours? The world that Ma desired just wasn't possible yet. We were still refugees living within certain borders. We would live and die in this amount of space and no more. Emerging from our mother's house, we smelled burning tires and bedding. (Our house was relatively unharmed.) I don't remember my mother crying; I remember entering that fetid air in silence. But you could hear our community mourning the loss of itself, if you knew how to listen; mourning was our language. The world around us was not the one we had worked hard to achieve but the quiet, degraded world that our not-country said we deserved. We couldn't keep nothing, the elders said, not even ourselves.

Had the uprising been a kind of temper tantrum? Acted out by a community that was, like me, looking for a Black man it could trust to protect and lead it? Rattley, Sealy, my only occasionally live-in father: there had been so many disappointments. Someone said that Sonny Carson had helped to quiet folks down. Someone said that a young Muslim man, a local youth-group leader, had also helped to calm things by serving as a liaison between the police and the crowds. Someone said that Mayor John V. Lindsay was around. And then there he was, our first celebrity, a tall white man, trailed by a group of photographers and tired-looking Black people, walking through our streets, or someone's streets, surveying the damage. Lindsay also served on President Lyndon Johnson's National Advisory Commission on Civil Disorders, more commonly known as the Kerner Commission, which had been established after riots took place in Los Angeles, Chicago, and Detroit. He had access to a world beyond what we knew, and now he turned his attention to me, in this world. He took my hand. He was beautiful, like a star from a movie I had never seen. Mixed with the confusion and the vague erotics of the moment—it was a thrill to feel my small hand in his big one (was *he* my father?), though I had already learned to hide that part of myself—was my silent bewilderment over the fact that poverty and frustration could be an opportunity for a photograph, though no one asked us what it was like to lose a home or to dream of living in one.

Hope dies all the time. And yet we need to believe that it will come back and attach itself to a new cause—a new love, a new house, something that gives us a sense of purpose, which is ultimately what hope is. Ma always had hope, because she knew that it had helped to change the world, her Black world. But I had no clear examples, growing up, of what might make a difference in mine. Guns? Death? Poetry? Would any of it dismantle the economic discrepancies, for instance, that defined our de-facto underclass, that kept us scavenging for a lifeline, even if it was just a pair of sneakers snatched through a pane of broken glass? When I finally saw the National Mall, in Washington, DC, in person, the black-and-white pictures of King's historic gathering there played in my head, but alongside memories of 1975's Human Kindness Day. Established in 1972, Human Kindness Day—a series of exhibitions, concerts, and literary events meant to inspire racial pride—was spearheaded by the National Park Service, the DC Recreation Department, and Compared to What?, Inc., a nonprofit organization for the advancement of the arts. Each year, a concert by a great Black artist capped off the festival—Roberta Flack the first year, Nina Simone the next. But in 1975, when Stevie Wonder was the headliner, vandalism broke out. Hundreds of folks were robbed and injured. It's cited as an early example of "wildin'," but, when discussing it, people rarely mention the recession of the mid-seventies, or the way that bringing together haves and have-nots lent a stage, yet again, to the drama of inequality.

It was a drama that I saw play out, over and over again, as I was growing up. I don't remember when we moved to Bedford-Stuyvesant, but demonstrations and riots followed us there. Then, after a time, we moved to Crown Heights again; riots followed us there too. No place was safe, because wherever we congregated was unsafe. The laws of real estate, economics, and racism made us unsafe. To cops. To landlords. To social workers, who "visited" our houses whenever they felt like it to see if our mothers were entertaining men (and, by implication, getting paid for it). To shopkeepers, who didn't understand that the deprivations of poverty were a pretty good incentive for us to take what we'd never be able to buy. To schoolteachers, who weren't paid to care. To a society that demanded our gratitude for the dried gruel at the bottom of the bowl, which it tossed us after years of scarcely remunerated labor. To the Black men whom we wanted to stay, but who couldn't for fear that our vulnerability would compound their own.

The question for me from Brownsville on was: How would I protect my mother and the other women in my family when the riots came again (and they always came)? Adults are supposed to protect children, yes, but when I was growing up it didn't necessarily work that way. It wasn't that your mother didn't care—you were all she had—it was just that she kept running out of time. In addition to her full-time job—and, often, a second job—there was the work that went into feeding you, listening to you, and making sure no one laughed at you or cracked you in the face because you had dreams.

As a boy in Brownsville and in Bed-Stuy, I was tormented by the question of protection, because, of course, I too wanted to be protected. Like any number of Black boys in those neighborhoods, I grew up in a matrilineal society, where I had been taught the power—the necessity—of silence. But how could you not cry out when you couldn't save your mother because you couldn't defend yourself? Although I had this in common with other guys, something separated me from them when it came to joining those demonstrations, to leaping in the air when Black bodies were threatened. My distance had to do with my queerness. The guys who took the chance to protect their families and themselves were the same guys who called me "faggot."

For a while, I thought their looting and carrying on had to do with enacting a particular form of masculinity: If white men and cops could wreak havoc in the world, why couldn't they? But, as I grew older, I realized that part of their acting out had to do with how we were brought up. They weren't trying to be men—they were already men—but in order to have the perceived *weight* of white men they had to reject, to some degree, the silence they had learned from their mothers. If they were going to die, they were going to die screaming.

The silence that I was taught as a means of survival no longer fits me either. But I know that I wouldn't have given it up entirely—it's hard to give up, Ma—if Christian Cooper hadn't shown me another way in Central Park last month, if that fifty-seven-year-old thinker hadn't woken up next to his slumbering boyfriend, then left their shared love to look at birds, which he loved too. By example, Cooper showed me that I was not alone. When a white woman tried to endanger him with a lying 911 call ("An African American man is threatening my life!"), he did not run, and he did not, on a profound level, engage with his attacker's theatrics of racism. Cooper's actions that day said, Listen to yourself, not to your accuser, because your accusers are always listening to their own panic about your presence. And if what they are saying—or shouting—threatens your personal safety, protect yourself by any means necessary. If you can protect yourself, you'll be around to love and take care of more people, and be loved and taken care of in return.

I don't entirely agree with the great Ralph Ellison when he says, in his 1989 essay "On Being the Target of Discrimination,"

> It isn't necessarily through acts of physical violence—lynching, mob attacks, or slaps to the face, whether experienced firsthand or by word of mouth—that a child is initiated into the contradictions of segregated democracy. Rather, it is through brief impersonal encounters, stares, vocal inflections, hostile laughter, or public reversals of private expectations that occur at the age when children are most perceptive to the world and all its wonders.

The truth is that nothing is impersonal when it comes to racism, or the will to subjugate. Every act of racism is a deeply personal act with an end result: the unmooring diminishment of the person who is its target. If you have suffered that kind of erasure, you are less likely to know who you are or where you live. My brother has suggested that we moved so much when we were kids because our mother kept looking for safety. I don't remember exactly how many times we moved; in those days, my focus was on trying to win people over, the better to protect my family, or—silently—trying to fend off homophobia, the better to protect myself. My being a "faggot" was one way for other people to feel better about themselves. My being a "faggot" let cops know what they weren't.

At present, I live in a predominantly white neighborhood in Manhattan. For a number of reasons, I was stuck at home when the demonstrations started downtown last month. Panic set in when I heard the helicopters flying low and the police sirens going. I was convinced that the cops would run across my roof and, on seeing my Black ass sitting in an apartment in a neighborhood where I had no business being, would shoot me dead. I asked a white male friend to come and be with me.

What I felt during that first wave of panic was a muscle memory of riots and rootlessness; the thought of those cops took away my feeling of being at home in my home. The real-as-hell feelings I had in my apartment that evening before my friend got there were also a metaphor, but I don't know for what kind of story—and if it is all a story, where do I put Richard Ross? Where do I put George Floyd, whose murder by a white police officer in Minneapolis launched those demonstrations? Where do I put Tony McDade, the Black trans man who was killed by a police officer in Tallahassee on May 27? Or Breonna Taylor, shot to death in her bed by Louisville police in March? Or Robert Fuller, whose death by hanging, in Palmdale, California, this month may have been a suicide or may have been a lynching, and how horrible it is that either is possible, in a world hell-bent on a certain kind of extinction? And why are these stories becoming conflated? That is, why have they become one story in the media's mind—a story of Black death and Black uprising and Black hope and regeneration? Inevitably, we are losing sight of the individual stories, because it takes too long to consider them one by one. The rope around Robert Fuller's neck becomes Billie Holiday trying to breathe out the choking words as she sings: "Here is a fruit for the crows to pluck . . . / Here is a strange and bitter crop."

Are we a strange crop, constantly provoking strange responses—which are now out in the open, because, truth to tell, Black people are also an important revenue stream, and Hulu wants to show us that, by streaming the "Black stories" in its archives? Hulu is only one of any number of media outlets that are rushing blindly to show their solidarity with the cause, without mentioning the financial and political benefits that may accrue to them. We all hurt, but some of us want to continue to be paid. And what will the world look like after this period becomes just another moment in history (and it will)? Will there be a backlash? Will culture become tired of his Blackness and her difference and revert to what it's always reverted to—Andrew Wyeth–tinted dreams, impatience, or downright amnesia once Black lives mattering doesn't pay, in all senses of the word? Is this all one story?

I keep looking for the loneliness inherent in Black life, our refugee status dressed up in self-protective decorum, because if you can get to your loneliness and articulate it you can also begin to talk about community, and why it is needed in life too. My community is my memory, which includes the image of my late best friend—he died of AIDS thirty years ago now—who was white and Catholic, being beaten up outside a gay Asian club he was exiting, and me asking later, when he showed up with blood on his jacket, if he'd called the police, and him staring me dead in the eye and saying, "Why bother?" I looked at him and heard the terrifying sound of him being punched in the head because he was interested not only in his own queerness but in Something Else, a gay world where he was not looking in a mirror but was a guest in someone else's home.

Is this all one story? As a writer, I inhabit a world or worlds where the prevalent ethos is presumed to be liberal, but I can't remember a time when the publishing industry, like other institutions devoted to the arts—museums, Broadway—didn't come down on the side of fashion and power. At meetings and parties, one spends a great deal of time with people I call the collaborators—functionaries in service to power—who'll step on your neck to get to the next fashionable Negro who can explain just what is happening and why. When white America asks Black artists in particular to speak about race, it's almost always from the vantage point of its being a sort of condition, or plight, and, if those collaborators can actually listen, what they want to hear is, Who are *we* in relation to *you?* In his powerful essay "Within the Context of No-Context," published in this magazine in 1980, George W. S. Trow described that phenomenon further:

> During the nineteen-sixties, a young black man in a university class described the Dutch painters of the seventeenth century as "belonging" to the white students in the room, and not to him. This idea was seized on by white members of the class. They acknowledged that they were at one with Rembrandt. They acknowledged their dominance. They offered to discuss, at any length, their inherited power to oppress. It was thought at the time that reactions of this type had to do with "white guilt" or "white masochism." No. No. It was white euphoria. Many, many white children of that day felt the power of their inheritance for

> the first time in the act of rejecting it, and they insisted on rejecting it . . . so that they might continue to feel the power of that connection. Had the young black man asked, "Who is this man to you?" the pleasure they felt would have vanished in embarrassment and resentment.

Why embarrassment and resentment? Because what passes for intellectual inquiry at cocktail parties and in many contemporary institutions is a way of masking the continued and seemingly endless grip that the cultural status quo has on Blacks and whites alike. And, if you confront your white interlocutor with that truth, he has to confront why he thinks that he and his culture are better than yours. You may have Blackness, but we have Rembrandt. Or, in the words of Saul Bellow, "Who is the Tolstoy of the Zulus? The Proust of the Papuans? I'd be happy to read them."

Who will tell this story? Many of us and none of us. Because the "exceptional" Black artists who are asked to sit around the fire and explain why riots, why death, or why a child has a mother and not a father, have a built-in expiration date: they function as translators of events and rarely as translators of their own stories, their own loneliness in a given place and time. As my friend sat with me earlier this month to help ease the terror I felt on hearing the helicopters, I thought about what certain other writers might have made of this place and time if life and our segregated society hadn't exhausted them long ago: Richard Wright, dead at fifty-two. Nella Larsen, prematurely silenced. Zora Neale Hurston, broke and forgotten by the time she was sixty. Wallace Thurman, drunk and disgraced, dead at thirty-two, and, of course, James Baldwin, fatigued and lonesome, dead at sixty-three. Imagine all the things they didn't say because they couldn't say them. All those journeys abroad, all the shutting themselves off from the world.

Was it worth it, Ma? (You yourself died at sixty-two.) Was it worth Richard Wright spending so long on his book-length essay, *White Man, Listen!* (1957), in which he wrote about racism and his hopes for African nationalism, with all the sense and confusion that was in him? Racism can break your heart, break your body. Did Wright, Baldwin, Chester Himes, W.E.B. Du Bois, and so many others forgive their country before the end, or did they die screaming? They were my parents too. Are destruction and hope my only models? Ma, tell me where to begin this story, which will have to include your fear of my death—I'm sorry. Because we are all dying. Shall I begin by showing the collaborators the wounds I've suffered on the auction block of gay and Black life and culture? Or should I shut up and learn forgiveness on top of forgiveness?

Okay, Ma, maybe forgiveness is the way, because I love you. But can I forgive myself for forgiving? For the temerity of wanting to be an artist and eating shit to support that impulse? An impulse, Ma, that you supported from the very beginning by writing your comments on the stories I shared with you ("Very good. Mommy"), just as you supported all those poems my sister wrote in her bedroom with the door closed in Brownsville. I've lived with forgiveness for so long—surely there is another language, a different weight on the soul?

Ma, can I forgive the white movie executive who thought it might be "fun" to tell our Black host at a luncheon that he'd confused him with another Black man? Can I forgive the white Dutch director who asked me to step in for a Black actor—to play the character of an old family retainer—since I was, you know, Black myself? Can I forgive the self-consciously "queer" white academic at a prestigious Eastern university who made disparaging remarks about my body in front of his class—I was his guest speaker—because he wanted to make a point about one of my "texts"? Can I forgive the white editors who ask me who the next James Baldwin might be, so that they can stay on top of the whole Black thing? Can I forgive the white female patron of the arts who, after I'd given a lecture in Miami, at a dinner that was ostensibly in my honor, turned the party against me because I hadn't paid more attention in my speech to an artist whose work she collected? Can I forgive the white former fashion-magazine editor who promised me a job but then discovered that his superiors would never hire a Black man? Can I forgive the white magazine writer who, a day or two after I was hired by this magazine, yelled at me in front of friends—with whom I was celebrating the occasion—that I had been hired only because I was Black? Can I forgive the white musician who "accidentally" faxed me a racist drawing that her child had made in school, which she thought was funny and his teacher saw no reason to criticize? Can I forgive the white couple who, at a memorial for a friend, made it a point to tell me they'd had no idea that I was so big and so Black? Can I forgive the white book editor who said on a first date that his family had had some financial interest in Haiti, where they had owned people "just like you"? Can I forgive the white arts benefactress in Boston who, at another dinner after another lecture, told the table how much she'd loved spirituals as a child, and said, rhetorically, "Who doesn't love Negro spirituals?" Can I forgive the white woman who sat next to me at a Chinese restaurant while I was enjoying a quiet dinner by myself and leaned over to ask if I was a cast member of *Porgy and Bess,* which was playing across the street? Can I forgive the white curator who shapes much of the city's, if not the world's, understanding of modern art, who, exhausted by the whole question of inclusion and apropos of an exhibition at her institution, said, "I'm just not into Chinese art"? Can I forgive the white editor who invited me to lunch and during the course of the meal defended his use of the word "nigger" in one of his predominantly white college classes with the Lenny Bruce argument that the only way to defuse the word is to take its power away by speaking it, and added that, besides, one heard it used all up and down Lenox Avenue, in Harlem, and what about that? The old model—Ma's model—was not to give up too much of your power by letting your oppressor know how you felt. But, Ma, I was dying anyway, in all that silence.

You get it only when the shit happens to you too; we all know that. And now the effects of our segregated democracy are happening to you. And now you can see or understand that, all along, I've been trying to get along, just like you. The way Ma taught me. To be independent and help my chosen family. I've tried to make a living at something I love and to explore the intricacies of love, just like you. I've lost friends and forgotten to pay a credit-card bill, just like you. But I wasn't allowed to be like you. And now my "other" is happening to you. Now degradation and moral compromise and your body breaking down are happening to you. Because Donald Trump has happened to you. Oxycontin has happened to you. Broken families have happened to you. Gun violence—in schools, in supermarkets, in movie theaters, at concerts—has happened to you, along with riots, and frustration, and cops who can't pass up an opportunity to flash their guns and their batons in your presence, even as you search for home, even as the dream comes tumbling, tumbling, tumbling down.

MOLLY McCULLY BROWN

The Broken Country

FROM *Virginia Quarterly Review*

THE FALL I was nineteen, I came into my college dining hall in California just in time to overhear a boy telling a table of our mutual acquaintances that he thought I was very nice, but he felt terribly sorry for me because I was going to die a virgin. This was already impossible, but in that moment all that mattered was the blunt force of the boy's certainty. He hadn't said, *I could never . . .* or *She might be pretty but . . .* or *Can she even have sex?* or even *I'd never fuck a cripple,* all sentences I'd heard or overheard by then. What he had done was, firmly, with some weird, wrong breed of kindness in his voice, drawn a border between my body and the country of desire.

It didn't matter that, by then, I'd already done my share of heated fumbling in narrow dorm-room beds; that more than one person had already looked at me and said, *I'm in love with you,* and I had said it back. It didn't matter that I'd boldly kissed a boy on his back porch in sixth grade, surprising him so much that the BB gun he was holding went off, sending a squadron of brown squirrels skittering up into the trees. Most of me was certain that the boy in the dining hall was right in all the ways that really mattered. He knew I'd never be the kind of woman anyone could really want, and I knew that even my body's own wanting was suspect and tainted by flaw. My body was a country of error and pain. It was a doctor's best attempt, a thing to manage and make up for. It was a place to leave if I was hunting goodness, happiness, or release.

I have the strongest startle reflex in the world. Call my name in the quiet, make a loud noise, introduce something sudden into my field of vision, and I'll jump like there's been a clap of thunder every time. It's worst, though, if you touch me when I'm not expecting it. I start the way a wild animal does. For years I thought only the bad wiring in my brain was to blame, the same warped signals that throw off my balance and make my muscles tighten, keeping me permanently on tenterhooks. Then I met Susannah, whose first memories are also of a gas mask and a surgeon's hands, of being picked up, held down, put under. She too jumps at the smallest surprise, the slightest unanticipated touch. Now I think that feral reflex also arises from something in that early trauma: all those years of being touched without permission, having your body talked about over your head, being forced under sedation, made to leave your body and come back to a version that hurts more but is supposedly better—the blank stretch of time when something happened you can't name. I think it matters that the first touch I remember is someone readying to cut me open, that when I woke up I was crying, and there was a sutured wound.

For the better part of my childhood, I was part of a study on gait development in children with cerebral palsy. At least once a year—and sometimes more frequently if I'd recently had surgery—I spent an afternoon in a research lab, walking up and down a narrow strip of carpet, with sensors and wires attached to my body so doctors could chart the way I moved. The digital sensors composed a computer model of my staggering shape, each one a little point of light, and when I peeled them off they left behind burning red squares like perfect territories. But the doctors also shot the whole thing on a video camera mounted on a tripod, and gave us the raw footage to take home. The early films are cute; I'm curly-haired and chatty. The bathing suit I wear so that my legs and arms are bare is always either a little too small or a little too big, a hand-me-down from my older sister. I trundle happily down the carpet. As I get older, though, the tapes get more complicated. By the time I get to footage where I look anything like myself, I can't bear to watch it anymore. I'm a teenage girl in bike shorts or a bathing suit, being watched by a collection of men, walking what's essentially a runway like some kind of wounded animal.

Even today, I can't quite tell: Do I hope that when they looked at me back then, mostly undressed, they saw only a crop of defects that needed fixing, a collection of their best repairs? Or do I hope that one of them—maybe the redhead, not yet thirty—felt some small press of desire, knew I was a girl on the edge of womanhood and not a half-lame horse or subject #53? I know I hated being watched. I also know it never occurred to me that anyone watching would see something worth wanting. They took those videos throughout most of my adolescence. Do you know I still can't stand to watch myself walk? I put my eyes on the floor when I pass department-store mirrors or a window's reflective glass. I catch a glimpse of myself and my stomach turns. When I asked the first man I loved about the way I moved, he said, *It's nothing. It doesn't matter*—he meant it as a comfort—but I thought, *You're wrong. It makes me what I am.*

Chronic pain makes you good at abandoning yourself. It teaches you to ignore your body until it insists on being noticed, until your joints ache too badly to stand, until something buckles, until you fall and then you're bleeding hard enough to ruin your clothes. There's a certain low thrum of hurt I don't notice; it's just the frequency at the bottom of everything. A good day is one where I hardly think about my body, where I adjust for its flaws by instinct, where there isn't any sudden spike in that low pulse of pain.

On a good day, my body doesn't embarrass me. It does what I ask it, lets me walk short distances and do my job. I don't notice people staring, don't trip on my way in to teach a class, sending thirty-five student papers flying everywhere. I don't have to pause at a threshold and ask a stranger to help me lift my wheelchair up and through a door. No one I don't really know needs to put their hands on me. No one in the grocery store asks, *What happened, sweetie? You're so pretty to be in a wheelchair!* On a good day, my body pulls hard at the hem of my dress, and I hiss back, *You don't exist,* and it goes somewhere else, or I do.

In bed, a man pauses, puts a wide, gentle hand on my face and asks, *Honey, where are you? Come back here.* I want to, and also I don't.

Just as I hit adolescence, my body abruptly began to break down. I grew, and so did my physical instability. My tendons tightened, and my pain increased. The doctors scheduled another set of medical procedures: a surgery, a summer in a set of full-leg plaster casts and then a pair of heavy, bulky metal braces. Just as I began to learn I could feel sexual desire, I was splintered and in pain again, and the fact of it demanded most of my attention. My earliest experiences with lust feel shrunken by the trauma, vague and distanced, as if I watched through a scratched viewfinder while they happened to someone else. I can't identify them for you except as strange, dark shapes at an unreachable horizon line.

Those years I had to wear parachute pants—specially made by a tailor who regularly asked my mother to remind her what was wrong with me—and giant sneakers to accommodate the braces. Besides all that, I had the usual adolescent problems. I hadn't learned that you really just shouldn't brush curly hair, or that if you have hips and spend most of your time sitting or bent over, low-rise jeans are a terrible idea. Not only was I far from resembling the kind of girl I could imagine anyone finding desirable, I was so occupied with pain and with being a patient, perpetually hamstrung between taken-apart and put-back-together, that it would take me years to really look at myself and realize I was also a person. A woman. That there was a whole other way I could want to be touched.

I belonged to an adaptive skiing association and spent most of the time I wasn't in the hospital or physical therapy learning to hurl myself down snow-covered mountains with men who'd been paralyzed in car wrecks. But I didn't know a single adult woman with a disability really comparable to mine. Nowhere on television, or in any magazine, did I see any portrayals of disabled women as sexual and desirable (let alone as partners or as parents), and most of the solace that the early 2000s internet had to offer was in the form of assurances that I might one day be the object of some very particular fetish. It matters that when any adult spoke to me about my body, they did so in purely utilitarian terms, said that I should want the best range of motion, the least pain, the highest level of mobility, so that I could one day buy groceries, live independently, hold a job. Of course, nobody warned: You'll want your hamstrings to be loose enough that it doesn't hurt when your muscles tense before you have an orgasm. They also didn't say: We want to do all this to you so that one day your body can be a thing that brings you pleasure, a thing that you don't hate.

The truth is, my first real flushes of lust happened when my own body was a dangerous thing, one I couldn't trust not to fall to pieces or to lunge at the rest of me with its teeth bared, out for blood. So much of my somatic experience was agonizing and frightening. I had no idea what my body would look, move, or feel like five years down the line. Desire wasn't entirely crowded out by pain, but I distrusted it the same way I did everything that felt born in my body, as if it were an instant away from morphing into suffering, waiting only until I attended to it to become a thing that hurt me. I playacted at desire often—mimicking the adolescents around me when they traded gossip about crushes, had first kisses, held hands furtively underneath their desks in social studies class—but I couldn't afford to get to know its real contours in my life, to attend to my own sensations, or to believe in a future with real space for that kind of pleasure or intimacy, that kind of love. To survive, I had to stay unfamiliar to myself: neutralized, at arm's length. Sometimes, I think, all these years later, I'm still hunting the part of myself I exiled.

When I was newly seventeen, one of my closest friends put her head in my lap, said, *You're so gorgeous,* and then leaned up and kissed me. I would spend the better part of the next year alternately pushing her away and pulling her close, trying to figure out whether I wanted her too or only the plain, unapologetic fact of her desire for me. Her gentleness, her confidence in her own body and its hunger, the fact that when she watched me move, I felt like a painting come to life and not a patient or a busted windup toy. A decade later, I still feel guilty for all the secretive back-and-forth I put her through because I was unwilling to be open about our romantic relationship, and the answer to the question of my own desire still feels fraught and muddy.

A handful of years after that, I was in a coffee shop with a man I half-thought I'd marry, in a youthful, abstract way, and someone in line assumed he was my brother, though we couldn't have looked less alike. When we corrected her, she looked over my head at him and said, gently and admiringly: *She's so lucky to have found you.* He bit his tongue when I squeezed his hand. I didn't want to think about it anymore. We turned away.

We started dating after he attended a reading I gave. When it was over, he came up and kissed my cheek, said, *That was so incredible that I forgot to breathe while you were talking.* Then he turned on his heel and walked away. I rolled my eyes but couldn't get him out of my head. The way I moved was nothing. He was proof it didn't matter.

At a taffy shop on the boardwalk in San Francisco, the weekend we first say *I love you,* a middle-aged man is pushing a woman, clearly his wife, in a wheelchair. They are laughing and his head is bent so that their faces are close together as he walks, intimate and tender. We bump into one another in the aisle and pause —two couples exchanging smiles—while we make room for her wheelchair to get past mine. They walk on, and then we kiss, fierce and happy there. We're young and don't know anything. We both think *maybe.*

Later, we're in Florida at the beach, and I've been stiff and hurting for weeks from a summer of travel. In the bathroom, while we're changing into bathing suits, he looks me up and down. I'm prepared for him to try something—to kiss me—and I'm prepared to put him off, we don't have time; we have to meet my family by the water. Instead, he asks me tenderly, *Do you want help clipping your toenails, baby? They're getting kind of long.* That night, in bed, I roll away when he reaches for me. My body is no country for desire.

A couple of years later still, another man—charming, boy-next-door-beautiful, and quarterback-confident—has started spending evenings in my bed, or with me pinned to his couch. He tells me I'm sexy, asks to read what I'm writing, then asks quiet questions about poetry and movies that I love. But he won't be seen dating me in public. When I tell him I'm more than happy to be fooling around, but that I won't sleep with somebody I hardly know, he puts all his weight on top of me, says, *Oh, if I wanted to have sex with you, you'd know.* Then flips me over. Pushes my head down hard enough that it hurts. I think, *He's embarrassed to be seen with me. He gets off on how fragile I am. I'm too old to put up with this.* But I let him. I let it go on for weeks and weeks like that before I stop returning his late-night texts.

I want him to want me, and though I can't quite admit it to myself, I am also a little afraid. Always, I'm aware that I'm particularly vulnerable: I couldn't run if you came at me. I'd fall to the ground if you touched me even slightly roughly. I will always start at an unexpected hand.

But because some of you are wondering (I see you leering at me, stranger at the bank; I see you, terrible internet date), because we live in a world that often assumes disabled people are sexless or infantile, because I wish I had heard anyone who looked or moved like me say it when I was fourteen, I want to be very clear: I can, in fact, have sex. I am a woman who wants in ways that are both abstract and concrete. I have turned down advances from people I wasn't attracted to, and said yes to a few advances I'm sorry about now, and more that have been lovely, surprising, and good. I've had a date who didn't realize I was in a wheelchair turn and walk out of a restaurant when he saw me, and I've watched the light behind men's eyes turn from desire to curiosity to something else when they realize something's wrong with me. I've been hit on while on barstools by people who disappear once they've watched me get up and shuffle slowly to the bathroom. I've used that trick to my advantage. I've spent a summer weekend taking baths and eating overripe peaches in a seedy motel with someone I loved, and another getting lusty-whiskey-drunk with someone I didn't, but whom I was still perfectly happy to have unbutton my shirt. The explicit details I'll keep to myself, except to say that my familiarity with how to jump-rope the line between pleasure and pain has done me some favors. If you're listening, younger self, some of what you're learning will, I swear, eventually have uses no one's naming for you, uses that no one orbiting around you can locate, name, or even imagine.

In another kind of story, I would leave it there. Or I would say that I've arrived at a reconciled point, that no part of me ever still believes that the boy in the dining hall, who was certain I would die a virgin, hit on some real truth about the ways my body is defective and repellent; that, now, I can watch myself move without feeling some small wave of shame; that I've completely stopped abandoning my body out of instinct, or habit, or what feels like necessity, in moments when it should bring me pleasure and intimacy and joy. I'd have fully worked out how to be with a partner who I know really sees my body, its contours, its scars, and its pain, who I can let give me the kinds of help I need and still trust to see me as sexual and desirable. But that isn't where I find myself. I don't know exactly where the reconciled point is, or even what it looks like. Instead, things just get more complicated. I really want children, and in the last few years that prospect has collided with questions of intimacy and desire. I worry about finding a partner truly willing to parent with me in the ways I know my disability will necessitate, and to sign up for the medical uncertainties I know are around the bend in my own life. I worry about the toll pregnancy might take on my body, and about being physically capable of being a good parent once my children are born. I worry that my clock is ticking faster than most people's, my body wearing down and wearing out. And, in the hardest moments, that whatever small kind of beauty and desirability I might, in fact, possess is wearing away with it. I'm still surprised by my own limits, still frustrated and exhausted by pain. Sometimes I still feel suspicious of all my body's sensations, the good ones tangled too tightly with the bad. But not all moments are the hardest ones, and maybe the point is simply this: that I am still alive, still in the business of heading somewhere, still a woman who can stumble, hurt, and want, and—yes—be wanted. That there is no perfect reconciliation, only the way I hold it all suspended: wonderful, and hugely difficult, and true.

AGNES CALLARD

Acceptance Parenting

FROM *The Point*

BEFORE THE 1970S, the word "parent" was commonly used only as a noun; since that time, American parents have roughly doubled the amount of time they spend parenting, and each generation since seems to stress more about parenting than the previous one. The fact that modern parents are beleaguered by the emotional toil of parenting is now as familiar a trope as the opinion piece advising parents to relax, be less perfectionist, and be more forgiving of ourselves.

The economist Bryan Caplan supplements this advice with some science to ease the parental burden. Twin studies, he points out, suggest that genes are significantly more influential than parenting with respect to a wide variety of factors: future income, personality traits, educational attainment, religiosity, and marital status. This knowledge, Caplan hopes, ought to give parents permission to take shortcuts: given how minimally you can influence your children, you might as well buy more child care, ease up on those extracurriculars, let them watch TV, and take vacations without them. Let your children roam free outside! They are safer than they have ever been. Don't let them walk all over you, use discipline to set boundaries—it's ultimately harmless—and make your own life easier!

Why have parents turned parenting into self-torture? Caplan posits a peer pressure–based desire to keep up with the Joneses, and hopes to wrench people out of this collective mistake by showing them how easy parenting could be, if they just let it: "Intellectual error explains much of the decline in family size."

"Just relax" is the gentlest species of parenting commentary;

harsher critics scornfully characterize modern parents as "helicopters" for micromanaging our children's lives, and blame our "coddling"—excessive care, indulgence, and overprotectiveness—for turning our children into "snowflakes." The overall implication is that if only parents could muster up the wisdom and courage to defect from this "bad parenting culture," we could be happily and healthily enjoying our children instead of hovering anxiously and fruitlessly around them.

These critics of modern parenting—gentle and harsh alike—put me in mind of a person who, upon first seeing a car, demands to know where the horses are, and upon being assured there are no horses around, offers advice about where to find some and where to attach them. They simply don't seem to understand just how fundamentally and irreversibly the parenting game has changed. The easily observable changes, from the heightened attentiveness to the increased stress levels, are but the visible signs of a deep, tectonic shift in our conception of the basic tenets of the enterprise. Traditional parents weren't better at what today's parents are doing; traditional parents were tasked with doing something different—and easier.

If one wants to grasp the profundity of the shift, one is better off turning away from those who aim to intervene in parenting culture and toward those who concern themselves with a far more challenging task: accurately representing it. There is a wonderful scene in the British miniseries *Years and Years* in which a daughter nervously comes out as trans to parents who, having snooped on her Google searches, react with a prepared effusion of support: "Oh honey, it's all right, I swear. We're completely fine either way! Now look at us, we're fine! I know we might be a bit slow and a bit old and this is going to be confusing for us and we'll make a mess of it sometimes, but we love you. We absolutely love you. And we always will . . . And if it turns out we've got a lovely son instead of a lovely daughter, then we'll be happy."

She is momentarily confused, and corrects them: "No. I'm not transsexual, I'm trans*human!*" She explains that she aspires to first modify her body in various ways to integrate herself into the internet, and eventually to dispense with her body altogether by uploading herself into the cloud: "I don't want to be flesh."

The parents react with the shock, outrage, and screaming rejection that follows the classic "bad parent" script heard by countless children who have, over the years, presented themselves as diverging from their parents' expectations with respect to religion, marriage, career, etc. Parents have always been faced with the challenge of handling rebellious, wayward, disobedient children; but at no prior time have they—have we—been so pre-committed to acceptance. At no point in the past was the parental inability to accept that which strikes them as antithetical to their basic understanding of what is true and what is good perceived as a potential failure by the parents' *own* standards.

The consequences of the shift extend well beyond increased parental stress levels. When it comes to the question of whose job it is to conform to whom, the sign has gotten reversed. As a teenager coming of age in the 1990s, I watched the tide turn on homosexuality. From my vantage point, a lot of the change seemed to be driven by acceptance parenting: those who couldn't stomach rejecting their children rejected their own homophobia instead. As acceptance parenting takes hold culturally, we find ourselves speaking more and more about what it takes to be a "good parent" and less and less frequently of the virtues of a "good son/daughter." The more we expect the parents' acceptance, the less concerned we are with children's obedience.

This in turn helps explain why parenting has objectively become harder. If you want to understand why parents are so much more stressed than they used to be, just consider the slip between "transsexual" and "transhuman": you cannot predict what, at the end of the day, you will be asked to accept; and you know that from day one; and that knowledge—of your own ignorance—casts a shadow over every parenting decision you make.

I was struck by a recent *New York Times* piece offering scientifically grounded instruction in praising one's child. It warns against excessive praise: don't fuel "'praise addiction,' in which a child compulsively performs behaviors to earn approval." It offers advice on how to target one's praise: "praise the process, not the person," as "praising the outcome or the person encourages the child to focus on those things. She might feel performance anxiety. He might question the conditionality of your love." Also, be sincere: "children can sense when praise is not genuine." One might wonder who needs to read this: Why can't parents be trusted to simply praise what they think is praiseworthy and blame what is blameworthy? The answer is that praise and blame are ways of directing children, telling them which direction to go in and what outcomes to avoid. Acceptance parents know that they don't know the answer to those questions. The inclination to look to scientists for guidance in everything from baby sleep to teenager management suggests a self-awareness, on the part of parents, of our ignorance.

Parents have always justified themselves with reference to the future—you'll thank me later!—and parents have always aimed at the happiness of their child. What's radically new is not, at heart, how concerned or permissive we've become, but how fully we have given over to our children the job of defining happiness. For acceptance parents, neither instinct nor culture is a sufficient guide to what counts as acceptable behavior in a child. Instead of being able to draw on culture and tradition to set standards relative to which children are to be assessed, those standards now come from the people they are to be applied to—more specifically, from *future, which is to say, not yet existent, versions* of those people.

Traditional parents were in the business of handing to their children a settled way of life: values, habits, standards, practices, skills, sometimes a job. On this older picture, it was the role of the parent to give—"tradition" comes from *tradere,* "to hand over"—and the child to accept, obediently. If I were a traditional parent, I would be trying to give my child some version of *my* life; as an acceptance parent, I am trying to give my child something I don't have and am not familiar with—*his* life.

And yet parental resources are no greater than they have ever been. Apart from some desperate attempts at supplementation—all those after-school activities parents are mocked for enrolling children in—all that each of us has to give remains her own values and standards and practices and skills. The only thing we can change is how we "give" them, and so we've come to make our offerings with circumspection and delicacy. We hover around our children attentively, experimenting with what will or won't "take." Even though we acceptance parents are committed to tolerance, our resources are no less constrained than those of traditional parents: we are able to tolerate what we independently find tolerable. The difference is that now, when our children transgress our boundaries, we no longer feel sure whose side we should be on. Like all forms of freedom, acceptance parenting makes life more, and not less, stressful. If the parent is demoted from wise authority figure to tentative spokesperson for the child's future self, childhood and child-rearing become a nerve-racking quest to find one's own footing.

Once you flip the switch from tradition to acceptance, it doesn't flip back. And that's why acceptance parenting is not so much a style of parenting as the backdrop against which parenting battles are fought.

Consider the case of Amy Chua, the self-proclaimed "tiger mother" whose entertaining book records the intense time and effort she expends on her young daughters' musical training. Chua claims to be engaged in "traditional Chinese parenting," but the details of her book tell a different story. She fights with her daughters constantly and tolerates a level of insolence ("'She's insane,' I'd hear them whispering to each other, giggling") that does not accord with the respectful obedience required by "traditional Chinese parenting," as Chua herself characterizes it.

"I will not give up on you," Chua tells her rebellious younger daughter. And Chua reports: "'I *want* you to give up on me!' Lulu yelled back more than once." When push comes to shove, Lulu "wins" the battle over switching from violin to tennis. Chua views this concession as a break in her parenting philosophy—she laments her own weakness in capitulating to "Western parenting"—but in fact it is consistent with the justifications she has been giving, to herself and her daughters, all along.

Chua's musical training program was not aimed at turning her daughters into musicians; rather, music was a vehicle for "arming them with skills, work habits, and inner confidence that no one can ever take away." When tennis turns out to be a better vehicle, Chua readily adapts, "texting her [tennis coach] with questions and practice strategies . . . Sometimes, when Lulu's least expecting it—at breakfast or when I'm saying good night—I'll suddenly yell out, 'More rotation on the swing volley!' or 'Don't move your right foot on your kick serve!'"

Pre- and post-tennis, Chua's message is consistent. She tells her daughters, "My goal as a parent is to prepare you for the future—not to make you like me." The fact that preparing them for the future and making them like you are contrasted rather than identified is one hallmark of acceptance parenting. Another is the tendency to privilege confidence over obedience. When you don't know someone well enough to buy them a gift, you give them money; likewise, self-confidence and diligence are seen as the universal tool for the child who must "become someone"—you know not who.

The failure to acknowledge the revolutionary turn to acceptance parenting leads Chua to exaggerate the degree to which she diverges from "Western parents." And it leads many of the critics of parenting culture to misunderstand their audience. Traditional parents, ones engaged in "molding" children into the image of themselves, are the people who would have been reassured by Caplan's argument that most of the molding work has already been done by genetics. But for acceptance parents, there is no shape into which they are trying to mold their children at all. The fact that my child's DNA heavily influences many aspects of his future offers me little guidance as to what I mean—or rather, what he will mean—by "happy."

What makes parenting in a pandemic so difficult is not, first and foremost, the increased time commitment. It is not even the close-up view of your children's suffering—watching them become withdrawn, struggle to cheer themselves up, lose weight. The hardest part is the work of parenting itself, which is to say, the parts of one's engagement with one's child that concern their future. My youngest child boycotted Zoomschool in the spring; he's very social, but when we tried to appeal to his desire to see his friends, his response was irrefutable: "Those are not my friends! My friends are not flat!" My husband started teaching him Euclid, mostly so as to give us the feeling that he is learning . . . something.

My middle son is more willing to play along, and it is one of the bright spots of Zoomlife that I can snoop on his school day and learn that I have raised a Class Participator. But I can also hear the relief in his voice when he announces a fifteen-minute break between Zooms, and I see that he spends much of his day in a frustrated hunt for what folder another folder is supposed to go in. He's being occupied, but not necessarily educated.

My oldest watches multiple movies a day—they speak to him more than anything his teachers say over their screens—and when he's not watching movies, he's writing them: hundreds, probably thousands, of pages of scripts. Would a "good parent" be pushing him to be more invested in school? Spend more time outdoors? Reading? Something else? Would a good parent curtail his screen time, or would she encourage him to stay the course? Should I be blaming or praising him? Scientists who study praise don't have the answers for me.

And I don't think they could give any, even if they tried, unless they could answer questions like: Will movies even exist after this pandemic? What kind of a world am I sending him into? Which of his talents will be of most use—to himself and others—in it? How do I help him develop them?

The problem here is not my fear of employing discipline, or my inclination to micromanage. The problem is ignorance. Unlike my forebears, I don't know the things I need to know in order to be a good parent, and none of the people telling me to calm down know those things either. The only one who might know, my grown child, doesn't yet exist.

GABRIELLE HAMILTON

The Kitchen Is Closed

FROM *The New York Times Magazine*

ON THE NIGHT before I laid off all thirty of my employees, I dreamed that my two children had perished, buried alive in dirt, while I dug in the wrong place, just five feet away from where they were actually smothered. I turned and spotted the royal-blue heel of my youngest's socked foot poking out of the black soil only after it was too late.

For ten days, everyone in my orbit had been tilting one way one hour, the other the next. Ten days of being waterboarded by the news, by tweets, by friends, by my waiters. Of being inundated by texts from fellow chefs and managers—former employees, now at the helm of their own restaurants but still eager for guidance. Of gentle but nervous pleas from my operations manager to consider signing up with a third-party delivery service like Caviar. Of being rattled even by my own wife, Ashley, and her anxious compulsion to act, to reduce our restaurant's operating hours, to close at 9 p.m., cut shifts.

With no clear directive from any authority—public schools were still open—I spent those ten days sorting through the conflicting chatter, trying to decide what to do. And now I understood abruptly: I would lay everybody off, even my wife. Prune, my Manhattan restaurant, would close at 11:59 p.m. on March 15. I had only one piece of unemotional data to work with: the checking-account balance. If I triaged the collected sales tax that was sitting in its own dedicated savings account and left unpaid the stack of vendor invoices, I could fully cover this one last week of payroll.

By the time of the all-staff meeting after brunch that day, I knew I was right. After a couple of weeks of watching the daily sales dwindle—a $12,141 Saturday to a $4,188 Monday to a $2,093 Thursday—it was a relief to decide to pull the parachute cord. I didn't want to have waited too long, didn't want to crash into the trees. Our sous-chef FaceTimed in, as did our lead line cook, while nearly everyone else gathered in the dining room. I looked everybody in the eye and said, "I've decided not to wait to see what will happen; I encourage you to call first thing in the morning for unemployment, and you have a week's paycheck from me coming."

After the meeting, there was some directionless shuffling. Should we collect our things? Grab our knives? Stay and have a drink? There was still one last dinner, so four of us—Ashley and I; our general manager, Anna; and Jake, a beloved line cook—worked the last shift at Prune for who knows how long. Some staff members remained behind to eat with one another, spending their money in house. As word trickled out, some long-ago alumnae reached out to place orders for meals they would never eat. From Lauren Kois, who waited tables at Prune all through her PhD program and is now an assistant professor of psychology at the University of Alabama:

2 dark and stormies
shrimp w anchovy
fried oysters (we're pretending it's a special tonight)

Leo Steen Jurassic Chenin Blanc
skate wing
treviso salad
potatoes in duck fat
brothy beans

breton butter cake
2 black coffees

+ 50 percent TIP

Ashley worked the grill station and cold appetizers, while also bartending and expediting. Anna waited and hosted and answered the phone. Jake worked all ten burners alone. I was in a yellow apron, handling the dish pit, clearing the tables, and running bus tubs, and I broke into tears for a second when I learned of Kois's order. The word "family" is thrown around in restaurants for good reason. We banked $1,144 in total sales.

As our staff left that night, we waved across the room to one another with a strange mixture of longing and eye-rolling, still in the self-conscious phase of having to act so distant from one another, all of us still so unaware of what was coming. Then, as I was running a last tray of glassware before mopping the floors, Ashley leaned over to announce: "Hey, he just called it. De Blasio. It's a shutdown. You beat it by five hours, babe."

The next day, a Monday, Ashley started assembling thirty boxes of survival-food kits for the staff. She packed Ziploc bags of nuts, rice, pasta, cans of curry paste, and cartons of eggs, while music played from her cell phone tucked into a plastic quart container—an old line-cook trick for amplifying sound. I texted a clip of her mini-operation to José Andrés, who called immediately with encouragement: We will win this together! We feed the world one plate at a time!

Ashley had placed a last large order from our wholesaler: jarred peanut butter, canned tuna, coconut milk, and other unlikely items that had never appeared on our order history. And our account rep, Marie Elena Corrao—we met when I was her first account twenty years ago; she came to our wedding in 2016—put the order through without even clearing her throat, sending the truck to a now-shuttered business. She knew as well as we did that it would be a long while before the bill was paid. Leo, from the family-owned butchery we've used for twenty years, Pino's Prime Meat Market, called not to diplomatically inquire about our plans but to immediately offer tangibles: "What meats do you ladies need for the home?" He offered this even though he knew that there were thirty days' worth of his invoices in a pile on my desk, totaling thousands of dollars. And all day a string of neighborhood regulars passed by on the sidewalk outside and made heart hands at us through the locked French doors.

It turned out that abruptly closing a restaurant is a weeklong full-time job. I was bombarded with an astonishing volume of texts. The phone rang throughout the day, overwhelmingly well-wishers and regretful cancellations, but there was a woman who apparently hadn't followed the coronavirus news. She cut me off in the middle of my greeting with, "Yeah, you guys open for brunch?" Then she hung up before I could even finish saying, "Take care out there."

Ashley spent almost three days packing the freezers, sorting the perishables in the walk-in into categories like "Today would be good!" or "This will be good for the long haul!" We tried burying par-cooked chickens under a tight seal of duck fat to see if we could keep them perfectly preserved in their airtight coffins. She pickled the beets and the brussels sprouts, churned quarts of heavy cream into butter.

I imagined I would tackle my other problems quickly. I emailed my banker. For sales taxes, liquor invoices, and impending rent, I hoped to apply for a modest line of credit to float me through this crisis. I thought having run $2.5 million to $3 million through my bank each year for the past two decades would leave me poised to see a line of credit quickly, but then I remembered that I switched banks in the past year. Everyone in my industry encouraged me to apply for an SBA disaster loan—I estimated we wouldn't need much; for fourteen days, $50,000—so I sent in my query.

In the meantime, I made a phone call to Ken, my insurance broker of twenty years, who explained—in his patient, technical, my-hands-are-tied voice—that this coronavirus business interruption wouldn't likely be covered. He intended to file for damages, as he would if this shutdown had been mandated because of a nearby flood or a fire, but he doubted I would get any money. That afternoon, I saw the courtesy email from our workers'-comp carrier that the next installment of our payment plan would be drafted automatically from our bank in six days.

Knowing the balance, I snorted to myself: *Good luck with that.* I called Ken about this, and he got them to postpone the draw.

And then, finally, three weeks of adrenaline drained from me. I checked all the pilot lights and took out the garbage; I stopped swimming so hard against the mighty current and let it carry me out. I had spent twenty years in this place, beginning when I was a grad student fresh out of school, through marriage and children and divorce and remarriage, with funerals and first dates in between; I knew its walls and light switches and faucets as well I knew my own body. It was dark outside when Ashley and I finally rolled down the gates and walked home.

Prune is a cramped and lively bistro in Manhattan's East Village, with a devoted following and a tight-knit crew. I opened it in 1999. It has only fourteen tables, which are jammed in so close together that not infrequently you put down your glass of wine to take a bite of your food and realize it's on your neighbor's table. Many friendships have started this way.

What was I imagining twenty years ago when I was working all day, every day at a catering job while staying up all night every night, writing menus and sketching the plating of dishes, scrubbing the walls and painting the butter-yellow trim inside what would become Prune? I'd seen the padlocked space, formerly a failed French bistro, when it was decrepit: cockroaches crawling over the sticky Pernod bottles behind the bar and rat droppings carpeting the floors. But even in that moment, gasping for air through the T-shirt I had pulled up over my mouth, I could see vividly what it could become, the intimate dinner party I would throw every night in this charming, quirky space. I was already lighting the candles and filling the jelly jars with wine. I would cook there much the way I cooked at home: whole roasted veal breast and torn lettuces in a well-oiled wooden bowl, a ripe cheese after dinner, none of the aggressively "conceptual" or architectural food then trendy among aspirational chefs but also none of the roulades and miniaturized bites I'd been cranking out as a freelancer in catering kitchens.

At that point New York didn't have an ambitious and exciting restaurant on every block, in every unlikely neighborhood, operating out of impossibly narrow spaces. There was no *Eater,* no Instagram, no hipster Brooklyn food scene. If you wanted something expert to eat, you dined in Manhattan. For fine dining, with plush armchairs and a captain who ran your table wearing an Armani suit, you went uptown; for the buzzy American brasserie with bentwood cane-backed chairs and waiters in long white aprons, you stayed downtown. There was no serious restaurant that would allow a waiter to wear a flannel shirt or hire a sommelier with face piercings and neck tattoos. The East Village had Polish and Ukrainian diners, falafel stands, pizza parlors, dive bars, and vegetarian cafés. There was only one notable noodle spot. Momofuku opened five years after Prune.

I meant to create a restaurant that would serve as delicious and interesting food as the serious restaurants elsewhere in the city but in a setting that would welcome, and not intimidate, my ragtag friends and my neighbors—all the East Village painters and poets, the butches and the queens, the saxophone player on the sixth floor of my tenement building, the performance artists doing their brave naked work up the street at P.S. 122. I wanted a place you could go after work or on your day off if you had only a line cook's paycheck but also a line cook's palate. And I thought it might be a more stable way to earn a living than the scramble of freelancing I'd done up until then.

Like most chefs who own these small restaurants that have now proliferated across the whole city, I've been driven by the sensory, the human, the poetic, and the profane—not by money or a thirst to expand. Even after seven nights a week for two decades, I am still stopped in my tracks every time my bartenders snap those metal lids onto the cocktail shakers and start rattling the ice like maracas. I still close my eyes for a second, taking a deep inhale, every time the salted pistachios are set afire with raki, sending their anise scent through the dining room. I still thrill when the four-top at Table 9 are talking to one another so contentedly that they don't notice they are the last diners, lingering in the cocoon of the wine and the few shards of dark chocolate we've put down with their check. Even though I can't quite take part in it myself—I'm the boss, who must remain a little aloof from the crew—I still quietly thrum with satisfaction when the "kids" are chattering away and hugging one another their hellos and how-are-yous in the hallway as they get ready for their shifts.

But the very first time you cut a payroll check, you understand quite bluntly that, poetic notions aside, you are running a business. And that crew of knuckleheads you adore are counting on you for their livelihood. In the beginning I was closed on Mondays, ran only six dinner shifts, and paid myself $425 a week. I got a very positive review in the *New York Times*, and thereafter we were packed. When I added a seventh dinner in 2000, I was able to hire a full-time sous-chef.

When I added weekend brunch, which started as a dreamy idea, not a business plan, it wound up being popular enough to let me buy out all six of the original investors. I turned forty-three in 2008 and finally became the majority owner of my restaurant. I made my last student-loan payment and started paying myself $800 a week. A few years later, when I added lunch service on weekdays, it was a business decision, not a dream, because I needed to be able to afford health insurance for my staff, and I knew I could make an excellent burger. So suddenly, there we were: fourteen services, seven days a week, thirty employees. It was a thrilling and exhausting first ten years, with great momentum.

But Prune at twenty is a different and reduced quantity, now that there are no more services to add and costs keep going up. It just barely banks about exactly what it needs each week to cover its expenses. I've joked for years that I'm in the nonprofit sector, but that has been more direly true for several years now. This past summer, at fifty-three, in spite of having four James Beard Awards on the wall, an Emmy on the shelf from our PBS program, and a best-selling book that has been translated into six languages, I found myself flat on my stomach on the kitchen floor in a painter's paper coverall suit, maneuvering a garden hose rigged up to the faucet. I'd poured bleach and Palmolive and degreaser behind the range and the reach-ins, trying to blast out the deep, dark, unreachable corner of the sauté station where lost egg shells, mussels, green scrubbies, hollow marrow bones, tasting spoons and cake testers, tongs and the occasional sizzle plate all get trapped and forgotten during service.

There used to be enough extra money every year that I could close for ten days in July to repaint and retile and rewire, but it has become increasingly impossible to leave even a few days of revenue on the table or to justify the expense of hiring a professional cleaning service for this deep clean that I am perfectly capable of doing myself, so I stayed late and did it after service. The sludge of egg yolk seeped through the coverall, through my clothes to my skin, matted my hair and speckled my goggles as my shock registered: It has always been hard, but when did it get *this* hard?

Two weeks after we closed, Ashley still had not got through to unemployment, and I had been thrice thwarted by the autofill feature of the electronic form of the loan I was urged to apply for. I could start to see that things I had thought would be quick and uncomplicated would instead be steep and unyielding. No one was going to rescue me. I went into the empty restaurant for a bit each day to push back against the entropy—a light bulb had died, a small freezer needed to be unplugged and restarted. Eleven envelopes arrived, bearing the unemployment notices from the New York State Department of Labor. The next stack of five arrived a week later. And then another six.

The line of credit I thought would be so easy to acquire turned out to be one long week of harsh busy signals before I was even able to apply, on March 25. I was turned down a week later, on April 1, because of "inadequate business and personal cash flow." I howled with laughter over the phone at the underwriter and his explanation. Everything was uphill. Twenty-one days after we closed, Ashley still hadn't been able to reach unemployment. They now had a new system to handle the overload of calls: You call based on the first letter of your last name, and her next possible day would be a Thursday. If she didn't get through, she would have to wait until the next day allotted for all the M's of the city.

Links to low-interest SBA disaster loans were circulated, but New York City wasn't showing up on the list of eligible zones. I emailed my accountant: This is weird? She wrote back with a sarcastic smiley emoticon: *I believe it will be updated. It's the government—they are only fast when they are collecting your taxes.* The James Beard Foundation kicked into high gear and announced meaningful grants of up to $15,000, with an application period that was supposed to last from March 30 to April 3, but within hours of opening, it was overwhelmed with applications and had to stop accepting more.

Ashley texted me from home that our dog was limping severely. This was the scenario that made me sweat: a medical emergency. We could live for a month on what was in the freezer, and I had a credit card that still had a $13,000 spending limit, but what if we got hurt somehow and needed serious medical care? Neither of us was insured. My kids are covered under their father's policy, but there was no safety net for us. Among us chefs, there have been a hundred jokes over the decades about our medical (and veterinary) backup plans—given our latex gloves and razor-sharp knives and our spotless stainless-steel prep tables—but my sense of humor at that moment had become hard to summon.

Meanwhile, my inbox was loaded with emails from everyone I've ever known, all wanting to check in, as well as from colleagues around the country who were only now comprehending the scope of the impact on New York's restaurants. Hastily, fellow chefs and restaurant owners were forming groups, circulating petitions, quickly knitting coalitions for restaurant workers and suppliers and farmers. There were surveys to fill out, representatives to call, letters to sign. Some were turning their restaurants into meal kitchens to feed hospital workers. There was a relief bill before Congress that we were all urgently asked to support, but it puzzlingly left out small, independent restaurants even as it came through pretty nicely for huge chains and franchises. The other option, the Paycheck Protection Program, would grant you a loan with forgiveness, I learned, but only if you rehire your laid-off staff before the end of June. With no lifting of the mandatory shuttering and the COVID-19 death toll still mounting, how could we rehire our staff? I couldn't really use the loan for what I needed: rent for the foreseeable future and the stack of invoices still haunting me in the office.

And right when I started to feel backed against the ropes, I got a group email from a few concerned former Prune managers who eagerly offered to start a GoFundMe for Prune, inadvertently putting another obstacle in front of me: my own dignity. I sat on the email for a few days, roiling in a whole new paralysis of indecision. There were individual campaigns being run all over town to raise money to help restaurant staffs, but when I tried to imagine joining this trend, I couldn't overcome my pride at being seen as asking for a handout. It felt like a popularity contest or a survival-of-the-most-well-connected that I couldn't bring myself to enter. It would make me feel terrible if Prune was nicely funded while the Sikhs at the Punjabi Grocery and Deli down the street were ignored, and simultaneously crushed if it wasn't. I also couldn't quite imagine the ethical calculus by which I would distribute such funds: Should I split them equally, even though one of my workers is a twenty-one-year-old who already owns his own apartment in Manhattan, while another lives with his unemployed wife and their two children in a rental in the Bronx? I thanked my former managers but turned them down: I had repeatedly checked in with my staff, and everybody was okay for now.

It would be nigh impossible for me, in the context of a pandemic, to argue for the necessity of my existence. Do my sweetbreads and my Parmesan omelet count as essential at this time? In economic terms, I don't think I could even argue that Prune matters anymore, in a neighborhood and a city now fully saturated with restaurants much like mine, many of them better than mine —some of which have expanded to employ as many as a hundred people, not just cooks and servers and bartenders but also human-resource directors and cookbook ghostwriters.

I am not going to suddenly start arguing the merits of my restaurant as a vital part of an "industry" or that I help to make up 2 percent of the US gross domestic product or that I should be helped out by our government because I am one of those who employ nearly twelve million Americans in the work force. But those seem to be the only persuasive terms—with my banks, my insurers, my industry lobbyists and legislators. I have to hope, though, that we matter in some other alternative economy; that we are still a thread in the fabric that might unravel if you yanked us from the weave.

Everybody's saying that restaurants won't make it back, that we won't survive. I imagine this is at least partly true: not all of us will make it, and not all of us will perish. But I can't easily discern the determining factors, even though thinking about which restaurants will survive—and why—has become an obsession these past weeks. What delusional mindset am I in that I just do not feel that this is the end, that I find myself convinced that this is only a pause, if I want it to be? I don't carry investor debt; my vendors trust me; if my building's co-op evicted me, they would have a beast of a time getting a new tenant to replace me.

But I know few of us will come back as we were. And that doesn't seem to me like a bad thing at all; perhaps it will be a chance for a correction, as my friend, the chef Alex Raij, calls it.

The conversation about how restaurants will continue to operate, given the rising costs of running them, has been ramping up for years now; the coronavirus did not suddenly shine light on an unknown fragility. We've all known, and for a rather long time. The past five or six years have been alarming. For restaurants, coronavirus-mandated closures are like the oral surgery or appendectomy you suddenly face while you are uninsured. These closures will take out the weakest and the most vulnerable. But exactly who among us are the weakest and most vulnerable is not obvious.

Since Prune opened in the East Village, the neighborhood has changed tremendously in ways that reflect, with exquisite perfection, the restaurant scene as a whole. Within a ten-block radius of my front door, we have the more-than-hundred-year-old institutions Russ & Daughters and Katz's Delicatessen. We have hole-in-the-wall falafel, bubble tea and dumpling houses, and there's a steakhouse whose chef also operates a restaurant in Miami. There's everyday sushi and rare, wildly expensive omakase sushi, as well as Japanese home cooking, udon specialists, and soba shops. There's a woman-owned and woman-run restaurant with an economic-justice mission that has eliminated tipping. Bobby Flay, perhaps the most famous chef on the Food Network, has a 125-seater two avenues over. We have farm-to-table concepts every three blocks, a handful of major James Beard Award winners and a dozen more shortlisted nominees, and an impressive showing of *New York Times* one- and two-star earners, including Madame Vo, a knockout Vietnamese restaurant just a few years old. Marco Canora, who started the country's migration from regular old broth to what is now known by the name of his shop, Brodo, has published a couple of cookbooks and done a healthy bit of television in the course of his career. He still runs his only restaurant, seventeen-year-old Hearth, on First Avenue.

But block after block, for so many years now, there are storefronts where restaurants turn over so quickly that I don't even register their names. If COVID-19 is the death of restaurants in New York, will we be able to tell which restaurants went belly up because of the virus? Or will they be the same ones that would have failed within sixteen months of opening anyway, from lack of wherewithal or experience? When we are sorting through the restaurant obituaries, will we know for sure that it was not because the weary veteran chef decided, as I have often been tempted myself in these weeks, to quietly walk out the open back door of a building that has been burning for a long time?

It gets so confusing. Restaurant operators had already become oddly cagey, and quick to display a false front with each other. You asked, "How's business?" and the answer always was, "Yeah, great, best quarter we've ever had." But then the coronavirus hits, and these same restaurant owners rush into the public square yelling: "Fire! Fire!" They now reveal that they had also been operating under razor-thin margins. It instantly turns 180 degrees: even famous, successful chefs, owners of empires, those with supremely wealthy investors upon whom you imagine they could call for capital should they need it, now openly describe in technical detail, with explicit data, how dire a position they are in. The sad testimony gushes out, confirming everything that used to be so convincingly denied.

The concerns before coronavirus are still universal: The restaurant as we know it is no longer viable on its own. You can't have tipped employees making $45 an hour while line cooks make $15. You can't buy a $3 can of cheap beer at a dive bar in the East Village if the "dive bar" is actually paying $18,000 a month in rent, $30,000 a month in payroll; it would have to cost $10. I can't keep hosing down the sauté corner myself just to have enough money to repair the ripped awning. Prune is in the East Village because I've lived in the East Village for more than thirty years. I moved here because it was where you could get an apartment for $450 a month. In 1999, when I opened Prune, I still woke each morning to roosters crowing from the rooftop of the tenement building down the block, which is now a steel-and-glass tower. A less-than-five-hundred-square-foot studio apartment rents for $3,810 a month.

The girl who called about brunch the first day we were closed probably lives there. She is used to having an Uber driver pick her up exactly where she stands at any hour of the day, a gel mani-pedi every two weeks, and award-winning Thai food delivered to her door by a guy who braved the sleet, having attached oven mitts to his bicycle handlebars to keep his hands warm. But I know she would be outraged if charged $28 for a Bloody Mary.

For the past ten years I've been staring wide-eyed and with alarm as the sweet, gentle citizen restaurant transformed into a kind of unruly colossal beast. The food world got stranger and weirder to me right while I was deep in it. The "waiter" became the "server," the "restaurant business" became the "hospitality industry," what used to be the "customer" became the "guest," what was once your "personality" became your "brand," the small acts of kindness and the way you always used to have of sharing your talents and looking out for others became things to "monetize."

The work itself—cooking delicious, interesting food and cleaning up after cooking it—still feels as fresh and honest and immensely satisfying as ever. Our beloved regulars and the people who work so hard at Prune are all still my favorite people on earth. But maybe it's the bloat, the fetishistic foodies, the new demographic of my city who have never been forced to work in retail or service sectors. Maybe it's the auxiliary industries that feed off the restaurants themselves—the bloggers and agents and the "influencers," the brand managers, the personal assistants hired just to keep you fresh on "Insta," the Food & Wine festivals, the multitude of panels we chefs are now routinely invited to join, to offer our charming yet thoroughly unresearched opinions on. The proliferation of television shows and YouTube channels and culinary competitions and season after season of programming where you find yourself aghast to see an idol of yours stuffing packaged cinnamon buns into a football-shaped baking pan and squirting the frosting into a lace pattern for a tailgating episode on the Food Network.

And God, the brunch, the brunch. The phone hauled out for every single pancake and every single Bloody Mary to be photographed and Instagrammed. That guy who strolls in and won't remove his sunglasses as he holds up two fingers at my hostess without saying a word: he wants a table for two. The purebred lapdogs now passed off as service animals to calm the anxieties that might arise from eating eggs Benedict on a Sunday afternoon. I want the girl who called the first day of our mandated shutdown to call back, in however many months when restaurants are allowed to reopen, so I can tell her with delight and sincerity: No. We are not open for brunch. There is no more brunch.

I, like hundreds of other chefs across the city and thousands around the country, are now staring down the question of what our restaurants, our careers, our lives might look like if we can even get them back.

I don't know whom to follow or what to think. Everyone says: "You should do to-go! You should sell gift cards! You should offer delivery! You need a social media presence! You should pivot to groceries! You should raise your prices—a branzino is $56 at Via Carota!"

I have thought for many long minutes, days, weeks of confinement and quarantine, should I? Is that what Prune should do and what Prune should become?

I cannot see myself excitedly daydreaming about the third-party delivery-ticket screen I will read orders from all evening. I cannot see myself sketching doodles of the to-go boxes I will pack my food into so that I can send it out into the night, anonymously, hoping the poor delivery guy does a good job and stays safe. I don't think I can sit around dreaming up menus and cocktails and fantasizing about what would be on my playlist just to create something that people will order and receive and consume via an app. I started my restaurant as a place for people to talk to one another, with a very decent but affordable glass of wine and an expertly prepared plate of simply braised lamb shoulder on the table to keep the conversation flowing, and ran it as such for as long as I could. If this kind of place is not relevant to society, then it—we—should become extinct.

And yet even with the gate indefinitely shut against the coronavirus, I've been dreaming again, but this time I'm not at home fantasizing about a restaurant I don't even yet have the keys to. This time I've been sitting still and silent, inside the shuttered restaurant I already own, that has another ten years on the lease. I spend hours inside each day, on a wooden chair, in the empty clean space with the windows papered up, and I listen to the coolers hum, the compressor click on and off periodically, the thunder that echoes up from the basement as the ice machine drops its periodic sheet of thick cubes into the insulated bin. My body has a thin blue thread of electricity coursing through it. Sometimes I rearrange the tables. For some reason, I can't see wanting deuces anymore: No more two-tops? What will happen come Valentine's Day?

It's no mystery why this prolonged isolation has made me find the tiny twenty-four-square-inch tables that I've been cramming my food and my customers into for twenty years suddenly repellent. I want round tables, big tables, six-people tables, eight-tops. Early supper, home before midnight. Long, lingering civilized Sunday lunches with sun streaming in through the front French doors. I want old regulars to wander back into the kitchen while I lift the lids off the pots and show them what there is to eat. I want to bring to their tables small dishes of the feta cheese I've learned to make these long idle weeks, with a few slices of the *saucisson sec* I've been hanging downstairs to cure while we wait to reopen, and to again hear Greg rattle the ice, shaking perfectly proportioned Vespers that he pours right to the rim of the chilled glass without spilling over.

I have been shuttered before. With no help from the government, Prune has survived 9/11, the blackout, Hurricane Sandy, the recession, months of a city water-main replacement, online reservations systems—you still have to call us on the telephone, and we still use a pencil and paper to take reservations! We've survived the tyranny of convenience culture and the invasion of Caviar, Seamless, and Grubhub. So I'm going let the restaurant sleep, like the beauty she is, shallow breathing, dormant. Bills unpaid. And see what she looks like when she wakes up—so well rested, young all over again, in a city that may no longer recognize her, want her, or need her.

TONY HOAGLAND

Bent Arrows: On Anticipation of My Approaching Disappearance

FROM *Ploughshares*

THEY COME ARCHING over the horizon from distant places, like bent, crooked arrows dispatched from many directions.

They arrive in thin blue envelopes on folded stationery, or in fat, feverishly duct-taped packages. By overnight mail—sent prepaid by FedEx—($26.00!)—containing, say, three little misshapen onyx pebbles, which, I am told, should be placed in the corner of my sleeping room to ward off negative spirits.

A brass Turkish medallion from a person I hardly know, accompanied by a three-page letter explaining how she acquired it in Bulgaria, during her sexually promiscuous 1990s.

An ironed-flat wax-paper packet of pressed dried lavender and rosemary from someone's garden in Indiana.

A passionate testimonial to the healing power of spirulina.

A tribute CD of Gay Clark songs.

A handmade cedar-scented candle. A whoopee cushion.

The Irish friend from New Jersey sends a three-hour recording called "Long Healing Prayer"—a nonstop, droning dirge, performed, it seems, by three widows who have broken into the instrument closet of a medieval Celtic monastery. Wailing voices that float endlessly on a slick of fiddle music, like an Irish oil spill. It should be called "Suicide Note on Forlorn Bagpipe."

The reason I am the recipient of these exotic attentions is simple: I went on hospice service a month ago, and word leaked out. My cancer is no longer being treated, my narrative is fixed, the time uncertain but not distant. Now acquaintances and friends and even utter strangers are cleaning out their emotional cabinets, like midwives tying an umbilical knot between the dead and the living. Although I am the one dying, it is clear that they are the ones speaking their last words.

In a flat, heavy box, three Ziploc baggies, full of sand scooped and labeled from three different beaches: one in Florida, one on Cape Cod, one in Michigan.

From California, a message from the widow of a friend arrives: "I hope the end comes fast for you, as it did for Y."

Person X writes to tell me how good morphine is, and how she hopes those stingy bastards in the medical profession are giving me the good stuff. Her tone is one of barely disguised fury.

Then there is the genre of blithely delivered misinformation: the cheerful note that says, "Heard you are doing much better! So great to hear!"

Not all of the messages are whacky projections. Some are carefully worded, unexaggerated statements of friendship and memory (this turns out to be the essence of the business).

Others are like saturated handkerchiefs, soaked and dripping with sentimentality; monologues in which the mourner is so carried away by her capacity to emote deeply, I feel I should avert my eyes from such a private moment.

Persons I haven't heard from in decades want to visit and renew our friendship. But, isn't it a little late for that, I wonder? I imagine them standing over my couch, looking down at my diminished body, and I wonder what it is that they believe they have to say, what they have to bring, what they imagine they would like to take away. I wonder what they would see.

By email someone else writes, "I've discovered this wonderful anthology: *200 Greatest Zen Death Poems!* I'm sending them to you immediately."

I drift on my polka dot couch, I read and write. I watch the ceiling and the skies, and the strange missives—some touching, some bizarre—arrive. People I once considered close evaporated months ago; others, whom I thought as peripheral, have appeared and stayed: sane, stalwart, and present. Their voices are oddly reassuring. Most of the time now, dying doesn't seem like such a big thing.

How do you feel? I sometimes ask myself, not really knowing.

I have this image: I am floating on my back on a great body of water, buoyed comfortably by some kind of life vest. My gaze on the sky; seagulls and birds drift high overhead, on their way elsewhere; the clouds keep changing. I feel lonely, but calm. This is not so bad, I think. This sensation, of being held up by water, is something I have always loved.

In the distance, I can see the huge ocean liner from which I seem to have fallen overboard. With its many, many remaining passengers, it is moving away from me. Soon it will be out of sight. A ship that size, I understand, is simply too big to turn around for one person.

Even so, I can still glimpse the figures of people standing at the stern railing of that great ship—my friends—and in addition, some other people I don't recognize. Over the railing they are tossing bouquets, messages in bottles, pieces of chocolate cake in Tupperware containers; old photographs, bundles of dried sage. These are their goodbyes, their farewell gifts.

Once in a while, something splashes with a *thunk* and a ripple into the water near me. I am the passive participant in these transactions. No response is required of me. And these strange bent arrows keep arriving.

I gaze up at the endlessly interesting, endlessly changing sky.

Here comes another. There it goes.

I think someone is looking for me.

GREG JACKSON

Vicious Cycles

FROM *Harper's Magazine*

This is what I feared, that she would speak about the news . . . about how her father always said that the news exists so it can disappear, this is the point of news, whatever story, wherever it is happening. We depend on the news to disappear . . .

—Don DeLillo, "Hammer and Sickle"

What a story. What a fucking story.

—Dean Baquet, on the election of Donald Trump

A Circular Conversation

WHAT IS THE news? *That which is new.* But everything is new: a flower blooms; a man hugs his daughter, not for the first time, but for the first time *this* time . . . *That which is* important *and new.* Important in what sense? *In being consequential.* And this has been measured? *What?* The relationship between what is covered in the news and what is consequential. *Not measured.* Why? *Its consequence is ensured.* Ensured . . . ? *It's in the news.* But then who makes it news? *Editors.* Editors dictate consequence? *Not entirely.* Not entirely? *It matters what people read and watch—you can't bore them.* Then boredom decides? *Boredom and a sense of what's important.* But what *is* important? *What's in the news.*

I.

In his 1962 book *The Image,* Daniel J. Boorstin explains, "There was a time when the reader of an unexciting newspaper would remark, 'How dull is the world today!' Nowadays he says, 'What a dull newspaper!'" The first American paper, Benjamin Harris's *Publick Occurrences Both Forreign and Domestick,* committed to appearing only once a month—or "oftener 'if any Glut of Occurrences happen.'" Clearly, things have changed. "We need not be theologians," writes Boorstin, "to see that we have shifted responsibility for making the world interesting from God to the newspaperman." The chief tool in this new labor is the pseudo-event.

What is a pseudo-event? They are everywhere; we hardly notice. Some familiar examples: the speech, the rally, the press conference, the briefing, the ribbon cutting, the political announcement, the political response, the interview, the profile, the televised debate, the televised argument, the televised shouting match, the televised roundup of other televised events, the official expression of outrage, remorse, righteousness, fear, sanctimony, jingoism, smarm, or folksiness. The talking point is its handmaiden. News analysis is a second-order pseudo-event, not an event per se but the dissection of pseudo-events: that is, theater criticism. It is not that pseudo-events are always uninteresting or meaningless but that they are always *not news.* They exist only to be reported on. To supply a format. To make up for the non-glut of occurrences. Take away the pseudo-event and what is left to fill the news?

II.

To meet our demand for newness and stimulation, we refashioned public life as a ritual sequence of pseudo-events. This transformed politics from an industry of policy and legislation into an industry of emotion and entertainment. If the news covered only the proposal and passage of specific legislation—or the proposal and enactment of specific policy—we would have little news, and audience interest would quickly fade. But the work of politicians might become the work of governing. As things are, the job of politicians is to feed the emotional-entertainment industry that we call "news," which is accomplished by grandstanding and self-promotion. Reporters and pundits cover politics by analyzing how politicians succeed and fail as spokespeople and media figures. Interest shifts, by turns, to how the game is played, how the media fits into this game, and, eventually, how journalists do their jobs. The news today, properly understood, is about the careers of politicians and journalists. It is career drama.

III.

Television news aims to alert you to problems. In life, when someone alerts you to a problem, the problem's meaning takes shape within an implicit context, answering: (1) How important is this problem? (2) Where does it fit into the rest of my life? (3) What should I do about it? News shows cannot answer these questions because their format and their content are at odds. Their content says, "This is very important," but their format says: (1) No more important than the next segment; (2) In a time slot; (3) Keep watching. If you are a teacher or a car mechanic or a doctor, your job is not simply to identify a problem but to connect people to a solution. The news media doesn't do this. It *believes* it does—insofar as its audience members vote—but hundreds of hours spent consuming news in a given year put to the service of one vote in one election is a terrible use of any person's time. Consider what all these people, with all these hours, might otherwise accomplish. Consider that most viewers would vote similarly, and not necessarily less well, with much less information. The principal effect of TV news is to create engagement through distress. News shows cannot connect viewers to meaningful actions they might take in their own lives to relieve this distress because these actions would mean ceasing to watch TV. And this is the goal to which all others will be sacrificed: to keep you watching.

IV.

> Entertainment is the supra-ideology of all discourse on television. No matter what is depicted or from what point of view, the overarching presumption is that it is there for our amusement and

> pleasure. That is why even on news shows which provide us daily with fragments of tragedy and barbarism, we are urged by the newscasters to "join them tomorrow." What for? One would think that several minutes of murder and mayhem would suffice as material for a month of sleepless nights. We accept the newscasters' invitation because we know that the "news" is not to be taken seriously, that it is all in fun, so to say.
>
> —Neil Postman

Analyses of the news tend to focus on how the internet has changed things, and there is no doubt that the intrusions of Facebook's news feed and Google News, online aggregation and free content, real-time reporting, YouTube, blogging, podcasting, and Twitter have roiled and remade the news business. But the crisis in news *as an industry* is not the same as the crisis in news *as a cultural institution.* The latter took root long before we connected online. It is for this reason, because so much media today represents the continuation, even the culmination, of trends that originated in the late seventies and early eighties, that writers such as Neil Postman remain relevant. They saw that the news was moving in two directions even then: toward entertainment and away from the local reality of people's lives. For all the intervening technological change, entertainment on TV remains the dominant modality of all twenty-first-century news.

And while the news may not feel like fun, it is fun in the sense that it is stimulating without demanding effort—that doing anything else would require more energy and commitment, even turning off the TV. Watching television leaves no meaningful residue of knowledge or skill. When I visited Amsterdam many years ago, kids staying at the hostels liked to tour the Heineken brewery for an afternoon. They wanted to do something "cultural," an activity that justified having traveled to the Netherlands, but really they wanted to drink beer. This is the logic of all infotainment, all TV and most internet news: it soothes the mind's demand for constructive activity while delivering entertainment—a sugary drink sold on its vitamin content. Prestige TV works the same way: by convincing people that they are engaging with art. Make no mistake—well-wrought entertainment can require as much talent as art to create, but that alone does not make it art. Likewise, not all experiences of information are the same, since more or less passive forms of learning involve us differently. What distinguishes art (or knowledge) from entertainment (or infotainment) is that art asks something of its audience, and that its form serves the artwork, and not the other way around. Until the news can say, "We have no show (or paper) today because there is nothing of significance to concern you," the news will build its monument to truth on a lie.

V.

When you think you are doing something serious but you are doing something trivial and fun, you grow to believe that serious things are effortless and enjoyable. You are experiencing a format, while believing you are experiencing a content. The content suggests you are learning about truth, when you are really learning how to *feel*. You are learning how you should feel in the presence of certain information. These feelings go on to determine your expectations and worldview.

The formal message of the news is simultaneously the vital importance and utter triviality of everything that is happening. For weeks leading up to the 2018 midterm elections, the media covered the "migrant caravan" as the central story of the moment. Journalists understood that its salience as a crisis had been manufactured, and they devoted pages and segments and podcasts to debunking this salience, to exposing it as, in effect, a peripheral real event being turned into a central pseudo-event. These debunkings of course contributed to the critical mass of coverage, until the story, or nonstory, took up significant space in our minds: in our idea of the world "out there." Then the election took place; the migrant caravan had served its purpose as an object of media attention, and it disappeared. Presumably it did not disappear from the face of the earth, but to judge by the sole connection it had to most people who attended it—its life as a news item—it might as well have.

Which was the truth: That it was news, and it did belong in our minds? Or that it was an irrelevant sideshow? What we can say for certain is that this question was not decided in the real world of human necessity but in the virtual world of the news. The caravan story may be notable for how precipitously it disappeared, but the same uncertainty hangs over every news story: What space does this deserve in the limited sphere of our awareness? Since media attention rarely solves the problems it fixates on, in time the news must move on, letting every story vanish like the caravan—even wars. The raw matter and proportions of the world "out there" take shape in our minds in relation to the imperatives of an industry. This proportionality, rather than fact or truth, decides the image of the world we construct: what Jean Baudrillard calls a "hyperreality," the inseparable amalgam of the virtual and the real. The news narrativizes the world, but distortedly, according to the proclivities of its format, and so the story the news tells is always at heart the story of news: the story of curating what we recognize as news.

VI.

Is it a problem that our mental representation of the world is the product of a for-profit entertainment industry? Yes. Our government, for instance, cannot be dully competent if what we demand of it is that it not be boring. (After the first day of open testimony in the impeachment hearings, NBC News noted that the witnesses "testified to President Trump's scheme, but lacked the pizzazz necessary to capture public attention.") Journalists often rightly claim that the engaged polity should focus more on state and local politics, but people follow national politics for the same reason journalists and pundits do: because it's interesting. Were we to take their advice, they would be out of a job. Our attention sustains them, as it sustains politicians, and so when journalists wring their hands over the unfortunate necessity of covering Trump's tweets—to choose another example—they mistake their own complicity in what they, again rightly, find toxic. For there is no noncircular logic that ordains the newsworthiness of the president's tweets. As the celebrity is famous for being famous, so Trump's tweets are news because they get covered as news. If the news media chose to report only on concrete actions and orders emanating from the White House, the activity of governing would once again become the proper object of political contemplation.

What news outlets appear to mean by insisting that they must cover Trump's tweets and other provocative ephemera is that if they don't, someone else will and will thereby steal their audience, or that they feel obliged to report on what their audience seems to want. But this only draws attention to the central flaw in their industry. They are not, they reveal, reporting "the news"—an expert and principled curation of what they believe is important—but seeking to win audience share, like any other entertainment business, by trading on the inherent prestige of and misconceptions about what we have come to call "news."

On the podcast *Stay Tuned with Preet,* Preet Bharara asked Christiane Amanpour whether the media underestimates people in assuming they want to be entertained rather than informed. It is a confused question and received a confused answer:

> I think maybe that was the case in the past several years. But I do believe that since we've entered this vortex of a different kind of politics, I think many, many people are actually looking for real news, facts, truth. Clearly, there's a lot who don't really care, who buy into conspiracy theories, who still go to Facebook and other places where they can find fake news. I do think that people have to take on a responsibility of their own right now. . . . They go out and they shop around, and they get the best that they can. And they must do that right now when it comes to information because we are being inundated by charlatans who don't give a damn about the effect they're having on people. And they just care about clickbait and just care about racking up their own dollars, their own profit margins. It is a disgrace. It is immoral. It is the marketplace. So I think that people need to be responsible and choose their destination carefully, and come to people like us who are tried and true and tested and proven brand names in this sphere.

Amanpour's show is on PBS, which may partially insulate it from the market. Still, her assumptions and elisions are striking, if predictable. She does not ask whether meaningful or essential truth may be different from "real news, facts, truth" as dictated by a TV news show. She glides over the question of whether she is supplying facts and information to an audience that would otherwise not have this information or fall prey to conspiracy theories and fake news. She assumes, against all reasonable belief, that people are drawn to her show because they are searching for truth or facts in a morass of confusion and deceit. She suggests, with no apparent irony, that being "responsible" means choosing your TV news "destination" carefully. Finally, while denigrating the charms of less "true and tested and proven brand names in this sphere," she seems utterly (or conveniently) incurious about what people actually get out of her program and others like it. What she must know—just as Bharara knows it—is that she is not principally the purveyor of unique information but a media personality, someone people like to spend time with, and that her show, while presumably made up of real news and facts and truth, is a fantasy, a shimmering hyperreality, one that in this case happens to be a fantasy *about* how facts and news and truth are treated, with emphases and mores that signal seriousness and importance within well-understood and fairly rigid parameters. What she is selling, in other words, is not an experience of reality but of what her viewers wish reality were like—that is, therapy, not news.

VII.

The coincidence of trauma and therapy, alarm and comfort, is the essence of today's news, which requires emergency, high-stakes drama, breaking stories, updates, and alerts to keep its audience engaged, but which must then solve the problem it has created by offering explainers and analyses to give coherence to so much terrifying chaos and by employing informational docents, in the form of likable media figures, to soothe our fear of a world on fire with their good humor, their intelligence, and the reassuring whisper embedded in their format: *the news exists so it can disappear.* And the news does disappear, inevitably, because its salience in the virtual sphere of our apprehension is so disproportionate to its salience in our lives. But what does not disappear is the residue of the experience and how this primes us for our next encounter with news of politics and the world out there.

One consequence of inflating the stakes of ongoing political activity in order to fill formats and draw audiences is that people are afraid of politics: afraid of politicians—the government—actually doing anything. Large constituencies stand ready on either side to denounce any new policy or law as the end of everything they cherish. The potential effect of policy gets subsumed into the virtual space of the news, where it languishes as an untested proposition, an object of endless, futile debate. Instead of implementing policy and evaluating it in practice, we remain paralyzed, and the more paralyzed we get—the less able to enact or amend policy—the more the case for paralysis grows, since the chances of fixing a mistake diminish. This grants an asymmetric power to the forces that want the government to do less, not more.

But the more pernicious effect is a psychic cancer introduced into the culture as a whole. The extreme coincidence of urgency and irrelevance, terror and impotence, turns into a maddening unsettledness and contradiction in the conceptual sphere of life, authoring fear, anger, and confusion everywhere. The essential experience of a hyperreality is angst: dread, hushed panic, ambient foreboding. A disturbing fiction at least comforts you that it is fiction. A needling friend may finally admit, "I'm just fucking with you." The news is, on balance, just fucking with us, but it can never say so because it draws its stimulating power from the pretense that it isn't entertainment, isn't just "fun," but is deeply consequential. It rigorously blurs the line between entertainment and public service, since its market share and prestige depend on this confusion. But when you ask yourself what you can *do* with what you have learned on the news, you see that it only permits you to consume subsequent news more conversantly.

VIII.

Whether as a news show, a podcast, or an article, chances are today the news came to you through a screen. Online news platforms differ from traditional broadcast media and newspapers in significant ways. When clicks and engagement define the metrics of success, prompts and alerts, listicles, clickbait, most-read or "top story" sections, and otherwise manipulative headlines and teasers become predominant aspects of the experience. The graphic layouts of news on TV and on websites converge, with chyrons mimicking banner ads and vice versa. Red-letter "breaking news" gets more common (and less likely to be urgent, or even news) as the thirst for constant stimulation grows. When you buy a physical newspaper, what you do with it next—what you read—is your business. Not so with news on the internet; here the publication's interest does not end but begins at the "point of sale," and everything about the architecture of the product is designed to attach you to more of it.

But even old-school newspapers succumb to the tyranny of format, worshiping, in their way, a less glitzy hyperreality we call "the news of the day." This is what a newspaper is and has been—a kind of composite pseudo-event—since the telegraph and other technologies of communication freed information from limits imposed by space and time. The news of the day comprises real- and pseudo-events and even, sometimes, real news, but it is only one of infinite possibilities of how we might narrativize the world. It strives to be factual but adheres to strict conventions of format about what can and can't appear. It collapses the dimensionality we rely on to judge the world around us so that the proportions of the world it presents cannot agree with the proportions of our lives—"cannot" because the news *is* above all else this proportionality, this idiosyncratic condensation of the world out there.

This is what Neil Postman meant when he wrote, "The news of the day is a figment of our technological imagination." Our means of apprehending reality determine the reality we apprehend. What few could foresee was that, as technological and business pressures drew the news further toward stimulation and away from representing immediate life, at a certain point the value of the news' being true, its hewing as close as possible to an accurate picture of the world, would fall away. The news' relationship to people's lives had grown perilously virtual and its meaning, on an emotional level, nearly indistinguishable from entertainment. That no feedback mechanism existed to discourage people from getting their facts wrong, or to correct them when they did, underscored how deeply insignificant and remote the subject matter of the news—trumpeted for its significance and immediacy—was to the lives of its audience. In the immediate and practical sense, news and fake news became a distinction without a difference.

IX.

What we call "news" is less and less the meaningful historical facts —*this happened*—and more and more "opinion": argument to substantiate an ideology or worldview. Have you noticed a recent profusion of ideology? Here's why: ideology is an answer to the problem of conceptual questions destined to remain in the conceptual sphere. It fills a vacuum of action. You can argue using ideology, but you can't build a bridge with it. If you spend more time arguing than building bridges, it's very useful.

One way to tell you're in the presence of ideology is when an entire industry of opinion exists to bolster and substantiate beliefs that people do not know how to justify on their own. Its nature is to confuse the question of who is thinking for whom and where thought or belief began. Ideology flatters people that their beliefs are their own precisely when they are not, and thus the sort of opinions and analyses that present themselves as ideology's correctives are in fact its enablers. The consumer of opinion does not ask himself "Why do I believe this?" but "Who can remind me why I believe this?"

Much has been made of the dichotomy between news and opinion in the case of Fox News or the *Wall Street Journal,* but almost all news today comes with a lacing of opinion or ideology, a framing, at the very least, that helps sort through the implications of a piece of information and put it in the context of a prior ideological framework. Rarely are you left to wonder whether a given idea matches Republican or Democratic, conservative or liberal ideology. Rarely are you left to wonder what you yourself think, or what else you would like to know before forming an opinion, without someone swooping in to think for you.

Guidance from those who know more than you do is often a good thing: the substance of education. But education means to empower you to think for yourself, not indoctrinate you. The signs of education and of ideology mirror each other inversely: curiosity, open-mindedness, and self-doubt on the one hand; quickness to anger, defensiveness, and tenacity of belief on the other. One welcomes new information; the other fears it.

Most Americans are not significant consumers of news and are not especially ideological. One might hope that if news were performing the educational function it sets for itself, news-savvy, high-information Americans would be still more open-minded and less ideological. Studies suggest the opposite is true—that more "informed" voters are more partisan and often have less accurate, more ideologically skewed ideas about the world. This isn't necessarily the news' fault. Nonetheless, the news seems not to counteract or mitigate but to abet our ideological drift. It gives us the tools not to interrogate but to taxonomize belief, not to develop policy preferences but to identify to which political identity and tribe a policy belongs. In the internet age it gives us just enough to cobble together our own take—demonstrating our wonkish bona fides, unleashing a snarky dismissal or the sickest burn—just enough, that is, to pass off the scraps of other people's expertise as an ersatz identity of our own.

X.

Ideology grows stronger for our belief in a lie: that information has an additive property whereby at some point it becomes knowledge. This simply isn't true. Outside the contextual frameworks that give information a place in life and a relationship to other information, it is quite literally meaningless. Would more state-issued facts about the Soviet economy in 1980, or more pages of talking points from an industry lobby, get you closer to the truth simply for not being untrue? Does knowing more trivia help someone build a better car or advance particle physics or write a more touching ballad? If we judge the "informed" as those who possess more information—more disembodied or decontextualized bits of trivia that are "true" in the sense of not being demonstrably false—we may find we have created a vacuous category ("conversance") and that we need invented contexts, like the proliferating "news quizzes," to put these incoherent facts to use. "Think You're Smarter Than a *Slate* Senior Editor? Find Out With This Week's News Quiz," *Slate* suggests. "Did you stay up to date this week?" the *New York Times*'s news quiz more gently wonders. It's only one step further to propose the news business itself and the practice of journalism as the proper object of the news connoisseur's attention and interest. Asking such people's opinions in polls, then, may do less to draw out "informed" commentary than to hold up a mirror to the culture's own confusion.

"Truth" and "fact" in isolation do nothing to combat ideology and error. It merely benefits the news industry to pretend they do. I understand why people object to false equivalencies between MSNBC and Fox News, but to focus on veracity blinds us to the deeper effect of opinion and punditry per se. The pertinent question concerns the terms of the implicit contract between audience and commentator. If commentators serve the sensibility of their audiences—which the necessity of attracting and retaining viewers (or listeners or readers) in a competitive media environment ensures—it hardly matters that they traffic in fact or avoid untruth since the overall message people receive is: *Your worldview is substantially right, and here are the arguments to insulate and fortify it.* The purpose is to justify ideological frameworks as a way of dealing with uncertainty and to reinforce the complex social agreements on which these consensuses are built. When the Fox News anchor Shepard Smith debunked what conspiracy theorists had dubbed the Hillary Clinton "uranium scandal" in 2017, his audience did not thank him for elucidating the truth, but suggested he belonged on CNN or MSNBC and that, for exposing a false story, he was anti-Trump. In other words, he had violated the terms of their contract, which was not to provide fact or best judgment but corroboration. Truth was welcome, but only truth that confirmed one view.

Thus while ideology and entertainment may seem at odds—entertainment is reputedly fun and lighthearted, where ideology is deadly serious—they are in fact flip sides of the same coin. Entertainment means to transfix, to keep you in place: watching, tuned in. It cannot ask you to endure discomfort, and the comfort it offers is often an uncomplicated intimacy, even a vicarious identification, with a celebrity—in the case of news, with the commentator or host. Because this person's primary concern is your comfort—which is to say your attention and approval—a subtle con exists at the heart of the exchange. This person does not know who you are or, in any but the most superficial sense, care about you. But the illusion of a relationship is nonetheless paramount. It goes one step further, since part of the illusion, in the face of political confusion and distress, is that the news celebrity's competence and clarity are your own. Her power is briefly yours, and while you inhabit the aura of her expertise you are safe from your own ignorance and the frustration of life among other people. The most fervent devotees of a cult or demagogue are those who mistake courtship for love and the power of a leader for their own. But when you step outside the aegis of a leader's power, the aura of a pundit's companionship, you realize, suddenly, that you are alone and unprepared. You were misled into thinking you were getting help when you were giving worship. Ideology takes root in this disappointment because the alternative is more painful: accepting that you've been conned.

XI.

Newspapers begin with the most serious and sober news, which, though it has little to do with your life, understands that you show up with good intentions. You mean to do something civic, or at least to cast a glance over those more serious headlines on your way to controversy and gossip, celebrity and human drama.

The news, like a fractal, repeats this betrayal of good intentions on every scale. This is the poignancy and tragedy of the news. We need it: the Fourth Estate, complement to government, scourge of corruption, orchestrator of public discourse. No one thinks we could get by without a press. No one who understands the work of journalism has anything but admiration for its honest practice.

But this work—to hold power to account, to safeguard the truth, to comfort the afflicted and afflict the comfortable, in Finley Peter Dunne's immortal words—has entered into a fatal bargain with an effluvium that demeans and yet supports it. Traditional reporting becomes the loss leader. It exchanges its status for a subsidy, and slowly a reluctant embrace of this co-optation—by the very forces a profession that stands in opposition to power should repel—turns into an erotic grapple, because the apotheosis of market logic is the jittery Stockholm syndrome that makes the prisoners of the market insist that it has set them free.

So we find ourselves in a situation in which an entertainment industry of specious value (called "news") subsidizes a much smaller and less popular subindustry (real news), which lends its prestige to the former and permits it to call itself by the same name. As this entertainment industry subsumes and replaces the news industry, a little game takes place, more or less in public. The game involves pretending—journalist and audience alike—that they have gathered to discuss a truth that exists outside the media, when, except in the rarest cases, they intend to discuss the processes of the media itself: the drama of how information and sentiment evolve and are influenced within a media environment. Like sports fans, news consumers learn the subtleties of the game. They grow "media-savvy," and media-savvy becomes the hope of an industry. Members of the news business (and practically they alone) call for greater "media literacy"—a solution to a problem they have created that expects the reformation of their audience but not of their industry—because they do not want to choose between responsibility and popularity, or principle and career. They are selling a healthy product, they imply, which people are using the wrong way. But this is confused. No one *wants* the healthy product. They want its misuse. They want to believe something so stimulating can be healthy, and they rely on media members to help perpetuate this lie.

As civic discourse—the news—becomes increasingly shaped by media-savvy and game-play, as it becomes a metadiscourse not about actual events but about the translation and distortion of actual events within a virtual sphere, the little lie about what the news is and why we follow it permits bigger lies. Charlatans, con men, demagogues, and cheats crawl out of the woodwork and operate with impunity, knowing they need not win on truth or merit, but simply win the news cycle, win within the rules of a confected game. Playing the game well, being stimulating and likable in a media environment, suffices to justify one's ascendancy within it, because—despite protestations to the contrary—this logic of celebrity explains why anyone is a media figure in the first place, and why we attend them. The sober, responsible news, now in its watchdog guise, enters here—when the mechanism of its own industry has elevated a crook or a scoundrel to a position of power—promising to solve, through exposure, a problem it helped create. But it can't undo the media mechanism without relinquishing its own power and profitability by copping to the lie on which its prestige rests.

XII.

But we need the news, don't we? We need information spreading through society. We need people digging into convenient stories to check the facts. We need to uncover what power seeks to hide and discourage those who can abuse their power from doing so.

Of course, we can't judge the soldier, the police officer, the watchdog only by what they do, but also by what would happen without them.

And yet no one would suggest we fund the military by watching it wage war on TV, that the size of its audience should determine its budget. We understand where such incentives would lead.

But this is the way the news works. Its greatest social benefit rests in discouraging the sensational and scandalous from happening, but it needs the sensational and scandalous to attract the audience that supports it. No one would propose we fund cancer research through tobacco sales or link heart-disease treatment to McDonald's revenue. No one would say that the CIA should partner with TMZ to run a celebrity-gossip site. But with the news we are not so far from these fanciful scenarios. Breitbart and right-wing talk radio belabor fake scandals to create a salable emotional product, but the mainstream media, for all its understandable concern about Trump, cannot stop helping him when it boosts their bottom line. They can't limit themselves to reporting on concrete actions by the White House but must breathlessly amplify every ephemeral utterance, every remark designed to cause a little flurry of reporting and nothing more. They can't stop saying "Trump" and broadcasting his likeness, when his likeness has nothing to do with the news and when they could as easily say "the White House" or "the executive branch." They are puppeteered by their own game, caught in a bind whereby their abhorrence of Trump and their audience's abhorrence of Trump elevated him to such cacophonous prominence that he had a shot of winning the presidency. And when he did win and the mood among reporters at the *New York Times* turned bleak, the paper's executive editor, Dean Baquet, was surprised at the response: this was the story of a lifetime. "Great stories trump everything else, right?" he says in the documentary miniseries *The Fourth Estate.*

But only someone besotted with the news as an end in itself could believe that—another executive clinging to the delusion that he's a celebrity and a civic hero at once. The privatization of a public good has progressed to a far-gone place when market success and moral success are so confused that you congratulate yourself for selling both antidote and toxin.

XIII.

The news may be judged by what it crowds out. "Democracy dies in darkness,"the *Washington Post* motto reads. For billions who live in countries without a free press, this is true. But our problem in the United States is not an absence but a glut. Truth dies in darkness, but it also dies in blinding light. Separating what's important from what's trivial is as essential as revealing what's important. A needle in the haystack isn't much better than no needle.

The problem of distinguishing the important from the trivial is a problem for all of us—for our educators, our politicians, our leaders, for us as individuals, as citizens, as friends. To lay this problem at the feet of the news industry is unfair. The news is trapped in a business model that makes no sense, that rewards it for its worst behavior and refuses to pay it for what of greatest value it contributes. But the news can be blamed for confusing the issue. We need to know when we are being entertained and when we are having a different experience. Being fed trivialities when we need importance, like empty calories when we need nourishment, makes us sick. We grow to mistake bigness for importance, when importance is a measure of our involvement. Big trivialities make us psychically obese, with nowhere to expend this pent-up energy. "What a story. What a fucking story," Dean Baquet said, watching Trump's inauguration.

The essayist Lauren Hough writes about being a "cable guy" and describes the clenched-teeth white-knuckling of a customer who hears he will have to forgo Fox News for a week. A junkie without a fix. What is this hunger, this addiction? An addiction is a hunger briefly satisfied, then redoubled, by its object. But hunger for *what?* Hunger for something much more significant than the news. An answer to the incommensurable. To the incommensurability of the scope of the world and the scope of our lives. The vastness of our hopes and the range of our capabilities. Meaning and place. I feel it too. It does not begin in anger or fear, but it can be twisted into these by a cynical exchange—too many cynical exchanges, one after the next. Too many trivialities passed off as sustenance. Too much fake intimacy. Too much stimulation to no end.

William Carlos Williams wrote that while people rarely get their news from poems, it is "for lack / of what is found" in poetry—this deeper sounding of what concerns us—that they perish daily. Good luck getting anyone to turn away from the news to a poem, but this is the lack—and the surfeit, the glut—of which we die miserably every day.

Something Missing

When we turn away from the news, we will confront a startling loneliness. It is the loneliness of life. The loneliness of thinking, of having no one to think for us, and of uncertainty. It is a loneliness that was always there but that was obscured by an illusion, and we will miss the illusion. We will miss the illusion that we had a place in history, the sense that we were celebrities ourselves, actors on the grand stage. We will miss the voices and images that came to us daily and convinced us they were our friends. We may, if we listen closely to the echo inside this loneliness, hear the expectant beating of our own hearts and understand that what we longed for, what we asked for, and what was given us was a story—a story of such grand metaphysical proportions that reality could never meet it. Reality could only meet it by inflaming itself, and this was the danger—the danger that made our hearts beat faster and the story grow stronger. Then we will see the news for what it was: the narrator of our national epic. "The news of the day" was the next chapter in an evaporating book. And we will miss tuning in each day to hear that voice that cuts boredom and loneliness in its solution of the present tense, that like Scheherazade assures us, the story is still unfolding and always will be. I don't know whether we can give it up. We may need it too much, miss it too sharply. We may never get to the quiet place where we can read a poem, because this will mean distinguishing happiness from pleasure and understanding that happiness means boredom, means loneliness. Means life among one another, in the world: a place where drama subsides and horizons of time stretch to months, to years. Are you not bored already? Who will narrate our epic now? Will we have one? What will bind us? No one knows. What we do know is that some part of us longs for our dreams to come true. Dream of monsters long enough and you bring them into being. We make what we imagine real. And who then reminds us—and what must happen before we remember—that the drama we want in our stories is not the drama we want in our lives?

RUCHIR JOSHI

Clarity

FROM *Granta*

I'VE SPENT THE past five, six years, feeling I'm not getting things. At times I feel like I'm encased in some sort of prophylactic that prevents me from seeing or hearing him properly, from sensing everything I need to sense; at others it's as though he is trapped in a transparent silo and all I can do is circle around lecturing and hectoring him, all meaningless—or pointless—to use one of his favorite words.

"Why do you give a fuck? Why do you care so much?" he asks me from time to time.

"Because you're my son. Because I love you. Because I've never loved anyone more than you and your brother." It sounds oversweet and cheap when I play it back now in my head, but I've learned to keep what I say simple. And truthful.

Every now and then I think he's asking me this question because he himself wants to find a route to caring. At other times I think he wants to be divested of caring so much, that his love and anxiety for me, for his mother and his older brother, are too much of a burden.

Sometimes I bring up the fact that we've led these split lives since he was born. Me coming to London for a chunk of every year to be with the two of them. Them coming to India once, twice a year, first with both parents, then with their mother and then on their own, being fed into the airline system at one end by one parent, received on the landing end by the other. I tell him how I used to see them off at the airport and cry sometimes when I got home. His older brother has told me he used to miss me.

"Not me," he says, "I didn't think about it. Once you were gone you were gone. I thought it was normal."

Normal. Your parents dying before you is normal, that's what they are there for, to bring you up, and then to die well before you do, leaving you to live at least some part of your life free of their presence. The same applies to you and your children, overlapping like cross-fading soundtracks: your life before parenthood, your life with your children, your children's lives after you. I'm now looking at an alternative cross-fade, my life before my younger one was born, the years with him, and now life after him—which is not what I was designed for. Suddenly, I don't fit my life. Every corner is wrong, the size is suddenly incorrect, somebody else's life delivered to me by mistake, but now it's the only one available.

I was close to my own father, which many people are not. He died thirty-one years ago and I still miss him, not in a way that cripples me, but acutely nevertheless. I have vivid memories of time spent with him, of learning things, of great laughter, love, and joy. I don't need to dig up those moments, they are inside me, woven into the fabric of my being. What I regret about my father's death is that it came too early. I feel sad that he never saw my sons, never played with them or watched them grow up. Then again, on days when I unsubscribe from the rational, I feel he *has* seen all this, and that he's still there, somewhere, and comes to visit from time to time. Had he lived a bit longer he would have directly exchanged sight and touch and love with his grandsons; but the way things turned out I've always felt he and the kids could only reach each other through me.

Thinking about what my son went through before he killed himself, at times I feel I didn't let enough of my father through, or of my mother either, to help him take a different route. I feel I failed as a medium—as a channel I allowed myself to be blocked.

One of the things I find myself missing is the fear. Even now I hesitate to leave my laptop where you might find it and smash it, or my mobile phone where you might take it and walk off, to listen to music, to drop it and break it, to have it slip out of your pocket and not even notice, to sell it to a dealer for a few quids' worth of some shitty low-grade shit, or my wallet with whatever small amount of cash and the house keys, which are far more important.

It's true that you never actually walked off with my phone, and the only laptops you smashed were the ones you considered your own, but one never knew: I could never take the risk, and I'm still not sure that someday you wouldn't have done to my stuff what you did to your own. But now that tension has worn thin. The putting away, the hiding of stuff, comes from habit that's now emptied of proper anxiety, and I find myself wishing it wasn't so. I find myself wishing I was still afraid.

I'm sitting on a bus when an ambulance goes by, siren on. Then a police car, roof on blue fire, going in the other direction. There's a stab of anxiety, but the knife is one of those trick ones kids play with, with a plastic blade going back into the handle. The sirens aren't for you, they can never again be for you.

Over the past five years I've rehearsed the sirens many times. Ambulance tearing through the night, me gripping your hand as you lie on the stretcher, prayers stuck in my throat, unable to break out. Police siren stopping outside the door, and then the doorbell. Me nine thousand miles away in India, too far to hear the siren, which, in fact, is what finally happens. Me not there for the police standing outside your mother's front door, no siren, just bringing the news. Me back in Calcutta when they actually come the first time, three years ago. The photos I receive of you all tubed up in the ICU—induced coma to counter huge overdose, life saved because of timely intervention—the drug traces they find coming out of you unidentifiable, Chinese whispers, outside their range of tests.

When you come out of the ICU and go back into the mental ward everybody weighs up those two bruiser-words—suicide and self-harm—and then rejects them. At the times you do admit to doing the drugs, you say you were just trying to have a blast, pushing the limits, taking this new substance, popping three small squares of this paper when you were supposed to take no more than one—because you'd read that some guy had swallowed nine and survived.

Nevertheless, over the past few years whenever I arrive from India, among the first things I always do is hide the really sharp Japanese knife and the small, lethal German paring knife in your mother's kitchen. I'm not thinking you'll use the knives on yourself, I'm not thinking that I or someone else might be at the wrong end of the blade, I'm not thinking anything specific, I'm just thinking if there was a bottle of aspirin, an electric drill, or car keys, I would hide those too.

When I was little I fell ill often, sometimes seriously, and each time I remember my mother praying that the illness be transferred to her. I understand that now, properly only now. It's not that I wanted to take over your "madness," as you called it, but I often found myself wishing there was some way it could be siphoned entirely into me, like I was some kind of Neelkanth Shiva able to quarantine poison in his throat, or, like with some water-purifying plant, processed through me and out as waste.

Now the only way I can process your death, put it through the computation of my still being here and your not, is to try and think of everything as magical. Every single thing, every moment, every encounter, every sight that crosses my eyes. Everything magical, unreal, impossible, and impossibly insulting to logic and reason.

You and I, we talked a lot about logic and reason. I sometimes felt that Logic-and-Reason was a faraway country that you would now and then consider visiting, but that you were not convinced by the recounting of my travels over there.

I think of the skin between the rational and the irrational. That skin that we all have, that skin of yours that got scraped away and never grew back.

The first psychiatrist who sees him is in India. I take him to the appointment when he's just turned seventeen. It's a disorder, but definitely not schizophrenia or anything long-term like that. He should get better with medication and he must stay off the illegal substances. After that it's mostly back in London where the doctors treat him. Again, no psychiatrist wants to give it a name. "We wouldn't like to slot him into a particular condition." But for the benefits forms they do need a label and his is "paranoid schizophrenia."

Some of the signs were there much earlier, but from seventeen the layers really start to thicken and surround him: whatever different brain-wiring he was carrying from birth; what the ever-present screens—TV, laptop, and phone—were bringing him; the street drugs; the mental health services protocols and medication; the benefits money coming into his bank every two weeks; different nets enmeshing him, pulling him away from his mother, his brother, and me, from his friends and the other grown-ups who cared desperately for him. Pulling him away from imagining a different future, one for which he might want to wake up again and again.

The anger sits close at hand, like some obsolete object now uselessly taking up space. Anger at him, at the mental health services, and the ward where he accessed the more serious drugs for the first time, at the pushers and dealers circling around the wards and the streets, anger at Fuckfacebook and GlyouTube. At all these layers of netting in which he was trapped, for which I didn't have the scissors, the knives, wire cutters, laser cutters.

There was the facility for languages and accents that showed up early. A clustered gift for language, music, and mathematics that was startling, almost scary. When things start to turn, the talent for language also starts biting into itself. Words become bombs, become booby traps, entanglements in which he always seems trapped. But, even in the middle of the turmoil, there are moments of crazy clarity.

In late 2013 we are in Calcutta for a couple of weeks. He is seventeen, already in pain, trying to make sense of quotidian things. He speaks nothing but his Northlondonese to everyone; he certainly speaks no Bengali. Eight months later, in London, he tells me: "I think I'll learn Bengali." I give some response about how he should go back to working on his Spanish, which he gave up. I tell him Bengali might be difficult to pick up. "Hyan! *Koto* mushkil!" he sneers—"Yes! *How* difficult!" but in a perfect Bengali accent, the sarcastic-aunty tone precise to the context. Where did he get it from?

And where did it go?

There are the scrawled notes I keep finding: "Disbelief of Belief, Belief of Disbelief," repeatedly worked out sums between "ego," "traveler," and "desire," scrawled seesaws between "emotion" and "thoughts," the pen pushing against commonly accepted meanings and valences of simple words, trying to map the "I," set a net to trap the self.

Language is also a skin. My skin is different from his. When our skins rub against each other, sometimes it's like two bits of sandpaper scraping. He's angry with others about various things; with me he fights against my voice and words. His loud voice smashing into mine—same voice box; his skill with words fencing with mine—very different swords.

At some point a couple of years ago, he develops a volcanic anger at the word "consequences," when I tell him that just as actions do, words too have consequences, like billiard balls glancing and sending each other in directions not entirely predictable.

When the November 2015 attacks happen in Paris he takes it personally. "I fucked up," he says. "I could have saved them." Likewise with Trump getting elected—he takes it as his personal failure. "I should not have let that happen." He can handle PlayStation games all right, but the TV bothers him; often he'll ask, "Is that live? Is that TV live?"

Through the seven-odd years of his worsening condition, there is the business of the "signal": something getting to him that he demonstrates by rubbing together his thumb and forefinger. "Can't you feel it? The signal?" he asks his mother, his brother, me, others. When we say we can't feel it, he explodes. "Don't *lie!* How can you not feel it? Why are you lying to me?"

The nets tangle and tighten around him and I can't tell if it's the drugs talking or the psychosis, can't tell which comes first, the anxieties and delusions or the substances he constantly reaches for to counter them. The metaphors get tangled in my head: on the one hand there are the nets; on the other hand, layers peeling off a rain-soaked wall, first the paint of reality flaking away, then the base plaster of the will to live, and finally the cement of logic, brittle now, falling out from between the bricks of words.

Sometimes I find myself thinking that by snatching yourself away, you also took away the just-walking baby I danced with, the three-year-old I read to, the eight-year-old I wrestled with, the fourteen-year-old with whom I'd argue happily about music, all those kids of mine that were you. And then I think, no, those boys were long gone, happily and correctly; and yet again no, there is nowhere those boys are going, they will always be inside me just as they would have been had you grown older and moved into your own "normal" life.

I think of one of those Russian dolls, except this one is reversed—you open a small one and a bigger one comes out and then a bigger one from that, till your kid reaches adulthood, taller than you, walking faster than you, knowing more and knowing better than you, often looking at you with pity and fraying patience.

Maybe for a child growing up, each parent is like a normal Russian doll, going down from the big, hollow outer one to ever smaller, ever more distilled and diminishing versions. In this imbalanced yin and yang of two lives there is never a point when both parent and child are exactly the same size, or with the same power; something is always askew, always some asymmetrical osmosis taking place.

They fuck you up your girl and lad, they don't mean to but they do. They find the cracks you never had, and make some new ones too.

When I tell a friend about you, about your going, she—herself a mother—says, "I don't know how you are alive after this."

It's true. This body of mine is a strange place to be in when you're no longer in yours.

When the postmortem reports come in three months later they find no intoxicants in your body. None of us, your mother, your brother, or I, are surprised. The drugs have had their say already; we have each sensed that you did what you felt you had to do, completely stone-cold sober. For me, you had a small window of your kind of clarity and you made it pay. I wish it had been a different clarity, closer to mine.

In the garden of your mother's house in London. A warplane slicing into sky, knifing open the blue, the contrail-wound sharp for a few moments before it opens and the universe pours in. Or pours out.

In your grandmother's house near the Himalayas. I draw a portrait of you. You watch, and then you take the pencil and paper and draw one of me.

AMY LEACH

Oh Latitudo

FROM *Granta*

"I LOVED BEING young," says the chorus in *Heracles*, written around 420 BCE, and to this day people are still chorusing about how they loved being young, insisting that someday young people too will have loved being young. Nobody goes up to old people and says, "I loved being old," or if they do you can't hear them or see them. I know of a bear who didn't love everything about being young, the bear who his first winter built a den for himself, but it wasn't big enough, so all winter he hibernated with his bottom sticking out.

Platypuses could say to us, "I loved being young," since compared to platypuses humans are whippersnappers. Platypuses may condescend to us but we must not condescend to them. If we want to condescend to somebody we can condescend to petunias. Petunias are ridiculously young, having been cultivated in the nineteenth century. (Their parents are old and wild.) But even though they are young and inexperienced, I have seen petunias rallying after a hailstorm, putting themselves back together. I imagine if the supervolcano a little south of here erupted, there would be the insouciant petunias afterward, shaking the ash off their purple.

Flying around over a supervolcano, the dragonflies of Yellowstone are so insouciant you might think they were superyoung. However they are three hundred million years old and over that time have seen plenty of supervolcanos erupt. Maybe that is why their heads are all eyeballs. Anyway, rather than organizing a superbucket brigade in preparation for another eruption, the flame skimmers, cherry-faced meadowhawks, and mountain emeralds are zooming backward, zooming forth, zooming up and down, zooming in place. They possess the insouciance of the old.

The supervolcano has a supersecret underneath the surface, magma and hot mushy crystals. On the surface that secret is expressed in the bluest pools, the most experimental rocks, the burpiest mud and the rainbowiest steam. Looking toward the Grand Prismatic Spring from far off, you can see its prismatic steams rising into the air, red steam, green steam, tangerine steam. The steams are the supervolcano letting off steam, and the colors are the colors of the swimmers in the spring.

Of course in the swimming-pool biz the tradition is to keep the water "safe," with a pH of 7.4 and a temperature between 83 and 86 degrees F to make it "comfortable for your swimmers." However, it depends on what type of swimmers you're wanting—if you want fragile big loud pink and brown swimmers, then those are good parameters. If on the other hand you keep your pool at 450 degrees F with a pH of 2, like lemon juice, you will get flinty little green and orange swimmers who never shout.

So extreme pools attract extreme patrons; so much for toning things down. Still, the supervolcano is probably at its most brilliant when not erupting. A kept secret is an engine of invention, and Yellowstone's supervolcano is flamboyantly secretive. Because it does not eject its secret, its secret is ever-imminent, effecting pools so turquoise, so russet, so lime, so lemon, waters so swashbuckling and rocks so imaginative, those beehives and mammoths and urchins and elephants and hoodoos. Landscapes with no secret can be a snore.

Hoodoos are imaginative rocks; they are people-looking columns with a hard little limestone cap that keeps their softer sandier torsos and legs from eroding. Actually the hoodoos of Yellowstone are not hoodoos but boulders that tumbled down a hill. However they resemble hoodoos, and hoodoos resemble hooligans. Hoodoos resemble hooligans both externally and in a deeper way: as a hooligan is not just a hooligan, so a hoodoo is not just a hoodoo. That is why hoodoos and hooligans are never disappointing.

Sandhill cranes fly up from Arizona to Yellowstone to have their babies on the supervolcano. Their babies are destination babies. The cranes must know what they are doing because, like the dragonflies, they are very old, dating from the Pleistocene, when some extinct humans appeared. As it turns out, those humans were fifth wheels—who misses them now?—who cares if a fifth wheel falls off? Anyway, maybe they went extinct because they were impatient. The patience of the sandhill crane is exemplified by that mother sitting on her egg in the spring blizzard. While the snow piles up to her eyes, her baby bird never even knows it's snowing. She is patient like Monteverdi, who had terrible headaches but you'd never know it from his music. (With some music, you can tell the composer had headaches.) Here's to all you mothers out there sitting on your babies in the snow.

Our mother the world is very old, and like a lot of old and wild parents—Abraham Lincoln and God and the parents of petunias—she is quite permissive. She gives us plenty of latitude and longitude and endless examples of what is permissible. The bubbly fresh springs give us permission to think bubbly fresh thoughts; the boiling mud gives us permission to think boiling muddy thoughts. Winter gives us permission to think dark icy thoughts, especially if our dens aren't big enough. The aspen, immovable of trunk and movable of leaf, gives us permission to be both movable and immovable and dragonflies give us permission to zoom in place in the presence of great explosivity.

These authorities like dragonflies and coyotes outnumber the bigwigs, and are worthier of respect. The coyote authorizes us to possess some bite and the bump on the log authorizes us to be a bump on a log. The petunia authorizes us to be ridiculously young and the platypus to be ridiculously old as well as ridiculously ridiculous. The volcano erupting authorizes you to erupt, even if you are no longer three, even if you are a million years old. The volcano that abstains from erupting authorizes you to contain your volcanic feelings and thus to bubble up the "Ode to Joy" in arpeggios or watercolors or spumone or whatever your medium might be. I know some people whose medium is mud. Composing the "Ode to Joy" is better than burning down Wyoming. Wyoming has all those beloved forest-floor animals.

In my house lives a toy rabbit holding a basketball who, I am told, likes everything except for death. He is friends with a macaroni penguin who likes everything including death. She is the kind of penguin who would not only say "I loved being young" but also "I loved being old" and "I loved being dead." Somehow the rabbit and the penguin have resisted the pressure to rue everything. We live in a world so full of quality bears and quality beers, quality skunks and clowns and thimbleberries, quality Waynes and walnuts and whatnots, and we have such a quality satellite, such a quality star. The basketball rabbit and the macaroni penguin are good examples, good Emersonians, to like everything including headaches and sleeplessness and snowstorms and then even after death —to maybe go on liking.

PATRICIA LOCKWOOD

Insane After Coronavirus?

FROM *London Review of Books*

MY STORY WILL be that John Harvard gave it to me. "Who's that?" I asked, pointing at a bronze bust in the reading room where I had arrived to give my lecture, and was told that it was the university's founder, John Harvard. "Damn," I said. "It never even occurred to me that Harvard was a guy." It was the night of March 3, and traveling didn't seem so foolhardy as it would even a week later; at that point the accepted wisdom was that hand sanitizer was the great necessity and that the virus was being mostly spread by touch. (On a Q&A message board I frequent, there were multiple questions in those early days from people desperately wondering how to stop picking their noses. *Something* was coming for us eventually.) It was a pleasure to be in the reading room, a pleasure to note that the carpet was ugly, a pleasure to learn that Harvard was a guy, a pleasure to send the controlled flow of my voice into the microphone and out to the hundred or so people in the room. The fireplace was big enough to roast me in; there was a statue of Kronos in the corner, spreading inflexible wings from a soft central nakedness. It was, according to the new formula, the last normal thing I did.

"It's *barely a flu,*" my friend said when she came over the next night to watch *Titanic* with me. I've always been partial to disaster movies, particularly ones where a volcano erupts and people have to run really slowly away from rivers of lava, but *Titanic* is the granddaddy of them all, and the situation seemed to call for it. "Why isn't he turning the wheel? *Why isn't he turning the wheel?*" we screamed, when the opaque iceberg of history first appeared in view, and the ship of the people couldn't swerve in time. "Fools," I said, delighted, and coughed the hot breath of John Harvard into my elbow. "Look at them. They're about to get so wet."

The first real symptoms were not mine, but my cat's. Miette, who kisses me on the lips each morning to see if I have become food yet, became deathly ill with a stomach virus two days after my return; my other cats soon contracted it as well. I know what you're thinking, but please let my husband have this. It pleases him so much to believe that our cats might have had coronavirus "before those cats in Belgium." If I one day win the Nobel, it could not confer a greater distinction.

Miette was back to her usual self a week later, but I had developed a low-grade fever. My head ached, my neck, my back. My eyes ached in their orbits and streamed tears whenever I tried to read or watch television. My mouth tasted like a foreign penny. "You reek," I mentioned to Jason once or twice in passing. "Like a swamp thing." Since a "swamp thing" is not a typical thing for a man to reek of—even a man who subsists entirely on mysterious powders from the health food store, and who every day drinks a shake that claims to contain All Known Nutrients—this should perhaps have been a tipoff, but it wasn't. "Does it . . . feel like this to be alive?" I asked him hesitantly one morning, and he shook his head feebly, flat on his back on the couch.

"No tests," a blurry telehealth doctor informed me, and advised me to go to the ER if my symptoms became severe. What counted as severe? What, for that matter, was a symptom? The pain was like a long, steady sunburn inside my chest; the weight was like a lead apron. It seemed more sensible to crawl from place to place rather than walk. My mind had moved a few inches to the left of its usual place, and I developed what I realized later were actual paranoid delusions. "Jason's cough is fake," I secretly texted a friend from the bathtub, where I couldn't be monitored. "I . . . don't think his cough is fake," she responded, with the gentle tact of the healthy. "Oh it is *very, very fake,*" I countered, and then further asserted the claim that he had something called Man Corona.

The love of my life is now my enemy, I thought to myself, crawling out of the bedroom on hands and knees to take one million mg of vitamin C, because what the hell else was I supposed to do—apply leeches? What kind of man would fake a cough while his wife was in the next room perishing? Hadn't he discouraged me from going to the hospital? At the beginning of lockdown, had he not thrown away the empty detergent bottle I set aside for use as an Apocalypse Bidet, telling me I was being a lunatic? Look at him, I thought to myself evilly: fit as a fiddle and playing video games all day—though later, of course, it turned out that he was *also* delirious and had been playing the same twenty minutes of *Skyrim* over and over without ever progressing. When he checked later he saw he had saved 130 games, and that all of the characters he had so painstakingly created had ripped abs, leather outfits, and huge cat heads. In between these feline exertions, he lay on the couch trying to summon the energy to make a will, so that I would have access to all of our financial information when he died.

The first wave subsided, and I thought I'd escaped, but the second hit with redoubled intensity a week later. My delusions became even more bizarre. I came to believe that someone "had put a Godzilla statue outside my window on purpose to freak me out"—this, it transpired, was the silhouette of two black streetlights, one superimposed on the other. I spent two weeks adding 143 words to my novel, about peeing next to Rob Roy's grave, feeling further from coherence with every draft. Local news graphics of the virion floated through the air, along with glimpses of originating animals: overlapping scales and flickering tongues, wings like black maple leaves. All this happened, it should be said, with a fever that never went higher than 100 degrees F. The persistent feeling was that I would die in the night. I woke fighting to breathe, with the sense of a red tide moving slowly up my chest toward my neck. And all the while strange music marched. A sentence I had seen on Twitter, part of a letter written by a chief surgeon at a New York hospital, kept breaking through my delirium like a line of sled dogs through a blizzard: "Anyone working in health care still enjoys the rapture of action. It's a privilege! We mush on."

I knew I was out of immediate danger when I stopped worrying about what my corpse would look like and allowed my husband to shave my head to the skin with cat clippers while I stood naked in the bathtub. (By night I resembled the hot alien from *Star Trek: The Motion Picture;* by day, more unfortunately, I resembled Jared Loughner of the Tucson shootings.) Euphoria set in, and I began to putter around the apartment singing Creed's "With Arms Wide Open" at the top of my lungs, placing special emphasis on the lyrics "Welcome to this *place,* I'll show you *everything.*" I knew Jason was out of immediate danger when my offer to make him soup was met with a long silence and then the hideous response: "*You're* the one who likes soup." Creed didn't enter into it for him at all.

Shy kleenexy flowers had opened all over the trees. Beauty played outside the window like a movie. I hadn't left the apartment in six weeks, except to sit on a bench in the nearest square. As soon as I ventured out, I saw that real life had been going on the whole time, and along with it the narrative, the living organism of *what's going on, what's happening*. As far as organisms go, this one is unhealthy. "Good COVID to Ye, Person of Space!" a group of crusties hollered at me as I passed them, wearing a mask. My downstairs neighbor, whose apartment looks like a commercial for meth addiction and who commences playing EDM every night at nine o'clock, so that my previously relaxing evenings have been transformed into reenactments of "The Tell-tale Heart," informed my husband out by the dumpsters that there was no need to worry: only people "with a very specific genetic profile" can get it. He is a nurse. He also owns a custom surfboard designed by Elon Musk, so maybe that has something to do with it.

My sister-in-law, who is a nurse practitioner, mentioned that her best friend, a COVID denier, was persistently badgering her about whether any of her patients *had* COVID, whether she'd ever actually seen a patient with a positive swab. Her best friend is, yes, a nurse. A man who sits on the board of the museum where my husband works was also denying its existence, even though his friend was one of the first people in town to die of it, back in the early days.

"Florida and Ohio, man," the barista at the local café said to my husband, when he asked about the tourist trade. "People here at least acknowledge that it's real. But people from Florida and Ohio don't even seem to think it's happening." Having lived in both places, I believe him: I have long had a theory that the surrealism that has overtaken the political landscape in America can be traced back to the poisoned ground of Ohio Facebook.

A friend's father informed her that the virus was "engineered and set loose by Obama." The peculiar phrasing, and the film strip it set playing in my mind, made me realize that I kind of missed those old conservative email forwards that had Obama tiptoeing around hospitals dumping newborn babies into trash cans, presumably while wearing a stolen doctor's coat and laughing a low, rich laugh. (Incidentally, I'm not sure why he was tipping them into the trash when he could have made a lot of money selling choice morsels of them to Planned Parenthood, but the heart wants what it wants.) "Conspiracy theories always get worse in an election year," my mother told me sagely: in 2016 the ads she saw on Facebook were mostly images of Hillary Clinton in a mandarin collar Photoshopped to have laser eyes.

As for my father, for the past few years I haven't pressed him on the specifics of any of his own most cherished conspiracy theories, fearing what I might find. (This is a man who, after a rash of high-profile shootings, doubled his donations to the NRA and received in return a custom NRA jacket that he actually started wearing in public. Over his cassock, and along with an Audi hat, for some reason.) "Are you questioning my knowledge of epidemiology?" he shouted at my sister, in the course of one conversation. She is a research pharmacist. He is a Catholic priest. She had asked him whether it was safe to administer communion to people on the tongue; he countered that it was the *only* safe way. It should be stated that my father, in the early days of lockdown, was in his absolute glory. The only thing he's ever wanted to do his entire life is hold a Secret Mass that is also illegal, and for a month or two he got his chance, operating through the loophole that a priest was allowed to celebrate the rite himself, and if he left the doors open and people happened to come in and witness it, and if a crumb of the body of Christ happened to fall off his fingertips directly into their mouths at the opportune moment, he could hardly be held responsible.

Yet when I was ill, he texted me multiple times a day, asking how I was doing, and bought me a stuffed aardvark when I mentioned that I missed the one I had as a teenager. (It was black and nearly as big as my body, and after I bought it I used to carry it around the mall under my arm, delightedly making machine-gun noises at people: heredity crops up in the strangest places.) This replacement aardvark might be the only gift he's ever bought me. I took to cradling it as I sat on the couch, trying to remember walking through that mall, being that person, thinking all the while that I was not the same.

I was under the impression that I had taken detailed notes throughout the experience, but when I opened the file called "quarantine" I found it to be 158 words long and full of cryptic particles: "Masque of the Red Death. Statue of Pericles. Tigers." Fine, whatever: I'll reconstruct the time line using my photo roll, I thought, but that was even worse—instead of the screenshots of headlines and news stories I usually save, I found photo sets of obscene ceramics featuring Kermit going down on Miss Piggy, and a bootleg T-shirt with Garfield lounging in a hot tub and uttering the statement I SEE SOME LADIES TONIGHT WHO SHOULD BE HAVIN' MY BABY. These still wore a faint aura of hallucination, which was all that I could remember about them. Texts too were useless. To one friend I had sent a screenshot of Sinéad O'Connor's statement "I had been a Muslim all my life and I didn't realize it," with no further comment. The tesserae failed to form a picture, merely sat in the sun and winked. It seemed to mirror the fracture of information that had led us here in the first place—hence the people who appear actually to believe that the virus is being spread by 5G. I understand it. It would make so much sense if the internet was the thing that gave me this.

When I examined my history, I found the following search: *insane after coronavirus? coronavirus made me insane?* This can't be entirely blamed on the illness. A few years earlier I had indulged in a similar query: *insane after book deal? book deal made me insane?* Other search strings of interest were: "Christy Turlington," "the Balkans," and "those things they use to shock people back to life."

Some people write *Pale Horse, Pale Rider* after living through a pandemic; other people don't. Still, I had promised to dash off a breezy diary of the lockdown, in that period after immediate recovery when I was certain I was 100 percent back to normal. "How's it going?" my editor tactfully asked me at one point—generally, when your editor asks you how it's going, you tell her it's going fine, and that she'll have the pages in her hand first thing Monday. Instead, I was truthful, and told her it was as if I was living in that terrible movie *Regarding Henry,* in which Harrison Ford gets shot in the head during a convenience-store holdup and afterward becomes a mental child and can no longer make love to his wife. I used to be able to do this; I know I used to be able to do this. I used to be able to make love to Harrison Ford's wife!

During a telehealth appointment, I explained to a different blurry doctor that after three months I was still experiencing intermittent symptoms: low-grade fever and difficulty breathing, mysterious arthritic nodules that had developed all over my hands, and for three weeks an almost total numbness in my legs, feet, arms, and face. I was aphasic, stumbling in my speech, transposing syllables, choosing the wrong nouns entirely. Some of the delusions I had developed during the most severe phase of illness persisted: that my vision was a picture that had been pasted in front of my eyes, that my floorboards, creaking with the expansive spring humidity, were going to fall through. Hours, days had fallen out of my memory like chunks of plaster. Some of this was the effect of lockdown, I knew; just as everyone was having vivid dreams of forgotten classmates—did I, as a second-grader, actually date a pair of hot twins called Michael and Kevin?—so everyone had suffered a falling-out with time. But much of it seemed to be the continuing effects, or aftereffects, of the virus itself.

One day I realized I couldn't remember my phone number, another that I couldn't remember my brother's middle name. But the most stubborn fact seemed to be that I had forgotten how to read. So I set myself a syllabus of maniacal intensity, as if to put the alphabet back in order after a tower of blocks had tumbled down. There was no particular logic governing the books I chose, and more than a hint of lunacy: at one point I plowed my way through both *Marjorie Morningstar* and *Shogun*. Sentences were sometimes as clear as if they had been blown by bugles; at other times they were dribble that barely stayed fastened on the page. *An African in Greenland* I read in one shining burst of comprehension, each word as firm in my mouth as a bite of whale blubber. I remember all of *The Corner That Held Them* and none of *Dead Souls*—I just kept underlining sentences where Chichikov was described as neither fat nor thin. I recall little of the revolutionary second half of *Summer Will Show*, but the first section, with its descriptions of Sophia Willoughby's children feverish and dying of smallpox after being dangled over the lime-kiln by an infected man, seems highlighted on the page with real sun: "Don't drop me, don't drop me! My mouth's hot. I looked at hell with my mouth, my mouth's burning. Hannah! Come and take hell out of my mouth, take it out, I say!"

I have never been a straightforward reader, preferring to linger inside the cupboards of those paragraphs that describe Aunt March's turquoise rings. Yet all of a sudden I wanted to read a book from cover to cover and be able to say what it was about. What is this about, I thought, what are books about? I read crazily, as if I were a train and the last page was Anna Karenina. I broke down crying one afternoon over *Mani,* knowing that if I were to take a test on the book after I finished, my page would read simply, "He . . . went . . . to . . . Greece?" (And to be honest, even the Greece part I'm not sure about.) But some automatic force must still have been at work in me, because looking at it now I see this lone paragraph highlighted:

> The air in Greece is not merely a negative void between solids; the sea itself, the houses and rocks and trees, on which it presses like a jelly mould, are embedded in it; it is alive and positive and volatile and one is as aware of its contact as if it could have pierced hearts scrawled on it with diamond rings or be grasped in handfuls, tapped for electricity, bottled, used for blasting, set fire to, sliced into sparkling cubes and rhomboids with a pair of shears, be timed with a stop watch, strung with pearls, plucked like a lute string or tolled like a bell, swum in, be set with rungs and climbed like a rope ladder or have saints assumed through it in flaming chariots; as though it could be harangued into faction, or eavesdropped, pounded down with pestle and mortar for cocaine, drunk from a ballet shoe, or spun, woven, and worn on solemn feasts; or cut into discs for lenses, minted for currency or blown, with infinite care, into globes.

Now that's it, I thought, that's what I remember about reading, about life: real air, so real you can write words on it, sliced into cubes and strung with pearls.

There were times, in my childhood, when I was sure I had forgotten how to breathe, and concentrating on the sheer mechanics of it—a set of matching velvety billows inside my chest, draw in, release—always carried me further away from the automatic function. But I highlighted the same paragraph I would always have highlighted, my heart leaped in the same place it always would have. And now, writing this, the tesserae are moving into place the way they always do, as if they are aware of the pattern they ought to be making—little red cells arranging themselves into an organism, the stars and spots and animalcules that swarm together to make up vision. I used to be able to do this, I know I used to be able to do this, I will be able to do it again.

BARRY LOPEZ

Love in a Time of Terror

FROM *Literary Hub*[1]

> This world is just a little place, just the red in the sky, before the sun rises, so let us keep fast hold of hands, that when the birds begin, none of us be missing.
>
> —Emily Dickinson, in a letter, 1860

SOME YEARS BEFORE things went bad, I arrived in an Aboriginal settlement called Willowra, in Australia's Northern Territory. A small village, it's haphazardly situated on the east bank of the Lander River, a dry watercourse. (I'd driven into the area several days before with a small team of restoration biologists. They were intent on reintroducing a small marsupial in the vicinity, the rufous hare-wallaby [*Lagorchestes hirsutus,* or *mala* in the local language]. The animal had been eliminated locally by feral house cats, domestic pets left behind decades before by white settlers.) When I arrived in Willowra, I was introduced to several Warlpiri people by a friend of mine, an anthropologist named Petronella Vaarzon-Morel. She'd been working for some years around Willowra and when the biologists dropped me off—that work now completed—she helped move me into a residence in the settlement, a guesthouse where she had been living. Petra then returned to her home in Alice Springs and I was on my own.

Before she left, Petra had pointed out numerous places in the countryside nearby that I should neither approach nor show any interest in. These were mostly innocuous-looking spots to my eye—rocks, trees, small sand hills—but they were important elements in the Dreamtime narratives that form the foundation of Warlpiri identity. Many of these sites were close to the Lander. When I asked my hosts, then, if I might walk out into the desert a few miles, in the direction that I was indicating, and then return along roughly the same track, the man I was speaking to pointed in a slightly different direction and said simply, "Maybe better."

I set off that afternoon on a walk north and west of the village, across a rolling spinifex plain that stretched away to hills on the horizon in almost every direction. The flow of the bland, uniform colors of the countryside was only broken up by an occasional tree or a copse of trees.

This universe of traditional Warlpiri land was completely new to me. I had no anxiety, however, about getting lost out there. At a distance of several miles, the settlement and the Lander, with its tall gallery forest of gum trees growing along its banks, remained prominent, in a land that displayed to my cultural eyes no other real prominences.

It was midday when I left so if I happened to walk too far to the west (on what would soon be a moonless night in June) darkness might conceivably force me to lie down and wait for dawn. (I could easily have strayed unawares into some broad, shallow depression on that plain, from which all horizons would appear identical.) But getting lost seemed most unlikely. Starlight alone, in this sparsely populated country lying on the southern border of another, much more stark, challenging, and enormous desert, the Tanami, would be enough to guide me home.

My goal that day was intimacy—the tactile, olfactory, visual, and sonic details of what, to most people in my culture, would appear to be a wasteland. This simple technique of awareness had long been my way to open a conversation with any unfamiliar landscape. Who are you? I would ask. How do I say your name? May I sit down? Should I go now? Over the years I'd found this way of approaching whatever was new to me consistently useful: establish mutual trust, become vulnerable to the place, then hope for some reciprocity and perhaps even intimacy. You might choose to handle an encounter with a stranger you wanted to get to know better in the same way. Each person, I think, finds their own way into an unknown world like this spinifex plain; we're all by definition naive about the new, but unless you intend to end up alone in your life, it seems to me you must find some way in a new place—or with a new person—to break free of the notion that you can be certain of what or whom you've actually encountered. You must, at the very least, establish a truce with realities not your own, whether you're speaking about the innate truth and aura of a landscape or a person.

I've felt for a long time that the great political questions of our time—about violent prejudice, global climate change, venal greed, fear of the Other—could be addressed in illuminating ways by considering models in the natural world. Some consider it unsophisticated to explore the nonhuman world for clues to solving human dilemmas, and wisdom's oldest tool, metaphor, is often regarded with wariness, or even suspicion in my culture. But abandoning metaphor entirely only paves the way to the rigidity of fundamentalism. To my way of thinking, to prefer to live a metaphorical life—that is, to think abstract problems through on several planes at the same time, to stay alert for symbolic and allegorical meanings, to appreciate the utility of nuance—as opposed to living a literal life, where most things mean in only one way, is the norm among traditional people like the Warlpiri, in my experience. In listening to negotiations, for example, between representatives of industrialized societies and representatives of traditional societies, it has always seemed to me that the latter presentation is meant to be more open to interpretation (in order not to become trapped in literalness), while the former presentation too often defaults to logic and "impressive" data sets, but, again, perhaps this is only me.

The goal in these conversations, from a traditional point of view, is to put off for a good while arriving at any conclusion, to continue to follow, instead, several avenues of approach until a door no one had initially seen suddenly opens. My own culture—I don't mean to be overly critical here—tends to assume that while such conversations should remain respectful, the outcome had to conform to what my culture considers "reality."

My point here is that walking off into what was for me anonymous territory, one winter afternoon in north-central Australia, was not so much an exercise in trying to improve myself as a naturalist as it was an effort to divest myself of the familiar categories and hierarchies that otherwise might guide my thoughts and impressions of the place.

I wanted to open myself up as fully as I could to the possibility of loving this place, in some way; but to approach that goal, I had first to come to know it. As is sometimes the case with other types of acquaintanceships, to suddenly love without really knowing is to opt for romance, not commitment and obligation.

The evening before I went off to explore the desert around Willowra, I finished a book called *The Last of the Nomads* by William John Peasley, published in 1983. Peasley recounts here a journey he made into the Gibson Desert in Western Australia with four other white men in the winter of 1977. They were accompanied by an Aboriginal man named Mudjon. The group was looking for two Mandildjara people believed to be the last of the Mandildjara living in the bush. Mudjon, a Mandildjara elder living at the time in a settlement on the western edge of the Gibson called Wiluna, had known for decades both of the people they were searching for—a hunter, Warri Kyango, and his wife, Yatungka Kyango. These two had refused to "come in" to Wiluna with the last of the Mandildjara people during a prolonged drought in the seventies. Mudjon respected their effort to continue living a traditional life under these very formidable circumstances but he feared that at their ages—Warri was sixty-nine, Yatungka sixty-one—they were getting too old to make their way successfully in the outback without the help of other, younger people.

The search for this couple, across hundreds of square miles of parched, trackless country, interrupted in various places by areas of barren sand hills, culminated with the party's finding the couple, together with their dingos, at a place called Ngarinarri. (The dingos helped them hunt and huddled up close with them on cold nights to share their warmth.) A few palmfuls of muddy water every day from a seep, and a small store of fruit from a nearby stand of quandong trees, was all that was sustaining them. Warri was injured and sick, and they were both emaciated.

An argument later ensued in Wiluna and then spread far and wide about the insistence of the rescue party that the couple travel with them back to Wiluna instead of leaving them there to die at Ngarinarri, which it seemed they preferred to "civilized" life in Wiluna.

I wasn't party to this, of course, so can offer no judgment, but this is an old story, characterizing many encounters over the years between "civilized" and traditional styles of living in the Australian bush. Like many readers, I brooded over the fate of these people for days after reading the book. (They both passed away within a year of their arrival in Wiluna, despite the availability there of food, water, and medical treatment.) This is a story of injustice, of course, and too a tragedy that virtually anyone can understand. What really stuck in my mind, though, was how love dramatized this narrative, a narrative as profound in its way as the other narrative, the one about colonial indifference and enduring harm.

Because Warri and Yatungka were both born into the same moiety among the Mandildjara, they were prevented by social custom from marrying. When they defied this custom and married anyway, their lives from then on, after their formal banishment, became far more difficult. They knew if they attempted to return to the society of their own people, they risked being physically punished. So they chose a life on their own. Even when they learned, years later, that they had been forgiven, and that their Mandildjara culture was unraveling further in the face of colonial intrusion, and even though they learned that a terrible period of widespread drought had brought most all of the "desert tribes" into white settlements like Wiluna, they continued to choose their marriage and their intimately known traditional country.

Warri and Yatungka looked after each other over all that time, and they took care of their beloved country according to the prescriptions and proscriptions in the Dreamtime stories, observing their obligations to it. They also knew, I have to think, that the watering places their people had traditionally depended on for generations had now withered and dried up or, in the case of the animals they regularly hunted, their food had simply departed the country. And yet they refused to succumb, even at what you might call the point of their natural end. It would be arrogant and certainly perilous to subscribe to any theory of what the two of them might have been thinking at the end, at Ngarinarri. What stood out for me as obvious, however, was their fierce allegiance—to their Mandildjara country and to each other. Death in this case was not for them tragic but inevitable, onerous but acceptable; and death in this place was preferable to lives lived out in Wiluna.

But, of course, again, this is not for me to determine.

The day I walked out into the desert in the direction I was pointed I was intent on immersing myself in the vastness of something I didn't know. I carried in my backpack a few books about recognizing and preparing "bush tucker," the desert plants and small creatures that could sustain Aboriginal people; a dependable bird book; and some notes about marsupials and poisonous snakes. In terms of what governed the line of my footsteps, my many changes of direction, my pauses, my squattings down, it was primarily my desire to pursue immersion—letting the place overwhelm me. Drifting through my mind all the while, however, was the story of Warri and Yatungka, or at least the version of it that was written up and that I had read.

At some point late that day, I came upon several dozen acres of land more truly empty than the desert landscape I'd been walking through for hours. It consisted of an expanse of bare ground and coarse sand with shattered bits of dark volcanic rock scattered about. I walked as carefully here as I might have through an abandoned cemetery. Silence rose from every corner of the place, and the utter lack of life here drew heavily on my heart. As I walked on, I saw no track of any animal, no windblown leaf from a mulga tree, no dormant seed waiting for rain. Other images of bleakness came to mind: bomb-shattered rubble that buried the streets of Kabul; a small island in Cumberland Sound, a part of Baffin Island in Nunavut, Canada, where dozens of large whale skeletons lay inert in acres of tawny sea grass rolling in the wind like horses' manes; the remains of a nineteenth-century whaling station; tiers of empty sleeping platforms, each bunk designed to hold four men, rising to the ceiling in a derelict barracks at Birkenau, where every night exhausted men lay in darkness, waiting to be carted off in wheelbarrows to the nearby ovens and burned on the day they could no longer wield their tools.

I had halted with these images pushing through my mind and in the moment was toeing a stone the size of my fist when another thought burst in, that most of the trouble that afflicts human beings in their lives can be traced to the failure to love.

In the summer of 1979, I traveled to an Eskimo village in the central Brooks Range in Alaska called Anaktuvuk Pass. My friend Bob Stephenson had a sod home in this settlement of 110 Nunamiut people, and in the days following our arrival we spent many hours listening to stories about local animals: wolverines and snowy owls, red foxes and caribou. The Nunamiut were enthusiastically interested in their lives, as were we. We spent a few days too hunting for active wolf dens in the upper reaches of the Anaktuvuk River. Then we flew several hundred miles west to the drainage of the Utukok River. Bob was a large-mammal biologist with the Alaska Department of Fish and Game, and the department maintained a temporary summer camp there on the middle Utukok, where field biologists could regularly observe tundra grizzlies, caribou, wolves, gyrfalcons, wolverines, and other creatures during the summer months. Bob and I stayed a few days with them and then helicoptered south to a place in the De Long Mountains farther up the Utukok called Ilignorak Ridge. We camped there for a week, watching a wolf den across the river from us—five adults and five pups.

Whenever I'm asked what I love, I think of the aggregate of relationships in that place that summer. Twenty-four hours of sunshine every day at 68° northern latitude. Cloudless skies, save for fair-weather cumulus. Light breezes. No schedule for our work but our own. Large animals present to us at almost every moment of the day. And, this far north of the treeline, looking through a gin-clear atmosphere with forty-power spotting scopes, we enjoyed unobstructed views of their behavior, even when they were two or three miles away. I had daily conversations with Bob about the varied and unpredictable behavior of wild animals (or, as I later came to think of them, free animals, those still undisturbed by human interference). We reminisced about other trips we'd made together in the years before this, on the upper Yukon River and out to St. Lawrence Island, in the northern Bering Sea.

The mood in our camp was serene, unhurried. We were excited about being alive, about our growing friendship, about this opportunity to watch free animals in good weather, and about the timelessness of our simple daily existence. I loved the intensity of our vigil. Every day we watched what was for us—probably for anyone—the most spectacular things: wolves chasing caribou; a grizzly trying to break into the wolf den, being fought off by a single young wolf; thirty caribou galloping through shallow water in the Utukok, backed by the late evening sun, thousands of flung diamonds sparkling in the air around them; an arctic fox sitting its haunches ten yards from the tent, watching us intently for twenty minutes.

When we returned to base camp, we enjoyed meals with the other scientists and talked endlessly with them about incidents of intriguing behavior among the animals we all watched every day. One afternoon someone brought in a mammoth tusk she had dug out of a gravel bank close by. Somehow, we no longer felt we were living in the century from which we had arrived.

During those days we all resided at the heart of incomprehensible privilege.

Evidence of the failure to love is everywhere around us. To contemplate what it is to love today brings us up against reefs of darkness and walls of despair. If we are to manage the havoc—ocean acidification, corporate malfeasance and government corruption, endless war—we have to reimagine what it means to live lives that matter, or we will only continue to push on with the unwarranted hope that things will work out. We need to step into a deeper conversation about enchantment and agape, and to actively explore a greater capacity to love other humans. The old ideas—the crushing immorality of maintaining the nation-state, the life-destroying belief that to care for others is to be weak, and that to be generous is to be foolish—can have no future with us.

It is more important now to be in love than to be in power. It is more important to bring E. O. Wilson's biophilia into our daily conversations than it is to remain compliant in a time of extinction, ethnic cleansing, and rising seas. It is more important to live for the possibilities that lie ahead than to die in despair over what has been lost.

Only an ignoramus can imagine now that pollinating insects, migratory birds, and pelagic fish can depart our company and that we will survive because we know how to make tools. Only the misled can insist that heaven awaits the righteous while they watch the fires on Earth consume the only heaven we have ever known.

The day of illumination I had in the spinifex plain west of Willowra, about a world generated by the failure to love, which was itself kindled by the story of the lovers Warri and Yatungka, grew out of my certain knowledge that, years before, I had experienced what it meant to love, on those summer days with friends in the Brooks Range. The experience delivered me into the central project of my adult life as a writer, which is to know and love what we have been given, and to urge others to do the same.

*

In this trembling moment, with light armor under several flags rolling across northern Syria, with civilians beaten to death in the streets of Occupied Palestine, with fires roaring across the vineyards of California, and forests being felled to ensure more space for development, with student loans from profiteers breaking the backs of the young, and with Niagaras of water falling into the oceans from every sector of Greenland, in this moment, is it still possible to face the gathering darkness, and say to the physical Earth, and to all its creatures, including ourselves, fiercely and without embarrassment, I love you, and to embrace fearlessly the burning world?

Note

1. This essay originally appeared as the foreword to an anthology, *Earthly Love: Stories of Intimacy and Devotion from Orion Magazine,* published by *Orion* in 2020.

JESSICA LUSTIG

What I Learned When My Husband Got Sick with Coronavirus

FROM *The New York Times Magazine*

"HOW ARE YOU doing, love?" I call to my husband from the living-room floor, where I now sleep each night on a roll-up foam sleeping pad that my daughter has used on camping trips, topped with a couple of thin blankets. It's quite literally hard to sleep on the floor, but after trying the couch and then, on the floor, the couch mattress—a bit of fabric stretched over some coiled rings—the floor itself has been a relief.

"I need some help," he whispers hoarsely, shivering inside the wool undershirt and sweater he insists on wearing. "I didn't want to wake you." I forgot to put the Advil in the plastic dish in the bathroom that is now his. I can't leave the bottle in there; it has to stay uncontaminated in the other bathroom, so that I can dispense the capsules into the dish and keep the bottle protected. Anything my husband, T, touches has to stay in his room or be carefully taken from his room to the kitchen, where I stand holding dishes while our sixteen-year-old daughter, CK, opens the dishwasher and pulls out the racks so I don't have to touch anything before she closes it again. She turns on the faucet for me, and I hit the soap dispenser with my elbow to wash my hands.

My husband, a tall, robust fifty-six-year-old who regularly goes—who regularly went—on five-hour bike rides from our Brooklyn neighborhood to Jamaica Bay in Queens and back, has been lying on his back, staring at the ceiling, or curled on his side, wearing the same pajama bottoms for days because it is too hard to change out of them, too hard to stay that long on his feet, too cold outside the sheets and blankets he huddles beneath. It has been twelve days since T woke up in the middle of the night on March 12 with chills. The next day, just as reports were growing more urgent about the coronavirus spreading in the United States, he thought he felt better, but then the chills came back, along with aches and a fever of 100.4.

Since then, T has been confined alone in our bedroom at the front of the apartment, where he complains of hearing trucks idling at the curb just outside and long blasts from the ships in New York Harbor a few blocks west. He creeps out only to go to the bathroom. The bedroom door stays firmly shut to keep out the cat, who is determined to get in and who howls outside it at night. "What to do if you are sick with coronavirus disease 2019 (COVID-19)" reads the sheet T is handed at the clinic two days after his symptoms begin. "Separate yourself from other people and animals in your home." By then he has a fever of 101.5. He tests negative for the flu. Then, because he is considered high risk with what his medical chart calls "severe" asthma that sent him to the emergency room with an acute attack a few months ago, he is tested for COVID-19, the disease caused by the coronavirus—just days before a national shortage of testing supplies emerged and the restrictions were tightened further.

Now we live in a world in which I have planned with his doctor which emergency room we should head to if T suddenly gets worse, a world in which I am suddenly afraid we won't have enough of the few things tempering the raging fever and soaking sweats and severe aches wracking him—the Advil and Tylenol that the doctors advise us to layer, one after the other, and that I scroll through websites searching for, seeing "out of stock" again and again. We are living inside the news stories of testing, quarantine, shortages, and the disease's progression. A friend scours the nearby stores and drops off a bunch of bodega packets of Tylenol. Another finds a bottle at a more remote pharmacy and drops it off, a golden prize I treasure against the feverish nights to come.

His doctor calls three days later to say the test is positive. I find T lying on his side, reading an article about the surge in confirmed cases in New York State. He is reading stories of people being hospitalized, people being put on ventilators to breathe, people dying, sick with the same virus that is attacking him from the inside now.

CK and I had settled in to watch *Chernobyl,* the HBO series about the 1986 nuclear accident and its aftermath, when T first felt sick and went to lie down in the bedroom. We stopped after three episodes. That time, when we would sit on the couch watching something together, is behind us. Now there is too much rushing back and forth, making sure T has a little dinner—just a tiny bowl of soup, just an appetizer, really, that he is unable to smell, that he fights nausea to choke down—taking his temperature, monitoring his oxygen-saturation levels with the fingertip pulse oximeter brought by a friend from the drugstore on the doctor's advice, taking him tea, dispensing his meds, washing my hands over and over, texting the doctor to say T is worse again, standing next to him while he coughs into the covers, rubbing his knees through the blankets.

"You shouldn't stay here," he says, but he gets more frightened as night comes, dreading the long hours of fever and soaking sweats and shivering and terrible aches. "This thing grinds you like a mortar," he says.

CK's high school, closed on March 13, is now preparing with the rest of New York City's public schools to begin distance learning. For days she and her classmates have received instructions about what to expect, turning administrator and teacher directives into endless memes, feeds filling with repeated admonitions: This is regular school. This is not vacation. I start an email to her principal, guidance counselors, and teachers. "I am writing to let you know what CK has been going through at home." The draft sits open all day.

I am texting the doctor. I am texting T's five siblings on a group chat, texting my parents and my brother, texting T's business partner and employees and his dearest friends and mine, in loops and loops, with hearts and thankful prayer-hands emoji. He is too exhausted, too weak, to answer all the missives winging to him at all hours. "Don't sugarcoat it for my family," he tells me. He has asked for the gray sweater that was his father's, that his father wore when he was alive. He will not take it off.

It's as if we are in a time warp, in which we have accelerated at 1½ time speed, while everyone around us remains in the present—already the past to us—and they, blissfully, unconsciously, go about their ordinary lives, experiencing the growing news, the more urgent advisories and directives, as a vast communal experience, sharing posts and memes about cabin fever, about homeschooling, about social distancing, about how hard it all is, while we're living in our makeshift sick ward, living in what will soon be the present for more and more of them. "I took out the kitty litter," CK says, "and I saw some people standing on the corner, and I was like, I want to see strangers! And then I heard them saying: 'It's actually been really nice. It's been a chance to connect as a family.' And I was like, No, actually, I don't want to see strangers, and I came back in."

CK and I confine ourselves to the half bathroom, the one with the litter box, which she is now in charge of. Over the past days and days, drifty, dreamy CK has become my chief assistant on my nursing/housekeeping/kitchen rotations, feeding the cat and cleaning the litter box, folding laundry, preparing T's small meals, washing dishes and pots, coordinating with me in a complicated choreography when I come out of the sickroom holding dishes so we can get them into the dishwasher without my touching the handles or having to wash my dry, raw hands even more. "I feel like we're talking to each other more like equals now," she says. She is right.

I am consumed with trying to keep us safe. I wipe down the doorknobs, the light switches, the faucets, the handles, the counters with disinfectant. I swab my phone with alcohol. I throw the day's hoodie into the laundry at night as if it were my scrubs. I wash all our towels, again and again. When CK wants to shower, I wipe down the whole main bathroom—where T refills his water cup, where he has had diarrhea, where he coughs and spits out phlegm—with bleach, take out T's washcloth, towels, and bath mat, and replace them with clean ones, telling CK to try not to touch anything, to shower and go right back to her room. Then I do the same. If T needs to use the bathroom before we're ready to shower, I do the whole bleach routine again before we go in. Twice, in the first week of the illness, I eased him into an Epsom-salt bath. But not since then. He is too weak. It would be too much. There is no way. When he shuffles down the hall from the bedroom to the bathroom, he lists against the wall. He splashes water on his face in the bathroom, and that has to be enough.

I run through possibilities. I'm not so worried about CK getting sick. I can nurse her too. It's if I get sick. I show her how to do more things, where things go, what to remember, what to do if —What if T is hospitalized? What if I am? Could a sixteen-year-old be left to fend for herself at home, alone? How would she get what she needed? Could she do it? For how long?

The one thing I know is that I could not send her to my parents, seventy-eight years old and nearby on Long Island. They would want her to come, but she could kill them, their dear grandchild coming forward to their embrace, radioactive, glowing with invisible incubating virus cells. No. Not them. Someone else would have to take her, someone who has a bedroom and a bathroom where she could isolate and be cared for. Someone would. I lie awake at 4 a.m., on the floor, listening, thinking, wide awake with adrenaline.

The nights are hardest, when the fear and dread descend, T feverish, lying on his back, murmuring hoarsely about "anomie," saying he almost just called CK by the name of his twenty-years-ago ex-girlfriend. Three times we have tried to decide whether we need to go to the emergency room while on speakerphone with the doctor, once after I burst into sobs in the bathroom, saying out loud, "I'm afraid to make the wrong call." Each time we decided to stay at home. He doesn't have trouble breathing, and that would be the reason to go to the hospital.

We do a video call on one of these nights with a New York University emergency-room doctor, one of 250 who have been mobilized to do urgent-care video calls with patients who have flulike symptoms. She tells us that they are seeing this illness run two to three weeks. She tells us that T is okay to stay home if his oxygen-saturation reading doesn't get too low, if he is not struggling to breathe. He is not. When I open the bedroom door to check on him and find him sleeping, I tiptoe closer and bend to make sure he is alive, to make sure he is still breathing, as I used to do when CK was an infant, asleep in her crib.

On one of the worst nights, I stay next to the bed, rubbing his body through the piled-on blankets, trying to comfort him. I hear myself start to hum, low, the only song I would: the song both my mother and my grandmother used to sing to me. When my mother sang it, it was "Tura Lura Lura," with "When Irish Eyes Are Smiling" cut into it after the words "That's an Irish lullaby." When my grandmother sang it to me, it was "Tura Lura Lura" with the words changed to "That's a Russian lullaby." That is the song of my early childhood, and more than four decades later I am humming it to my gravely ill husband.

"Now we live in a dystopian story," I say to CK in the kitchen.

"Yeah," she says. And then: "Lots of people already did."

Out on the street, T somehow looks even more frail, his six-foot-one frame stooped and swaddled in his winter jacket over another jacket over his father's gray wool sweater over a Duofold wool undershirt over a white ribbed tank. He says it's cold, blinking in the March sun over the white surgical mask he wore at the clinic when he was tested.

We both wear disposable gloves. I put my hand through the crook of his arm, and we slowly start for the clinic. The day before was one of the harder ones, with T lightheaded and nauseated most of the day, eating only if I spoon-fed him, coughing more and using his albuterol inhaler more, then coughing more again. He was soaked in sweat in the morning and by evening was lying curled up, looking apprehensive. "I coughed up blood just now," he told me quietly.

We talked to his doctor on speakerphone. "We are all kind of working blind," he told us. Many patients, he said, seem to begin to feel better after a week. But others, the more serious and severe cases, take a downturn, and the risks rise as the virus targets the lungs. Pneumonia is a common next step in that downward progression. We read about it in the patients admitted to the hospital. Now the doctor called in a prescription for antibiotics to the CVS pharmacy that would close in less than an hour. I texted T's friend down the block, and he texted back that he would pick up the medicine. I asked if he would get oranges too; T has been accepting a little fresh-squeezed juice or cut-up pieces, and we were down to one last orange. They suddenly seemed an unimaginably exotic treat.

The doctor told us to go back to the clinic for a chest X-ray first thing in the morning. Now we slowly walk the three blocks, T coughing behind his mask. As we move along the street, we see some other people too—fewer than a few days ago, before Governor Andrew Cuomo directed New Yorkers to stay indoors as much as possible. Some joggers go by. Just over a week ago, that was still me. Now I point out the buds about to bloom on the branches we pass, drawing T's attention away from the few passers-by so we won't see if they start or turn around. A few are wearing their own masks, but they are walking upright, striding along, using them as protection for themselves. Not like us.

At the clinic, another couple wearing masks opens the door and walks in. A man in a mask sits in the waiting area. T eases into a chair and leans against the wall with his eyes closed. I go to the desk. "My husband has already tested positive for COVID-19," I tell the attendant, whose eyes meet mine over her mask.

She hands me a mask. T's doctor is working at a different clinic today, so we'll see another doctor, and they will compare notes. We wait, wearing our masks. T's eyes are still closed. I look out the window behind us, where people on the street are walking along as if it were an ordinary day. A man opens the door of a tiny café across the street with his bare hand and goes inside.

Another attendant comes to the desk, and the first attendant murmurs quietly to her. The second attendant puts on a mask.

We're called inside. The nurses, in masks, check T's vitals. He has a slight fever, just over 99 degrees, but that may be lowered because of the recent ibuprofen and acetaminophen in his system. His blood pressure is fine. His pulse is fine. His oxygen saturation is fine. We tell them about the fevers, the sweats, the nausea, the coughing, the spots of blood he is continuing to cough up, the lower oxygen-saturation number we recorded at home this morning.

When the nurses leave, T leans back in the examination chair, resting his head with his eyes closed. Out in the hall, I hear someone telling a patient that he has been sick for a long time. It's time to go to the hospital five blocks away.

The doctor comes in, wearing a mask and a plastic shield over it. T, shivering in a paper gown, follows her out for the X-ray. "That was strangely difficult," he says when he returns. "Just holding my arms above my head." The X-ray looks different from the one a week ago, the doctor tells us after consulting with the radiologist. Now it shows pneumonia in the left lung. T's doctor was right to order the antibiotics last night. T's lungs sound all right when she listens through a stethoscope—he is not wheezing. He is not having breathing problems. He can keep being treated at home. "But now we're going to be watching you even more closely," she says.

At the door of the clinic, we stand looking out at two older women chatting outside the doorway, oblivious. Do I wave them away? Call out that they should get far away, go home, wash their hands, stay inside? Instead we just stand there, awkwardly, until they move on. Only then do we step outside to begin the long three-block walk home. I point out the early magnolia, the forsythia. T says he is cold. The untrimmed hairs on his neck, under his beard, are white. The few people walking past us on the sidewalk don't know that we are visitors from the future. A vision, a premonition, a walking visitation. This will be them: either T, in the mask, or—if they're lucky—me, tending to him.

DAWN LUNDY MARTIN

What Money Can't Buy

FROM *Ploughshares*

> If, in William Penn's words, America was "a good poor Man's country" and remained the dream of a promised land for Europe's impoverished up to the beginning of the twentieth century, it is no less true that this goodness depended to a considerable degree on black misery.
>
> —Hannah Arendt

ON A STEAMY August day, I return to the city of my birth to take my two youngest nieces on a back-to-school shopping trip they haven't asked for. Both their parents—my brother and his ex-wife—are undereducated and poor, and my youngest niece, Taj, who's twelve, lives with my brother in my mother's house. My mother told me that Taj was kicked out of her own mother's house for threatening to hit her. I'm not sure what the truth is about that. It occurred to me, however, given money problems and her displacement, that no one would buy her new underwear and bras and sneakers, and I wanted her to feel like a normal kid, one inside that space between excitement and anxiety about the new school year. For fairness's sake, I take her slightly older sister, Nara, too, who does not live at my mother's house. I'm nervous about the whole thing, never having taken kids shopping for anything ever. And I've never spent hours of alone time with my nieces. I've witnessed their conflict and treachery when my nieces all visit my brother on weekends and holidays—there are four of them in total—and the chaos of yelling and fighting that ensues between the girls and the adults trying to control them. Beyond that, my nervousness is about the fact that I will have to visit my mother's house, the place I escaped from at eighteen and rarely looked back.

To run your wild days,
I always said, is you a leaf,
return, as uncertain as what
we hold when the jaw clinches.
Door, ajar,
home, they say, is where the heart is.

I'm trying to wrangle something unwranglable. I'm channeling my savior complex toward the one kid, the youngest one, in an effort to give her a boost so that she might be able to catapult herself up and out, and toward some bright future. I'm not optimistic. She cannot see that future from inside the house where she's been cocooned all summer. She's been sitting in front of the old-fashioned no-cable TV set in my mother's living room. Her eyesight is bad, so she sits up close to not squint. My friends' children all have soccer, overnight camp, days of frolicking in the ocean, drawing classes, trips abroad, movie outings, trips to the aquarium or natural history museum, friend sleepovers, and the like. Taj, though, has no one to pay for her, enroll her, or take her to any activity outside the house. My mother, now eighty-six, would have been that person a few years ago, but her arthritis and other inexplicable pain have made her crippled and feeble, so it's difficult for her to walk more than a few paces. My brother works most of the time as a motel janitor, but even when he's not working, his inclination is not to parent in the ways of outside exposure. His way is smallness and enclosure. He doesn't want Taj to explore the neighborhood on her bicycle. He won't let her walk the six blocks to school alone. Up until a few weeks ago, she slept on a cot in his bedroom instead of inhabiting the empty bedroom next door, which used to be mine. And my mother's way is shame and religion. She believes that girls must be modest so as not to invite male attention, and that God will take care of things beyond our control.

Weeks before my shopping spree visit, I researched the middle school that Taj is about to enter. It's ranked two on a scale from one to ten. Only 13 percent of its students read and write at grade level. I alerted both my mom and my brother with an urgency bordering on hysteria. My mother has never been one to speak truth to power and she's certainly not going to as an old woman. "Well, maybe things will work out," she said. "Things don't just work out for poor Black kids," I said. "Someone has to actually do something to even their playing field." My mother shrugged. "Well, I don't know what to do." I tried convincing my brother, realizing that the hill for that battle would be steep. This happened in a text exchange:

ME: Hey bro, Did mom tell you that I think we should work hard to get T in a better middle school? The one she's about to enter has the worst reputation. It's ranked very, very low.

BROTHER:

ME: I have a plan to try to get her into a much better school but since you are the parent, you MUST be involved. Please call me as soon as possible. It would be horrible for T to linger in a shitty school and have no future prospects just because no one acted. She's a smart kid. She just needs better opportunities.

BROTHER: I will call you later. I'm busy putting in ac. But I will call you.

Four days later:

ME: Hey did you ever call me?

BROTHER:

ME: I have some ideas to help you get T into a better middle school. Middle school is the exact right time for this to happen. It would be a shame for her to linger in a horrible school situation for no reason. Please let me know when there's a good time to call you.

BROTHER:

In order for some people in this country to rise, some others have to be the backs upon which rising occurs. That's the American way—*the haves and the have nots,* as my mother is fond of saying. Almost everyone in my immediate and extended family is a have not. When my father was alive, I thought of us as working class. My parents worked nearly all the time and never had much extra money for anything frivolous or luxurious. My dad liked to gamble at the Hartford Jai Alai, which made my mother want to murder him, even though his winnings probably made it so that overall he ended up breaking even. If my parents wanted a vacation, they saved for it the way you save when you put your change in a big jar and count it all up at the end of the year—a few dollars every so often adds up. What I had seen in my extended family was my cousins dying in their fifties from lack of access to health care, other cousins ending up in jail, others opening up storefront churches in an attempt, I guess, at a spiritual rise up and out of one's situation. The girls got pregnant too early and without partners, and some lived as their parents lived, in the Black projects when there were projects. My aunt Willie Mae, my mother's sister, is an exception. Like my mother, she graduated from college. Unlike my mother, she married a Howard-educated dentist. She sees ghosts now, but she sees them from her house, which she and her husband had built in Titusville, Florida. She sees them hovering over her swimming pool. And, though they are not friendly ghosts, the vantage point from which she sees them is notable.

When I arrive to pick the girls up, they are dressed and almost ready but wearing head wraps of some sort because their mother has yet to braid their hair. "Are you guys going out with those hair hats?" I ask them. "Because we're going to the mall." It hadn't occurred to me that for most of the summer, no one had done their hair. Taj appears embarrassed. "My hair is a mess," she shrieks, hiding behind her door while she tucks her hair under the black scarf. "People are going to think we're Nation of Islam, or something" I say. "What's wrong with that?" asked Nara. I had some experiences with Nation of Islam people in my youth. My aunt Shirley and uncle Jimmy changed their names to Sakina and Jamil after joining. They talked constantly about the white man keeping them down. So, I guess there's nothing wrong with it. But my class shame is showing and I'm already experiencing the imagined ignominy of the imagined future at the fancy mall, toting two kids wearing black cultlike hair sacks.

We head to the Westfarms Mall in Farmington, head wraps and all, and suddenly the adult me appears and I feel immense empathy for the girls as we enter the glimmering apparatus renovated from when I was a kid to include Louis Vuitton and Nordstrom. There are still a few low-budget stores like JCPenney and Claire's too, but the general attitude is *bring your black card.* Walking through the entrance at Macy's the girls seem struck, a little like those recently released from a long incarceration. Their eyes are wide and they walk a few steps behind me next to each other. When we reach the escalator, Taj proclaims her fear of escalators and sits down on the stairs as we descend, refusing my offered hand. She's wobbly as we reach the bottom and I have a tiny fear that she's going to lose her balance and fall on her face. The mall shines with white marble floors, carpeted sitting areas with big comfortable chairs, silver framed lamps that hang from the ceiling, and giant skylights that let natural light in. On this day, a weekday the week before school begins, the mall is teeming with young people and parents, and everywhere we go the checkout lines are long and slow. The girls stand like frozen fawns in front of the crowded stores until I coax them inside, saying simply, "Come on."

I get exhausted after the very first store, Lady Foot Locker, where the girls get their feet sized and try a bunch of sneakers. A pair of Nikes Nara loves turns out to be very expensive. "Oh my God," I say, "these sneakers are $160!" I probably would have purchased them anyway if her heart was set on them, but she gets immediately turned off because of the price. "I don't want them," she says, "too expensive." I note this moment. I note it because it's clear to me that the cost of things is a conversation they've been having all their lives. I remember it from my childhood too. To desire something you can't have is futile, so Nara lost her desire completely when she assumed the cost was too much. There were other moments similar to this one. At Claire's, where we were buying headbands for Taj, Nara picks out a tiara, but I tell her that I don't think a $20 tiara is really necessary back-to-school wear. No disappointment registers on her body. She simply puts it back on the shelf. In the end, we spend three hours at the mall. Each girl gets sneakers they love. Nara ends up with the new high-top Air Jordans just displayed for the first time that day, and Taj picks out a pair of Nike Air Huaraches. We buy hoodies, jeans, T-shirts, socks, body wash and lotion, windbreakers, and underwear and bras from Pink, where the girls are measured for the first time ever. They are both given cards from the sales clerk with their bra sizes so that they can remember them. And this small gift, I notice, is an extraordinary one. "Can we keep the card with our sizes?" Nara asks, hopeful. Because shopping for kids is new to me, I'm surprised at how fast it all adds up. Even so, I pretty much buy them what they want—the $55 hoodie and $65 fall jacket at Vans, the completely unnecessary Ocean Extracts gel body wash from Pink. After all, just a few days ago, I spent $250 at Whole Foods without a blink. My own body wash from Aesop costs $45. It's completely evident that buying things on a whim is a wonder to them. They check with me before they put anything in the basket, hopeful that I'll say yes, and, with the exception of items not age-appropriate, I say yes.

Still, I worry. Pink was crowded with girls and young women, and Taj, for some reason, expresses shame at looking at the panty bar. "I don't want to touch those," she says. I ask her why and she just shakes her head as if the answer is obvious. Nara negotiates this scene more comfortably. She picks out ten pairs of underwear and puts them in the shopping bag handed to her upon entering. She's eager to find out her real bra size and picks out bras with flowers on them. Taj, however, expresses deep trepidation about the whole scene. She doesn't want the sales clerk to measure her at first and only acquiesces after the bras she tries on don't fit. "It will only take a minute," the young clerk assures Taj, "and it's over the shirt." This part of the trip is blackout to me because the rules are that only one person is allowed in the dressing rooms at a time. They spend more than a minute in the dressing room, and exit, finally, with the needed information. But a girl's life is a treacherous journey, and I can't tell if her shame around the undergarments and avoidance of being touched is normal preteen aversion or if there's a problem of the invasive sort that needs attention. I worry about the well-being of girls in general, but this girl, the one I'm trying to save from the fate so often traversed by those in my family, is one I'm watching closely whenever I see her. To be abandoned by one's mother is an abandonment that one never forgets. It's how my brother, Bruce, became my brother in the first place, given to my mother when he was a young boy by her sister, Helen, because her house was filled with children already and she was scrapped of means. His being given away, as I understand it, was an original trauma for Bruce. He was always a part of our four-person family and not. Who takes good care of the abandoned children beyond the things necessary for mere existence? Who makes them feel like they are more than just excess? Who watches over them and asks them about their inner lives and what they desire? After being measured, Taj finally looks at me, her big brown eyes suddenly alert, and says, "I want sports bras, not these other kinds." I feel that she trusts me a little, and now I have too been given a gift. "Do you want to take the stairs?" I ask her, when we reach the escalator. "No," she says, "I'm okay."

Come into the light, little one,
feel its bruise, its warmth too.

Whenever I go home these days, I rent a hotel room nearby. We used to have relatively normal furniture before my mother became crippled by disease and grief—even given some unfortunate design choices, such as carpet in the kitchen. Now the carpeting is worn and dirty, and several cabinet doors have fallen off. Because my mother has trouble bending over, she often keeps a plastic bag of trash on the kitchen counter. The living room furniture crumbles with decay, and piles of everything grow in corners and next to failing recliners. There's a white sofa that someone gave my brother. It was probably $300 new but is now brown and soiled, its coarse fabric violent on the skin.

Last year, I won a $100,000 poetry award and wanted to use some of the money to help my mother buy new furniture for the living room—a sofa and a rug, at the very least, given that she disposed of the Oriental rug she bought for $3,000 with her G. Fox & Co. credit card when I was a kid and replaced it recently with a plastic outdoor "rug" that bunches and twists at any pressure. I'd buy chairs too, if she'd let me, and new lamps so the room isn't always dark save the glow of the TV.

It's hard to know what old age is. I don't know what it does to the mind because I haven't experienced it yet. I only know what it's doing to my mother from watching her and from my encounters with her. She does not appear senile at all. She seems more deeply the part of herself that insists on things that make no sense. She gets an idea in her head and sticks with it, no matter how improbable. This has always been a part of who she is. Instead of accepting the gift I offered, my mother said she wanted a rug in the dining room. The dining room is a room in the house that isn't an eyesore. There's a Hitchcock table and chairs, a bench with a landline phone so you can take your calls right at the source, and a china cabinet where Mom stores things she wants to keep out of her grandchildren's clutches. "But, Mom," I insist, "there's really no place for guests to sit in the living room when they come over, including me, because that sofa is repulsive." There was no arguing with my mother about the dining room rug, so I order the one she wants—a thick jute/wool rug from The Company Store in Wisconsin, a store that prides itself on making things built for harsh winters. The color is sage and she's right, it does look great. I hoped this purchase would quell my mother's obsession with the dining room, but it didn't. She wants curtains next and to refinish the floors under the area rug. It's as if she's creating a museum for a past when she perceived she was in control, the agent of her own life and surroundings.

I can no longer bear its current disarray or the old hauntings that invade me whenever I'm inside the house. I witness Taj in this cluttered space and watch her adopt my brother's ways of cluttered hoarding, her bedroom stacked with unwashed clothes, one of the broken recliners in the living room surrounded by her disorderly piles of books and games. To my mother's feeble annoyance, my brother is collecting items all over the house. The basement refrigerator is filled to bursting with beverages—beer, soda, hard cider, water, juice—that he's brought home from the motel after he's cleaned the rooms. "People leave them behind," he tells me, "so I take them and sell them—a little side business." The truth is that he's not selling them; he's just obsessively building a beverage nest. The refrigerator is so full, he's started stacking bottles and cans adjacent in a giant heap. I could not invent a better symbol for stuckness and immobility than the stuff my brother accumulates despite there being no more space for it. The stuff—the sheer weight and diversity of it—is like a physical manifestation of Bruce's inability to do almost anything at all. He is trapped by objects but he is also held by them. He cannot stop gathering objects even though they literally prevent his movement around his bedroom. Symbols, though, always stand in for something else.

When we return from the shopping trip, the girls, carrying their bags of loot, and I bump into Bruce, who is preparing for work. "Hey," I say to him, "why didn't you ever call me?" His reply is "I don't know." I stare at him. "You don't even know, do you?" I say. "No," he says, "I don't even know." He looks away. I can't tell if he feels bad or confused or helpless. He slouches a little. All the anger I have been carrying around for weeks dissolves in an instant. Bruce, as far as I know, has never been to see a psychologist or been told he might benefit from medications that affect the ill-alignment of the psyche. No one has tested him for a learning disability, though after recently tutoring him for the GED, I'm sure he has one. What we call the white patriarchy is so insidious in this way. We think "patriarchy" and we think "all men," but some of us, me sometimes, included, forget what happens when Blackness and boyness intersect—the perception of it, already, as unworthy of gentleness and care and attention. Together, Bruce and I are the reification of, the made material of, the real Americanness—not the grand ideals of the country but the way things really are. One sibling in constant movement so far away from home with the freedom to sit and think and write all summer; the other off to his job at which by an act of the state government his minimum wage of $10 an hour will over a number of years, slowly, be raised to $15. I'm not standing on his back, but I might as well be. And maybe he senses the pressure. Maybe his saying I don't know and not knowing is a way of saying "unfair." And maybe this unfairness triggered his being stuck. They say that clutter when it's pathological sometimes stands in place of a personal connection with humans, affection transferred to objects. Leaving, however, is sometimes the strongest thing a person can do.

The girls are giddy in the living room, pulling their items from shopping bags and displaying them for my mother. "Nana," teases Taj, who knows exactly how to get under my mother's skin, "these biker shorts and this sports bra are going to be my new outside outfit." My mother tells her that there's no way she's wearing that outside. "People are crazy," she says, "you can't go around half naked." I become seventeen in this moment and ask my mother why the girls have to wear clothes to deal with other people's craziness. Taj should be able to be free in front of her own house. Young women sunbathe in bikinis at parks in New York City and why not? Etc. As an elderly woman, frustration is my mother's primary displayed emotion. It's rising now. It's bubbling up. And then, clothes and sneakers are being yanked from bags when Nara says, unprompted, "Some of the teachers at school look at our tooshes." I want to ask her about this, but before I can, my mother chimes in. "Don't say that!" she exclaims. "They do not!" I glare at her. "You shouldn't negate the girls' realities," I say, "especially when it comes to sexual violation. That's how sexual violence against children is able to take place, when adults don't listen to what they say." My tone is perhaps too strident, and my mother makes muffled sounds of frustration and uses her arms to catapult herself out of her broken lounger. She's mumbling some words when she grabs her cane and heads slowly, gruntingly upstairs to the bathroom. I look at Nara but I'm talking to both of them when I say, "If anyone ever does something inappropriate to your body, it doesn't matter if it's an adult or someone your age, you tell me immediately, okay?" She nods, and looks away, but I know she hears me.

"Oh my God, look!" says Taj, pointing at the security panel next to the front door. It reads: "The National Weather Service in Boston/Norton has issued a tornado warning for Southeastern Hartford County." Taj starts to freak out. "I don't want to die!" she screeches. I have no idea whether we're in Southeastern Hartford County but the sky looks weird—big, low pillowing clouds with holes for blue sky, yet it's dark at the same time. "Let's order a pizza!" I say. I don't want them to be afraid of everything in the world they can't control. I want to model adventure, and even though it's a little reckless in this particular moment, I suggest we go pick the pizza up in fifteen minutes, and we do. It's Mr. Pizza, the pizza shop I'd walk to when I was about nine years old, having made money from my snow-shoveling business or some other racket, where I'd go with my friends to play video games and eat subs using our newly made money. I tell the girls this story too. "You've never been here?" I ask. They shake their heads no, and the clouds get darker and the air strangely still.

We make it the eight or so blocks home and munch happily in the pristine dining room on the pizza of my youth. I'm still plagued by what I see of the girls' futures when I notice a drawing on Taj's new bedroom door. With crayons she's drawn a brown girl with puffy hair to her shoulders, wearing a black short-sleeved T-shirt and blue overalls. Instead of using crayons for the eyes too, she's drawn those separately in pencil and cut them out to paste on the figure. I stare at it for a long time. "Who's Maria Haydn?" I ask her. "Oh, that's her name," she says. I'm struck by the figure's expression, achieved mostly with the contours of the mouth, and also by the deep emotional blue of the jumper, the arms straight down by the sides. Self-portrait? Maybe. She's also written in a true preteen way, "Do not disturb! I mean it" at the top of the image. "You're a really great artist," I tell Taj. She shows me other drawings in a notebook, some beautifully rendered odd faces from her imagination and others drawings of comic book figures she's copied. The comic book figures are perfect renderings, as if she's training herself to draw with an attention to the line.

Maybe I can't wrangle the thing I want to happen. And maybe

my mother is right in this case. Maybe things will work out. Or maybe not. When I was in college, my second cousin, Khalil, the grandson of my Nation of Islam aunt and uncle, would come over to our house and sit in that chair in front of the TV set that Taj sits in. Just a boy, he too was farsighted and sat up close, a couple of feet away, engrossed in whatever network show that interested him. My mother was active then and took him to the children's museum, to the library downtown, and on outings at Bushnell Park. She read to him and bought puzzles for him just as she did for me when I was a kid. She fed him and let him sleep over whenever the electricity got cut off for nonpayment at his grandparents' house, where he lived. I was a junior in college when I took Khalil out with my ice cream truck where we ate ice cream until our bellies were sick and memorized Robert Frost poems.

Everyone keeps telling me how one person can make a big difference in a child's life. They say to me, *You don't have to be a constant presence, just a presence in your nieces' lives in order to inspire them and show them that existences far from what they see every day are possible.* "They'll remember the back-to-school shopping trip for the rest of their lives," one friend who is a high-school principal tells me. "They will remember that you care about them, that someone cares." I wonder, however, what it really takes to escape what you see every day. That witnessing, that being inside of, is like any indoctrination. It affects the person beyond their knowing, in what some might call the soul. Khalil got a girl pregnant when he was fifteen, and another girl entirely a few years later, and another, still, a few years later. Like his father, he saw no reason to act responsibly toward the girls or the children. He simply walked away as if nothing had happened. His father, whose name is also Khalil, is a registered sex offender in Memphis, Tennessee, for something called Second Degree Criminal Sexual Conduct. In Tennessee, this means he did something very bad. But before that, he did other bad things, the least of which is probably abandoning his son shortly after birth.

Resistance, I believe, has to come from some deep inner reserve. It's a thing only you know, a little god inside yourself. So when the outer voices come with their nonsense and the clutter of your experience threatens to pull you under, you have a secret buoying something that refuses to let you go. It might be where art comes from—that inexplicable opening of the mind.

Taj has a cool sense of style that seems to come from nowhere. The sleeves on the white hoodie she picked out from Vans are patterned abstractly with checkerboard and thick colored lines. Sitting on the sofa, she puts her new locker organizer on her head and wears it for a hat. I'm reminded of the '80s band Devo. Then she takes the pins gifted to me by the Gap with my new credit card and puts one on her backpack. The pin says something like NOTHING HERE IS ORDINARY. She is, as my mother puts it, "hardheaded" and doesn't listen to anything anyone says. Though my mother hates this hardheadedness and obstinacy, I had both of these traits as a girl too. I was dragged to church most Sundays, but nothing could convince me that the stories the preacher retold from the pulpit were more than that, stories. I knew not to speak of this. I disappeared into books to the point where those realities were more real than the one I actually inhabited. I was a trickster teenager and did whatever I wanted, lying and scheming in order to live the life I believed I deserved. When my mother told me that I couldn't sleep at the doors of the Civic Center to buy Prince concert tickets as soon as they went on sale, I snuck out in the middle of the night and pushed my father's car down the driveway and into the street. I drove downtown anyway and with friends camped out in a snowstorm, returning the car before my parents woke, while my friends held my spot. So desperate was I for liberation, I'd steal from the earth itself for a taste of it. What I wish for Taj is something far better, devoid, perhaps, of guile and guilt—that she, as well, has an inner reserve of strength and her own ideas about things, and will be able at some point to wrench herself from the clutches that confine her, even if that confining comes from love. My wish for her is that the artist I see inside her will be able to emerge, and that that, not me, will be what pulls her up and out. This is a prayer for the growth of the inner god, no matter how much it hurts.

CLAIRE MESSUD

Two Women

FROM *A Public Space*

WHEN MY FATHER was first dying—that's to say, in the time we thought he would die but he did not; the time when he made a belated and miraculous recovery and was returned to us, like a character in a fairy tale, for two years, three months, and five days—my aunt, his younger sister, tried to insist upon a visit from the priest. My mother, although diminished (as yet undiagnosed, she was already undermined by the Lewy body dementia that would fell her), resisted valiantly, because my father (at that time off with the fairies, as the expression has it; apt, for the fairy-tale-like nature of that time) could not; and the priest was kept at bay.

But two years later, when he was actually dying, fully and utterly presently himself, my father—my obdurate and fierce father, whose will we feared and admired in equal measure—could not resist his sister in her zeal. Which is how he came, in the nursing home, reluctantly to take communion from Father Bob, the once-a-week visiting Indian pastor in a baby-blue open-collared short-sleeved summer shirt, who, with short, plump fingers, unwrapped the host from a rolled hankie in his breast pocket like a wee snack saved from lunch.

"Isn't there someone," my father asked me pleadingly, "who could do this in French?"

Alas, I shook my head, I did not think so.

Being a man of his word, having promised his sister, my father opened his mouth for the host with all the enthusiasm he might have shown for a cyanide tablet. It was, of course, in addition to a display of religiosity from one who abhorred falsity and religion both, the first moment in which he had performatively to acknowledge that he accepted his imminent death. There were many reasons to balk at the preposterous scene of which he was unwillingly a part, carefully shaved and combed though his skin was a blotched mess, his Brooks Brothers button-down tidily ironed, his torso pinned awkwardly in his wheelchair, in the antiseptic white-tiled room overlooking verdant gardens in Rye Brook, New York, where the nursing aides, all as Catholic as my aunt, were visibly relieved to see my father saved from damnation at the last. One woman in fuchsia scrubs, standing out in the hallway, clasped her hands and gave thanks to God. The morning of this encounter was almost the last time my father forced himself from bed, his pain by then too great. A few days later he would be transferred to the hospital, and thence to the strange, liminal calm of hospice, to be granted the benison of morphine, and soon thereafter, of eternal rest.

But he accepted all this—the muttered prayers of Pastor Bob, who drew the sign of the cross upon my father's inviolable forehead, and the aides' hallelujahs—only when my mother was not in the room. Even half-witted—by then she'd lost many of her wits, though she'd struggled so valiantly and for so long not to let it show that I feel a traitor even now to acknowledge it—she would not have permitted my aunt's meddlesome Catholic hand. After the fact, she fumed; and remembered that betrayal longer than, by then, most things.

They had vowed when they married to keep religion out of it: she was a mild Anglican, and he a lapsed Catholic, child of passionately devout parents. (My French grandparents, their unconventional union blessed by papal dispensation, slept all their married lives beneath a crucifix draped with a rosary from the Vatican.) For each of my parents, the other's religion carried swathes of meaning—or, in the case of my mother's for my father, of meaninglessness. My father had rebelled against the swaddling quotidian faith in which he had been raised, but considered my mother's watery Christianity to be no faith at all. My mother, meanwhile, raised petit bourgeois and socially aspirant in midcentury Toronto, fully of her place and time, considered Catholicism sentimental and vulgar—by which she meant working class. We had at home a framed professional portrait of my French grandparents, black and white, both in profile: "It's very Latin," my mother would whisper, with evident distaste. "Very Catholic." She would have turned it to face the wall if she could.

This meant, in practice, that the pact against religion had been against Catholicism, first and foremost. I don't know whether my father knew, when he and my mother married, how the edict might shape their lives and ours. I don't know whether he ever wanted, before his deathbed, to return to the church of his childhood; but in that moment it was to his childhood that he returned: he longed for the prayers in French because only in French did they have meaning for him; it was only to his French self that they could speak.

His sister, my aunt, our Tante Denise, never left the church. She, like her parents, slept beneath her crucifix, and indeed ultimately died beneath it, watched over by nuns paid to pray at her bedside, rather than by us, her faithless North American nieces. Years before, contemplating retirement, she wondered often aloud whether to join a convent; in fact, when she stopped working, she gave herself—her time, her love, what little money she had—to the church, and more specifically to a particular priest, the fantastically named Père Casanova, with whom she more or less fell in love. Always meticulous, she undertook for years, pro bono, the accounts for his parish; but more indulgently, she fed him—gorged him, even, upon luxuries: filet mignon, truffles, expensive cognac—and lavished him with gifts; an expensive Aubusson carpet was, we came to know, among her donations. She blushed and grew giddy when he waved his carved ivory cane or swirled his embroidered raiment in her direction and praised her piety, or when, in mufti, he stopped by her apartment for an aperitif or two. She spoke so earnestly of leaving her property and worldly goods to the church that we assumed she'd written it into her will.

This was late in life, of course, when my sister and I had spouses and children of our own. We made fun of my aunt behind her back for being so perfectly like an aging spinster from a Trollope novel—by we I mean my mother, of course, and my sister and I. Our father remained silent, his face darkening when we joked about his sister: her lifelong defender as well as ours, he was, in such moments, rudely torn. With distance, I have to acknowledge that he was thus torn throughout his life, possibly almost all the time. After they'd all died—first our father; then, two years later, within months, my mother and my aunt—my sister observed that it was as if he'd been married to both of them, as if he'd shuttled all his life between two competing women. Needless to say—and it was never said—they hated each other.

As the story went, my mother met my father on a bus in the rain at Oxford, where they both attended summer school in 1955. Their first date was a picnic with an intimidatingly sophisticated American woman also in my mother's program named Gloria Steinem, and a Texan chap she brought along. My Canadian mother, tall and slender, resembled Ingrid Bergman; my father, who then had (albeit briefly) a full head of hair, was Latinly handsome. Both were shy. Their romance blossomed not only in Oxford but over the subsequent months in Paris, my mother's European foray prolonged on my father's account. By letter, she threw over her Canadian boyfriend—a young solicitor of the society to which she had been elevated, in adolescence, by her family's improved fortunes; my sister and I knew his name because our Canadian grandmother, when cross with our father, would mutter darkly that Margaret should have married Armstrong instead—and did not return home until she and my father were engaged.

Margaret's parents were far from entranced by the match: for starters, François-Michel was French, not to mention Catholic—in their small world the French were reputedly philanderers. He was only a student (and would remain one for some years), his prospects unclear. Apparently his parents—then en route to Buenos Aires, a city the very existence of which may have seemed doubtful to the Canadians—had no money.

Margaret's parents, amusingly surnamed Riches, had only lately risen from scrimping modesty to modest grandeur (my grandfather, a patent attorney, wrote the insulin patent for Banting and Best): a mink, a sheared beaver, and a belated diamond engagement ring for Marjorie; a Jaguar and a convertible both, for Harold; a lakeside summer cottage for all three to enjoy, though they remained in their same little house in their then-dowdy neighborhood in Toronto's West End: their expansion had its limits. My Canadian grandparents promptly wrote a letter to their future in-laws inquiring about their son's future plans, about how he proposed to keep their only daughter in the style to which she was accustomed. I've seen the letter; they actually used that phrase.

My parents were in touch only by correspondence for over a

year, until my father arrived in Toronto a few days before their wedding, in late July 1957. Algeria, the land of his forebears going back over a century and the complicated home of his later childhood, was at that time in violent turmoil; his parents, recently resettled in Argentina, could not afford the journey to Canada. They sent instead my father's younger sister, Denise, my only aunt, to represent the family.

In the photos, she smiles gamely. She'd had a horrendous crossing from Paris by plane, with severe turbulence and a long layover in Gander (this, her first air travel, instilled in her a permanent aerophobia); and once she'd arrived, with only minimal English, she had to put on a dumb show of eager jollity. Still plump then —her obsessive thinness came later, a lifelong near-anorexia made possible by chain smoking—she was pale and rather horsey-looking, but you can see the courage and willing with which she stands alongside her brother, among these strapping, alien Canadians: my grandfather Harold, who died before I was born, looks like a bona fide giant. And yet it's strange, surely, that in so many photos my father is flanked on one side by my tall mother—in her pristine cream peau de soie faux-Dior dress that accentuates her fine waist, her elegant calf, her swanlike neck—and on the other by my plain and solid aunt (whose physique I unfortunately inherited), in floral chintz.

From the beginning, my father had two women to take care of: in his old-school, patriarchal worldview, that was how he understood it. At the time of their wedding, he and my mother surely didn't know that my aunt would never marry; they did not anticipate her imminent nervous breakdown, nor her subsequent lifelong fragility—she was never not on lithium after that; even when, toward the end, she drank so heavily that she'd collapse naked in her own vomit in the front hall of her apartment, even then she was on lithium—nor her inability to be alone. Although even as a child, nicknamed Poupette, little doll, she'd been timorous and highly strung, asthmatic and sickly, and had been billeted for months to an aged relative in the Algerian countryside because she was so traumatized by the bombardments in Algiers. And she was, except as a young girl, plain, and as I say, at that point in her young womanhood, plump, with thick ankles—the sort of thing that my grandfather surely pointed out to her (he told me, when I was a teenager, that I'd be good-looking were my legs not so heavy and wondered whether there existed an operation whereby my ankles might be slimmed). She would have been clear in her own mind that she wasn't readily marriageable.

Immediately after my parents' wedding, they boarded a ship for Le Havre. I can only imagine their bafflement: having known each other intensely for just a few months, they then hadn't seen each other for many more; had met again in the flurry of festivity and wedding preparation; had married; and were suddenly cast into greatest intimacy, in a tiny cabin on a rolling ship upon the high seas. My aunt doesn't feature in the shipboard photographs; I assume she had a return ticket by airplane, though there's nobody left to confirm this. I think of my prudish mother, my extremely private father, embarked not only upon a newly sexual life in their tiny cabin, but sharing seasickness too—vomit? diarrhea?—at a stage of uncertainty when they may still have eyed one another warily, thinking, "You don't look quite as I remembered. Your left eye is smaller. Your skin is a bit bumpy. Your laugh sounds strange." And at the same time: "Here we are, joined for life, till death do us part." Of these early months, my mother confessed that she'd have turned tail and fled for home were it not for her mother's voice in her ear muttering "I told you so." Though it might, of course, have been the best move for all concerned.

Their first months together were spent in a small town in northern France, where my father completed his military service, and my mother—her French still a work in progress—spent such lonely days that she welcomed the pair of black-clad Mormon missionaries when they rang the bell and chatted with them for an hour. They then moved for a time to my grandparents' apartment in Paris, where my father had a job—though they would soon decamp again, for Boston, where he enrolled in graduate school at Harvard, in Middle Eastern studies.

The salient fact about their Paris sojourn is that they shared the small flat with my aunt. She'd been living in Paris for some months by then. There, working in an office, she fell in love with her married boss. This love, like all the romantic loves in her life that we know about—including her passion for the Père Casanova—proved unrequited. Denise spiraled into depression. It was 1958, and as she told it, the hostility toward her *pied-noir* background was everywhere palpable, sometimes even malicious. The Algerian War raged. The famous Pontecorvo film *The Battle of Algiers* describes events of 1956–57, culminating in the arrest of the FLN leaders in September of '57; the following months saw the rise of the OAS, a right-wing colonial terrorist organization fighting against the FLN with the support of certain military factions. The attempted coup in Algeria on May 13, 1958, led to the collapse of the Fourth Republic in France—Algeria's troubles brought France to the brink of civil war—and precipitated the return of an aging Charles de Gaulle to the French presidency. A new constitution was drafted; the Fifth Republic was launched. But the Algerian War would not end for another four bitter years.

A lyrical or mythic narrative of what resulted, for lonely young Denise, might glancingly propose that the violence and distress of the nation—France's inability to maintain power over its colony, Algeria, while at the same time being unable to liberate it—manifested as a crisis in my aunt's psyche, she a young woman who could neither be free from her abandoned homeland (whence her parents also had departed, of course, first for Morocco and then Argentina) nor at home in metropolitan France. Whether her collapse was precipitated by unattainable love of a man; a family; or a country, her Algeria; or whether by the political unrest around her, and the ways in which she saw herself as implicated in that unrest, as a young *pied-noir* woman in Paris passionately committed to a French Algeria, surrounded by peers who largely felt otherwise and considered her, a colonial in the metropole, an interloper—it's impossible now to know, and was perhaps impossible to know even then. She fell, through no fault of her own, on the wrong side of history. She fell through the cracks of history, perhaps. And she fell alone, while around her, for better or worse, her family was coupled: woebegone, she slid between her parents (their union legendarily happy), and mine (theirs not).

Which is to say: when my aunt's breakdown began, on the cusp of twenty-five (she was four months older than my mother; in 2010, she would die just two months after her), she was alone in Paris: her parents on another continent, in another hemisphere; her brother and his new wife some distance away. But then they moved into the flat on the avenue Franco-Russe along with her: Denise, François-Michel, and Margaret. My still newlywed parents—less than a year married; I think: they hardly knew each other!

They tried to make room for themselves—my mother tried to make room for herself, I should say—among my grandparents' furniture and the matter of Denise's troubled life. Denise quit her job; she stayed in, sitting, when not sleeping, on the sofa; she wept; she smoked; she did not eat the meals that my mother prepared (because my mother understood preparing meals to be her wifely role); she shed the extra weight that had so discomfited her; she stared into space; she wept some more.

This too I try to imagine, from my mother's point of view, or even from my father's. Many years later, my mother would say to my sister and me, apropos apparently of nothing, "Always remember that when you marry someone, you marry their family too." Those months in that small flat: a month is comprised of weeks, a week of days, a day of many hours, each hour of many minutes. My father out between breakfast and supper; my mother and my aunt at home, together, bridging the language gap as best they could, harboring and hiding their mutual dislike. My aunt histrionic; my mother cool to the point of unresponsiveness; my father, in the evenings, the go-between, himself tempestuous and hardly intuitive, nightly mixing cocktails, his sole domestic talent, in an effort to keep the peace.

Eventually my aunt was dispatched to Buenos Aires, to the care of her parents. There she spent an exhilarating decade, made great friends, became fluent in Spanish, and again fell fruitlessly, impossibly, in love, once more with a married man, always with lithium as her guardrail. She never again left her parents: they traveled the world as a trio, and when the old couple retired to Toulon, she went with them and found employment nearby. They signed their letters "Pamande"—Papa, Maman, Denise.

These two women, Denise and Margaret, so profoundly different, were yet not wholly unalike. Each lived by a set of unspoken rules, complex webs of necessity inferred by my sister and me, internalized and absorbed without explanation. Figuring out the world, in childhood—figuring out how to be a girl, how to be a person—meant learning these women's signals and, in time, attempting to parse their meaning. (Our father loomed large in our lives, but, during those years, in the way of a Greek god: he was rather frightening, and usually not at home. Many fathers then weren't: a business suit, a sort of passport, liberated them to travel.) We were issued occasional Delphic pronouncements—such as our mother's about marrying families; or another of her infamous comments, about my aunt: "Getting the idea she was a good person is the worst thing that ever happened to her." Sometimes we encountered instead inexplicable actions, as when my aunt, the night after my wedding, in a crowded hotel elevator in London, attempted to press into my hand a wad of French francs—a gift? Why, in that moment? Why at all, when she and my grandfather had already presented us with an expensive set of luggage? When I declined to accept it, she flew into a rage, the quelling of which required our best diplomatic efforts—not only mine and my husband's but also those of my sister and my father and my grandfather too. My mother, needless to say, did not get involved, and later simply rolled her eyes. After threatening to return to her room, Tante Denise was eventually persuaded to join us for supper, and in the photos at the Greek restaurant she smiles as if nothing had happened. Years later she said, out of the blue, "If I'd known you were going to keep your name, I would never have come to your wedding."

The rules that shaped my aunt's world were those of devout Catholicism above all; but also those of petit-bourgeois *pied-noir* society in the first half of the twentieth century, influenced too by the rigid French naval order of my grandfather's profession. Denise was profoundly devout; she collected religious artifacts, rosaries and holy water, and believed in signs and wonders. She kept secrets only, as she saw it, to make others' lives better: she hid the worst, which is why, in the end, we heard about her terminal diagnosis only from her doctor—she never mentioned it. We were always told that her terrible (solo) car accident occurred because she fell asleep at the wheel; though the timing suggests, in retrospect, greater volition. Still, she maintained a sunny face for as long as she possibly could. She had a terrible temper—what could she say? God had given it to her—but she was loyal. Deference to the patriarch, and to all elders, was absolute. The role of women in her world was clear, and fixed: we were on earth to marry and bear children. My aunt, a spinster with a successful career—a lawyer, which was the profession that my mother longed to practice, Denise worked also as an accountant—was referred to by her parents as "*pauvre* Denise"—in part because of the breakdown, the lifelong lithium, but chiefly because she'd failed to fulfill her role. They were sad that she was childless; sadder still that she remained unmarried. Theirs was not a secret pity, but overt, accepted. It was understood that in her single, childless state, Denise would stay close to home: caring for aging parents had been, for centuries, the lot of unmarried daughters. They had resigned themselves to this as far back as Buenos Aires—Pamande!—and took care of her at least as much as she did them.

After my grandmother died, my aunt guarded my grandfather like a wolf: when, at a restaurant with a close friend, he tripped and fell while my aunt was parking the car, she banished that friend from their lives. Ensuring his welfare and longevity became her focus, and she did her job well: at ninety-four, my grandfather died in his sleep, after a short illness, with all his wits—and his family—about him. After which, my aunt turned her attention to her older brother: thereafter, she rang François-Michel daily. They discussed the weather, their ordinary activities, her parish, her neighbors. She did not complain, not to him, not ever, no matter how desperate she felt. Theirs was *"la famille du sourire"* and her job was to bring him happiness. From across the Atlantic, Denise would care for him, in spite of my mother (who clearly didn't know properly how to do so). She would do so in a spirit of religious and relentless self-abnegation and self-sacrifice.

Meanwhile, her own existence grew ever more monastic and spartan: having saved very little, she embraced poverty almost like a child playing at being poor. She accepted gifts from my parents—from my father, really—as her birthright: an emerald ring, an amber necklace, a Burberry raincoat, her apartment—but for herself, she ate little, bought nothing, wore clothes and shoes until they fell apart, dried her husk of a body with rough and threadbare ancient towels. She did keep up always her Clarins foundation, her expensive lipstick—a deep dried-blood color, from Yves Saint Laurent: my mother loathed it, called it ghoulish—and her weekly *mise en plis;* these appearances were a matter of Catholic dignity, of French patriotism almost, a sunk cost. Beyond that, with the exception of cigarettes, she could forgo almost anything. She could, and she would, want less, use less, need less, demand less than anyone else: in this, at least, in being last, she would be first.

Even as she whittled down ever farther her person and her material desires, she grew desperately needy and enraged. She became a hurricane of fury. This was when and why she took to drink, the drink that would ultimately, along with the cigarettes, kill her; but which proved the only means by which she could allow herself unfettered. She drank Johnnie Walker when my parents bought it for her, but otherwise Label 5, a lowly brand of scotch sold in chunky embossed bottles, some of which she saved to refrigerate tap water—not for herself, who preferred all drinks tepid, but for her visitors.

Drunk, Denise became greedy, garrulous, avid. When we were away, she kept count of how long since we'd visited, and a few drinks in would throw out the exact tally in astringent reproach. She quarreled with lifelong friends, taking issue with their inconstancy, their insufficient attention. When we were there, she'd force our arms around her neck, pull us close, plant loud, soggy kisses on our cheeks, rumbling in our ears in her raspy Louis Armstrong fag-end of a voice, in a fug of tobacco smoke—French Marignys had, with time, turned into Marlboro Reds. Scrawny in age, and haggard, she developed particular tics when drunk, a way of tucking her hands into her waistband and rocking back and forth in unseemly pelvic thrusts; a way of thoughtlessly licking her forefinger, then pawing with the saliva at a raw, red patch on her face; a way of grinding her loose lips, ruminating almost, so that you couldn't ignore the prominent teeth behind them. Her pale-blue eyes, always watery behind their thick glasses, grew filmy and red-rimmed—and frightened, and sad.

Repelled by her, we were also guilty, even loving, in our repulsion: Tante Denise became a doppelgänger, a part of me that I feared, abhorred, accepted, and defended in equal measure. God forbid we should end up like Tante Denise—*pauvre* Denise. She was our Christian test, or one of them—mad, pathetic, noble, generous, oppressive, funny, deluded, brave, so lonely, and trying, always trying, until she couldn't try anymore. In her ignominious last years, of her naked drunken self, I was reminded always of Jane Bowles's character Mrs. Copperfield, who wants to drink gin until she can roll around on the floor like a baby. Being a woman was too difficult; in the end, maybe all along, Denise wanted only to renounce.

My mother's set of life rules, on the other hand, was that of a Protestant Anglophile with social aspirations in the Toronto of her youth. Effortless superiority and keen wit were de rigueur: you were supposed to be beautiful (or not, if you weren't) without making a fuss about it; wear practical, sturdy shoes; get straight A's without being seen to work; you were to be always polite and, when necessary or even amusing, cutting in your politesse. Gentle and considerate, even passive by nature, Margaret had nevertheless developed the sharp tongue her adolescent milieu (a private girls' school) had required, and often spoke like a character out of Anthony Powell or Muriel Spark. Of a college friend of mine, she memorably said, after the girl's one visit, "I've never met such a nonentity. I kept forgetting she was in the car." Insecurity could make her mean; matters superficial got under her skin: she envied her friends their mink coats, their Caribbean vacations, their husbands' deaths. She enlisted us, her daughters, as her defenders in arguments with our father and raised us to understand that her life had been ruined by marriage to a man who didn't support her liberation or believe in her capabilities. "Never, never be financially dependent on a man," she would hiss, or, because she felt our father dismissed her intellect, "Never, ever marry anyone who isn't as smart as you are." "I've wasted my life on his dirty socks," she said. "Don't ever get stuck like me."

But the messages confused, because she never left him—she never so much as went overnight to a friend's house or a motel. She railed against François-Michel, but when we criticized our father, she'd defend him; when we told her our secrets, she'd pass them on to him. We came to know that her allegiances were more complicated than she wanted to let on. Moreover, for someone who bitterly described being a wife and mother as "the waste of a life," she mastered the housewife's tasks with stellar preeminence: a magnificent cook, she prepared three-course meals even on weeknights (my favorite dessert was zabaglione, an egg yolk and marsala confection whipped over heat into a fiery, airy froth: it took twenty minutes over the stovetop at the last minute, but she'd make it sometimes just for the four of us, for fun); she kept house impeccably; everything was ironed, from shirts and dresses to sheets and pillowcases, nightgowns, underpants, my father's linen handkerchiefs. She could remove any spot from any fabric, darn socks, invisibly repair moth holes. She saved leftovers in tiny dishes in the fridge, and old twist ties, and washed out plastic bags and hung them up to dry.

She taught us that good stewardship was a moral strength; so too was thrift. This was not incommensurate with her sense of superiority and her sharp judgments of others—for a child of the Depression, greater continence was an expression of superiority, indeed. She came from, aspired to, a Canadian society of hardy, broad-shouldered women, capable and resilient. She eschewed makeup and fine clothes: when my father bought her beautiful things, she stuffed them, tags on, in the back of her closet. She used Eucerin as her face cream, and in my entire life, possessed one ancient blue eye shadow; her waxy lipsticks came from the drugstore. She never paid more than thirty dollars for a haircut and seemed almost to take pride in having great bone structure (Ingrid Bergman!) but looking shabby—the perfect counterpoint to Tante Denise, who, although homely, always made the most of herself. (My sister and I thought of it—think of it still—as Protestant versus Catholic and Canadian versus French.) She knitted elaborate sweaters; she created and tended beautiful gardens; she trained beloved dogs, and walked them for miles, and played ball with them, and talked to them: she adored dogs. She read thousands of books, developed unexpected areas of erudition (for example, nineteenth-century female travelers in Asia and Africa; histories of fonts and presses; all facts about the Bloomsbury Group). And she wrote letters, amazing letters, many of which I am fortunate still to possess.

Both women formed me, even as they shaped my father's life. Albeit differently, they taught my sister and me that we should ask for, and expect, less, even as they encouraged us to strive for more, lessons that seem quaintly old-fashioned now. In the parking lot of the nursing home where Father Bob delivered the last rites to my father, my mother, mildly demented, remarked, with sadness in her voice, but also with considerable calm, "There's still so much of life to get through, once you realize that your dreams won't come true." She'd never taken up much space, but in those last years she took up less and less, ever polite, obliterated but gracious to her ten-month-bedridden end. Tante Denise, meanwhile, erased herself little by little in a different, uglier way, with the help of Label 5. She called the Atlantic "that accursed ocean" but managed nevertheless to cross it to be with her brother when he was dying. She largely ignored her sister-in-law at that point and picked fights instead with my sister. Once François-Michel was gone, Denise saw no reason to hold on, and her alcoholic suicide began in earnest.

My father had, all his life, two women to take care of (four, if you count my sister and me). He was devoted to his sister, and he adored his wife; though they irked him, each in her way. He, who had no time for gossip, said nothing behind their backs; in fact, I never heard him criticize my aunt at all; though he and my mother rowed a great deal over the years.

Denise knew what she was supposed to be (married, a mother, sweet, submissive), approved wholeheartedly, even judgmentally, of those traditional ideals, but couldn't for the life of her fulfill them. We've often wondered whether her unrequited heterosexual loves were for show, and whether, in our era, or without the pressures of her Catholic faith, her intimate life might have unfolded differently. Margaret, in contrast, despised what she was supposed to be (married, a mother, sweet, submissive) and yet was most successfully all of these things. What she wanted instead, she was too submissive to attain. From the two of them I learned that to hope for happiness, or peace, even, I should strive to be everything, but also that I was probably doomed: there's still so much of life to get through when you realize that your dreams won't come true.

Painfully, both my mother's and my aunt's identities involved profound self-loathing: they believed, as so many women have been brought up to believe, that they were inadequate as they were. I have struggled, with uncertain success, to divest myself of that legacy. Yet much that I internalized from these two women I still uphold: the joy and dignity of small pleasures, the gift of requiring less in order to find contentment, the Christian ethics that teach us to put others before ourselves, to be humble, to be kind. Curiosity, openness, fearlessness, generosity of spirit, above all, love—these things I also learned from them. To live with an open heart and an open mind, and to live with kindness—truisms, perhaps, but not less admirable goals for that. If there's an afterlife, I don't believe access to it lies in the hands of Father Bob, with his hankie-wrapped host; nor do I believe there's particular merit in my mother's urge to banish potentially assuaging rituals of faith. If I'd only found the priest between Stamford and White Plains who could deliver the last rites in French, my father might have been consoled. Even without believing, he might have been consoled.

Here's how I like to remember them, my aunt and my mother. When I was small, perhaps six or so, I knocked over my water glass on the table in the Vietnamese restaurant in Le Pradet, near my grandparents' home in the south of France. My father, who couldn't tolerate mess and still less embarrassment (he too carried a lot of anxiety), roared at me, and I broke into tears.

"Don't be sad," said Tante Denise, putting an arm around my shoulder. "Accidents happen. They can happen to anyone—even to grown-ups." (She spoke in French, of course, and so the words she used were deliciously literal to my childhood self: *grandes personnes,* "big people.") She grasped her full wineglass by the stem and turned it over on the table, so that the red wine mixed with my water on the textured white-paper cloth in an expanding red swirly sea. "See?" she laughed, "it doesn't matter!"

And my mother, Margaret Riches Messud: her gentle soul, even to the end, before and after the bitterness and disappointment. She stood, or rather teetered slightly, in our kitchen, in the last year of her life, beatific while I, in my turn, fumed: I'd taken her three times within an hour to the bathroom because she kept forgetting she'd already been ("Are you sure, Mama?" "Yes, I'm sure"): each trip was a lengthy ordeal on account of the Parkinson's; she couldn't manage any of the practicalities herself.

"Isn't it wonderful," she whispered, eyes alight, apropos of nothing. I was aware that she spoke in all sincerity and yet, at the same time, that she perhaps didn't know entirely that she lived with us, nor perhaps quite who I was, that I was her daughter. "I just love being here," she said, "and I just wish I could spend all my time with you." And she smiled at me, at the world, like a blessing, and she reached out to hold my hand.

WESLEY MORRIS

My Mustache

FROM *The New York Times Magazine*

LIKE A LOT of men, in pursuit of novelty and amusement during these months of isolation, I grew a mustache. The reviews were predictably mixed and predictably predictable. "Porny"? Yes. "Creepy"? Obviously. "'70s"? True (the 18- *and* 1970s). On some video calls, I heard "rugged" and "extra gay." Someone I love called me "zaddy." Children were harsh. My eleven-year-old nephew told his Minecraft friends that his uncle has this . . . *mustache;* the midgame disgust was audible through his headset. In August, I spent two weeks with my niece, who's seven. She would rise each morning dismayed anew to be spending another day looking at the hair on my face. Once, she climbed on my back and began combing the mustache with her fingers, whispering in the warmest tones of endearment, "Uncle Wesley, when are you going to shave this thing off?"

It hasn't been all bad. Halfway through a quick stop-and-chat outside a friend's house in July, he and I removed our masks and exploded at the sight of each other. *No way: mustache!* I spent video meetings searching amid the boxes for other mustaches, to admire the way they enhance eyes and redefine faces with a force of irreversible handsomeness, the way Burt Reynolds never made the same kind of sense without his. The mustache aged me. (People didn't mind letting me know that, either.) But so what? It pulled me past "mature" to a particular kind of "distinguished." It looks fetching, for instance, with suits I currently have no logical reason to wear.

One afternoon, on a group call to celebrate a friend's good

news, somebody said what I didn't know I needed to hear. More reviews were pouring in (thumbs down, mostly), but I was already committed at that point. I just didn't know to what. That's when my friend chimed in: "You look like a lawyer for the NAACP Legal Defense Fund!"

What I remember was laughter. But where someone might have sensed shade being thrown, I experienced the opposite. A light had been shone. It was said as a winking correction and an earnest clarification. *Y'all, this is what it is.* The call moved on, but I didn't. That *is* what it is: one of the sweetest, truest things anybody had said about me in a long time.

My friend had identified a mighty American tradition and placed my face within it. Any time twentieth-century Black people found themselves entangled in racialized peril, anytime the roots of racism pushed up some new, hideous weed, a thoughtful-looking, solemn-seeming, crisply attired gentleman would be photographed entering a courthouse or seated somewhere (a library, a living room) alongside the wronged and imperiled. He was probably a lawyer, and he was likely to have been mustached.

Thurgood Marshall started the National Association for the Advancement of Colored People's Legal Defense and Education Fund eighty years ago. (It still exists. Sherrilyn Ifill is in charge.) The LDF's most famous cases include *Shelley v. Kraemer,* which, in effect, forbade landlords from refusing to rent to Black people, and *Brown v. Board of Education,* the crown jewel in the fund's many school-desegregation challenges. Marshall was, essentially, the civil rights movement's legal strategist, and in case after case, he arrived at the Supreme Court in elegant tailoring and sharp haircuts. A decade later Marshall was on the court. And any time he donned that robe and those horn-rimmed spectacles, every time he shined at oral arguments, he did so wearing a mustache. The glasses and jowls emphasized his famous air of wisdom. The mustache bestowed a grounding flourish.

In 1954, when the court ruled in *Brown,* it wasn't so rare to see a mustached man. They were a common feature among blue-collar joes. Charlie Chaplin and Errol Flynn had been stars; and the country hadn't quite finished with Clark Gable. Ernest Hemingway had aligned the mustache with distinctly American ideas of masculine bravado, concision, and sport. But a mustache could also be a softener, a grace note. A mustache advertised a certain commitment to civility. On a man like Gable, it embellished his rough edges, gave his characters' chauvinism a classy place to land.

On Black men, a mustache told a different story. It was fashionable, but it was more than that. On a Black man, it signified values: perseverance, seriousness, rigor. Ralph Ellison, Langston Hughes, Jacob Lawrence, Gordon Parks, Albert Murray, John Lewis, C. T. Vivian, Martin Luther King Jr., Ralph Abernathy, Bayard Rustin, Joseph Lowery, Fred Shuttlesworth, Julius L. Chambers, Jesse Jackson, Hosea Williams, Adam Clayton Powell Jr., Elijah Cummings: mustaches all. Classics. (It should be noted that the superstar ideological iconoclast among the freedom fighters, Malcolm X, did battle accordingly. He was the only prominent American leader, of any race, with a goatee.)

In the days after that congratulations video call, the euphoria of having been tagged as part of some illustrious legacy tapered off. The mustache had certainly conjoined me to a past I was flattered to be associated with, however superficially. But there were implications. During the later stages of the movement, a mustached man opened himself up to charges of white appeasement and Uncle Tom–ism. Not because of the mustache, obviously, but because of the approach of the sort of person who would choose to wear one. Such a person might not have been considered radical enough, down enough, Black enough. The civil rights mustache was strategically tolerant. It didn't advocate burning anything down. It ran for office—and sometimes it won. It was establishmentarian, compromising, and eventually, come the infernos at the close of the 1960s, it fell out of fashion, in part because it felt out of step with the urgency of the moment.

The Black mustache didn't end with the disillusionments of the post-civil-rights era. Jim Brown, Stevie Wonder, Richard Roundtree, Billy Dee Williams, Lionel Richie, Sherman Hemsley, Carl Weathers, James Brown, Arsenio Hall, and Eddie Murphy wore one. It's just that no higher calling officially united them. Their mustaches were freelance signatures, the mark of an individual rather than a people's emblem. At some point in the 1970s and through at least 1980, Muhammad Ali grew one you could attach to a broom handle. Donnie Simpson hosted BET's *Video Soul* with a tapered number and a silky smoothness that could line a tuxedo jacket. Throw a rock at an old *Jet* magazine from the 1980s, you'll hit somebody's mustache. But well before then, the politics of self-presentation had coalesced around grander, less deniable hair. They migrated to the Afro. A mustache might have been a dignified symbol in the pursuit of equality. But there was nothing inherently Black about it. A mustache meant business. An Afro meant power.

I knew before the summer's Black Lives Matter protests that my mustache made me look like a bougie race man: a professional, seemingly humorless middle-class Negro, a moderate, who believes that presentation is a crucial component of the "advancement" part of the NAACP mission, someone who doesn't mind a little respectability because he believes his people deserve respect. It's a look to ponder as the country finds itself churning once again over ceaseless questions of advancement and justice and the right to be left the hell alone. I live a street over from a thoroughfare where the protests happened almost nightly in June and July. I could hear their approach from my living room. One evening, I stood at a corner, moved, as thousands of people passed: friends, colleagues, coworkers, some guy I went on a blind date with a million years ago, chanting, brandishing banners and buttons. Some protesters had their fists raised in a Black Power salute. So I raised mine. Not a gesture I would normally make. But there was something about seeing so many white people lifting their arms that goaded me into doing it too. Mine kept lowering itself, so I had to jerk it to its fullest, most committed extension. I felt out of control, like Edward Norton throwing himself around his boss's office in *Fight Club;* like the kleptomaniac that Tippi Hedren played in Alfred Hitchcock's *Marnie,* trying to palm a stack of cash but her arm. Just. Won't. Pick. It. Up. At some point, I stopped straining. This wasn't the struggle I came for. Plus, a friend told me later that I had made my fist wrong.

The Black Power salute is not a casual gesture. It's weaponry. You aim that arm and fire. I aimed mine in solidarity—*with* white people instead of at a system they personify. And that didn't feel quite right. But how would I know? I had never done a Black Power salute. It always seemed like more Blackness than I've needed, maybe more than I had. I'm not Black Power Black. I've always been milder, more apprehensive than that. I was practically born with a mustache.

I grew up in Philadelphia in the 1980s. My mother left my father when my sister and I were small. I took the divorce just fine. Except for the stealing. I used to pluck quarters from my mother's change purse and, before class, feed them to the arcade consoles at the 7-Eleven near school. First, though, I would discreetly jam handfuls of one-cent candy into my pockets. The quarters were never meant to cover that. For two weeks in the second grade, this is how my mornings began—until I got caught. The store manager called my mother, and in the uncomfortably long wait for her arrival, I sat there, wallowing in regret. But she never showed. My father did. She must have phoned him. He walked me home to the house he no longer lived in and spanked me (a first, for us both). Then he calmly walked me to school. On the way, he explained, with uncharacteristic gravity, that because I was Black, I needed to be very careful about my behavior. Nobody should steal. And we especially shouldn't. He was a track coach, and that was one of the few times he ever coached me.

It's perhaps absurd to point to one childhood incident and declare it decisive, but I've always found that story useful. It's rich in disappointment, embarrassment, shame, and guilt (my mother needed those quarters; they were carfare; and the kids at school now knew I was a thief). I was so ashamed that I vowed, at six, that I never wanted to feel like that again. I'd had a moral near-death experience. From there on, I would be good. That was the vow.

"Good" meant trying hard and helping out and listening and being a devoted friend. It meant only the best news for my parents and being liked. But goodness as a personal policy is strange for a child to have. It's for grown-ups, not for kids. Teachers like good kids; some teachers prefer them. The kind of goodness I'm talking about is suspicious to other kids. Kids don't want to catch you abstaining from trouble or raising your hand or staying behind after school to help out or, worse, to *hang*. I went to the same small, mostly Black private school from third grade until graduation. That kind of goodness sometimes got classified as "white." It wasn't pejorative, exactly. Kids liked me. But we all seemed to realize that now I had a genre.

I don't recall making a conscious equation between goodness and whiteness. But I watched TV and went to movies and devoured comic books and music videos in which most of the people were white. I made identifications. I internalized things. I watched almost every episode of two popular sitcoms in which rich white people adopt Black orphans. Hip-hop had only begun its pursuit of world domination; it was still just rap. But I preferred pop music and liked it when a rap song—"Push It," "Just a Friend," "Going Back to Cali"—crossed from Black radio to everybody else's. The crossing over was validating. Pop was proof not of selling out, but of a kind of goodness.

I never suffered any major drama about being Black or being gay. (A stretch of the sixth grade featured me talking like Jackée Harry, who played the flamboyantly congested sexpot, Sandra, on *227*.) I just understood that there were strata and somewhere among them were my "proper" diction and pegged jeans. I had made myself an individual and was never tortured too terribly for it. I had a little room of my own in a wider Black world. Then Carlton moved in.

Carlton was Will Smith's rich, conservative cousin on *The Fresh Prince of Bel-Air.* The show ran on NBC from 1990 to 1996 and was another Black-adoption sitcom, only the rich family was Black. Carlton was the middle kid: bellowingly enunciative, preppy in Ralph Lauren everything, deafened by the setting on Will's Blackness. To Will, Carlton's familiarity with whiteness made him indistinguishable from it. Early in season 1, when a family friend chooses Carlton and not Will to drive his fancy car to Palm Springs as a favor, a miffed Will asks, "This is a Black thing, isn't it?" On the road, Carlton offers Will a snack: "What do you say to an Oreo?" Will answers: "What's up, Carlton?"

Carlton's erudition and country-club style panic Will, whose own approach to Blackness becomes an overcompensation for his proximity to affluence. His Blackness is a thing he performs—for an audience, but mainly for himself. In season 2, Uncle Phil tells Will that he's proud of him, that he's just like his son. It's a compliment that induces a nervous breakdown. "I'm turning into Carlton," Will says. "No more of these sissy sandwiches. No more valet parking. And no more of these preppy parties, man." He then destroys the $200 check that he kissed up to Uncle Phil to write him and says, "Yo, the funky fresh is back in the flesh with a vengeance, Holmes!" It's stunning enough, the equation of intelligence with emasculation and whiteness with lunch (Will: *sandwiches?*). But when he's finished, the audience erupts in cheers. Nobody watching wanted Will to become "good." They wanted him to stay Black.

I didn't know who Carlton was until I was presumed to be him:

in school, at my weekend movie-theater job, in the checkout line at the Gap. He equipped the young and perplexed with a shorthand for bright, square oddballs who weren't quite nerds. (Nerds were easy. They were Steve Urkel, the geek from *Family Matters.*) In high school, there were a few of us oddballs. I, alas, was the lone Carlton. But a crucial part of the equation always felt off. Carlton epitomized the hazardous comedy of racial estrangement. Even his assertions of Blackness were meant in irony. Like the time, in season 1, when Will bets that his cousin wouldn't last long in Compton, and Carlton winds up dressed like a gangsta. His sudden abundance of Blackness was supposedly funnier because we were well versed in his alleged lack of it.

But sometimes I wondered, Was he really an exemplar of Blackness's rigidity or could he have been an exploration of its parameters? Could I? I don't think it mattered back then. These were teenagers. They weren't looking for the nuances of who anybody was. They were Will, in search of the easiest path to jokes that distracted from their insecurities. And the path from Carlton to me was, admittedly, not an arduous one to forge. This would have been asking a lot of a network sitcom, but I sometimes wondered about the Blackness of Carlton's inner life and its correspondence to mine.

One of the proudest secondhand moments of my adolescence was the Wimbledon tennis tournament in which an unseeded Lori McNeil stopped Steffi Graf's title defense *in the first round* and almost made it to the final. I liked Steffi Graf, but Lori McNeil? How? Did Carlton catch any of that? Did he love it when a curmudgeon like Stanley Crouch, a reality checker like Julianne Malveaux, or a sage like Toni Morrison would show up on some talk show and just go on and on about whatever? The hosts might have seemed prepared for the erudite truth of what they had to say but often seemed taken aback by the precise Blackness of its deployment. The joke of Carlton was that he adored Tom Jones and danced like Belinda Carlisle. But surely he could sense that the 1980s and 1990s were a bounteous age for an anything-goes kind of Blackness: Prince, Whoopi Goldberg, Jermaine Stewart, Janet Jackson, Flavor Flav.

The first time I saw a wet suit was on Corey Glover, who sang in the band Living Colour, four Black guys who built their hard rock on a base layer of rhythm and blues. Rap's menu had diversified enough to include Afrocentric hippies like Arrested Development and hippie-dorks like De La Soul. Lenny Kravitz was another hippie but nobody in my life seemed to take his funk-rock as spiritually as I did. To them, it was cheesy and ripped off. I inspected this music for a Blackness that comported with mine and every time felt the thrill of pure identification.

Carlton rarely got to make any such discovery. His cluelessness was too useful an asset. He was the bane of my adolescence, but I came to feel for him and despise the trap he was in. Every once in a while, though, somebody involved with that show would let him the littlest bit loose. At the end of Compton episode, this happens:

CARLTON: "I never judge you for being the way you are. But you always act like I don't measure up to some rule of Blackness that you carry around."

WILL: "You treat me like I'm some kind of idiot just 'cause I talk different."

CARLTON: "'Different*ly*.'"

The show just kept shaking the Etch A Sketch, resetting Carlton's self-awareness and Will's insensitivity to it. But I understood what Will's ilk ignored. The Oreo had a soul.

During that stretch in high school, I grew a mustache. It was a classic rite of male puberty: I grew it because I could, kept it because it didn't violate a dress code, and was grateful for it because it probably helped tame the homophobes. Just about every boy in my graduating class had something sprouting above their lip. Wispy, ghostly, "cheesy," but certifiably masculine. That's also why people called me Carlton: because I bore the vaguest resemblance to Alfonso Ribeiro, the actor who played him. We both talked funny, dressed funny, danced funny. And we both, it must be said, had a mustache.

On my way to college, I got rid of it, hoping to exorcise Carlton. And it didn't go with the look I wanted to take with me: baggy T-shirts and baggy pants, with either Doc Martens or a pair of Chuck Taylors. I had two beloved T-shirts: Travis Bickle, the *Taxi Driver* psycho, was printed on one; the other was striped thin in red, green, black, and yellow, which struck me as in some way African even though it was not. My older cousin Leon bought me a 40 ACRES AND A MULE baseball cap from Spike Lee's merchandise shop. No filmmaker mattered more to my teenage self. But I was perpetually concerned that somebody might ask what the 40 ACRES were all about. Here I was, nervous about the call for reparations atop my head when there was a homicidal maniac staring out from my chest. Even then, I couldn't. Make. A. Fist.

I went to Yale, which, until recently, offered an orientation camp for several dozen nonwhite students to bond. It was a week of sitting around, exploiting the pretext of food and talent shows to luxuriate in the personalities and tastes and lives of potential new friends. It was exciting, finding these kindred souls. Every once in a while, one of us would pause our little paradise to laugh at the absurdity of it all (the program's acronym was PROP) and ponder the looming menace: Were we being warned? The program was a rather stunning admission on the college's part: this is a white place; you all are going to need to keep one another from drowning. Lots of us had gone to integrated schools. We could swim. I swam.

But there's a way that, for certain nonwhite people (especially if you're poor), life at a liberal arts college (especially a so-called elite one) can feel like the reward for all of that being good. Maybe you've beaten some odds to get there, and your prize for all of the effort and, let's face it, all of the luck is, yes, a premium education but also living among white people. But first—ha, ha —*first* you must exemplify your people, be a diplomat for them and an ambassador to the white people to whom your ways might seem foreign.

No one ever puts it that way. The structure does the talking. No Black first-year student I knew at Yale had a Black roommate. If a professor put James Baldwin or Toni Morrison or Ntozake Shange or August Wilson on a syllabus, you, as the section's sole Black person, would be gazed at until you got the discussion started, expected to approve your sectionmates' analysis and withstand their insinuations. There were several ways to receive such a position: aghast, aggrieved, in acquiescence, with authority.

I eventually owned the situation. But it created delusions. I, at least, went through a brief, shameful period of high peacock during which my stage name could have been Mr. Black Experience. Prolonged only-ness winds up abutting exceptionalism. The alternatives never felt, to me, like improvements. Take the athlete from

Southern California whom I ran into during a terrible evening he was having our first year. The pressure to declare his Blackness had snapped him. He didn't want to be merely some Black guy; he just wanted to be him. There was no consolation. We ran into each other from time to time. He pledged one of the big white fraternities and seemed to enjoy its spoils. I still think about him. What were the rest of his four years like?

Mine remain four of my best. I was happy. Only this summer have I taken any deep stock of the time I had there, how acculturation can breed estrangement, how I ended up with the comfortable life I've got. One urgent demand of this moment is for people, workplaces, and institutions to reckon with their whiteness. Why not reckon with mine? Day after day of video calls will do that. I sat there on work meetings, in friend hangouts and family catch-ups, and stared into people's homes, tallying who's in my world, regretting nothing but simply absorbing how solidly white and discretely nonwhite the parties are and how it all feels traceable to a morning I got caught stuffing my pockets with Jolly Ranchers.

After graduation, during the decade and a half I spent working at newspapers in San Francisco and Boston, I embarked on a life that featured increasingly fewer Black people—at the office, in restaurants, on the streets. It was less an ambition than ambition's consequence. Some days it felt as if the Rapture had occurred and taken all the Black people to Atlanta or Houston. Even as I basked in the fortune of my life, loneliness performed its gentle tintinnabulations. San Francisco once had a good, Black-run soul-food place called Powell's. I sat down there almost every month just to have a base to touch. I talked about moving to Oakland but never did. In Boston, I had a couple of weird years with men. After a political convention, in 2004, I took home a guy from South Carolina who seduced me with talk about the difference he planned to make as a Black politician. On the walk to the subway the next morning, I all but asked him to take me to Charleston. That was the end of that.

I wasn't thinking of the people in my life as just white people; these were my coworkers, my friends. One of those friends applied a similar logic to me. The same week that a Minneapolis police officer killed Philando Castile, he found me in grief, and I told him that I've always harbored a murmuring awareness that I could be shot. He was incredulous. How could that happen to *me?* I went to a good school and had a good job. I was Black but not "killed during a police stop" Black. I was good.

I can imagine a version of myself that, having completed Yale and succeeded professionally, would've heard that response and felt relieved. That I was one of racism's carve-outs. I was me. Only I've always felt more lucky than exceptional. I can now see that my vow of goodness was an existential shift of shape. Having been told, early on, that unreasonable obstacles awaited, I set about finding a form that could easily evade them.

There is, I suppose, an other hand, wherein I take further stock and declare a folly. The entire affair of race is a joke. My life is mine, no strings, no speed traps. Why overthink it? And the mustache. Come on. It's called a pandemic trend. I made bread on my face. One's race is not one's self. I know this and strive to leave it at that. But I never get far. In the United States, a Black self eventually discovers his race is a form of credit (or discredit, as it were). You can't leave home without it.

Yet for as long as Black Americans have been conscious of their Blackness, some public intellectual has cried "Hoax." *You, Black person, are free—free to be a Person.* You can Rapture yourself. American literature reserves a corner for characters who've plotted escape: the passing novel, wherein Black people eke out a sad white life. Certainly, a logic for leaving exists. I must admit I do feel free, often in precisely the way that friend of mine insisted I must, because my fears haven't yet come true. I could, in theory, join the Black exit campaign and leave, if not the race, then certainly the sort of thinking that believes racism is a form of determinism, affecting the choices we make as individuals.

I've tried to empathize with this thinking and am always surprised that I can't close the deal.

You might recall that before he became America's most notorious double-murder acquittee, O. J. Simpson insisted he wasn't Black, either: he, alas, was O. J. But ensnarement within the criminal-justice system has this tragic way of clarifying who you are. Simpson emerged from that national disaster redefined by the Blackness he forsook. Lately and most cantankerously, it's Kanye West who has been daring to level with us. His early musical pushes against Black orthodoxy have mutated, over the last four years, into pleas for Black people to stop it with the racism talk, to get over it, essentially. His vision for transcendence of racism, if not race itself, would be easier to share if it didn't appear to lead straight into the arms of racists.

I don't believe in that kind of transcendence. I'm not a Blexiteer, some person who is still convinced that we live in postracial times. If anything, I'm a Blexistentialist. I encounter something like Barack Obama's *Dreams from My Father,* which is steadfastly the opposite of the passing experience, and feast on his decades-long search for a Black self that suits him. It's a finding book, a story of becoming. As the Black tent expands, the people beneath it can keep doing as they've always done—widening its poles.

I have wondered, though, what kind of spiral I would have taken, had the friend on that video call not said "NAACP lawyer," if she had looked at my face and said, "You look like Clarence Thomas" or Herman Cain or Ben Carson (Carson's goatee has, on occasion, been only a mustache). What if she had pinned me to a bootstraps mentality that rejects racism as a root of injustice, that believes you're your own responsibility? I would have felt cornered, I suppose. Personal accountability isn't nothing. This country just won't let it be all. The extant number of Black firsts, rares, onlys, nevers, not yets, and not quites attests to that, as do the chronic too manys, too oftens, and too soons.

I like to think that I would have absorbed her "Clarence Thomas" and regaled her with a separate lineage. I would have told her that I hail from a long line of family mustaches. Uncle Gene's made him look famous. Uncle Jack's got bushy after World War II and pretty much stayed that way. My grandmother's last husband, Jimmy, wore his in a style best described as "sharpened." How did she kiss that thing and not need stitches? Her first husband, my grandfather, kept his barely there. Both their sons had one. Her brother Marcellus liked his thin. My mother loved my stepfather's, because, well, she loved him. My father had his phases. Three of his brothers had them too; the fourth, Uncle Bill, had an ascot —had you ever met Uncle Bill, you would conclude that the ascot essentially was a mustache.

It might just have been simpler to say who didn't have one than who did. I don't know what everybody's politics were, but as a clan, we were a Thanksgiving spread, a little of everything yet nothing so outrageous that the advancement for colored people would ever be off the table. These were workingmen, providers, not activists but voters, certainly. Their mustaches strike me now as a generational phenomenon. These people were all born between 1920 and 1950. Of their children, only my cousins Butchie and Kyle are describable as mustache men.

This is why I've kept mine. It's me squeezing my way into a parallel heritage. In this small sense, the work I do caring for it feels connected to a legacy of people who did and do the work chipping at and thinking with this nation. The good work.

Something obvious in just about any photograph taken of Black Americans during the civil rights era is how put-together everyone is. They wore to war what they wore to church. The country was watching. People got dressed up to withstand being put down. They dressed with full awareness that an outfit risked ruin: skirts twisted round, glasses cracked, ribbons undone, hair soaked, fabric stained with mustard, cream, and blood. What hat didn't stand a good chance of permanent separation from its wearer? What fine pair of shoes didn't risk meeting its doom? A mustache, though? Hard to mar one of those. It was a magisterial vestige of elegance in defiance. It couldn't be snatched at or yanked. It held its ground, no matter how many times a nightstick or fist might attempt to remove it.

I look at those pictures and wonder about getting dressed—for contempt—about grooming oneself for it. Maintaining a mustache requires a surgical delicacy, a practiced lightness. I tend to save it for last, strenuously avoiding that part of a shave, for as delighted as I am by the sound of the scraping of the blade against my skin, some doubt never fails to creep into the mustache stage. It's a dismount, match point. *Can I close this out? Is this going to be the shave the mustache doesn't survive?* I have dreamed that I've lost it, that it just leapt off my face and I chased it around my house. Destroying it is always possible, but you're more likely just to turn it into something else, something you would be terrified to wear. Mine is actually a pre-emption. I go with the Denzel Washington in *Philadelphia* because I don't trust that I have the hands for the Denzel of *Devil in a Blue Dress.*

This is also to say that, for the righteous and wayward alike, the process entails a disturbance of the line between vanity and knowledge of self. In 2018, Martin Luther King Jr.'s former barber, Nelson Malden, spoke to Alabama Public Radio about grooming

King: "He was more concerned about his mustache than his haircut. He always liked his mustache to be up off the lip, like a butterfly. He would tell me, 'Make it like a butterfly this time.'"

It's grueling work, the business of becoming a butterfly. Long, ugly periods of churn and slog. But then you have this light, fluttering thing. It might have seemed inadequate—or incongruous, at least—for King to grip the sides of a lectern to tell congregants that they were all striving to bring the nation closer to embodying the hair beneath his nose. But when you know that he thought of his look as bespeaking a kind of weightlessness, you could also surmise that he knew the price of such flight might be life itself. He was trying to align the country with that mustache. We're not there yet. But we're working on it.

Make it like a butterfly next time.

BETH NGUYEN

Apparent

FROM *The Paris Review*

WHEN MY FIRST child was a year old, I took him to Boston to meet my mother. She didn't show up. It turned out that she had gone to Foxwoods Casino instead, which sounds bad and maybe was, but it had been three years since I'd seen her or even spoken to her; we wouldn't see each other for seven more. I couldn't blame her for trying her luck elsewhere.

"Birth mother" doesn't seem the right term for her and neither does "biological mother," which implies an adoption story. "Real mother" forgets my stepmother, who has been in my life since I was three. I never know how to refer to the woman who gave birth to me, who was my first mother, who did not leave me but was left by me. Sometimes I say "Boston mother," deflecting any sense of claim onto geography even though she ended up there not by choice, exactly, but by resettlement efforts years after the end of the war in Viet Nam.

This is a story I keep having to tell because I'm trying to understand it. Because there is no getting away from our origin stories.

What I tell people is that my family left Saigon the day before its fall, on April 29, 1975. What I don't always say is that *family* meant my dad, uncles, grandmother, older sister, and me. We left because my father and uncles had been in the South Vietnamese military and the end of the war meant reeducation camps or worse. We left because we had a chance. We had motorcycles that took us to a boat on the river that went out to the sea, to a US Navy ship that took us to the Philippines, where airplanes took us to Guam and then Arkansas and then Michigan. Three refugee camps in all.

What I don't usually say is that my mother stayed behind in Viet Nam. Or was left behind in Viet Nam. I don't know the truth, or if there is such a thing. I can't frame what happened as a decision or a choice. It was wartime, and half my family became refugees and half did not.

In 1975 I was a baby; what happened was not my conscious experience. My memories, instead, are of growing up in Michigan, with a strong grandmother and a strong stepmother. The summers were short and the winters went on and on. Icicles lengthened from the eaves and fell like daggers into the snow. My sister and I knew the vague story about our mother in Viet Nam, but ours was a family that preferred silence over questions, especially when there were no simple answers. We lived in a mostly white community that wasn't happy about a sudden influx of Vietnamese refugees, and our mode of safety was silence. No one talked about the war. It was better to look forward, not back. It was better not to ask and not to know.

Sometime in the eighties, when my sister and I were in elementary school, our mother in Viet Nam became our mother in Boston. My father told us that she had written him a letter to say that she had come to America with her two older children. I remember how surprised I was—at her existence being mentioned, at her having other kids. At the same time, I felt relieved. It helped to think of her as being less alone in Viet Nam. Less abandoned, because she had a whole other life. My sister and I saw the envelope—I remember the neat, script-like handwriting of the return address, Swarthmore, Pennsylvania—but we never saw the letter, which must have been in Vietnamese, a language neither of us could read. I feel like I should know the exact moment that my father told us this news, bringing to light a subject that was supposed to be in permanent shadow, but I don't. It just happened that one day my mother was no longer a distant someone in a country I didn't know much about, but a real person in this country that we now shared.

My father said that she'd been able to come to the United States because her son was, as people said back then, "Amerasian"; his father had been a white American soldier. What had happened to that guy or who he was, no one knew or would say. But because of this status my mother, her teenage son, and her twenty-year-old daughter had arrived in Pennsylvania, where their sponsoring organization was based, and then moved to Boston, where they stayed.

My father and stepmother thought it best that my sister and I wait until we were older to meet our mother, because it was all just too complicated and confusing. My sister and I did not object; again, we did not ask questions or wonder aloud why we were getting this information. Even then I understood that my father could just as easily have not said anything at all. So my sister and I waited, and didn't mind the waiting. We didn't know our mother so we didn't know what it was, really, to miss her. Sometimes I think we knew that whatever we would learn or gain would alter us, and maybe we didn't want that just yet. It was troublesome enough being Vietnamese in our conservative white town. There was already so much to conceal from our white friends, so many ways to pretend that we were just like them.

Or maybe we knew that it wouldn't alter us. That we would go on as we were no matter what.

I met my mother the summer after my second year of college. I'd had a chance the summer before, when my sister, father, and stepmother traveled to Boston, but I used my receptionist job as an excuse not to go. I was afraid to face her, afraid to let anyone else see me facing her. I might have kept putting it off if I hadn't agreed to attend a friend's wedding in Boston.

My father was the one who arranged for my mother to meet me outside the suburban hotel where I was staying. The first thing she said to me was You are so late. She had brought her daughter, her daughter's husband, and their two little kids—my niece and nephew. We piled into their maroon Plymouth Sundance, which looked just like the ones from driver's ed in high school. My mother and I were dropped off in Chinatown, where we walked around for an hour, browsing the shops. I pretended to admire all the jade and gold jewelry. We talked about school, and about the construction going on in Boston. I learned that my father and stepmother had been in communication with her over the years, sending money. I tried to ask a couple of questions about Viet Nam, my birth, my sister's birth, but my mother brushed them away. *That was so long ago* was her stance then, and it is still. We kept walking. Anyone who saw us might have assumed we were mother and daughter. We were the same size, the same height. I realized I'd never thought about that possibility, that I could see something in her that was something of me, and that she could do the same. I found myself looking anywhere else—the street signs, the way all the other women seemed to be carrying plastic bags with the handles tied so tight they would have to be cut. I couldn't wait to get back to the hotel, to go to a wedding filled with people I didn't know. My mother insisted on buying me a Buddha-shaped mooncake and I didn't tell her that I have always hated the heavy sweetness of mooncakes. I pretended to save it for later, then threw it away when I was alone.

In real life, when I tell people about my Boston mother—only when needed, when an explanation seems required—I say that she and I are not close, which is true. It is hard to describe how this has happened. It is hard to describe but, I see now, easy to experience: how distance creates distance. We saw each other, we said goodbye, we went back to our regularly scheduled lives. It was not dramatic. It was simple. Once you are gone, it gets easier to stay gone.

Over the course of my American life I have spent less than twenty-four hours with my mother. We have never spent more than an hour or two together at a time. If I see her it's only because I'm in Boston for some other reason and I'll call my father so he can call her to arrange a visit. I need his easy Vietnamese to figure things out, to decide the time when I must show up at her apartment. And then she and I just sit there, maybe drink some tea, maybe talk about her pet cockatiels. I ask her questions she won't really answer.

Once, after a visit, I walked with her to the paper factory where she worked regular shifts, doing something with envelopes and sealant. I remember leaving her there and walking away—but to where? Where was I going, and why? I remember thinking about paper, about envelopes, and thinking it was too obvious. I had once held the envelope containing the letter my mother had sent my father all those years ago. Swarthmore, Pennsylvania. I had taken note of her handwriting, the blue ink. But not of the letter itself. That was gone, and who can say when or how such artifacts slip away and disappear, lost in the shuffle of our lives.

The paper factory went out of business ten years later, undone by the paperless revolution. My mother does not have email or a computer. She has a cell phone but the number I have for her is a landline. I wrote it down on a piece of paper that I keep in my desk. Once, I called and no one answered. Once, I called and she said she was on her way out to the market and then to the casino in Connecticut. I could try tomorrow, she said. I didn't.

In the first years of my children's lives I was awake so often at two and three and four in the morning, hours I had always felt were the most sorrowful. We were living in Chicago, on the seventh floor of a thirty-story building, and sometimes at three in the morning I would look out at the other buildings nearby, counting the lit-up windows. I would decide that within each of those windows was another mother, nursing or cleaning or somehow taking care, and that we all shared a silent connection through our various windows, our various lights.

To be a mother is to form a new understanding of time. It is to form a new relationship with all that you know about your body and its spaces. It is not quite a do-over of your own childhood, but close enough.

I have always hated being up at the hour of the street sweepers. I have never cared to hear the earliest birds start their songs. I don't want to see the sky turning toward day. Being a mother has meant learning time as a function of someone else's needs. When my babies slept next to me they would turn to me, to my body, for milk. I would wake up just enough to be aware, enough to stay afloat in a near dream state. Often, I didn't even open my eyes. I knew my children by heart. The normal measures of time—traffic, sunrise—seemed an affront, a demand to return to the outside world where who you are might be someone else entirely.

And sometimes in that half-awake state I would try to imagine the weeks after the fall of Saigon, my mother traveling across the city, from her own mother's house, to see us—my sister and me, her two youngest children. Looking up for someone at an open window. Maybe she knew before she got there that the house would be empty. A neighbor told her that my father had left word: we were going to try for America. For a long time, that's all she knew. I have no idea when she heard from my father next. One day my mother had four children in Saigon and the next day two of them were gone.

*

When I took my kids to meet my Boston mother, my older son had just turned eight and my younger son would soon turn six. Once again I planned the trip through my father, who called my Boston mother and let her know that we would be visiting. I booked a hotel near the Public Garden, thinking my kids would enjoy the swan boats, but didn't tell them why we were there. To them it was just a jaunt from New York, where we'd been staying before one of my teaching gigs.

On the morning of the visit my kids and I walked through the rain to the nearest T stop. We didn't have umbrellas. We hurried down the steps, purchased our fares, then lingered by the map, watching trains come and go. We were on the Green Line, the oldest subway in America, and my kids were fascinated, as I had been years ago on my first trip to this city, at the streetcars skidding along the embedded tracks. My children were delighted by the old-fashionedness, how people had to climb up into the cars rather than board from a platform. Quickly they memorized the system—which train letters corresponded with which destinations—because that's what they liked to do. We often took train and subway rides for fun, with no real destination.

I had been putting off telling them where we were going in case she canceled, though I also knew that if she were to cancel, I wouldn't know; she simply wouldn't be home. At Park Street we changed to the Red Line and I pointed out the Porter Square stop on the subway map. That's where we're going, I said. When they asked why, I told them, Because we're going to visit my mother—your other grandmother.

Oh, Michigan grandma is here? my older son asked. That's what he and his brother, of their own devising, have always called my stepmother. They have a Michigan grandma and a Michigan grandpa, a DC grandma and a DC grandpa. Sometimes geography makes more sense than the abstraction of family lineage.

Not Michigan grandma, I said. Your other grandma, the one you haven't met yet. My mother.

You have another mother? he asked. As the older child, he often ends up speaking for both of them.

They knew the story of how my family had left Viet Nam as refugees, but I'd always avoided the part about my mother staying behind. I guess I thought it was too traumatic for them to handle; in hindsight, I wonder if I was just replicating the silence I'd been taught.

My older son looked at me with thoughtful curiosity in his eyes —the same look I'd seen since his baby days. The child who would study every person in a room. Assessing, wondering. Often worrying.

So, he said, we have another grandmother?

Yes, I said.

It was midmorning on a Saturday in June, and the outbound Alewife train was mostly empty. The man sitting near us was clearly listening, with great interest, to everything I was saying to my children. I couldn't blame him.

My younger son, who is less of a worrier than his brother, smiled and said, We're going to visit Boston grandma!

Yes, I said, hoping I sounded enthusiastic.

Oh, okay, my older son said, the way he does when he asks what's for dinner and I answer. Like, sounds good, no big deal.

My children looked out at the grayness of the day and the grayness of the Charles River—they love it when trains cross bridges —and we didn't say much more until we pulled into the station. I met the eye of the man who'd been listening to our conversation and he nodded a little, which I interpreted as good luck.

From the station we took a Lyft to the complex where my Boston mother has lived since the eighties. Over the years she has moved from one apartment to another without ever really leaving the place. It was still raining when my kids and I walked toward what I thought was the correct building. They all looked the same —brick, surrounded by parking spots. No one else was outside. We huddled under an awning while I checked my phone to make sure I had the right address, then walked to the next building, which was also wrong. Finally I called my mother's number.

Where are you? she said. Supposed to be here by now.

We're here, I said, but I can't find the right building.

She tried to give me directions but soon the kids and I were standing in the middle of a parking lot.

Then I saw her: she had a fuchsia umbrella and was waving to us from a curb near the farthest apartment building. She had come out to find us.

Hiiii, she called to my kids, give Grandma a hug! She held her arms open and they went into them, hugging her as if they already knew her.

She had the same delicate frame, the same thin skin around her eyes, that I had kept in my mind from the first time I saw her all those years ago. It was hot and we had walked around Chinatown slowly, turning to pass the same stores. Now she wore a houndstooth coat and satiny heels and a jade-and-gold necklace and the kind of flowy pants that I associate with all Vietnamese women of a certain age, that I sometimes think of as waiting for me too.

My sister says that our relationship with our Boston mother only goes one way. We're the ones who have to visit, who have to call, who have to do everything, she says. If we don't, then we'll never hear from her.

This is true. And yet.

We are the ones who left her. Even if it wasn't our choice. We left; we are the leavers. And we don't even regret it because we are glad to have grown up in America because that is what we know.

I say to my sister: Maybe we are the ones who must make amends. In truth, I'm not even sure what I mean by this. Maybe what I'm trying to say is that we are the lucky ones, and with luck comes responsibility.

What I don't say to my sister: Maybe because we know we can never correct the absence that defines our shared past, that pictures and money don't ease the fact of such absence—maybe that's why we keep leaving. Why I keep leaving. I have gotten so used to that feeling of being gone that I can hardly imagine returning.

It was easier when we didn't know the truth.

It was easier when we didn't ask questions.

In America my mother has always lived in small one-bedroom apartments. The window blinds are drawn and partly broken; the altar for Buddha and the ancestors gets central space in the living room; there are piles, everywhere, of what my mother would call things she needs where she needs them to be. Here, she had spread a blanket on the floor in front of the altar and covered it with an assortment I couldn't figure out: stacks of paper napkins printed with casino logos, boxes of tea, tin buckets and mixing bowls, mini water bottles, hairbrushes and toiletries, a plastic bag filled with other plastic bags, a large scale.

Before I could think to ask about this, my older son did: What is all this for?

For this and for that, she said.

This is how she has always answered questions, and I remembered how when I first met her I asked her to tell me the story of how she met my father and she said, Oh, who can remember.

Now that my kids had finally met my mother and we were in her apartment, I didn't know what to do next. I'd brought her a gift bag, filled with tea and sweets and some money, and she set it aside without opening it. She seemed in no hurry to do anything besides sit on her pink sofa, so my kids and I sat down too. When I asked what she usually did with her days she said, This. We sit here, we relax. She smiled at her boyfriend, who was texting on his phone.

Did I mention her boyfriend? In truth, I'd forgotten about him. As my mother explained it, he was Chinese and spoke very little English and no Vietnamese, and she was Vietnamese and spoke decent English but no Chinese. Over the years, she had learned enough Mandarin to communicate with him.

Has he learned Vietnamese, or more English? I asked her. She laughed.

I asked how long they'd been together and she said more than ten years. Actually, she said, we're married. He's my husband.

Oh, I said. When did you get married?

Years ago. I never told your daddy, I don't know why.

My mother was eager to give my kids bottles of mango juice, which they happily accepted. We continued to sit on the pink sofa. We took pictures of each other. I peeked into the small kitchen—more piles of things—but didn't go in. My mother kept asking my kids if they wanted something to eat but didn't say what she had. My kids were far more interested in the piles in front of the altar—the paper napkins, the scale. To amuse themselves, they started weighing various items around them.

I tried to make conversation with my mother. I asked questions I'd asked before. Do you remember anything about the day I was born, or when my sister was born? Not really.

Are you going to visit Viet Nam again soon? She'd spent months there last year and would probably go again in the winter. What's Viet Nam like now and what was it like back then? Oh, so very different. I asked about my half brother; I asked about my half sister and her kids. Where were they? What were they doing? I had all this family that didn't seem like mine, stretched out across Boston, across the United States, across the world to Viet Nam.

We talked about the pictures of her parents on the altar. Along with fruit and incense, candles and fake flowers, there were mini bottles of whiskey and champagne glasses filled with dusty Life Savers.

She lived a long time, my mother said of her own mother. Age ninety-something. You remember her?

I did. I had met her once, fifteen years ago when I visited Viet Nam, the one and only time I've been there since leaving as a refugee baby. I met my maternal grandmother in her home in Saigon. I can still see her teeth stained from betel nut, a light shawl draped around her shoulders even though it was the hot season. We sat on a cushionless wooden sofa. An oscillating fan turned toward me and I thought about counting how many times it would in five minutes, ten. My Vietnamese wasn't strong enough to ask questions and my grandmother's English wasn't strong enough to answer so we smiled and stared at each other over cups of tea. I didn't stay there long. We didn't know each other at all, and never would.

My mother was getting agitated by my kids' efforts to weigh whatever objects they could find, so they stopped and wandered into her bedroom, where plastic storage boxes were filled with shoes and makeup and an open closet revealed a tight row of dresses and jackets. The bed was layered with clothes. I wondered if I had gotten my own messy, keep-everything tendencies from her, or if this was a consequence of refugee, immigrant life: having as much as possible nearby, just in case.

My mother shooed the children out of her room and they went back to the pink sofa. There wasn't much else to do. We'd been there less than an hour but it was clear the visit was over. The boyfriend, now husband, stood up. My mother asked my kids if they wanted to take more mango juice with them.

Bye-bye, my mother said to my kids when they had put on their shoes. She gave them another hug and they gave her another hug. Bye, they said. Everyone was smiling. She patted their heads and said they were good boys, handsome boys, and told me to send pictures in the mail. Sure, I said, though I was also pretty sure I wouldn't get around to it because I never had.

When my sister and I were twelve and ten we sent school pictures of ourselves to our mother. We put them in a greeting card, our response to the letter she had sent our father. We were excited at first but within a couple of weeks we forgot to keep checking the mailbox. Soon, we forgot to think about a reply at all. As far as I knew she never wrote to us, and we never wrote her again. But I recognized those pictures—me in a striped dress I had loved, my tortoiseshell glasses crooked on my face; my sister with too much hairspray in her bangs—among pictures of her other children, all of us in a basket near her front door.

Byyyye, my kids said again. They waved. My mother and her husband waved back. My kids and I left the building and stood outside waiting for a Lyft to take us back to the subway station.

My kids were in a good mood, happy to get back on a train. They seemed to have simply accepted the fact of another grandmother and now their attention was on what was next: lunch, more transportation. They did not know what I was thinking, which is that I am always leaving my mother.

When my children were eight months old, the age I was when I left Viet Nam, I would try to imagine them disappearing, bound for another country, a different life. It felt impossible only because it felt unbearable. Unbearable to think of my children having no memory, no imprint of me.

Is it better, is it lucky, even, that my sister and I were too young for memory, too young for the imprint of imagery? We might have left in fear, we might have cried, but we keep no memory of this. We have vague anxieties, nightmares, but we don't have the active pain our mother must have had, must have still, even if she will never speak of it.

I've never seen my mother show strong emotion. She is no-nonsense; she is a wave of the hand—*Eh, who can remember how things were?* She is not one to tell stories. She will resist the very idea of a narrative. Maybe because this is a story that no one would want. But I suppose we just don't get to choose. We must contend. I am trying to contend. If my childhood was all about silence then my parenting, my now, is all about questions.

Here's what happened that time in Boston when my only son was a year old and my mother didn't show up to meet him: her daughter, my half sister, showed up instead. She explained about the casino. The way she spoke, it sounded like a necessity, a fact of life. She had to go to Foxwoods, you see. Then she gave me an envelope—a gift from all of us, she said. I knew it was money. We're Vietnamese; there was a new baby; that meant money in an envelope. I didn't want to accept but even as I protested, I knew I had no choice.

My half sister stayed only a few minutes. She admired the baby. She said she was in a hurry because of parking.

After she left I looked at the envelope in my hand. Inside was one hundred dollars.

I'm not sure I ever expected my mother to show up. I wasn't hurt, wasn't surprised. If I ever feel bitterness toward her, it is so fleeting that it leaves only a slight impression, an almost-ness that doesn't take shape. Always I think: I have no right to want anything or expect anything from her.

After all, my mother didn't know me. Why would she need to know my children? She had children and grandchildren already. They were her actual life, the daily being together around a table, eating and laughing and watching the same television. These became the memories of how her family has lived out, is living out, its life. I'm not there. My sister isn't there. My children aren't there. We aren't in their thoughts and they aren't in ours. It's the people who are there, in front of you, who get to be your actual life.

Mothers aren't supposed to take up so much space. They're supposed to do the work—quietly, efficiently, and behind the scenes—and then get out of the way. Mothers are dismissed and disdained; they are helpers and helpmeets. This is the clear message I have always seen and now get to experience. I feel it most when I have the urge to tell someone I'm not just a mother and then realize what I have internalized in even thinking that phrase, *just a mother.*

One day at my kids' school I had to identify myself and instead of saying, I'm a mother, I said, I'm a parent. I don't remember the circumstances or why this needed to be stated, but as I spoke I saw the words in front of me: *I'm apparent.* I had become, in parenthood, apparent to myself in a way that I was not before—in a way so deep, so intense, I know I will spend the rest of my years turning it over in my mind, trying to understand it. Instead of slipping into the background, being the coordinator of all things who then hurries out of view, I was the opposite: I was present; I was here. I was being seen—at least by me.

If I don't make the effort to see my mother in Boston, we will never see each other again. We aren't estranged, just separate. But I now know the strange secret of this kind of separation: absence gets easier, not harder.

And if nothing happens, who will care? My sister tells me that I'm the only one who cares. She thinks I am making this circumstance of life more difficult than it is. That sometimes families are made rather than given.

Perhaps it's true that I am bothered by the narrative mess and messiness of my family's story, which, like all family stories, can never have a resolution. I see myself trying to fix the messiness through my own mothering, right down to chaperoning field trips and sewing tae kwon do badges. The concreteness of mothering, I think, surely will affix me to their lives and memories. Because a foundational truth of parenthood is that you raise children for the rest of *their* lives. Not for yourself. The point of raising children is to let them leave. To help them leave. Because they will; they must.

I think about how so much of my life harks back to a time that I can't remember and didn't choose: that time I left my mother in Viet Nam and then didn't know or see her until I was twenty years old. There is no returning, no repairing. Every mother knows that because motherhood is all about time, about waiting and watching. *The days are long but the years are short,* people keep saying to me. Complete strangers on playgrounds, on public transportation. Only other parents would say such a thing. My relationship with my children is also my relationship with time, with the concept of motherhood, with the mothers I have known, with the mother I have never known. It is a catch in the throat. It is the edge of tears. It is the wanting to be here, in this moment, so that I will stay in my children's minds. We cannot control what our children will remember, what they won't. We are always hedging our bets against the future.

Before I go to sleep, I check on my children. This is a universal thing that parents do. Sometimes it is very late, and I do that thing of standing in the doorway or sitting on the edge of the bed to watch the children sleep. What are we doing when we do this? We're checking to make sure they're literally alive, for one thing. We're checking to make sure they're not sleeping half on the floor, because we know they sometimes contort themselves in their sleep. We're checking to make sure they've got their blankets and pillows and stuffies. We're making sure that they are safe as we understand the idea of safe, which is to say within reach of us. Sometimes all I want is this: to be in the same room, at the same time, together. A brief thing I can know as true. At such times, in darkness, I can't help thinking about how far our bodies have traveled, keep traveling, will travel. What we go through to get here, to remain. Sometimes I feel like I'm just shoring up these moments of being a mother. Like insurance, because to be a mother is to be in a permanent state of fear of loss. So I want them to know I was there. Here. I never wanted to leave. I will stay as long as they let me.

FINTAN O'TOOLE

The Designated Mourner

FROM *The New York Review of Books*

MOURNING BECOMES JOE Biden. "I have found over the years," he writes in his recent best-selling memoir *Promise Me, Dad,* "that, although it brought back my own vivid memories of sad times, my presence almost always brought some solace to people who have suffered sudden and unexpected loss . . . When I talk to people in mourning, they know I speak from experience." The most moving thing in that book is not even Biden's restrained and heartbreaking account of the slow death of his beloved son Beau. It is the two brief appearances of Wei Tang Liu, whose son, Wenjian Liu, was one of two police officers murdered in New York City on the Saturday before Christmas 2014. Biden visited the family home in Brooklyn to pay his respects.

The father, an immigrant from China, had little English, but Biden picked up on his need for physical intimacy, for the consolation of touch: "Occasionally he would lean into me so that his shoulder touched my arm . . . I did not pull away, but leaned in so that he could feel me there." When Biden finally made to leave, Liu walked outside with him and embraced him in front of the line of policemen standing watch. "He held on to me tightly, for a long time, as if he could not bear to let me go." Five months later, when Beau was dead, Biden was leaving the public wake at St. Anthony's church in his hometown of Wilmington, Delaware. He saw, in the long line of mourners, Wei Tang Liu. Neither man spoke to the other: "He just walked up and gave me a hug. It meant so much to me to be in the embrace of somebody who understood. He held on to me, silently, and wouldn't let go."

Joe Biden is the most gothic figure in American politics. He is haunted by death, not just by the private tragedies his family has endured, but by a larger and more public sense of loss. Richard Ben Cramer, in his classic account of the 1988 presidential primaries, *What It Takes,* wrote how even then it was a journalistic cliché to define Biden by the terrible car crash that killed his first wife, Neilia, and their daughter, Naomi (and injured Beau and his brother, Hunter), in 1972, shortly after Biden was elected to the Senate at the age of twenty-nine. Cramer refers to the "type that fell out of the machine every time they used Biden's name: '. . . whose life was touched by personal tragedy . . .' Joe Biden (D-Del., T.B.P.T.)."

Even now, as Hunter Biden's name is threaded through Donald Trump's impeachment hearings, there is a ghost behind it: Hunter is Neilia's maiden name. Trump's preoccupation with Hunter's presence on the board of the Ukrainian energy company Burisma hinges on a reality that is certainly worthy of scrutiny: Joe Biden was, as he recounts in some detail in *Promise Me, Dad,* deeply involved in the Obama administration's relations with Ukraine, and it seems implausible that Hunter's position with Burisma was merely coincidental. But the frenzied inflation of this story, like so much that involves the Bidens, is freighted with both dread and grief. The dread is Trump's (arguably misplaced) fear of Biden as a competitor for the presidency in 2020, an anxiety that became a manic fixation that has led to his impeachment. The grief drives Biden's fierce need to protect his living son, not just for himself, but for Hunter's dead mother and brother.

Yet even if those horrible losses had not befallen his family, Biden would have a very public relationship to the dead. He is haunted by the murdered Kennedys. In his campaign speeches he has evoked the image of himself and his sister, Valerie, weeping openly as Robert Kennedy's funeral train passed by. For the first decades of his political career, his pitch was essentially that these dead men could rise again through him. The speech that first made people talk of Biden as a potential presidential candidate was at the New Jersey Democratic Convention in Atlantic City in 1983, when he brought the house down with his evocation of the slain: "Just because our political heroes were murdered does not mean that the dream does not still live, buried deep in our broken hearts." Biden recalled in his 2007 memoir, *Promises to Keep,* "I remember the feeling in the room when I delivered that line; its effect on the crowd washed back at me as a physical sensation. I could see people in the audience crying." He also realized that in channeling the dead, he allowed each listener to "fill in my words with his or her own meanings . . . After all, each person has a little something different buried in a broken heart."

Here was Biden the consoler and at the same time the ambitious politician, for what he really meant was that the Kennedys lived on in him. Biden's biographer Jules Witcover writes of Biden in 1987, early in his campaign for the Democratic primaries, "Casting himself as the next young and rising John F. Kennedy, Irish Catholic Biden told the cheering Iowa Democratic faithful . . . 'I think 1988 is going to be about 1960.'"[1] That, of course, was the year of JFK's coming. Biden even repeated exactly JFK's slogan, "Let's get America moving again." The ghost of the other dead Kennedy hovered around him too. Of the campaign managers who were trying to shape a grand story for Biden in 1988, Cramer writes:

> It wasn't that they wanted to make Joe into Robert Kennedy . . . it just happened that Robert Kennedy was important . . . to the *time,* to a whole generation. And *that was the message:* that a whole generation was lost, submerged, driven off from the struggle for a better world, twenty years ago, in '68, bloody '68, the Year of the Locust, and the Tet Offensive, the Chicago Convention, and Richard Nixon, and the murders of Martin Luther King and . . . Bobby KENNEDY! That was the whole fucking point! . . . That a whole generation had to come back now, that they had to wake up!

There is something eerie in this notion. Biden becomes not just the reembodiment of the dead Kennedys but a kind of political necromancer, calling forth an entire generation that has been wandering in a civic Hades, lost to the world of democratic engagement. He also becomes the man who can imaginatively reverse time, who can take us all back to 1960, back to the beginning of the story so that it can be told again without the blood-soaked pages.

The most important question, though, is what gave Biden the right to make this vast claim? It was not the authority of experience—*I was there by the side of our murdered hero.* In the two great mass movements of the 1960s, the campaigns against the Vietnam War and for civil rights, Joe Biden was conspicuously not there.

There were large protests against the war in Wilmington—he does not seem to have attended any. College deferments saved him from any danger of being drafted for Vietnam.

In 1968 and 1969 Wilmington was placed under military occupation by the Delaware National Guard for fully nine months after riots following King's assassination. In *Promises to Keep,* Biden recalls passing "six-foot-tall uniformed white soldiers carrying rifles" on his way to work at a law office every day. He acknowledges that, in the Black neighborhoods of East Wilmington, these white soldiers were "prowling" the streets and that "mothers were terrified that their children would make one bad mistake and end up dead." But he then folds their terror into an anecdote about how he got to know Black people for the first time while working as a lifeguard in a Black district six years earlier. The extraordinary political event—an American city under military occupation—becomes an intimate tale of awakening sympathy.

This lack of personal involvement in the struggle did not stop Biden, when he was seeking national office, from inventing a civil rights past for himself. Cramer reported on his rhetoric in the primaries in 1988: "Joe was off on his life . . . how he started in the civil rights movement . . . *remember? . . . The marches? Remember how that felt?* . . . And they're nodding in the crowd, and he's got them, sure." Even when his handlers warned him to stop saying this because it was not true, he couldn't help himself: "Folks, when I started in public life, in the civil rights movement, we marched to change attitudes." The plain fact, as Witcover notes, is that "he avoided street protest or anything else that smacked of civil disobedience." He was a concerned observer of, not a participant in, the great dramas of the 1960s.

So how could Biden imagine himself as the reincarnation of the Kennedys? Those two words: Irish Catholic. His claim to that legacy is not experiential or particularly ideological. It is ethnic and religious. The Kennedys defined an Irish American Catholic political identity—white (even in their case conspicuously privileged), yet by virtue of the grimness of Irish history and the outsider status of Catholics, supposedly not guilty of the grave crimes of racial oppression. Its promise was to act as the bridge across the great divide of US society, being mainstream enough to connect to the white majority but with a sufficient memory of past torment to connect also to the Black minority. Its underlying appeal was to the very thing that Biden would come to embody—"a sense of the depth of their pain" rooted in "vivid memories of sad times." This is what Biden chose when he defined himself as he has throughout his public career: "I see myself as an Irish Catholic."[2]

And this was indeed a choice. Biden is not an Irish name—he recalled in *Promises to Keep* his Irish American aunt, Gertie Blewitt, telling him: "Your father's not a bad man. He's just English." Nor is his middle name, Robinette. The Robinettes, his paternal grandmother's kin, traced their ancestry in America to a tract of land near Media, Pennsylvania, originally granted by William Penn. So Biden could have presented himself, had he chosen, as an all-American boy. Instead he identified with his mother's ethnic ancestry, making himself, as he puts it in *Promise Me, Dad,* a "descendant of the Blewitts of County Mayo . . . and the Finnegans of County Louth, on a volatile little inlet of the Irish Sea." Part of the attraction was undoubtedly the devout Catholicism that has been Biden's great consolation. But another part was the great escape from American history and its burdens of guilt. Biden recalled the same aunt telling him about the notorious British irregulars sent to put down the Irish nationalist revolt in 1920:

> I'd go upstairs and lie on the bed and she'd come and scratch my back and say, "Now you remember Joey about the Black and Tans don't you?" She had never seen the Black and Tans, she had no notion of them, but she could recite chapter and verse about them. Obviously there were immigrants coming in who were able to talk about it and who had relatives back there. She was born in 1887. After she'd finish telling the stories I'd sit there or lie in bed and think at the slightest noise, "They're coming up the stairs."[3]

This is a fine description of vicarious oppression. Biden grew up in relatively prosperous middle-class American comfort and went to Archmere, a privileged fee-paying Catholic high school in Wilmington. Even as a national politician, he seems to have been largely shielded from anti-Catholic venom. But one of the advantages of being an Irish American Catholic is that you can attach yourself to a history of oppression in Ireland and release yourself from white guilt in America. Your forefathers are sinned against, not sinning. As Biden put it in 1974, defending his opposition to busing in Wilmington, "I feel responsible for what the situation is today, for the sins of my own generation. And I'll be damned if I feel responsible for what happened three hundred years ago." By "what happened" it is clear that he meant slavery. How could the Irish be responsible for that?

Above all, though, being Irish Catholic created the possibility of reincarnating the Kennedys. Biden's desire was there from his coming of age. He told Neilia that he would be a senator by the time he was thirty and then president of the United States. He achieved the first through sheer chutzpah, taking on the incumbent Republican, Cale Boggs, who had won seven straight elections and had held state and federal office for twenty-six years. Biden got the nomination because no serious Democrat even wanted to run against Boggs. But the Kennedy magic worked. And it is clear that Biden thought it might work all the way. Cramer reported on Biden's fantasy project in the 1980s to buy a seventeen-acre plot and have his extended family all together in different houses:

> Joe and Jill and the kids would take the big one, and then a guest house . . . it was a compound, it was . . . *Hyannis Port!* He could see the goddam thing in *Life* magazine, he could just about lay out the photos *right now* . . . The Bidens. First Family.

And like the Kennedys, this First Family was to be dynastic. As Biden wrote in *Promise Me, Dad,* "I was pretty sure Beau could run for president some day and, with his brother's help, he could win." The reader is invited to imagine, through the evocation of the brotherly bond, that Hunter might then succeed Beau. The Irish Catholic dynasty of which the United States was robbed by the murders of the Kennedys in the 1960s would return in the 1980s and last, perhaps, for decades.

But in gothic stories, dreams of the dead shade into nightmare. On the political level, the second part of the Biden plan—becoming president—has made him a revenant. Cramer, writing about Biden's discussion of a run for the 1988 primaries, describes Jill Biden wondering, "What if Joe did break out and made a run for the finish, and came in . . . just short. Then they'd run again . . . and again. That was her nightmare: that he'd run, come close, and then it would never stop." Her nightmare became real. Biden filled out papers for the New Hampshire primary of 1984, ran for the 1988 nomination, ran again for 2008, and is running yet again for 2020.

*

A major problem here is that Irish Catholicism, youth, and good looks were never enough to make Biden the heir to RFK. To return to that speech in Atlantic City in 1983, in which Biden invoked the murdered heroes, its appeal to unity is vastly blander than Kennedy's insurgent effort to forge a real unity of purpose between the Black and white working classes. Biden, like RFK, positioned himself as a figure who could transcend class, race, gender, and party, but this time in the name not of radical change but of a mere rhetorical figment. He urged Democrats to campaign "not as blacks or as whites; not as workers or professionals; not as rich or poor; not as men or women, not even as Democrats or Republicans. But as people of God in the service of the American dream." The utter vacuity of the last sentence points not to a transcendence of divisions but to mere evasion of all questions of power, privilege, and systematic oppression.

There is something almost too ghoulishly spectral—more Halloween than haunting—in the way Biden's most promising presidential bid, his first, was derailed by Robert Kennedy. Biden got into trouble when it was revealed that he had effectively plagiarized a speech by the then leader of the Labour Party in Britain, Neil Kinnock. But he might have weathered the storm, since he had actually credited Kinnock several times previously in using the same material. What destroyed him was the unearthing of an earlier speech in which he echoed, word for word but without attribution, a long passage in which RFK had attacked the idea of the "bottom line": "That bottom line can tell us everything about our lives . . . except that which makes life worthwhile." Adam Walinsky, who wrote the original speech, accused Biden of a "counterfeit of emotion." Instead of being a reincarnation, Biden appeared as a grave robber.

Yet the one Kennedy trait no one can accuse Biden of faking is tragedy. And within this tragedy, there is the other side of the Irish Catholic dream. The shadowy twin of the striving for success is an almost Greek sense of the capriciousness of fate. The Kennedys' dazzling success comes with a terrible toll of death. Biden, cruelly, endured the pain without ever quite matching the glamour of the ascent. He wears his dead son's rosary beads around his wrist and says that litany of prayers in his dark moments. It culminates in a great cry of despair directed to the mother of the crucified Christ:

"To thee do we cry, poor banished children of Eve. To thee do we send up our sighs, mourning and weeping in this valley of tears." Biden has had to live much of the time in the valley of tears, and in this long sojourn his Irishness is about something more than vicarious oppression. It is a way of framing sorrow.

In *Promise Me, Dad,* Biden quotes one of the grand figures of Irish American politics, Daniel Patrick Moynihan: "To fail to understand that life is going to knock you down is to fail to understand the Irishness of life." So while an African American choral group was chosen to play "joyful music" at Beau's memorial service, Biden notes that there were also "bagpipers to add the mournful, plaintive wail of Irishness." In his address at the service, Barack Obama quoted a line from a song by the Irish poet Patrick Kavanagh, in which mourning is as inevitable as the passing of seasons: "And I said, let grief be a fallen leaf at the dawning of the day."

It scarcely matters here whether there's much truth in the notion that the Irish have a particularly familiar relationship with grief. What does matter is that the "mournful, plaintive wail of Irishness" is the soundtrack for both the Kennedy and the Biden stories, in which triumph is always shadowed by calamity. There is in this structure of feeling no easy opposition of hubris and nemesis. There is just, as Obama said to Biden when Beau was dying, the awareness that "life is so difficult to discern"—difficult because it does not offer itself in the easy forms of the wonderful and the terrible but confuses the two by conjoining them as twins. The political manifestation of this awareness is not the upbeat rhetoric of the American dream; it is a politics of empathy in which the leader shares the pain of the citizen. While Biden seems hollow when he deploys the former, he has been a forceful practitioner of the latter. "We had to speak for those who felt left behind," he writes in *Promise Me, Dad.* "They had to know we got their despair." Biden has always been better at getting despair than at giving concrete, programmatic form to hope.

With Biden, fellow feeling is literal—he feels you. He is astonishingly, overwhelmingly hands-on. He extended the backslapping of the old Irish pol into whole new areas of the body—hugging, embracing, rubbing. In his foreword to Steven Levingston's engaging account of the Biden-Obama relationship, *Barack and Joe,* Michael Eric Dyson writes of the vice president's "reinforcing his sublimely subordinate position by occasionally massaging the boss's shoulders." But Cramer noted Biden doing the same thing to an anonymous woman at a campaign stop in 1987: "Gently, but decidedly, he put his hands on her. In Council Bluffs, Iowa! He got both hands onto her shoulders, while he talked to the crowd over her head, like it was her and him, through thick and thin." So not really a gesture of submission or of domination, perhaps, but a desperate hunger to connect, to touch and be touched, to both console and be consoled. "The act of consoling," Biden writes, "had always made me feel a little better, and I was hungry to feel better."

There is something religious in this laying-on of hands. It is an act of communion. But it is also profoundly problematic—and not just for the obvious reason that, in the Me Too era, touching is too apt to raise questions of gender, power, and consent that clearly did not occur to Biden in Council Bluffs or anywhere else. It too easily depoliticizes pain. To see how this can play out in practice, consider a phone call Biden made to Anita Hill in October 1991. Clarence Thomas had been nominated to the Supreme Court by George H. W. Bush. Biden, as chair of the Senate Judiciary Committee, was in charge of the process. Hill had written, in confidence, an account of Thomas's sexual harassment of her. Biden was calling her to invite her formally to testify at a hastily arranged public hearing. Hill was worried about whether she would be protected from verbal assault and whether witnesses who came forward to express similar concerns about Thomas would also be heard. Here is Hill's account:

> "The only mistake I made, in my view, is to not realize how much pressure you were under. I should have been more aware," Senator Biden confessed over the telephone line. ". . . Aw kiddo I feel for you. I wish I weren't the chairman, I'd come to be your lawyer," he added when I told him I had not secured legal counsel. I fought the urge to respond as I furiously took notes of our conversation, hoping for some useful information. Little concrete information was forthcoming. As he closed the conversation, I could almost see him flashing his instant smile to convince both of us that the experience would be agreeable.[4]

"Aw kiddo I feel for you" is pure Biden. If he could have reached through the telephone, he would surely have massaged Hill's shoulders. There is no reason to think he was disingenuous. The problem is that he felt for Clarence Thomas too. As Witcover puts it, "Joe seemed to be trying to convince both the judge and his female adversary that he was their friend." After receiving Hill's written allegations but before she testified, Biden went to the Senate floor to say that "for this senator, there is no question with respect to the nominee's character . . . I believe there are certain things that are not an issue at all." He then failed to call the two women who could corroborate Hill's testimony, Rose Jourdain and Angela Wright, to appear before his committee. Feeling is not enough: there were great questions of gender and power and the nature of public deliberation at play in the Thomas hearings, and "aw kiddo" was a brutally inadequate answer to any of them.

This is not to deny the power or the sincerity of Biden's empathy. It is real and rooted and fundamentally decent. It has at its core the baffled humility of the human helplessness in the face of death that makes life "so difficult to discern." As an antidote to Donald Trump's grotesquely inflated "greatness," it has authentic force. It is a different, and much better, way of talking about distress, of making pain a shared thing rather than a motor of resentment. But can a politics of grief be adequate to a politics of grievance? Can it deal either with the real grievances of structural inequality or with the toxic self-pity that Trump has both fostered and embodied? Biden's essential appeal as a candidate for 2020 is that he (not least being older, male, and white) is the only one who can heal a heartbroken and divided America. But he cannot embrace voters one by one. The United States cannot be made whole again because it has never been whole. Biden's core belief is that injustice is a failure of benevolence and effort: "There is nothing inherently wrong with the system; it's up to each of us to do our part to make it work." But division is real and profound and structural—it is not just a matter of feeling. The need is not to reconcile everyone to the balance of power but to alter that balance. Consolation is not social change. Solace is not enough.

When he was vice president, Biden became fixated on the digital clock outside his official residence in the Naval Observatory in Washington. As he recalls in *Promise Me, Dad,* "Red numbers glowed, ticking away in metronomic perfection . . . This was the nation's Precise Time, which was generated less than a hundred yards away, by the US Naval Observatory Master Clock." The young Biden thought he could turn the clock back to begin again at 1960, but the Master Clock moves in one direction only, and as the decades pass they bring the realization that there will be no Precise Time for President Biden. As his limousine pulls out onto Massachusetts Avenue, he sees it in his mind's eye: "The clock was behind us in a flash, out of sight, but still marking the time as it melted away." The years melt away and the presidential dream recedes as Biden keeps striving toward it, driven by a sense of destiny that has become, over the years, less shining and more tragic. What began in bold hope is now tinged with despair—what else but the presidency could make sense of all his suffering?

But the Master Clock has moved too far forward. The Kennedys are too long dead. "Irish Catholic" no longer carries that old underdog voltage of resistance to oppression. The center of gravity of Irish American politics now gathers around Trump: Mick Mulvaney, Kellyanne Conway, Brett Kavanaugh. A politics of white resentment has drowned out the plaintive wail of common sorrow. The valley of tears has been annexed as a bastion of privileged white, male suffering. Biden, who once promised to turn back time, is an increasingly poignant embodiment of its pitilessness.

Notes

1. Jules Witcover, *Joe Biden: A Life of Trial and Redemption* (William Morrow, 2010).
2. Niall O'Dowd, "Joe Biden's Irish Roots," *Irish Central,* March 15, 2009.
3. O'Dowd, "Joe Biden's Irish Roots."
4. Anita Hill, *Speaking Truth to Power* (Doubleday, 1997), p. 156.

MAX READ

Going Postal

FROM *Bookforum*

I QUIT TWITTER and Instagram in May, in the same manner I leave parties: abruptly, silently, and much later than would have been healthy. This was several weeks into New York City's lockdown, and for those of us not employed by institutions deemed essential—hospitals, prisons, meatpacking plants—sociality was now entirely mediated by a handful of tech giants, with no meat-space escape route, and the platforms felt particularly, grimly pathetic. Instagram, cut off from a steady supply of vacations and parties and other covetable experiences, had grown unsettlingly boring, its inhabitants increasingly unkempt and wild-eyed, each one like the sole surviving astronaut from a doomed space-colonization mission, broadcasting deranged missives about yoga and cooking projects into an uncaring void. Twitter, on the other hand, felt more like a doomed space-colonization mission where everyone had survived but we had to decide who to eat. Or like a drunken 3 a.m. basement fight club, a crowd of edgy brawlers circling each other, cracking their knuckles, waiting for an excuse. Only, it didn't have any of the danger, or eroticism, or fun you might expect from a fight club.

It seemed obvious that unless you were passing around a GoFundMe link, no good could come from social platforms at that moment. The main purpose of social media is to call attention to yourself, and it was hard to think of a worse time to be doing so. It wasn't like you were going to get a job thanks to a particularly incisive quote-tweet of President Trump; in the midst of a lockdown, your chances of getting laid based on your Instagram Story thirst traps plummeted. The already paltry rewards of posting disappeared, while the risks skyrocketed. And yet: people kept on going. Founders and executives at companies with "empowerment" brands posted vague bromides about social justice to their Instagram Stories, unwittingly calling attention to systemic racism and sexism at the companies they oversaw. An editor I vaguely know posted his salary and was swiftly accused of acting like a creep to women he'd worked with; a writer at the *New York Times* took to Twitter in the middle of a fraught meeting to condescendingly castigate her peers, thereby alienating herself from her workplace to the point of resignation. A student at Brown tweeted a long, excoriating list of the scions of wealth and privilege who had matriculated alongside her, and then capped it off by revealing that her mother is the president of ExxonMobil Chemical—like an aristocrat rushing to the front of a crowd of sans-culottes, shouting, "Don't forget about *me!*"

Rather than wonder ponderously if this is "cancel culture" or whatever, we might ask ourselves: Why the fuck were all these people tweeting? What were they thinking? What were they hoping to accomplish? What was the cost-benefit analysis that led them to think continued participation in social media was a good idea? Liberal and left-wing tech critics like to suggest that we post, even against our own self-interest, thanks to nefarious software design that has been built in service of a multibillion-dollar advertising industry. The right wing has a tendency to blame the incentives encouraged by a hardwired social hierarchy, in which "blue checks" "virtue-signal" to improve their standing within social platforms, even to the point of self-sabotage. Neither answer seems particularly satisfying. Viewing anecdotes of sudden social combustion according to comprehensive, deterministic accounts of neurochemical response, social dynamics, and platform incentives can certainly be clarifying, but such theories are incomplete. After all, Mark Zuckerberg is not pointing a gun at anyone's head, ordering them to use Instagram—and yet we post as though he is. Perhaps the best lens through which to examine compulsive, unproductive, inexplicable use of social media is not technical, or sociological, or economic, but psychoanalytic. In which case, rather than ask what is wrong with these systems, we might ask, "What is wrong with *us?*"

This is the question asked by Richard Seymour in his excellent new book *The Twittering Machine,* which takes its title from a Paul Klee drawing—a sketch of four stick-figure birds perched on an axle cranking above a fiery trench. In it Seymour sees an allegory for the tech megaplatforms he calls "the social industry": "Somehow," he writes, "the holy music of birdsong has been mechanized, deployed as a lure, for the purpose of human damnation." The Twittering Machine "confronts us with a string of calamities," among them increasing depression, fake news, the alt-right, and fast-food brands tweeting on fleek. And yet, despite the obvious fact that it's very bad for us, we, and about half the population of the earth, remain its inhabitants. Why do we stay on—just to pick an example—Twitter, while also referring to it as the "hell site"? "We must be getting something out of it," Seymour writes.

The writing and thinking emerging from the anti-social-media "techlash" of the past few years have tended to focus on malevolent design choices and business models that supposedly keep users hooked on the big platforms. "The problem," the ex-Google "design ethicist" Tristan Harris told *Wired* in 2017, "is the hijacking of the human mind." According to tech critics and industry apostates like Harris and former Facebookers Sean Parker and Chamath Palihapitiya, the brains of users are overtaken by "dopamine feedback loops" "exploiting a vulnerability in human psychology" to reap profits from an attention-driven business model. But as radical (and conspiratorial) as such explanations of social media's power might sound, they rely on the same techno-determinism that Silicon Valley's boosters have been pushing for decades: just as networks would inevitably turn everyone into a liberal-democratic subject, they now inevitably turn us into slavering zombies. Fundamentally conservative, this school of thought finds its solutions in narrow technical reformism: tweak this algorithm, move these numbers, ban these users, and everything will be fixed.

It's not that the accounts of people like Harris are illegitimate—the social industry was designed as a behavioralist casino; it relates to us, even constitutes us, as addicts, "users" whose natural state is devoted attention to the object of our addiction. But such techno-determinism renders all of us passive objects, our very brain chemistry at the mercy of a small handful of Harvard dorks with admin privileges. Are we really captive to our devices in quite so direct or helpless a way? Seymour doesn't buy it, and worries that just-so stories about addiction are disempowering and limiting. "To *reduce* experience to chemistry"—those dreaded dopamine feedback loops—"is to bypass what is essential to it: its meaning," he writes.

His rejection of determinism isn't a recourse to personal responsibility, but a warning: regulation will not cure us, and reform won't save us. If we live in a "horror story, the horror must partly lie in the user."

This is not a book with an accompanying TED Talk, a ten-step program, or One Weird Trick to Fix Everything. Seymour's pose here is that of a working analyst, not a confident diagnostician. He draws connections, he sketches notes toward a further diagnosis. You can imagine him steepling his fingers and saying, his brow a bit furrowed, "Isn't it interesting that . . ." or "You seem very upset about . . ." He deploys journalistic narrative and empirical data, but in general writes with a dense, aphoristic energy—"The telos of the clickbait economy is not postmodernism, but fascist kitsch"—that some will find unbearably pretentious. Personally, I found it charming. (And correct: the telos of the clickbait economy is fascist kitsch.)

The Twittering Machine is powered by an insight at once obvious and underexplored: we have, in the world of the social industry, become "*scripturient*—possessed by a violent desire to write, incessantly." Our addiction to social media is, at its core, a compulsion to write. Through our comments, updates, DMs, and searches, we are volunteers in a great "collective writing experiment." Those of us who don't peck out status updates on our keyboards are not exempt. We participate too, "behind our backs as it were," creating hidden (written) records of where we clicked, where we hovered, how far we scrolled, so that even reading, within the framework of the Twittering Machine, becomes a kind of writing. The rise of print, Seymour points out, played a crucial role in developing the idea of the modern nation, not to mention the bureaucratic state and "industrial civilization." Now that epoch is ending, and a new revolution in literacy is extending the ability to write in public to billions of people worldwide. What will our new digital-writing culture call into existence?

For many years, Silicon Valley's answer to that question has been freedom, prosperity, and digital utopia—an interconnected world in which progress and interchange wouldn't be obstructed or censored by the powerful. And, as Seymour acknowledges, our urge to write demonstrates "how much was waiting to be expressed" under the previous regime, during which access to large audiences was sharply limited by powerful gatekeepers, and the vast majority of ordinary people were relegated to the letters-to-the-editor page, if they were given a voice in print at all. In practice, however, what we have isn't a new political order, but a new kind of social life, one that is, in Seymour's words, "bent around the imperatives of states and markets." Where the repressive systems built on print media depended on and enforced our silence, the social industry wants us to keep writing—and writing, and writing, and writing, rendering legible, analyzable, and profitable nearly all our basic social interaction. And while massive Facebook server farms whirring away in Scandinavia might be able to make some vague sense of all that data, the rest of us can barely hear over the noise. Each new byte of information adds confusion and entropy, and takes us further away from meaning and consequence. The Twittering Machine "reduces information to meaningless stimuli which it jet-sprays at us"; it "habituates us to being the manipulable conduits of informational power." In this, Seymour grimly concludes, there is "a fascist potential."

Seymour is cautious here. As he points out, we've only just set aside prophecies of inevitable, internet-borne emancipation, and we should be careful not to make the same confident mistake in reverse, with moralizing, panicked screeds about inescapable algorithmic radicalization. What is scarier, anyway, than the idea that we're trapped on a collision course with TikTok totalitarianism is Seymour's insistence that we're not "trapped" at all—that, in fact, "we are part of the machine, and we find our satisfactions in it, however destructive they may be." Whatever dark future we hurtle toward, we are copilots on the journey.

It's for this reason that slavish devotion to the social or biological "incentives" of the platforms is an insufficient explanation of our "scripturience." If we are compelled to write, it is because of "something in us that is waiting to be addicted"—a lack, a desire, a deficiency that we seek to address. Is it a longing for connection? A yearning for fame? If so, posting is a poor strategy: you are as likely to lose friends as you are to make them, and online celebrity is only ever 240 characters away from online infamy. So why do we keep participating in an activity that acts against our interests and gives us no particular pleasure? "Is self-destruction, in some perverse way, the *yield?*" Seymour wonders. In other words: get in, loser, we're going beyond the pleasure principle. What if the urge lurking behind our compulsive participation in the Twittering Machine is not the behavioralist pursuit of maximized pleasure, but the Freudian death drive—our latent instinct toward inorganic oblivion, destruction, self-obliteration, "the ratio"? What if we post self-sabotaging things because we want to sabotage ourselves? What if the reason we tweet is because we wish we were dead?

On the one hand, that sounds like Freudian mumbo jumbo. On the other hand, speaking as a frequent user of social media, that . . . seems about right to me. What the Twittering Machine offers is not death, precisely, but oblivion—an escape from consciousness into numb atemporality, a trancelike "dead zone" of indistinguishably urgent stimulus. Seymour compares the "different, timeless, time zone" of the Twittering Machine to what the gambling-addiction expert Natasha Dow Schüll calls the "machine zone," in which "time, space, and social identity are suspended in the mechanical rhythm of a repeating process." You might say that "Twitter is not real life," a line intended as a kind of cutting warning, serves equally as an advertisement for the platform. But what is at stake here is not "reality." It's time. Seymour compares the Twittering Machine to the chronophage, "a monster that eats time." We give ourselves over to it "because of whatever is disappointing in the world of the living," but we do so at great cost. "Given the time this addiction demands of us," Seymour writes, "we are entitled to ask what else we might be doing, what else we could be addicted to."

It has been a good year to ask that question. If the punchy, claustrophobic antisociality of platforms in the early lockdown suggested a particularly dark vision of the future, the Movement for Black Lives street uprising of the late spring felt like its joyous opposite—a future in which platforms were responding to and being structured by the events on the ground, rather than those events being structured by and shaped to the demands of the platforms. This was something worth our time and devotion, something that exceeded our compulsion to write, something that—for a moment, at least—the Twittering Machine could not swallow.

Not that it was not trying. As people in the streets toppled statues and fought police, people on the platforms adjusted and refashioned the uprising from a street movement to an object for the consumption and reflection of the Twittering Machine. What was happening off-line needed to be accounted for, described, judged, and processed. Didactic story-lectures and photos of well-stocked antiracist bookshelves appeared on Instagram. On Twitter, the usual pundits and pedants sprang up, demanding explanations for every slogan and justifications for every action. In these concern trolls and reply guys, Seymour's chronophage was literalized. The social industry doesn't just eat our time with endless stimulus and algorithmic scrolling; it eats our time by creating and promoting people who exist only to be explained to, people to whom the world has been created anew every morning, people for whom every settled sociological, scientific, and political argument of modernity must be rehashed, rewritten, and re-accounted, this time with their participation.

These people, with their just-asking questions and vapid open letters, are dullards and bores, pettifoggers and casuists, cowards and dissemblers, time-wasters of the worst sort. But Seymour's book suggests something worse about us, their Twitter and Facebook interlocutors: That we *want* to waste our time. That, however much we might complain, we find satisfaction in endless, circular argument. That we get some kind of fulfillment from tedious debates about "free speech" and "cancel culture." That we seek oblivion in discourse. In the machine-flow atemporality of social media, this seems like no great crime. If time is an infinite resource, why not spend a few decades of it with a couple of *New York Times* op-ed columnists, rebuilding all of Western thought from first principles? But political and economic and immunological crises pile on one another in succession, over the background roar of ecological collapse. Time is not infinite. None of us can afford to spend what is left of it dallying with the stupid and bland.

DARIEL SUAREZ

In Orbit

FROM *The Threepenny Review*

IT MUST HAVE been in the early nineties, as the Soviet Union's collapse rippled its way to Cuba, that I decided to build a spaceship. The plan was to collect anything made of metal: nuts, bolts, rebar. Also spark plugs, doorknobs, loose cables. I hauled large sheets of tin blown off someone's shoddy roof, rusty steel pipes left behind by the neighborhood plumber, the rim and spokes of a bicycle's wheel. I even found the circuit board of a black-and-white television and the discarded innards of a radio, both of which, to my mind, possessed the dazzling intricacy of a computer. Within a few weeks, I accumulated enough to create an impressive mound of trash in my grandparents' yard. The sheer size of it was promising: no doubt I'd be able to fit inside once I put everything together.

I can't pinpoint a specific event or reason as the genesis of my idea, other than a general aspiration to explore and the belief that, in time, I could actually pull it off. I do remember being fascinated by space, something I inherited from my grandfather. He introduced me to astronomy and science fiction at an early age. He'd spend hours talking about what to him were the latest discoveries (information usually trickled into Cuba on years-long delay), the possible connections between ancient cultures and aliens, the Soviet Union versus the United States space race. He spoke with an infectious air of wonder about human achievements. He claimed we were on a precipitous path toward time travel and finding other dimensions. Once, he saw a documentary on black holes, and that's all he discussed for weeks. He liked to cite Hawking, Einstein, Newton, though I could never tell if he was doing so accurately. Regardless, he passed on enough of a quasi-scientific vocabulary for me to develop a ravenous curiosity for the astonishing, ruthless world beyond our sky.

When he saw the initial pile of garbage sprouting up in a corner of his yard, he chuckled and slowly shook his head. I explained my plan with the hope that he would offer his full support. Luckily, his chuckle had been one of approval. He chose to indulge me—as he would rarely have done for others, for my grandfather was an intransigent man, quick to lose his temper. He was, to put it as he might have, a man not averse to confrontation. He wasn't physically imposing. He was of average height for a Cuban, muscularly thin, and walked with a cautious, almost reserved manner due to his glass eye. He'd suffered an infection that nearly left him blind and that, for most of my life, I believed I had caused: the only time I saw my grandfather cry was after I accidentally poked his left eye, the functioning one, while horsing around. I must have been four or five years old. I carried this guilt with me until very recently, when my mother explained that my poke forced him to get the surgery he'd been stubbornly dodging, a surgery that, according to her, saved his vision.

Although I loved him and thought of him as a protector, there was a mythological aura about my grandfather, especially when he was trying to impose his will. Despite his unimpressive appearance, his personal history and reputation made him a foot taller and several pounds stronger in my youthful perception. He'd openly challenged a well-respected neighbor to a knife fight over a political argument (the neighbor declined and from then on refused to pass by the front of our house). He'd charged at one of my uncles with a lead pipe after this uncle had drunkenly yelled at my grandmother (my grandfather forbade him from entering the house again, and after separating from my aunt, my uncle never did). To help him build water tanks, he hired a friend of the family who'd been in prison for stabbing someone to death during an altercation, a man everyone in our neighborhood avoided and whom my grandfather—in what he likely saw as a defiant display of masculine empathy—treated as a protégé.

All of this is to say that I, a shy kid whose personality might be described as the direct opposite of my grandfather's, both worshiped and feared him. His approval of my spaceship-building endeavor meant so much because he, more than any other person, could undo it with the simplest of words or gestures.

The typical layout of a Havana suburb is unlike its North American counterpart. There are no white picket fences, no large swaths of lawn or ample driveways, no lines of mailboxes neatly arranged down a noiseless street. Instead, there are compact rows of decaying buildings, old houses whose windows are at arm's length from each other, potholed streets so narrow that two-way traffic becomes a challenge. Living in Santos Suarez—a heavily populated residential area nestled between two of Havana's smallest municipalities—was a confining experience, as though I were sequestered in a tiny corner of the world. Santos Suarez was a place from which even the stars seemed inadequately close, as if, like everything else in Cuba, a specific portion of the sky had been allocated to us, with no access to another. This claustrophobic feeling of isolation made me want to leave.

A child, if sufficiently exposed to it, is capable of understanding the ramifications of abject poverty—the sense that tomorrow and the day after, the struggle will be the same, regardless of your efforts or abilities. I recall a constant tension between the intellectually liberal atmosphere at home and the propaganda-riddled, duplicitous nature of Cuba's strict school system. I recall my family's frustrating interactions with Communist neighbors, all of whom were prospective informants for the state. Back then I also had a vague knowledge that life in other countries—and particularly in the United States—offered a more fruitful future, a knowledge that became more alluring by the mid-1990s, when the Special Period crisis gripped virtually every household and emigrating felt like the best solution to all our economic and socio-ideological woes.

A child is not supposed to be grappling with these sorts of questions, not to the extent that they lead to the thought of abandoning one's country. But when you witness the abrupt absence of friends, and later hear how well they're doing in Miami, New York, Madrid, Toronto, Mexico City; when you see photos of them wearing brand-new clothes, living in freshly painted houses, riding in polished cars, smiling with a joy so effusive it can only come from people who know they've escaped a lifetime of hardship and disappointment; then the hand-me-down shirts and crumbling buildings and sputtering old cars and sun-beaten faces and socialist dictums suddenly take on a demoralizing quality. I wanted to leave Cuba because I sensed, very early on, that my adult self would be unhappy otherwise.

I suppose building a spaceship would have been one way to accomplish this. Yet I never made a connection between migration and shooting off past Earth's atmosphere. What I do remember is the thrilling prospect of defying ridiculous odds. I remember picturing myself inside a metallic cocoon with beeping lights, hissing pipes, blinking screens. I remember imagining what it would be like to orbit our planet, to look back at its massive splendor, to drift toward distant stars. I was searching for a larger kind of escape.

Most Cubans know the name Yuri Gagarin. We know he was Russian, the first person to orbit Earth, even if we don't always remember that he did so in 1961, that the name of the flight was Vostok 1, that the spacecraft had a spherical design to protect it from extreme heat on atmospheric reentry, and that the entire mission lasted 108 minutes. Gagarin's trajectory around Earth clocked in at a little over an hour. That's more than sixty minutes in space relying on what is now more than half-a-century-old technology. Picture cars, planes, televisions, or phones from the same era, and it is remarkable that we accomplished such a feat with such rudimentary resources. That alone is worthy of genuine admiration. It should make us, regardless of politics or national affiliation or our personal relationship to science, proud of what humans are capable of achieving, of what a person like Gagarin was willing to do.

Unsurprisingly, he was turned into an international spectacle. Gagarin was a symbol not just of the Soviet Union's power, but of its purported superiority over the United States. He was presented to Cubans as a hero, *our* hero. He was an example of Communism's ability—through collaboration, ingenuity, and sacrifice—to attain the impossible. Most of my generation clumped his name alongside Laika (the first animal to orbit Earth) and *Sputnik* (the first man-made satellite to be launched into space), words that, in their sound and relevancy, evoked a sense of artificiality and imposition: a relationship between expansive, cold Russia and small, tropical Cuba that now feels like some historian's cruel idea of a joke. It's no wonder these words, like *tovarish* (Russian for "comrade") or *koniec* ("end"), became a subject of mockery in our vernacular, the first for its obvious Communist connotation, the latter for appearing at the end of many a Soviet film with unresolved plot lines. *Koniec* stood for inexplicable, illogical, absurd—for the almost comical, improbable tragedy of what it meant to live in a Russian-dependent Cuban society.

Sputnik, however, holds greater significance for me. My grandfather referenced it often when I was a child. He wasn't referring to the satellite, but to the magazine. The Soviet Union's version of *Reader's Digest,* poorly written and even more egregiously translated, *Sputnik* was one of the scarce access points we had to anything resembling international pop culture—science and literary news, political discussions, and thematic articles, all aesthetically mushed through a Soviet filter. Like others of his and my parents' generation, Grandpa used it as a source of information, particularly when it came to science.

But the irony of living under a despotic, propaganda-driven regime is that, once the idealist portion of the process has dried up and only the disappointment and poverty and oppression remain, the disenchanted youth gravitate toward what has been forbidden. In my generation's case, it was American mythology and products. We consumed Hollywood movies and longed for a refreshing Coke while Fidel Castro spoke of socialist principles and our island's defiance of imperialist threats. I was more fascinated by Neil Armstrong and NASA than by any of the Soviet stories we were told. I don't remember seeing what Gagarin looked like, or memorizing the dates of the Soviet Union's space exploits, but I could close my eyes and picture the iconic images of the moon landing. I could recognize the NASA logo from afar and knew the *Challenger* disaster had occurred on the year of my birth; I had vivid images in my mind of the heartbreaking footage, the dense trail of smoke expanding behind the disintegrating spacecraft as fire consumed it.

Recently I stumbled upon what felt like an important question: What if I stripped away the politically marred layers of my memory and allowed myself to explore this Soviet space history?

I learned that Yuri Gagarin was born into a peasant family in a Russian village near a town that would later be renamed after him. His father was a carpenter and bricklayer, his mother a milkmaid. During the Nazi occupation, the family was forced to live in a mud hut behind their home for nearly two years, while his two older brothers performed forced labor in Poland until the end of the war. As a young man, Gagarin volunteered as an air cadet at a local flying club and, after being drafted into the army, became a pilot. In 1960 the Soviet space program selected him as part of an elite training group. He was subjected to extensive training and tests designed to measure physical and psychological endurance. Because of his distinction in performance compared to the other pilots, and because of his diminutive stature (Gagarin was only five feet two inches tall), he was deemed the perfect candidate to fly into space.

By April 1961 he was aboard the Vostok spacecraft. There's a recording of his voice at the exact instant he was receiving final instructions for the launch. One can hear static and then Gagarin shouting *Poyekhali!*, which translates to "Let's go!"—a phrase that essentially marked the beginning of the Space Age. It's the informal nature of what Gagarin chose to say, though, that intrigued me. Communism has a way of making even the mundane or empty sound laboriously grand. While Americans dress power and exceptionalism in colorful television commercials and romanticized views of democracy, there's a crushingly bureaucratic and militaristic attitude behind the entire Communist enterprise, including the language. At such a pivotal moment for the Soviets, I'd expect Gagarin to sound official, stiff, contrived. Coming across his impatient "Let's go!" stirred something in me. I hit play, again and again, and listened: *Poyekhali! Poyekhali! Poyekhali!*

The hairs on my arms rose. I skipped a breath. I was genuinely moved. Although all of this had taken place in Eastern Europe almost sixty years ago, I felt connected to it. It was as if my history—or, more accurately, a history that is and isn't mine, but to which I'm irrevocably attached—was echoing from somewhere remote and shaking my present self. How do we define what's ours? I wondered. Why did I have such a strong response to Gagarin's voice? Why do I feel compelled to share both his story and my personal reaction, to explore them further? What am I, a Cuban-born American citizen caught between opposing mythologies, really trying to figure out?

There's a danger that, as we get older, our world, instead of becoming larger and more connected, will remain relatively narrow and fractured. I've rarely encountered anyone in the United States, and this includes many writers and intellectuals, who knows about Neil Armstrong *and* Yuri Gagarin, who knows the details of the moon landing *and* Vostok 1, who can speak about American and Soviet events with a comparable level of interest, skepticism, or passion. We've been made to believe that another place's history is someone else's history, to the extent that extraordinary amounts of curiosity and empathy are needed to break through the barrier. Then there are the narratives imposed on us, the single-layered distortions meant to fuel our sense of pride and belonging. Whether we reject or internalize them, these narratives inevitably become entangled with our identity. I am Cuban, but the Soviet influences on my sensibilities, my cynicism and humor, my sense of the past and formative education are undeniable. They linger in my conscience in ways that American acculturation has failed to erase. How much say do we really have in what we discard or accept? How does a Cuban-born individual living in America reconcile the feeling of personal recognition—of a strange but visceral link—to the sound of a Russian astronaut he's always associated with Communist indoctrination?

Maybe we're just at the mercy of our instinctive reactions. Maybe what resonates for us as authentic, as somehow ours, is all that matters. But I can't shake the suspicion that even in moments of recognition, I must continue to prod and question if I want to arrive at anything resembling a unified sense of self. Ultimately, I find solace in the little tokens history gives us. Neil Armstrong and Buzz Aldrin, at the heart of the Cold War in 1969, left a medallion on the moon commemorating Gagarin's contribution to space exploration. Their acknowledgment and appreciation of a fellow astronaut transcended politics. I choose to see this seemingly small gesture as a comforting metaphor for the complex, colliding realities that make up my immigrant life.

It wasn't a simple word or sweep of the hand that extinguished my spaceship-building hopes. My grandfather paced in front of all the parts I'd spent weeks gathering, and with a menacing tremor in his voice ordered me to throw it all out. He needed to build a water tank, he said, and there was no reason for so much trash to be in the way. He offered no other explanation, no alternatives. He didn't acknowledge all the effort I'd put in. He looked at the pile of metal with disdain and exasperation. His indulgence of my dream had reached its limit.

I pleaded with my mother to reason with him. I remember there being a brief argument. Then I was carrying everything to the dumpster on our street corner. I hid the circuit board somewhere in my home but threw it away soon after, for fear that he would find it.

Defying my grandfather was not an option. When I was in kindergarten, he supposedly saw my best friend, Roli, push me while we were in line waiting to be released from school. I don't recall the push. I can barely recount any instances of animosity between Roli and me. But something must have happened, because on the walk home (my grandfather had permission from Roli's mother to bring him with me), he made us fight. He said something about how I shouldn't allow others to disrespect me, about not going home until Roli and I fought. We mainly grabbed each other and tussled on the ground, holding back tears. A neighbor who was walking by called my grandfather an animal. He told her to mind her business and pulled us apart only when he realized there would be no winner.

Roli and I never talked about the incident. We didn't tell our parents. Our friendship continued until his family moved to a different neighborhood when we were in fourth or fifth grade. I also never spoke of it with my grandfather. He wasn't the type to dwell on the past, at least not in the context of personal growth—admitting a wrong, offering or receiving forgiveness. Vulnerability was counter to what he believed and practiced. What hurt me most was his lack of self-awareness, his inability to grasp how much damage he could do.

Though my interest in science continued even after I realized how foolish the spaceship idea had been, my relationship with my grandfather was never the same. Once I left Cuba, we barely spoke for over a decade. A few years back, he and my grandmother came to visit my family in Miami. Time hadn't been kind to him. Wrinkles had conquered the whole of his face. His glass eye had sunk deeper into his skull. His spine had developed a forward bend, his walk a sluggish drag. Following the initial hug and typical exchange between people whose distance has turned them into strangers, he said he had something important to ask me. We walked out to my mother's balcony and shut the sliding door behind us. We sat across from each other, let a pause accentuate the moment—he for gravitas, me because I was expecting an insidious question about my long hair, my decision to become a writer, the lack of phone calls on my end. He moved to the edge of his chair, a surprisingly nervous appearance in his posture, and with a sheepish voice said, "I want you to be honest with me: Do you believe in aliens?"

Science, and particularly anything related to astronomy, slowly faded from my life once I arrived in America. By high school graduation, I'd decided becoming an astronomer and working at NASA were out of the question. I dropped out of college within a semester, turning to heavy metal music as my escape and manual labor as my means of support. When I returned to school in my midtwenties, creative writing had become my passion. Science reappeared only in the form of brief affairs with magazine subscriptions. A few *Scientific Americans* still sit unread on my bookshelf.

I've done a fair amount of online research, but I've failed to find any copies in Spanish of *Sputnik*. Perhaps in a future trip to Havana I'll come across one, since these kinds of Communist memorabilia have a way of never completely disappearing. Perhaps I just need to reconnect with the person who, before getting on a plane in 1997, would look at the stars and wonder how it was possible for some of them to have died so long ago, how we're able to see something that isn't actually there.

I don't believe my grandfather will ever be that pathway for me. If anything, my relationship with him has deteriorated further. I've learned things about him: the way he betrayed my grandmother with other women, the years of psychological abuse, the disparaging comments he made about my now-deceased father's struggle with alcoholism. Suffice it to say, I don't respect him as I did in my younger days; I now wish to be the opposite of him. My mother tells me he asks about me often, about my personal and professional achievements. She says he loves me. Still, my default emotion toward my grandfather is anger. In moments I'm not proud of, I wish my connection to science had nothing to do with him. I'm glad that leaving Cuba released me from his influence.

But migration isn't only about escape. It's also about irreparable loss. I know that who I am today is not just what I've become, but what is no longer with me. One learns to cope. The knowledge that something cannot be regained eventually moves past grief and nostalgia into a more indefinable state, a state in which hope begins working its way back—in my case to childhood, to what will always be the most authentic version of oneself. There, I find myself having built that spaceship. And unlike Gagarin, with his certainty of return, soon I'm truly in orbit, on an almost endless threshold between the known and unknown, beyond it the entire cosmos and its delightful abundance of possibilities.

JESMYN WARD

Witness and Respair

FROM *Vanity Fair*

MY BELOVED DIED in January. He was a foot taller than me and had large, beautiful dark eyes and dexterous, kind hands. He fixed me breakfast and pots of loose-leaf tea every morning. He cried at both of our children's births, silently, tears glazing his face. Before I drove our children to school in the pale dawn light, he would put both hands on the top of his head and dance in the driveway to make the kids laugh. He was funny, quick-witted, and could inspire the kind of laughter that cramped my whole torso. Last fall, he decided it would be best for him and our family if he went back to school. His primary job in our household was to shore us up, to take care of the children, to be a househusband. He traveled with me often on business trips, carried our children in the back of lecture halls, watchful and quietly proud as I spoke to audiences, as I met readers and shook hands and signed books. He indulged my penchant for Christmas movies, for meandering trips through museums, even though he would have much preferred to be in a stadium somewhere, watching football. One of my favorite places in the world was beside him, under his warm arm, the color of deep, dark river water.

In early January, we became ill with what we thought was flu. Five days into our illness, we went to a local urgent care center, where the doctor swabbed us and listened to our chests. The kids and I were diagnosed with flu; my Beloved's test was inconclusive. At home, I doled out medicine to all of us: Tamiflu and promethazine. My children and I immediately began to feel better, but my Beloved did not. He burned with fever. He slept and woke to complain that he thought the medicine wasn't working, that he was in pain. And then he took more medicine and slept again.

Two days after our family doctor visit, I walked into my son's room where my Beloved lay, and he panted: *Can't. Breathe.* I brought him to the emergency room, where after an hour in the waiting room, he was sedated and put on a ventilator. His organs failed: first his kidneys, then his liver. He had a massive infection in his lungs, developed sepsis, and in the end, his great strong heart could no longer support a body that had turned on him. He coded eight times. I witnessed the doctors perform CPR and bring him back four. Within fifteen hours of walking into the emergency room of that hospital, he was dead. The official reason: acute respiratory distress syndrome. He was thirty-three years old.

Without his hold to drape around my shoulders, to shore me up, I sank into hot, wordless grief.

Two months later, I squinted at a video of a gleeful Cardi B chanting in a singsong voice: *Coronavirus,* she cackled. *Coronavirus.* I stayed silent while people around me made jokes about COVID, rolled their eyes at the threat of pandemic. Weeks later, my kids' school was closed. Universities were telling students to vacate the dorms while professors were scrambling to move classes online. There was no bleach, no toilet paper, no paper towels for purchase anywhere. I snagged the last of the disinfectant spray off a pharmacy shelf; the clerk ringing up my purchases asking me wistfully: *Where did you find that at?* and for one moment, I thought she would challenge me for it, tell me there was some policy in place to prevent my buying it.

Days became weeks, and the weather was strange for south Mississippi, for the swampy, water-ridden part of the state I call home: low humidity, cool temperatures, clear, sun-lanced skies. My children and I awoke at noon to complete homeschooling lessons. As the spring days lengthened into summer, my children ran wild, exploring the forest around my house, picking blackberries, riding bikes and four-wheelers in their underwear. They clung to me, rubbed their faces into my stomach, and cried hysterically: *I miss Daddy,* they said. Their hair grew tangled and dense. I didn't eat, except when I did, and then it was tortillas, queso, and tequila.

The absence of my Beloved echoed in every room of our house.

Him folding me and the children in his arms on our monstrous fake-suede sofa. Him shredding chicken for enchiladas in the kitchen. Him holding our daughter by the hands and pulling her upward, higher and higher, so she floated at the top of her leap in a long bed-jumping marathon. Him shaving the walls of the children's playroom with a sander after an internet recipe for homemade chalkboard paint went wrong: green dust everywhere.

During the pandemic, I couldn't bring myself to leave the house, terrified I would find myself standing in the doorway of an ICU room, watching the doctors press their whole weight on the chest of my mother, my sisters, my children, terrified of the lurch of their feet, the lurch that accompanies each press that restarts the heart, the jerk of their pale, tender soles, terrified of the frantic prayer without intention that keens through the mind, the prayer for life that one says in the doorway, the prayer I never want to say again, the prayer that dissolves midair when the *hush-click-hush-click* of the ventilator drowns it, terrified of the terrible commitment at the heart of me that reasons that if the person I love has to endure this, then the least I can do is stand there, the least I can do is witness, the least I can do is tell them over and over again, aloud, *I love you. We love you. We ain't going nowhere.*

As the pandemic settled in and stretched, I set my alarms to wake early, and on mornings after nights where I actually slept, I woke and worked on my novel in progress. The novel is about a woman who is even more intimately acquainted with grief than I am, an enslaved woman whose mother is stolen from her and sold south to New Orleans, whose lover is stolen from her and sold south, who herself is sold south and descends into the hell of chattel slavery in the mid-1800s. My loss was a tender second skin. I shrugged against it as I wrote, haltingly, about this woman who speaks to spirits and fights her way across rivers.

My commitment surprised me. Even in a pandemic, even in grief, I found myself commanded to amplify the voices of the dead that sing to me, from their boat to my boat, on the sea of time. On most days, I wrote one sentence. On some days, I wrote a thousand words. Many days, it and I seemed useless. All of it, misguided endeavor. My grief bloomed as depression, just as it had after my brother died at nineteen, and I saw little sense, little purpose in this work, this solitary vocation. Me, sightless, wandering the wild, head thrown back, mouth wide open, singing to a star-drenched sky. Like all the speaking, singing women of old, a maligned figure in the wilderness. Few listened in the night.

What resonated back to me: the emptiness between the stars. Dark matter. Cold.

Did you see it? my cousin asked me.

No. I couldn't bring myself to watch it, I said. Her words began to flicker, to fade in and out. Grief sometimes makes it hard for me to hear. Sound came in snatches.

His knee, she said.

On his neck, she said.

Couldn't breathe, she said.

He cried for his mama, she said.

I read about Ahmaud, I said. *I read about Breonna.*

I don't say, but I thought it: *I know their beloveds' wail. I know their beloveds' wail. I know their beloveds wander their pandemic rooms, pass through their sudden ghosts. I know their loss burns their beloveds' throats like acid. Their families will speak,* I thought. *Ask for justice. And no one will answer,* I thought. *I know this story: Trayvon, Tamir, Sandra.*

Cuz, I said, *I think you told me this story before.*

I think I wrote it.

I swallowed sour.

In the days after my conversation with my cousin, I woke to people in the streets. I woke to Minneapolis burning. I woke to protests in America's heartland, Black people blocking the highways. I woke to people doing the haka in New Zealand. I woke to hoodie-wearing teens, to John Boyega raising a fist in the air in London, even as he was afraid he would sink his career, but still, he raised his fist. I woke to droves of people, masses of people in Paris, sidewalk to sidewalk, moving like a river down the boulevards. I knew the Mississippi. I knew the plantations on its shores, the movement of enslaved and cotton up and down its eddies. The people marched, and I had never known that there could be rivers such as this, and as protesters chanted and stomped, as they grimaced and shouted and groaned, tears burned my eyes. They glazed my face.

I sat in my stuffy pandemic bedroom and thought I might never stop crying. The revelation that Black Americans were not alone in this, that others around the world believed that Black Lives Matter broke something in me, some immutable belief I'd carried with me my whole life. This belief beat like another heart—*thump*—in my chest from the moment I took my first breath as an underweight, two-pound infant after my mother, ravaged by stress, delivered me at twenty-four weeks. It beat from the moment the doctor told my Black mother her Black baby would die. *Thump.*

That belief was infused with fresh blood during the girlhood I'd spent in underfunded public school classrooms, cavities eating away at my teeth from government-issued block cheese, powdered milk, and corn flakes. *Thump.* Fresh blood in the moment I heard the story of how a group of white men, revenue agents, had shot and killed my great-great-grandfather, left him to bleed to death in the woods like an animal, from the second I learned no one was ever held accountable for his death. *Thump.* Fresh blood in the moment I found out the white drunk driver who killed my brother wouldn't be charged for my brother's death, only for leaving the scene of the car accident, the scene of the crime. *Thump.*

This is the belief that America fed fresh blood into for centuries, this belief that Black lives have the same value as a plow horse or a grizzled donkey. I knew this. My family knew this. My people knew this, and we fought it, but we were convinced we would fight this reality alone, fight until we could no more, until we were in the ground, bones moldering, headstones overgrown above in the world where our children and children's children still fought, still yanked against the noose, the forearm, the starvation and redlining and rape and enslavement and murder and choked out: *I can't breathe.* They would say: *I can't breathe. I can't breathe.*

I cried in wonder each time I saw protest around the world because I recognized the people. I recognized the way they zipped their hoodies, the way they raised their fists, the way they walked, the way they shouted. I recognized their action for what it was: witness. Even now, each day, they witness.

They witness injustice.

They witness this America, this country that gaslit us for four hundred fucking years.

Witness that my state, Mississippi, waited until 2013 to ratify the Thirteenth Amendment.

Witness that Mississippi didn't remove the Confederate battle emblem from its state flag until 2020.

Witness Black people, Indigenous people, so many poor brown

people, lying on beds in frigid hospitals, gasping our last breaths with COVID-riddled lungs, rendered flat by undiagnosed underlying conditions, triggered by years of food deserts, stress, and poverty, lives spent snatching sweets so we could eat one delicious morsel, savor some sugar on the tongue, oh Lord, because the flavor of our lives is so often bitter.

They witness our fight too, the quick jerk of our feet, see our hearts lurch to beat again in our art and music and work and joy. How revelatory that others witness our battles and stand up. They go out in the middle of a pandemic, and they march.

I sob, and the rivers of people run in the streets.

When my Beloved died, a doctor told me: *The last sense to go is hearing. When someone is dying, they lose sight and smell and taste and touch. They even forget who they are. But in the end, they hear you.*

I hear you.

I hear you.

You say:

I love you.

We love you.

We ain't going nowhere.

I hear you say:

We here.

Contributors' Notes

Notable Essays and Literary Nonfiction of 2020

Notable Special Issues of 2020

Contributors' Notes

ELIZABETH ALEXANDER—award-winning poet, educator, memoirist, scholar, and cultural advocate—is president of the Andrew W. Mellon Foundation, the nation's largest funder of arts and culture and of humanities in higher education. Dr. Alexander has held distinguished professorships at Smith College, Columbia University, and Yale University, where she taught for fifteen years and chaired the African American Studies Department. She is chancellor emeritus of the Academy of American Poets and a member of the American Academy of Arts and Sciences; she serves on the Pulitzer Prize Board and codesigned the Art for Justice Fund. Notably, Alexander composed and delivered the poem "Praise Song for the Day" for the 2009 inauguration of President Barack Obama and is the author or co-author of fourteen books. Her collection of poems *American Sublime* was a finalist for the Pulitzer Prize in Poetry in 2006, and her memoir, *The Light of the World,* was a finalist for the Pulitzer Prize in Biography in 2015.

HILTON ALS became a staff writer at *The New Yorker* in 1994 and a theater critic in 2002. Previously, Als was a staff writer for the *Village Voice* and an editor at large at *Vibe.* His first book, *The Women,* was published in 1996. His most recent book, *White Girls,* a finalist for the National Book Critics Circle Award and the winner of the Lambda Literary Award in 2014, discusses various narratives of race and gender. He won the Pulitzer Prize in Criticism in 2017 and served as the guest editor of *The Best American Essays 2018.*

MOLLY MCCULLY BROWN is the author of the essay collection *Places I've Taken My Body,* which *Kirkus Reviews* named a Best Book of 2020, and the poetry collection *The Virginia State Colony for Epilep-*

tics and Feebleminded, winner of the 2016 Lexi Rudnitsky First Book Prize. With Susannah Nevison, Brown is also the co-author of the poetry collection *In the Field Between Us* (2020). Her essays have appeared in *The Paris Review, The Yale Review, Virginia Quarterly Review, The Guardian,* the *New York Times,* and elsewhere. She is an assistant professor of English and creative nonfiction at Old Dominion University.

AGNES CALLARD is an associate professor of philosophy at the University of Chicago and the author of *Aspiration: The Agency of Becoming* (2018). She writes a monthly public philosophy column for *The Point* magazine. Her writing has also appeared in the *New York Times, The New Yorker, Boston Review, Liberties,* and elsewhere. She lives in Chicago and is writing a book on Socrates's discovery of a conversational method of inquiry into life's fundamental questions.

GABRIELLE HAMILTON is the chef-owner of Prune, which she opened in New York City's East Village in October 1999. Prune has received national and international press recognition. Hamilton's television appearances include segments with Martha Stewart, Mark Bittman, and Mike Colameco; she was the victor in her Iron Chef America battle against Bobby Flay on the Food Network in 2008. She won an Emmy for her role in season 4 of the PBS series *Mind of a Chef.* Hamilton has written for *The New Yorker,* the *New York Times, GQ, Bon Appétit, Saveur, Food & Wine, Afar, Travel and Leisure, Vogue,* the *Wall Street Journal, Elle,* and *House Beautiful.* Her work has been anthologized in *Best Food Writing 2001, 2002, 2003, 2004, 2005, 2006, 2011,* and *2013.* A winner of four James Beard Awards, she was named Outstanding Chef in 2018. Her *New York Times* bestseller, *Blood, Bones, and Butter: The Inadvertent Education of a Reluctant Chef,* has been published in six languages. Her recent cookbook *Prune* features 250 recipes from her restaurant. A monthly columnist for *The New York Times Magazine,* Hamilton is currently at work on a memoir.

TONY HOAGLAND (1953–2018) published seven books of poetry, including *What Narcissism Means to Me* (2003) and *Priest Turned Therapist Treats Fear of God* (2018); three collections of essays, including *The Art of Voice,* with Kay Cosgrove; and *Cinderbiter: Celtic Poems,* with Martin Shaw. *Turn Up the Ocean: New and Uncollected Poems* is forthcoming in 2022.

GREG JACKSON is the author of *Prodigals: Stories,* for which he received the National Book Foundation's 5 Under 35 award and the

Bard Fiction Prize. His fiction and essays have appeared in *The New Yorker, Harper's Magazine, Granta, Virginia Quarterly Review, Tin House,* and *The Point,* among other places. In 2017 he was named one of *Granta*'s Best of Young American Novelists.

RUCHIR JOSHI is a writer, a filmmaker and the author of a novel, *The Last Jet-Engine Laugh.* His forthcoming novel, *Great Eastern Hotel,* will be published in the UK and India.

AMY LEACH grew up in Texas and earned her MFA from the Nonfiction Writing Program at the University of Iowa. Her work has appeared in *Orion, A Public Space, Tin House, The Best American Science and Nature Writing,* and numerous other publications. She is a recipient of a Whiting Writers' Award, a Rona Jaffe Foundation Writers' Award, and a Pushcart Prize. She is the author of *Things That Are* and *The Everybody Ensemble.* Leach lives in Montana.

PATRICIA LOCKWOOD is the author of four books, most recently the novel *No One Is Talking About This* (2021). Her memoir *Priestdaddy* won the 2018 Thurber Prize for American Humor, and her poetry collections include *Motherland Fatherland Homelandsexuals* (2014) and *Balloon Pop Outlaw Black* (2012). She is a contributing editor for the *London Review of Books* and lives in Savannah, Georgia.

BARRY LOPEZ (1945–2020) published the novel *Horizon* in 2019. The *New York Times Book Review* called it ". . . beautiful and brutal —a story of the universal human condition." A celebrated writer of fiction and nonfiction, Lopez was awarded the National Book Award for *Arctic Dreams* and the John Burrows Medal for *Of Wolves and Men*; he received a Guggenheim fellowship among other honors. In 2020, Lopez was inducted into the American Academy of Arts and Letters and received the Sun Valley Writers' Conference's first Writer in the World Prize. Throughout his writing life, Lopez collaborated with dozens of international writers and artists and fostered the careers of many younger men and women. For fifty years, Lopez lived next to his beloved McKenzie River in Oregon yet also traveled to more than eighty countries, where he enjoyed rich friendships. He died in December 2020, surrounded by his family.

JESSICA LUSTIG is a deputy editor at *The New York Times Magazine.* She has written on subjects including guns, the criminal justice system, culture, and books, but most often works behind the scenes with other writers. She lives in New York City.

DAWN LUNDY MARTIN is an American poet and essayist. She is the author of four books of poems, including *Good Stock Strange Blood,* winner of the 2019 Kingsley Tufts Award for Poetry. Her nonfiction can be found in *n+1, The New Yorker, Ploughshares, The Believer,* and *The Best American Essays 2019.* Martin holds the Toi Derricotte Endowed Chair in English at the University of Pittsburgh and is the director of the Center for African American Poetry and Poetics.

CLAIRE MESSUD's books include the novels *The Burning Girl, The Emperor's Children,* and *The Last Life*; a collection of novellas, *The Hunters*; and, most recently, an autobiography in essays, *Kant's Little Prussian Head and Other Reasons Why I Write.* She has received numerous honors, including the Strauss Living Award from the American Academy of Arts and Letters. She teaches at Harvard University.

WESLEY MORRIS is a critic at large at the *New York Times* and a staff writer at *The New York Times Magazine,* where he writes essays about popular culture. He also hosts the culture podcast *Still Processing* with Jenna Wortham. For three years he was a staff writer at *Grantland,* where he wrote about movies, television, and the role of style in professional sports; he also cohosted the podcast *Do You Like Prince Movies?* with Alex Pappademas. Before that, he spent eleven years as a film critic at the *Boston Globe,* where he won the 2012 Pulitzer Prize for Criticism.

BETH (BICH MINH) NGUYEN is the author of *Stealing Buddha's Dinner,* the novels *Short Girls* and *Pioneer Girl,* and the forthcoming memoir *Owner of a Lonely Heart.* She has received the American Book Award and the PEN/Jerard Fund Award, and her work has appeared in *The New Yorker, The Paris Review,* the *New York Times,* and numerous anthologies. Nguyen is a professor in the creative writing program at the University of Wisconsin–Madison.

FINTAN O'TOOLE is a columnist for the *Irish Times,* a regular contributor to *The New York Review of Books,* and the Leonard L. Milberg Visiting Lecturer in Irish Letters at Princeton. His journalism has won both the Orwell Prize and the European Press Prize. His most recent book is *We Don't Know Ourselves: A Personal History of Modern Ireland.*

MAX READ's work has appeared in several publications with the words "New York" in the title, including *New York* magazine, the *New York Times,* and *The New York Times Magazine.* He is also the former editor of multiple defunct websites, including Gawker and Select All. In 2011, he was the recipient of the Best Personal Tumblr award from the *Village Voice.* He lives in Brooklyn.

DARIEL SUAREZ is the Cuban-born author of *A Kind of Solitude,* winner of the International Latino Book Award for Best Collection of Short Stories, and more recently the novel *The Playwright's House.* He is the education director at GrubStreet and one of the City of Boston's inaugural Artist Fellows.

JESMYN WARD received her MFA from the University of Michigan and has received a MacArthur fellowship, a Stegner fellowship, a John and Renée Grisham Writers Residency, and the Strauss Living Prize. She is the winner of two National Book Awards for Fiction, for *Sing, Unburied, Sing* (2017) and *Salvage the Bones* (2011). She is also the author of the novel *Where the Line Bleeds* and the memoir *Men We Reaped,* which was a finalist for the National Book Critics Circle Award and won the Chicago Tribune Heartland Prize and the Media for a Just Society Award. Ward is currently a professor of creative writing at Tulane University and lives in Mississippi.

Notable Essays and Literary Nonfiction of 2020

Selected by Robert Atwan

Marilyn Abildskov
Krushchyovka, *The Southern Review,* 56/2
André Aciman
Adrift in Sunlit Night, *The American Scholar,* 89/3
Kazim Ali
Naming Home, *Ecotone,* #29
Brooke Allen
The Shakespeareans, *The Hudson Review,* 73/1
Amy Amoroso
Your American Dream, *Mount Hope,* #17
Sam Anderson
Snowed Under, *The New York Times Magazine,* November 8
Antonia Angress
A Secret Love Hidden in the Pages of *The Price of Salt, Literary Hub,* February 25
Robert Archambeau
Concerning the Soul of Andy Warhol, *Copper Nickel,* #31–32
Megan J. Arlett
On Castration, *Prairie Schooner,* 94/2
Chris Arthur
Listening to the Music of a Vulture's Egg, *Water-Stone Review,* #23
Jabari Asim
The Douglass Republic, *The New Republic,* September
Rana Awdish
The Shape of the Shore, *Intima,* Fall

Andre Bagoo
In Praise of Corn-Pone Opinions, *Electric Literature,* January 29
Jasmine V. Bailey
Destiny of Cumin, *Ruminate,* #54
Aimée Baker
Beasts of the Fields, *Guernica,* February 19
Tim Bascom
Hiking into the Unknown, *Under the Sun,* #8
Jack Beatty
The Cleopatra's Nose of 1914, *Lapham's Quarterly,* 13/2
Nicky Beer
My Brother Says "What the Fuck" *The Cincinnati Review,* 17/2
S. G. Belknap
Lovers in the Hands of a Patient God, *The Point,* #23
Allison Field Bell
The Body, the Onion: A Balagan, *Shenandoah,* 69/2

GABRIELLE BELLOT
The Curious Language of Grief, *Catapult,* March 11

ROSALIND BENTLEY
The Blessing and Burden of Forever, *Oxford American,* #109–110

HEATHER BRITTAIN BERGSTROM
Valley, *Narrative,* January 17

EMILY BERNARD
From the Stranger in Me to the Stranger in You, *Image,* #106

ERICA BERRY
Everything Bright Is Something Buried, *The Yale Review,* 108/3

ANDREA BIANCHI
Fade from Red, *Witness,* 33/3

SVEN BIRKERTS
Serendipity: Notebook, *Arrowsmith,* September 29

TOM BISSELL
Nabokov's Rocking Chair: *Lolita* at the Movies, *ZYZZYVA,* #119

SEBASTIAN BITTICKS
Terra Incognita, *Chautauqua,* #17

GEORGE BLECHER
Ghosts on the Landing, *Tiferet Journal,* Spring/Summer

GARRETT BLISS
Accumulations, *Tahoma Literary Review,* #18

LUCIENNE S. BLOCH
Inside Stories, *Five Points,* 20/2

LOUISE A. BLUM
How It Ends, *The Sun,* #531

MICHAEL BOGAN
Indiana, Summer, 1984, *Indiana Review,* 42/1

JASWINDER BOLINA
Color Coded, *Shenandoah,* 69/2

SARI BOREN
He's a Rope, *Sycamore Review,* 31/2

BRITTANY BORGHI
A Delicate Strength, *The Iowa Review,* 50/1

ZOE BOSSIERE
Fear in the Time of the Javelina, *Guernica,* May 13

JENNY BOULLY
I Want This to Be True, *The Georgia Review,* 74/4

CHRISTINE BOYER
Second Person, *Tahoma Literary Review,* #19

WILL BRIDGES
Bloodlines and Bitter Syrup, *Creative Nonfiction,* #73

REBECCA BRILL
On Gurning, *Colorado Review,* 47/2

VICTOR BROMBERT
In Praise of Jealousy? *Raritan,* 40/2

DAVID BROOKS
The Nuclear Family Was a Mistake, *The Atlantic,* March

KEVIN BROWN
Criticism and the Age: James Wood's Essays of Two Decades, *The Decadent Review,* July 9

DAN BRUBAKER
Bands of Time, *Under the Sun,* #8

CHRIS BURSK
Last Writes, *The Sun,* #534

TARA ISABELLA BURTON
Real Love in the Attention Economy, *The New Atlantis,* #61

AMY BUTCHER
On Images of Violence, *Columbus Monthly,* April

BLAKE BUTLER
Molly, *The Volta,* Fall

FRANCISCO CANTU
Lines of Sight, *Virginia Quarterly Review,* 96/1

MAX KING CAP
Saving the Baby, *The Threepenny Review,* #162

A. D. CARR
Losing Composure, *CRAFT Literary,* October 21

LIANE KUPPERBERG CARTER
Culling My Library in the Time of COVID, *Covey Club,* September 24

MELISSA CHADBURN
The Forgotten Babies, *Alta,* April 6

MAY-LEE CHAI
Women of Nanjing, *New England Review,* 41/3

ANKITA CHAKRABORTY
Be Like Bernhard, *The End of the World Review,* October 19

AMANDA CHEMECHE
Chengdu, *Michigan Quarterly Review,* 59/3

K CHIUCARELLO
In the Five, *Longleaf Review,* Spring

SU CHO
Of Sesame Leaves and Sunflowers, *Black Warrior Review,* 47/1

GEORGE CHOUNDAS
Paylessness, *The Chattahoochee Review,* 40/1

NICOLE CHUNG
Grieving My Mother Without the Reassurance of Rituals, *Time,* November 30/ December 7

MICHAEL DEAN CLARK
Signal to Noise Ratio, *Jabberwock Review,* 40/2

ROBERT CLARK
On Fitzroy Road, *Image,* #104

EMANUELE COCCIA
All Species Have the Same Life, *Granta,* #151

PAUL COCKERAM
Shapes Not Living to My Ken, *The Turnip Truck(s),* 5/1

CATHARIA COENEN
Changing Trains, *The American Scholar,* 89/1

MICHAEL COHEN
Talking to Myself, *North Dakota Quarterly,* 87/1 & 2

TEJU COLE
On the Trail of Caravaggio, *The New York Times Magazine,* September 27

JACKIE CONNELLY
I Have Nothing to Say / and I Am Saying It, *Prairie Schooner,* 94/1

JOAN CONNOR
Portmanteau, *Hotel Amerika,* #18

ELLIOT CONNORS
Prone, *The Adroit Journal,* #34

HARRISON COOK
Atlas, *Phoebe,* 49/1

JULIA COOKE
Buried Deep, *Guernica,* October 28

JEANNETTE COOPERMAN
Stoicism as the Art of Learning How to Feel Without Fear, *The Common Reader,* July 27

BONNIE COSTELLO
Our Guide in Warsaw, *World Literature Today,* 94/1

GEORGE COTKIN
"A Kiss": Marianne Moore and Joseph Cornell, *Chicago Quarterly Review,* #31

DANIEL ALLEN COX
The Glow of Electrum, *The Malahat Review,* #211

PAUL CRENSHAW
Cold Cola Wars, *Ninth Letter,* 17/1

ANTHONY D'ARIES
No Man's Land, *Sport Literate,* 12/2

DAWN D'ARIES
The Super's Wife, *Crazyhorse,* 98

LYDIA DAVIS
On Translating Bob, Son of Battle, *The Believer,* #133

ORMAN DAY
When We Were Swashbucklers, *Potomac Review,* #66

JILL DEASY
The Afterdeath, *Creative Nonfiction,* #73

BATHSHEBA DEMUTH
Reindeer at the End of the World, *Emergence Magazine,* July 12

TANIA DE ROZARIO
There Will Be Salvation Yet, *New Ohio Review,* #28

CHRISTOPHER DERRICK
Sirens, *Guernica,* July 27

DANIELLE CADENA DEULEN
Driving Lessons, *Fourth Genre,* 22/2

COLIN DICKEY
Palindromes, Palindromes, Motherfucker, What! *The Believer,* #129

STEPHANIE DICKINSON
Girl-World Krystal, *Jelly Bucket,* #10

NICHOLAS DIGHIERA
Fern Canyon, California, *Under the Gum Tree,* #34

NICOLA DIXON
Just Like Johnny Cash, *Kenyon Review,* 42/4

JOE DONNELLY
Messiah Wolf, *ZYZZYVA,* #119

MARK DOTY
You Are Here, You Are Not a Ghost, *Granta,* #151

MICHAEL DOWNS
Neighbors Gathered, *Alaska Quarterly Review,* 36/3 & 4

JACQUELINE DOYLE
Madeline's Trunk, *Passages North,* #41

KATHLEEN DRISKELL
Keats in Your Time of Pandemic, *Appalachian Review,* 48/3

IRINA DUMITRESCU
How to Learn Everything: The MasterClass Diaries, *Longreads,* August

CAMILLE T. DUNGY
Dirt: A Love Story, *Orion,* 39/4

LENA DUNHAM
False Labor, *Harper's Magazine,* December

ROBIN STOREY DUNN
Gimme Shelter, *The Tusculum Review,* #16

GEOFF DYER
Home Alone Together, *The New Yorker,* April 13

DINA ELENBOGEN
Another Country, *The Examined Life Journal,* #8

THOMAS SAYERS ELLIS
Fo(lk)cal fr-aim, *Arrowsmith,* September 29

ANNE FADIMAN
All My Pronouns, *Harper's Magazine,* August

SARAH FALLON
The Secret History of the First Microprocessor, the F-14, and Me, *Wired,* December

JUIAYANG FAN
Motherland, *The New Yorker,* September 14

LATOYA FAULK
In Search of a Homeplace, *The Common,* #20

SARAH FAYE
On Solitude (and Isolation and Loneliness [and Brackets]), *Longreads,* May 17

MELISSA FEBOS
The Mirror Test, *The Paris Review,* #235

LIZZIE FEIDELSON
No Shelter, *n+1,* #38

LUCY FERRISS
Stitches in Time, *The American Scholar,* 89/3

ZACK FINCH
The Village Beautiful, *New England Review,* 41/4

GARY FINCKE
Appearances, *North Dakota Quarterly,* 87/1 & 2

CAITLIN FLANAGAN
I Thought Stage IV Cancer Was Bad Enough, *The Atlantic,* June

MILES FOLSOM
This Side of Paradise, *Notre Dame Magazine,* 49/3

PATRICIA FOSTER
Alabama Triptych, *The Louisville Review,* #87

ROBERTO JOSE ANDRADE FRANCO
The Desert Reclaims Everything, *Texas Highways,* November

GABRIELA DENISE FRANK
Bad Date, *Pembroke Magazine,* #52

RACHEL FRASER
Illness as Fantasy, *The Point,* #22

IAN FRAZIER
Rereading *Lolita, The New Yorker,* December 14

JOHN FREEMAN
Touchless, *The Sun,* #539

STEVE FRIEDMAN
A Letter to My Curmudgeonly Big Brother, *Outside Online,* April 9

REBEKAH FRUMKIN
Feeling Bullish: On My Great-Uncle, Gay Matador and Friend of Hemingway, *Granta* (online), June 29

CHARLOTTE TAYLOR FRYAR
Blackwater, *Southern Humanities Review,* 53/2

KAORI FUJIMOTO
Making Peace, *The Threepenny Review,* #161

DEREK FURR
Green Heron (On Dwelling in Possibility), *Raritan,* 39/3

MEGAN CULHANE GALBRAITH
Hold Me Like a Baby, *Tupelo Quarterly,* July 14

J. MALCOLM GARCIA
Hector's Choice, *Tampa Review,* 59/60

ROSS GAY
Have I Even Told You Yet About the Courts I Loved, *Literary Hub,* September 15

JENNIFER GENEST
The Mills, *Colorado Review,* 47/2

DIANA HUME GEORGE
A Performance of Innocence, *Chautauqua,* #17

DAVID GESSNER
Looking Back from the End of the World, *The American Scholar,* 89/3

HADIL GHONEIM
Hairdressing, *Zone 3,* 35/2

DAVID GILBERT
The Wheel, *The New Yorker,* November 30

ANITA GILL
My Father's Language, *Kweli,* August

D. GILSON
Exodus, *New Ohio Review,* #28

MIRRI GLASSON-DARLING
On Alaskan Literary Cartography, *Territory,* #12

RICHARD GOODMAN
Arina, *North American Review,* 305/2 & 3

CAROLINE GOODWIN
The Money Place, *Under the Gum Tree,* #37

NICK FULLER GOOGINS
Maine Escapes, *The Sun,* #540

JESSE GREEN
Now Be Witness Again, *The New York Times Magazine,* September 20

KENDRA GREENE
Upright Members in Good Standing, *The Common,* #19

MINDY GREENSTEIN
Maybe the Survivor's Daughter Could Survive, *The New York Times,* March 20

GARTH GREENWELL
Making Meaning, *Harper's Magazine,* November

ERIN GREER
Something That Would Have Been Somebody, *Salmagundi,* #208–209

SIAN GRIFFITHS
The World Within, the World Without: A Thought List, *Juked*, #17

PAUL GRIMSTAD
Miles the Mercurial, *Raritan*, 39/4

JOHN GRISWOLD
Requiem for a Young Soldier Who Vanished, *The Common Reader*, August 28

LAUREN GROFF
Waiting for the End of the World, *Harper's Magazine*, March

KELLE GROOM
Star Tables, *River Teeth*, 21/2

ANOUCHKA GROSE
Snap, *Granta*, #151

MELISSA GRUNOW
Marriage: A Grammar Exercise, *Hypertext Review*, #7

MARGARET MORGANROTH GULLETTE
Must the Father Die? Reading *King Lear* over a Lifetime, *Salmagundi*, #208–209

MYRIAM GURBA
It's Time to Take California Back from Joan Didion, *Electric Literature*, May 12

KATIE GUTIERREZ
The Weight You Knowingly Carry, *JMWW*, September 3

VIX GUTIERREZ
Dark Sky City, *Subtropics*, #28–29

DEBRA GWARTNEY
Suffer Me to Pass, *Virginia Quarterly Review*, 96/2

BARBARA HAAS
Alone in the Mist with Tchaikovsky, *Upstreet*, #16

CERIDWEN HALL
Submarine Reconnaissance: Bodies, Permutations, Voyages, *Southern Humanities Review*, 53/4

JANE EATON HAMILTON
The Dead Green Man, *Event*, 49/1

K. J. HANLON
On Plumbing, *Under the Sun*, #8

NIKOLE HANNAH-JONES
What Is Owed? *The New York Times Magazine*, June 28

MEGAN HARLAN
This 5,000 Year Old House, *River Teeth*, 22/1

CRIS HARRIS
Survivor, *Indiana Review*, 42/2

SHAMECCA HARRIS
The Blacker the Berry, the Quicker They Shoot, *The Rumpus*, June 15

SAIDIYA HARTMAN
The End of White Supremacy: An American Romance, *Bomb*, #152

ANDREW HENDRIXSON
Taboret, *Image*, #105

MARY HENN
Assemblies, *Hayden's Ferry Review*, #66

DEWITT HENRY
Long-Distance, *Juked*, September 7

LISA LEE HERRICK
I Am Not Your Peril, *Emergence Magazine*, May 1

GREGG HILLIARD
Geek Duende, Blithe Dread: How to Organize Books by Sector, *The Iowa Review*, 50/2

J. D. HO
In Noise, Feeling, *The Missouri Review*, 43/2

RICHARD HOFFMAN
Remembering the Alchemists, *Consequence*, #12

MARYBETH HOLLEMAN
More Than Ever: What Wilderness Means Now, *Deep Wild*, #2

KAREN HOLMBERG
"The Very Worst Ache / Is Not Knowing Why": Remembering

Madame Cluny, *The Briar Cliff Review,* #32

Jim Holt
In This Is All, *Lapham's Quarterly,* 13/1

Lars Horn
With the Moths' Eyes, *Kenyon Review,* 42/2

Jazmine Hughes
A Plunge into the Unknown, *The New York Times Magazine,* March 29

Gary Hunter
John in the Rain, *Intima,* Fall

Phillip Hurst
Aqua Vitae, *Water-Stone Review,* #23

Felix Imonti
A Cynic's Song, *Another Chicago Magazine,* December 28

Katie Ives
The Naming of Mt. Misery, *Alpinist,* November

Mitchell S. Jackson
Nomen Est Omen, *The Believer,* September 1

Marlon James
Another Country, *Departures,* October

Nahal Suzanne Jamir
Proof Sheet, *Gulf Coast,* 32/2

Leslie Jamison
When the World Went Away We Made a New One, *The New York Times Magazine,* May 24

Honorée Fanonne Jeffers
Things Ain't Always Gone Be This Way, *Kenyon Review Online,* November/December

Caleb Johnson
Granny and Loretta, *Southern Living,* July

Alex R. Jones
The Maricopa, *The Carolina Quarterly,* 70/1

Rachael Jordan
Our Lady of Refuge, *Emrys Journal,* #37

Pat Joseph
The World Ends Here, *California,* Summer

Fady Joudah
A Spider, an Arab, and a Muslim Walk into a Cave, *Image,* #106

Zeyn Joukhadar
Incantations for Unsung Boys, *Columbia Journal,* August 4

Anna Journey
My Vampires, *The Southern Review,* 56/4

Heidi Julavits
Why I Went to Avalanche School, *The New York Times Magazine,* January 5

James Jung
Chasing My Father's Ghost Through the Swiss Alps, *Bicycling.com,* October 30

Michiko Kakutani
Pandemic Notebook, *The New York Times Book Review,* May 17

Howard Kaplan
George at Work, *Splice Today,* December 21

Miriam Karmel
This Is the Way We Talk, *Prairie Schooner,* 94/4

Aruni Kashyap
My Brother and the Fortune Tellers, *The Chattahoochee Review,* 40/2 & 3

Ariana Kelly
Challenger, *The Threepenny Review,* #160

Devin Kelly
From a Window, *Wildness,* #23

Mark Kemp
The Green Book Guide to North Carolina, *Our State,* September

Christopher Kempf
Local Color, *Narrative,* October 30

ANNE KENNER
If You Like Rules, *Southwest Review,* 104/4

COURTNEY KERSTEN
The Ergonomics of Loss, *Southern Indiana Review,* 27/1

JENNYMAE KHO
Neither Here Nor There, *Solstice Literary Magazine,* Spring

JAMAICA KINCAID
A Heap of Disturbance, *The New Yorker,* September 7

KENNETH KING
Secrets and Ciphers, *The Antioch Review,* Winter

LINDSEY B. KING
The Viruses Among Us, *5280 Magazine,* June

TAYLOR KIRBY
The Scopophiliac's Gift Shop, *Cream City Review,* 44/1

MARSHALL KLIMASEWISKI
The Art of Oblivion, *New England Review,* 41/2

CATHRYN KLUSMEIER
Gutted, *AGNI,* #91

WILSON A. KOEWING
Woodstown, *Pembroke Magazine,* #52

DAN KOIS
I Walked All 1,114 Blocks of My Zip Code Just to Catalog How People Style Their House Numbers, *Slate,* June 25

JESSE KRAEMER
The Wright Brother, *Chicago Quarterly Review,* #32

KATIE KRESSER
An Aesthetic of Lack, or Notes on Camps, *Image,* #107

RAFIL KROLL-ZAIDI
Reason Not the Need, *Harper's Magazine,* October

HARI KUNZRU
The Wages of Whiteness, *The New York Review of Books,* September 24

BENJAMIN LABATUT
La Ville Morte, *Granta,* August 11

DON LAGO
Hubble Vision, *The Gettysburg Review,* 33/1

MICHEL LARKIN
Lunch with Borges, *Harvard Review,* #56

PETER LASALLE
My New Literary Credo, Via Hanoi, *Michigan Quarterly Review,* 59/1

ALLISON LASORDA
The Pain You Want to Know, *Southern Humanities Review,* 53/3

TRAVIS CHI WING LAU
What Preparations Are Due? *Lapham's Quarterly,* 13/3

DAVID LAZAR
My Two Oscars: On Melancholy and Wit, *The Cincinnati Review,* 17/1

ANNA LEAHY
A Brief Encyclopedia of My Mother's Cancer, *The Los Angeles Review,* Spring

EDWARD LEE
The Lines Blur, *Able Muse,* #27

WHITNEY LEE
Wait, *Booth,* #14

LAWRENCE LENHART
A Ferret by Any Other Name, *Willow Springs,* #86

JILL LEPORE
These Four Walls, *The New Yorker,* September 7

AYDEN LEROUX
The Art of Stillness, *Guernica,* June 25

SHARRA LESSLEY
Season of Mists, *Kenyon Review Online,* July/August

YIYUN LI
Make My House Your Inn, *The New Yorker,* November 16

RACHEL LINDLEY-MAYCOCK
And Begin, *Prism,* 58/2

NICOLE GRAEV LIPSON
Kate Chopin, My Mother, and Me, *River Teeth*, 21/2

GORDON LISH
Death and So Forth, *The Antioch Review*, Winter

SPENCER LITMAN
Like Falling Asleep, *The Forge Literary Magazine*, January 13

PHILLIP LOPATE
Untitled (Table Talk), *The Threepenny Review*, #161

JESUS LOPEZ
The Egg, the Witch, and the Cure, *The Dead Mule School*, August 1

CHRISTIAN LORENTZEN
Truckers, *The Sewanee Review*, 128/2

THOMAS LYNCH
What Takes Our Breath Away, *The Atlantic*, June

ROSA LYSTER
Lost Libraries, *The Paris Review Daily*, September 14

DAVE MADDEN
Behold Us Two Boys Sitting Together, *ZYZZYVA*, #118

KRISTINE LANGLEY MAHLER
Alignment, *Blood Orange Review*, 12/2

JANET MALCOLM
A Second Chance, *The New York Review of Books*, September 24

JONATHAN MALESIC
Drinking Alone, *Commonweal*, July/August

SARAH MANGUSO
Perfection, *The Paris Review*, #233

TERRANCE MANNING JR.
Break Down Easy, *New Letters*, 86/1 & 2

JAMES MARCUS
Channeling Emerson, *The American Scholar*, 89/1

BILL MARSH
Sentences, *Bayou Magazine*, #72

HUGH J. MARTIN
Shrapnel, *Gulf Coast*, Winter/Spring

LEE MARTIN
Bachelors, *Booth*, #14

GREG MARSHALL
Cory, *Southwest Review*, 105/1

SAGE MARSHALL
Cutting the Ice, *Sport Literate*, 12/2

ANDREW MARZONI
Commodity of Doom, *The Baffler*, #53

DAVID MASELLO
Backlit: Looking into Turner's Light, *Fine Art Connoisseur*, February 17

KEN MASSEY
Behind the Red Railing: My Childhood Isolation, *Scoundrel Time*, September 15

M. BOONE MATTIA
Transitions, *The Washington Post Magazine*, September 10

SHARA MCCALLUM
Through a Glass, Darkly, *The Southern Review*, 56/4

TOM MCCAULEY
Introductory Element Comma Independent Clause: A Study of the Moon and Bees, *Willow Springs*, #86

REBECCA MCCLANAHAN
The Bath Whisperers, *The Gettysburg Review*, 33/1

CLINT MCCOWN
Noo Jall, *Colorado Review*, 47/3

CAROLINE MCCOY
Well-Known Stranger, *Juked*, May 29

CAITLIN MCGILL
How to Disappear, *CutBank*, #92

CHARLES MCGRATH
Reading *Ovid*, *The Hudson Review*, 73/3

ERIN MCREYNOLDS
Train Songs, *The Sun*, #530

CHRISTINE MCSWAIN
Excavation of a Car Crash, *Fourth Genre,* 22/2
JOYELLE MCSWEENEY
A Shocking December Red, *Image,* #106
DANIEL MENDELSOHN
Sleepless Love, *Freeman's,* October
MAAZA MENGISTE
A Future Hope, *Freeman's,* October
JOE MENO
Between Everything and Nothing, *TriQuarterly,* July 15
ANDREA MEYER
Her Name Was Nina, *Pangyrus,* October 3
LULU MILLER
The Eleventh Word, *The Paris Review Daily,* October 5
LIGAYA MISHAN
The Sacrifice, *The New York Times Magazine,* December 6
PETER WAYNE MOE
To Flense, *Fourth Genre,* 22/2
DINTY W. MOORE
The Burning Bush, *Kenyon Review,* 42/6
ELLENE GLENN MOORE
Stories My Mother Tells, *Ninth Letter,* 17/1
STEVEN MOORE
Where I Was From, *The Normal School,* February 12
KYOKO MORI
A/part: Notes on Solitude, *Conjunctions,* #75
JEREMIAH MOSS
Open House, *n+1,* #36
E. J. MYERS
Sammy 4.0, *Stoneboat Literary Journal,* 10/2

AIMEE NEZHUKUMATATHIL
Octopus, *The Georgia Review,* 74/2
EMI NIETFELD
My Mom Claims I Had a Drink with My Rapist. I Investigate, *Boulevard,* 35/2 & 3
LISA NIKOLIDAKIS
Active Drowning, *New Orleans Review,* #44
MARY HEATHER NOBLE
Plume: An Investigation, *Creative Nonfiction/True Story,* #34
WENDY NOONAN
Weeping Woman, *Meridian,* #44
DEBRA NYSTROM
Dream of the Subjunctive, *AGNI,* #91

W. SCOTT OLSEN
Fair Warning, *Lake Effect,* #24
ANNE-MARIE OOMEN
Touched: From Notes Taken at the Facility, *Hypertext Review,* #6
DANIELLE OTERI
The Secret of the Unicorn Galleries, *The Paris Review Daily,* September 18
NADIA OWUSU
The Heat of Dar Es Salaam, *Bennington Review,* #8

NELL IRVIN PAINTER
Why "White" Should Be Capitalized, Too, *The Washington Post,* July 22
BRICE PARTICELLI
Alternative Facts, Post Truth, and the Great American Eclipse, *Salmagundi,* #208–209
LESLIE JILL PATTERSON
In the Moments Before Gunfire, *Hunger Mountain,* #24
JENNY PATTON
Katsu, *Iron Horse Literary Review,* 22/4
NICK PAUMGARTEN
Airport, *The Sewanee Review,* 128/3

ALEXANDRIA PEARY
Hello to All That, *Southern Humanities Review,* 53/3

ALYSSA PELISH
The Problem with Being a Final Girl, *New England Review,* 41/3

CLINTON CROCKETT PETERS
A Portrait of the Artist at His Home in Texas, *The Iowa Review,* 50/1

JESSICA LIND PETERSON
Strange Season, *Orion,* 39/2

EMILIA PHILLIPS
Targeted Audiences, *Cherry Tree,* #6

ROWAN RICARDO PHILLIPS
The 2020, *Virginia Quarterly Review,* 96/3

MELISSA HOLBROOK PIERSON
Smoking in Wartime, *Prairie Schooner,* 94/2

TAYLOR PLIMPTON
See Ovid, 19, Tricycle, April 27

ANN POWERS
Diary of a Fugue Year, NPR Music, December 16

KHADIJAH QUEEN
False Dawn, *Harper's Magazine,* August

DAVID RANEY
End Times for the Poker Face, *Green Mountain Review,* May 17

RACHEL RATNER
Josh and Rach 4Ever, *The Normal School,* March 9

ROBERT REBEIN
Welcome to the Hotel Sabra, *CutBank,* #93

ERIK REECE
Because It's There, *Oxford American,* #109–110

MARYBETH REUTHER-WU
Sores of the Realm, *Hypocrite Reader,* July 17

ENDRIA RICHARDSON
The Body of Climbing, *Alpinist,* November

MOLLY RIDEOUT
Father and Son Buried in One Grave, *River Teeth,* 22/1

LAURA JACKSON ROBERTS
The Imperfect Aquarist, *Bayou Magazine,* #73

JAMES SILAS ROGERS
Not Yet Able, *Literature and Belief,* 39/2

CHRISTOPHER M. ROSE
Sticks and String, *Uncanny Magazine,* September 1

KENNETH R. ROSEN
Death, Love, and the Solace of a Million Motorcycle Parts, *Wired,* November 17

ARRA LYNN ROSS
Near, and Nearer Now, *Conjunctions,* #74

JOSHUA ROTHMAN
In Another Life, *The New Yorker,* December 21

DANIEL ROUSSEAU
Catch Me, Daddy, *The Chattahoochee Review,* 40/2 & 3

JESS ROW
Despair Management: Thoughts on Commuting, *The Yale Review,* 108/1

NATHANIEL RUDAVSKY-BRODY
Rehearsal, *Raritan,* 39/3

BRANDON RUSHTON
Inarguably Au Sable, *Alaska Quarterly Review,* 37/1 & 2

RICHARD RUSSO
The Lives of Others, *Harper's Magazine,* June

JAY RUTTENBERG
Ladies and Gentlemen, Put Your Hands Together for the Most Vulgar, Viscous Comic Ever to Walk the Face of the Earth, Andrew Dice Clay, *The Lowbrow Reader,* #11

DAVID RYAN
The Landlord, *The Southampton Review,* #26

IBRAHIM SABLABAN
When Suicide Speaks Arabic, *Intima,* Fall

SCOTT RUSSELL SANDERS
The Woman Who Made Lye Soap, *Notre Dame Magazine,* 49/3

ANNA SANDY-ELROD
The Number of Hair, *The Threepenny Review,* #162

K. ROBERT SCHAEFFER
Tarkovsky by Count Light, *The Gettysburg Review,* 32/4

PETER SCHJELDAHL
Apart, *The New Yorker,* June 8/June 15

MATTHEW SCHNEIER
Now Is the Perfect Time to Memorize a Poem, *New York,* April

CHRISTINE SCHOTT
Bone-House, *The Gettysburg Review,* 33/1

BRANDON R. SCHRAND
The End of Something, *North American Review,* 305/2 & 3

DAVID SCHUMAN
Model Homes, *Colorado Review,* 47/1

CAROLYN SCHULTZ-RATHBUN
Rublev's *Trinity, Water-Stone Review,* #23

SOPHFRONIA SCOTT
Hope on Any Given Day, *Yankee,* March/April

DAVID SEARCY
Yellowbelly, *Oxford American,* #109–110

DAVID SEDARIS
Unbuttoned, *The New Yorker,* March 2

LEANNE SHAPTON
Still Life, *Granta,* #152

JOSHUA WOLF SHENK
The Curse of Cool, *Virginia Quarterly Review,* 96/1

AURORA SHIMSHAK
Woodswomen, *The Southampton Review,* #26

TABITHA SIKLOS
Half Scissor, *Prism,* 58/2

CHRISTINA SIMON
Closer to Home, *Columbia Journal,* February 19

ROSE B. SIMPSON
Mata la Arana, *The Massachusetts Review,* 61/4

ELIZABETH SIMS
Taking the Cure, *North American Review,* 305/2 & 3

ANN TASHI SLATER
My Father, Montaigne, and the Art of Living, *Catapult,* October 29

JAMIE L. SMITH
Mythology Lessons, *The Tusculum Review,* #16

MELANIE S. SMITH
A List of Songbirds, *Ruminate,* #55

ZOE SMITH-HOLLADAY
Redbone, *805 Lit + Art,* 6/2

ERIN SOROS
I Do, *Room,* 43/3

WOLE SOYINKA
Unsinkable City: Reflections on a Lifetime in Lagos, *Stranger's Guide,* #6

SPARROW
Sparrow's Guide to Meditation, *The Sun,* #529

CORINA STAN
Between Us, *The Point,* #22

MAUREEN STANTON
Through a Glass, Tearfully, *Longreads,* January

MOLLY WRIGHT STEENSON
A Series of Tubes, *The Missouri Review,* 43/4

MARGO STEINES
A Very Brutal Game, *The Sun,* #539

T. J. STILES
The Death of a Master, *The Sewanee Review,* 128/1

JENNIFER STOCK
Lighter Than Air, *Salmagundi,* #206–207

WILL STOCKTON
A Week of Recreation, *Hotel Amerika,* #18

WARREN STODDARD II
When This Plane Lands, *Into the Void,* #16

GENEVA BURROUGHS STONE
Remaining Silent: The Facts, *The American Poetry Review,* 49/2

PATRICIA STORACE
At Table with Meg, Jo, Beth, and Amy, *Book Post,* March 23–25

ANDREW SULLIVAN
A Plague Is an Apocalypse. But It Can Bring a New World, *New York Magazine,* July 20

MAUREEN SUN
Notes from a Childhood Without Words, *The Yale Review,* 108/3

MARK SUNDEEN
Utah Wanted All the Tourists. Then It Got Them, *Outside Online,* January 29

BARRETT SWANSON
The Worst Novelist in the English Language, *The New Republic,* August

BENJAMIN SWETT
VR, *Prism,* 58/3

JOHN TALBIRD
What Happens Next, *Potomac Review,* #66

SYDNEY TAMMARINE
Blue Hour, *Ploughshares,* 46/1

JERRINE TAN
The Problem of Silence, *The Margins,* January 15

LUCIA TANG
The Haunted Tenants of Henry James, *Ploughshares* (blog), November 11

DONNA TARTT
True Grit, *The New York Times Book Review,* June 28

KERRY TEMPLE
A Moment's Notice, *Notre Dame Magazine,* 49/1

JOSEPH EARL THOMAS
With Violence and Doubt, *Gulf Coast,* 32/2

ERIN THOMPSON
Museum Lover, *The Point,* #23

KELLY S. THOMPSON
A Knowing, *Room,* 43/2

WILLIAM THOMPSON
My Cowboy Cousin, *Zone 3,* 35/1

KATLYN TJERRILD
Vanity of Vanities, *Meridian,* #44

TJOA SHZE HUI
On Being in Love with a White Man, *So to Speak,* #29

ALISON TOWNSEND
An Alphabet of Here: A Wisconsin Prairie Sampler, *Kenyon Review,* 42/1

DAYNA TORTORICI
My Instagram, *n+1,* #36

MAI TRAN
Variants of Unknown Significance, *Epiphany,* Fall/Winter

ERIC TRUMP
Anchored, *The Smart Set,* July 13

DAVID L. ULIN
Drive, *ZYZZYVA,* #119

KATRINA VANDENBERG
Cherry Season, *Orion,* 39/3

TOM VANDYCK
Wonderwall: On Soccer, Stadiums, and Mortality, *The Under Review,* #2

JODI VARON
Augury, *Boulevard,* 36/1

RAKSHA VASUDEVAN
Room Service Economics: Seven Principles, *Bat City Review,* #16

MARCO VERDONI
When to Tell Someone You Went to Prison, *Fourth Genre,* 22/1

JODIE NOEL VINSON
In Circadia, *Harvard Review,* #56

MATTHEW VOLLMER
Three Essays, *South Carolina Review,* 52/2

EUGENIO VOLPE
Jesus Kicks His Oedipus Complex, *The Massachusetts Review,* 61/2

JULIE MARIE WADE
Fauntlee Hills Was My Roseburg: An Essay in Episodes, *Prairie Schooner,* 94/2

JERALD WALKER
The Kaleshion, *Creative Nonfiction,* #73

NICOLE WALKER
(Who Gets to) Just Up and Move, *Longreads,* January 3

WENDY S. WALTERS
Soup Can; or, On Hospitality, *The Yale Review,* 108/3

MARY WANG
Sad White Women, *Michigan Quarterly Review,* 59/1

GENE WEINGARTEN
In Search of Healing, *The Washington Post Magazine,* October 26

ALEXANDER WELLS
Perpetual Motion Machine, *Hypocrite Reader,* July 17

LISA WELLS
Occasional Poems, *The Poetry Foundation* (blog), April

KATHRYN WILDER
Lunar Red, *High Desert Journal,* #31

WYATT WILLIAMS
Would You Please Please Please Please Please Please Please Stop Talking, *The Believer,* January

CLAIR WILLS
Stepping Out, *The New York Review of Books,* August 20

KEITH S. WILSON
Lobster Sky, *Indiana Review,* 42/1

ANNA GENEVIEVE WINHAM
my mother // itch, *Ninth Letter,* 17/2

LINDSAY WONG
Furniture on the Brain, *Room,* 43/3

BARON WORMSER
The Happy Nation, *Hotel Amerika,* #18

JOHN WRONOSKI
The Best Revenge, *Arrowsmith,* September 29

AMY YEE
Searching for Walter, *The Massachusetts Review,* 61/1

JOHN YOHE
Pacific Blues, *Entropy,* February 1

MAKO YOSHIKAWA
Clothes Make the Man, *Southern Indiana Review,* 27/2

TALYA ZAX
Philip Roth Doesn't Live Here Anymore: A Writer, a Stonemason, an American Friendship, *The Forward,* May 17

RHONDA ZIMLACH
The Ritual of Smoking, *Dogwood,* #19

JESS ZIMMERMAN
It Doesn't Hurt, It Hurts All the Time, *Catapult,* August 11

Notable Special Issues of 2020

Aperture, Native America, ed. Michael Famighetti; guest ed. Wendy Red Star, #240

The Believer, The Survival Issue, ed. Joshua Wolf Shenk, #132

Black Warrior Review, Portfolio of Afterwords, guest ed. Renee Gladman, 47/1

Chicago Quarterly Review, The Australian Issue, guest eds. Shelley Davidow and Paul Williams, #30

Creative Nonfiction, Memoir, ed. Lee Gutkind, #73

Denver Quarterly, Collaboration, ed. Vincent James, 54/4

Ecotone, The Garden Issue, ed. David Gessner, #29

Epiphany, The Borders Issue, ed. Rachel Lyon, Spring/Summer

Forum, A Blind Eye, ed. Danny Heitman, 100/2

Freeman's, Love, ed. John Freeman, October

The Georgia Review, Census Communis 2020, ed. Gerald Maa, 74/1

Granta, Membranes, guest ed. Rana Dasgupta, #151; Still Life, ed. Sigrid Rausing, #152

The Massachusetts Review, A Gathering of Native Voices, ed. Tacey M. Atsitty, Laura Furlan, and Toni Jenson, 61/4

Michigan Quarterly Review, Persecution, guest ed. Reginald Dwayne Betts, 59/4

n+1, Transmission, ed. Mark Krotov and Dayna Tortorici, #37

The New Yorker, Dispatches from a Pandemic, April 13

The New York Review of Books, Notes from a Pandemic, eds. Emily Greenhouse and Gabriel Winslow-Yost, April 23

Oxford American, The Place Issue, ed. Eliza Borné, #109–110

Ruminate, The Everyday, ed. Rachel King, #54

Stranger's Guide, Texas, ed. Kira Brunner Don, #9

Territory, Alaska, eds. Nick Greer and Thomas Mira y Lopez, #12

The Turnip Truck(s), Belief, eds. Tina Mitchell, Monica Mankin, and Ivan Castaneda, 5/1

Vanity Fair, The Great Fire, ed. Radhika Jones; guest ed. Ta-Nehisi Coates, September

Wildfire, Survivorship, ed. April Johnson Stearns, 5/2

ZYZZYVA, The Los Angeles Issue, ed. Laura Cogan, #119

Note:
The following essays should have appeared in "Notable Essays and Literary Nonfiction of 2019":

MEGAN ARLETT, Horsepower Manifesto, *Southwest Review*, 104/4
CAROL CLAASSEN, Leatherface, *The Normal School*, October 31
LEE DURKEE, Little Green Men, *Southwest Review*, 104/4
LANGDON HAMMER, Still to Love: For J. D. McClatchy, *The Yale Review*, 107/4

A Notable Essay of 2019 contained two misspellings. Here is the corrected entry:
JUDITH HERTOG, Running with Montaigne, *Crab Orchard Review*, 24/1